STELLAR AMBUSH

The Boskonian pirate cruiser locked onto its quarry, and a space-armored horde swarmed through the open ports—expecting to be met by confederates on board the captured freighter.

But a blast of pure force met them—Lensman Kim Kinnison and the Patrolmen were waiting. In seconds the airlock was a shambles.

The surviving pirates broke and ran, but there was no place to hide. . . .

Third in the famous Lensman series

E.E. "DOC" SMITH
GALACTIC PATROL

BERKLEY BOOKS, NEW YORK

GALACTIC PATROL

A Berkley Book / published by arrangement with
the author

PRINTING HISTORY
Eleven previous printings
Jove edition / October 1977
Berkley edition / July 1982

ISBN: 0-425-05459-4

To
Clarrissa M. MacD. Hamnett
and
Clarrissa MacD. S. Wilcox

CONTENTS

CHAPTER 1   Graduation

DOMINATING TWICE A HUNDRED SQUARE MILES OF CAMPUS, parade-ground, airport, and spaceport, a ninety-story edifice of chromium and glass sparkled dazzlingly in the bright sunlight of a June morning. This monumental pile was Wentworth Hall, in which the Tellurian candidates for the Lens of the Galactic Patrol live and move and have their being. One wing of its topmost floor seethed with tense activity, for that wing was the habitat of the lordly Five-Year Men, this was Graduation Day, and in a few minutes Class Five was due to report in Room A.

Room A, the private office of the Commandant himself; the dreadful lair into which an undergraduate was summoned only to disappear from the Hall and from the Cadet Corps; the portentous chamber into which each year the handful of graduates marched and from which they emerged, each man in some subtle fashion changed.

In their cubicles of steel the graduates scanned each other narrowly, making sure that no wrinkle or speck of dust marred the space-black and silver perfection of the dress uniform of the Patrol; that not even the tiniest spot of tarnish or dullness violated the glittering golden meteors upon their collars or the resplendently polished ray-pistols and other equipment at their belts. The microscopic mutual inspection over, the kit-boxes were snapped shut and racked, and the embryonic Lensmen made their way out into the assembly hall.

In the wardroom Kimball Kinnison, Captain of the Class by virtue of graduating at its head, and his three lieutenants, Clifford Maitland, Raoul LaForge, and Widel Holmberg, had inspected each other minutely and were now simply awaiting, in ever-increasing tension, the zero minute.

"Now, fellows, remember that drop!" the young Captain

9

jerked out. "We're dropping the shaft free, at higher velocity and in tighter formation than any class ever tried before. If anybody hashes the formation—our last show and with the whole Corps looking on . . . . ."

"Don't worry about the drop, Kim," advised Maitland. "All three platoons will take that like clockwork. What's got me all of a dither is what is really going to happen in Room A."

"Uh-*huh*!" exclaimed LaForge and Holmberg as one, and

"You can play that across the board for the whole Class," Kinnison agreed. "Well, we'll soon know—it's time to get going," and the four officers stepped out into the assembly hall; the Class springing to attention at their approach.

Kinnison, now all brisk Captain, stared along the mathematically exact lines and snapped:

"Report!"

"Class Five present in full, sir!" The sergeant-major touched a stud at his belt and all vast Wentworth Hall fairly trembled under the impact of an all-pervading, lilting, throbbing melody as the world's finest military band crashed into "Our Patrol."

"Squads left—March!" Although no possible human voice could have been heard in that gale of soul-stirring sound and although Kinnison's lips scarcely moved, his command was carried to the very bones of those for whom it was intended—and to no one else—by the tight-beam ultra-communicators strapped upon their chests. "Close formation—forward—March!"

In perfect alignment and cadence the little column marched down the hall. In their path yawned the shaft—a vertical pit some twenty feet square extending from main floor to roof of the Hall; more than a thousand sheer feet of unobstructed air, cleared now of all traffic by flaring red lights. Five left heels clicked sharply, simultaneously upon the lip of the stupendous abyss. Five right legs swept out into emptiness. Five right hands snapped to belts and five bodies, rigidly erect, arrowed downward at such an appalling velocity that to unpractised vision they simply vanished.

Six-tenths of a second later, precisely upon a beat of the stirring march, those ten heels struck the main floor of Wentworth Hall, but not with a click. Dropping with a velocity of almost two thousand feet per second though they were at the instant of impact, yet those five husky bodies came from full speed to an instantaneous, shockless, effortless halt at contact, for the drop had been made under complete neutralization of inertia—"free," in space parlance. Inertia restored, the march was resumed—or rather continued—in perfect time with the band. Five left feet swung out, and as the right toes left the floor the second rank, with only bare inches to spare, plunged down into the space its predecessor had occupied a moment before.

Rank after rank landed and marched away with machine-like precision. The dread door of Room A opened automatically at the approach of the cadets and closed behind them.

"Column right—March!" Kinnison commanded inaudibly, and the Class obeyed in clockwork perfection. "Column left—March! Squad right—March! Company—Halt! Salute!"

In company front, in a huge, square room devoid of furniture, the Class faced the Ogre—Lieutenant-Marshal Fritz von Hohendorff, Commandant of Cadets. Martinet, tyrant, dictator—he was known throughout the System as the embodiment of soullessness; and, insofar as he had ever been known to show emotion or feeling before any undergraduate, he seemed to glory in his repute of being the most pitilessly rigid disciplinarian that Earth had ever known. His thick, white hair was roached fiercely upward into a stiff pompadour. His left eye was artificial and his face bore dozens of tiny, threadlike scars; for not even the marvelous plastic surgery of that age could repair entirely the ravages of space-combat. Also, his right leg and left arm, although practically normal to all outward seeming, were in reality largely products of science and art instead of nature.

Kinnison faced, then, this reconstructed potentate, saluted crisply, and snapped:—

"Sir, Class Five reports to the Commandant."

"Take your post, sir." The veteran saluted as punctiliously, and as he did so a semi-circular desk rose around him from the floor—a desk whose most striking feature was an intricate mechanism surrounding a splint-like form.

"Number One, Kimball Kinnison!" von Hohendorff barked. "Front and center—March! . . . . . The oath, sir."

"Before the Omnipotent Witness I promise never to lower the standard of the Galactic Patrol," Kinnison said reverently; and, baring his arm, thrust it into the hollow form.

From a small container labelled "#1, Kimball Kinnison," the Commandant shook out what was apparently an ornament—a lenticular jewel fabricated of hundreds of tiny, dead-white gems. Taking it up with a pair of insulated forceps he touched it momentarily to the bronzed skin of the arm before him, and at that fleeting contact a flash as of many-colored fire swept over the stones. Satisfied, he dropped the jewel into a recess provided for it in the mechanism, which at once burst into activity.

The forearm was wrapped in thick insulation, molds and shields snapped into place, and there flared out an instantly-suppressed flash of brilliance intolerable. Then the molds fell apart, the insulation was removed, and there was revealed the LENS. Clasped to Kinnison's brawny wrist by a bracelet of imperishable, almost unbreakable, metal in which it was imbedded it shone in all its lambent splendor —no longer a whitely inert piece of jewelry, but a lenticular polychrome of writhing, almost fluid radiance which proclaimed to all observers in symbols of ever-changing flame that here was a Lensman of the GALACTIC PATROL.

In similar fashion each man of the Class was invested with the symbol of his rank. Then the stern-faced Commandant touched a button and from the bare metal floor there arose deeply-upholstered chairs, one for each graduate.

"Fall out!" he commanded, then smiled almost boyishly —the first intimation any of the Class ever had that the hard-boiled old tyrant *could* smile—and went on in a strangely altered voice:

"Sit down, men, and smoke up. We have an hour in which to talk things over, and now I can tell you what it is all about. Each of you will find his favorite refreshment in the arm of his chair.

"No, there's no catch to it," he continued in answer to amazedly doubtful stares, and lighted a huge black cigar of Venerian tobacco as he spoke. "You are Lensmen now. Of course you have yet to go through the formalities of Commencement, but they don't count. Each of you really graduated when his Lens came to life.

"We know your individual preferences, and each of you has his favorite weed, from Tilotson's Pittsburgh stogies up to Snowden's Alsakanite cigarettes—even though Alsakan is just about as far away from here as a planet can be and still lie within the galaxy.

"We also know that you are all immune to the lure of noxious drugs. If you were not, you would not be here today. So smoke up and break up—ask any questions you care to, and I will try to answer them. Nothing is barred now—

this room is shielded against any spy-ray or communicator beam operable upon any known frequency."

There was a brief and rather uncomfortable silence, then Kinnison suggested, diffidently:

"Might it not be best, sir, to tell us all about it, from the ground up? I imagine that most of us are in too much of a daze to ask intelligent questions."

"Perhaps. While some of you undoubtedly have your suspicions, I will begin by telling you what is behind what you have been put through during the last five years. Feel perfectly free to break in with questions at any time. You know that every year one million eighteen-year-old boys of Earth are chosen as cadets by competitive examinations. You know that during the first year, before any of them see Wentworth Hall, that number shrinks to less than fifty thousand. You know that by Graduation Day there are only approximately one hundred left in the class. Now I am allowed to tell you that you graduates are those who have come with flying colors through the most brutally rigid, the most fiendishly thorough process of elimination that it has been possible to develop.

"Every man who can be made to reveal any real weakness is dropped. Most of these are dismissed from the Patrol. There are many splendid men, however, who, for some reason not involving moral turpitude, are not quite what a Lensman must be. These men make up our organization, from grease-monkeys up to the highest commissioned officers below the rank of Lensman. This explains what you already know—that the Galactic Patrol is the finest body of intelligent beings yet to serve under one banner.

"Of the million who started, you few are left. As must every being who has ever worn or who ever will wear the Lens, each of you has proven repeatedly, to the cold verge of death itself, that he is in every respect worthy to wear it. For instance, Kinnison here once had a highly adventurous interview with a lady of Aldebaran II and her friends. He did not know that we knew all about it, but we did."

Kinnison's very ears burned scarlet, but the Commandant went imperturbably on:

"So it was with Voelker and the hypnotist of Karalon; with LaForge and the bentlam-eaters; with Flewelling when the Ganymede-Venus thionite smugglers tried to bribe him with ten million in gold . . . . ."

"Good Heavens, Commandant!" broke in one outraged

youth. "Do you—did you—know everything that happened?"

"Not quite everything, perhaps, but it is my business to know enough. No man who can be cracked has ever worn, or ever will wear, the Lens. And none of you need be ashamed, for you have passed every test. Those who did not pass them were those who were dropped.

"Nor is it any disgrace to have been dismissed from the Cadet Corps. The million who started with you were the pick of the planet, yet we knew in advance that of that selected million scarcely one in ten thousand would measure up in every essential. Therefore it would be manifestly unfair to stigmatize the rest of them because they were not born with that extra something, that ultimate quality of fiber which does, and of necessity *must*, characterize the wearers of the Lens. For that reason not even the man himself knows why he was dismissed, and no one save those who wear the Lens knows why they were selected—and a Lensman does not talk.

"It is necessary to consider the history and background of the Patrol in order to bring out clearly the necessity for such care in the selection of its personnel. You are all familiar with it, but probably very few of you have thought of it in that connection. The Patrol is of course an outgrowth of the old Planetary Police systems; and, until its development, law enforcement always lagged behind law violation. Thus, in the old days following the invention of the automobile, state troopers could not cross state lines. Then when the National Police finally took charge, they could not follow the rocket-equipped criminals across the national boundaries.

"Still later, when interplanetary flight became a commonplace, the Planetary Police were at the same old disadvantage. They had no authority off their own worlds, while the public enemies flitted unhampered from planet to planet. And finally, with the invention of the inertialess drive and the consequent traffic between the worlds of many solar systems, crime became so rampant, so utterly uncontrollable, that it threatened the very foundations of Civilization. A man could perpetrate any crime imaginable without fear of consequences, for in an hour he could be so far away from the scene as to be completely beyond the reach of the law.

"And helping powerfully toward utter chaos were the new vices which were spreading from world to world;

among others the taking of new and horrible drugs. Thionite, for instance; occurring only upon Trenco; a drug as much deadlier than heroin as that compound is than coffee, and which even now commands such a fabulous price than a man can carry a fortune in one hollow boot-heel.

"Thus the Triplanetary Patrol and the Galactic Patrol came into being. The first was a pitiful enough organization. It was handicapped from without by politics and politicians, and honey-combed from within by the usual small but utterly poisonous percentage of the unfit—grafters, corruptionists, bribe-takers, and out-and-out criminals. It was hampered by the fact that there was then no emblem or credential which could not be counterfeited—no one could tell with certainty that the man in uniform was a Patrolman and not a criminal in disguise.

"As everyone knows, Virgil Samms, then Head of the Triplanetary Patrol, became First Lensman Samms and founded our Galactic Patrol. The Lens, which, being proof against counterfeiting or even imitation, makes identification of Lensmen automatic and positive, was what made our Patrol possible. Having the Lens, it was easy to weed out the few unfit. Standards of entrance were raised ever higher, and when it had been proved beyond question that every Lensman was in fact incorruptible, the Galactic Council was given more and ever more authority. More and ever more solar systems, having developed Lensmen of their own, voted to join Civilization and sought representation on the Galactic Council, even though such a course meant giving up much of their systemic sovereignty.

"Now the power of the Council and its Patrol is practically absolute. Our armament and equipment are the ultimate; we can follow the law-breaker wherever he may go. Furthermore, any Lensman can commandeer any material or assistance, wherever and whenever required; upon any planet of any solar system adherent to Civilization; and the Lens is so respected throughout the galaxy that any wearer of it may be called upon at any time to be judge, jury, and executioner. Wherever he goes, upon, in, or through any land, water, air, or space anywhere within the confines of our Island Universe, his word is LAW.

"That explains what you have been forced to undergo. The only excuse for its severity is that it produces results —no wearer of the Lens has ever disgraced it.

"Now as to the Lens itself. Like every one else, you have known *of* it ever since you could talk, but you know nothing of its origin or its nature. Now that you are Lensmen, I can tell you what little I know about it. Questions?"

"We have all wondered about the Lens, sir, of course," Maitland ventured. "The outlaws apparently keep up with us in science. I have always supposed that what science can build, science can duplicate. Surely more than one Lens has fallen into the hands of the outlaws?"

"If it had been a scientific invention or discovery it would have been duplicated long ago," the Commandant made surprising answer. "It is, however, not essentially scientific in nature. It is almost entirely philosophical, and was developed for us by the Arisians.

"Yes, each of you was sent to Arisia quite recently," von Hohendorff went on, as the newly commissioned officers stared, dumbfounded, at him and at each other. "What did you think of them, Murphy?"

"At first, sir, I thought that they were some new kind of dragon; but dragons with brains that you could actually *feel*. I was glad to get away, sir. They fairly gave me the creeps, even though I never did see one of them so much as move."

"They are a peculiar race," the Commandant went on. "Instead of being mankind's worst enemies, as is generally believed, they are the *sine qua non* of our Patrol and of Civilization. I cannot understand them; I do not know of anyone who can. They gave us the Lens; yet Lensmen must not reveal that fact to any others. They make a Lens to fit each candidate; yet no two candidates, apparently, have ever seen the same things there, nor is it believed that anyone has ever seen them as they really are. To all except Lensmen they seem to be completely anti-social; and even those who become Lensmen go to Arisia only once in their lives. They seem—although I caution you that this seeming may contain no more of reality than the physical shapes you thought you saw—to be supremely indifferent to all material things.

"For more generations than you can understand they have devoted themselves to thinking; mainly of the essence of life. They say that they know scarcely anything fundamental concerning it; but even so they know more about it than does any other known race. While ordinarily they will have no intercourse whatever with outsiders, they did consent to help the Patrol, for the good of all intelligence.

"Thus, each being about to graduate into Lensmanship is sent to Arisia, where a Lens is built to match his individual life force. While no mind other than that of an Arisian can understand its operation, thinking of your Lens as being synchronized with, or in exact resonance with, your own vital principle or ego will give you a rough idea of it. The Lens is not really alive, as we understand the term. It is, however, endowed with a sort of pseudo-life, by virtue of which it gives off its strong, characteristically changing light as long as it is in metal-to-flesh circuit with the living mentality for which it was designed. Also by virtue of that pseudo-life, it acts as a telepath through which you may converse with other intelligences, even though they may possess no organs of speech or of hearing.

"The Lens cannot be removed by anyone except its wearer without dismemberment; it glows as long as its rightful owner wears it; it ceases to glow in the instant of its owner's death and disintegrates shortly thereafter. Also —and here is the thing that renders completely impossible the impersonation of a Lensman—not only does the Lens not glow if worn by an imposter; but if a Lensman be taken alive and his Lens removed, that Lens kills in a space of seconds any living being who attempts to wear it. As long as it glows—as long as it is in circuit with its living owner—it is harmless; but in the dark condition its pseudo-life interferes so strongly with any life to which it is not attuned that that life is destroyed forthwith."

A brief silence fell, during which the young men absorbed the stunning import of what their Commandant had been saying. More, there was striking into each young consciousness a realization of the stark heroism of the grand old Lensman before them; a man of such fiber that although physically incapacitated and long past the retirement age, he had conquered his human emotions sufficiently to accept deliberately his ogre's role because in that way he could best further the progress of his Patrol!

"I have scarcely broken the ground," von Hohendorff continued. "I have merely given you an introduction to your new status. During the next few weeks, before you are assigned to duty, other officers will make clear to you the many things about which you are still in the dark. Our time is growing short, but we perhaps have time for one more question."

"Not a question, sir, but something more important," Kinnison spoke up. "I speak for the Class when I say that we have misjudged you grievously, and we wish to apologize."

"I thank you sincerely for the thought, although it is unnecessary. You could not have thought otherwise of me than as you did. It is not a pleasant task that we old men have; that of weeding out those who do not measure up. But we are too old for active duty in space—we no longer have the instantaneous nervous responses that are for that duty imperative—so we do what we can. However, the work has its brighter side, since each year there are about a hundred found worthy of the Lens. This, my one hour with the graduates, more than makes up for the year that precedes it; and the other oldsters have somewhat similar compensations.

"In conclusion, you are now able to understand what kind of mentalities fill our ranks. You know that any creature wearing the Lens is in every sense a Lensman, whether he be human or, hailing from some strange and distant planet, a monstrosity of a shape you have as yet not even imagined. Whatever his form, you may rest assured that he has been tested even as you have been; that he is as worthy of trust as are you yourselves. My last word is this —Lensmen die, but they do not fold up: individuals come and go, but the Galactic Patrol goes on!"

Then, again all martinet:

"Class Five, attention!" he barked. "Report upon the stage of the main auditorium!"

The Class, again a rigidly military unit, marched out of Room A and down the long corridor toward the great theater in which, before the massed Cadet Corps and a throng of civilians, they were formally to be graduated.

And as they marched along the graduates realized in what way the wearers of the Lens who emerged from Room A were different from the candidates who had entered it such a short time before. They had gone in as boys; nervous, apprehensive, and still somewhat unsure of themselves, in spite of their survival through the five long years of grueling tests which now lay behind them They emerged from Room A as men: men knowing for the first time the real meaning of the physical and mental tortures they had undergone; men able to wield justly the vast powers whose scope and scale they could even now but dimly comprehend.

CHAPTER 2   *In Command*

BARELY A MONTH AFTER HIS GRADUATION, EVEN BEFORE HE
had entirely completed the post-graduate tours of duty mentioned by von Hohendorff, Kinnison was summoned to
Prime Base by no less a personage than Port Admiral
Haynes himself. There, in the Admiral's private aero, whose
flaring lights cut a right-of-way through the swarming traffic, the novice and the veteran flew slowly over the vast
establishment of the Base.

Shops and factories, city-like barracks, landing-fields
stretching beyond the far horizon; flying craft ranging from
tiny one-man helicopters through small and large scouts,
patrol-ships and cruisers up to the immense, globular superdreadnaughts of space—all these were observed and commented upon. Finally the aero landed beside a long, comparatively low building—a structure heavily guarded, inside Base although it was—within which Kinnison saw a
thing that fairly snatched away his breath.

A space-ship it was—but what a ship!* In bulk it was
vastly larger even than the superdreadnaughts of the Patrol;
but, unlike them, it was in shape a perfect teardrop,
streamlined to the ultimate possible degree.

"What do you think of her?" the Port Admiral asked.

"Think of her!" The young officer gulped twice before

---

* In the "big teardrops"—cruisers and battleships—the driving
force is always directed upward, along the geometrical axis of the
ship, and the artificial gravity is always downward along that same
line. Thus, throughout any possible maneuvering, free or inert,
"down" and "up" have the same significance as within any Earthly
structure.

These vessels are ordinarily landed only in special docks, but in
emergencies can be landed almost anywhere, sharp stern down, as
their immense weight drives them deep enough into even the hardest
ground to keep them upright. They sink in water, but are readily
maneuverable, even under water.   E.E.S.

he attained coherence. "I can't put it in words, sir; but some day, if I live long enough and develop enough force, I hope to command a ship like that."

"Sooner than you think, Kinnison," Haynes told him, flatly. "You are in command of her beginning tomorrow morning."

"Huh? Me?" Kinnison exclaimed, but sobered quickly. "Oh, I see, sir. It takes ten years of proved accomplishment to rate command of a first-class vessel, and I have no rating at all. You have already intimated that this ship is experimental. There is, then, something about her that is new and untried, and so dangerous that you do not want to risk an experienced commander in her. I am to give her a work-out, and if I can bring her back in one piece I turn her over to her real captain. But that's all right with me, Port Admiral —thanks a lot for picking me out. What a chance—*What* a chance!" and Kinnison's eyes gleamed at the prospect of even a brief command of such a creation.

"Right—and wrong," the old Admiral made surprising answer. "It is true that she is new, untried, and dangerous, so much so that we are unwilling to give her to any of our present captains. No, she is not really new, either. Rather, her basic idea is so old that it has been abandoned for centuries. She uses explosives; of a type that cannot be tried out fully except in actual combat. Her primary weapon is what we have called the 'Q-gun.' The propellant is heptadetonite: the shell carries a charge of twenty metric tons of duodecaplylatomate."

"But, sir . . . . ." Kinnison began.

"Just a minute, I'll go into that later. While your premises were correct, your conclusion is not. You graduated Number One, and in every respect save experience you are as well qualified to command as is any captain of the Fleet; and since the *Brittania* is such a radical departure from any conventional type, battle experience is not a prerequisite. Therefore if she holds together through one engagement she is yours for good. In other words, to make up for the possibility of having yourself scattered all over space, you have a chance to win that ten years' rating you mentioned a minute ago, all in one trip. Fair enough?"

"Fair? It's fine—wonderful! And thanks a . . . . ."

"Never mind the thanks until you get back. You were about to comment, I believe, upon the impossibility of using explosives against a free opponent?"

"It can't be impossible, of course, since the *Brittania* has been built. I just don't quite see how it could have been made effective."

"You lock to the pirate with tractors, screen to screen—dex about ten kilometers. You blast a hole through his screens to his wall-shield. The muzzle of the Q-gun mounts as annular multiplex projector which puts out a Q-type tube of force—Q47SM9, to be exact. As you can see from the type formula, this helix extends the gun-barrel from ship to ship and confines the propellent gases behind the projectile, where they belong. When the shell strikes the wall-shield of the pirate and detonates, *something* will have to give way—all the Brains agree that twenty tons of duodec, attaining a temperature of about forty million degrees absolute in less than one micro-second, simply cannot be confined.

"The tube and tractors, being pure force and computed for this particular combination of explosions, will hold; and our physicists have calculated that the ten-kilometer column of inert propellent gases will offer so much inertia and resistance that any possible wall-shield will have to go down. That is the point that cannot be tried out experimentally—it is quite within the bounds of possibility that the pirates may have been able to develop wall-screens as powerful as our Q-type helices, even though we have not.

"It should not be necessary to point out to you that if they *have* been able to develop a wall-shield that will stand up under those conditions, the back-blast through the breech of the Q-gun will blow the *Brittania* apart as though she were so much matchwood. That is only one of the chances—and perhaps not the greatest one—that you and your crew will have to take. They are all volunteers, by the way, and will get plenty of extra rating if they come through alive. Do you want the job?"

"You don't have to ask me that, Chief—you *know* I want it!"

"Of course, but I had to go through the formality of asking, sometime. But to get on with the discussion, this pirate situation is entirely out of control, as you already know. We don't even know whether Boskone is a reality, a figurehead, a symbol, or simply a figment of an old-time Lensman's imagination. But whoever or whatever Boskone really is, some being or some group of beings has perfected a mighty efficient organization of outlaws; so efficient that we haven't even been able to locate their main base.

"And you may as well know now a fact that is not yet public property—that even conveyed vessels are no longer safe. The pirates have developed ships of a new and extra-ordinary type; ships that are much faster than our heavy battleships, and yet vastly more heavily armed than our fast cruisers. Thus, they can outfight any Patrol vessel that can catch them, and can out-run anything of ours armed heavily enough to stand up against their beams."

"That accounts for the recent heavy losses," Kinnison mused.

"Yes," Haynes went on, grimly. "Ship after ship of our best has been blasted out of the ether, doomed before it pointed a beam, and more will be. We cannot force an engagement on our terms; we must fight them where and when they please.

"That is the present intolerable situation. We *must* learn what the pirates' new power-system is. Our scientists say that it may be anything, from cosmic-energy receptors and converters down to a controlled space-warp—whatever that may be. Anyway, they haven't been able to duplicate it, so it is up to us to find out what it is. The *Brittania* is the tool our engineers have designed to get that information. She is the fastest thing in space, developing at full blast an inert acceleration of *ten gravities*. Figure out for yourself what velocity that means free in open space!"

"You have just said that we can't have everything in one ship," Kinnison said, thoughtfully. "What did they sacrifice to get that speed?"

"All the conventional offensive armament," Haynes replied frankly. "She has no long-range beams at all, and only enough short-range stuff to help drive the Q-helix through the enemy's screens. Practically her only offense is the Q-gun. But she has plenty of defensive screens, she has speed enough to catch anything afloat, and she has the Q-gun—which we hope will be enough.

"Now we'll go over the general plan of action. The engineers will go into all the technical details with you, during a test flight that will last as long as you like. When you and your crew are thoroughly familiar with every phase of her operation, bring the engineers back here to Base and go out on patrol.

"Now we'll go over the general plan of action. Then engineers will go into all the technical details with you, during a test flight that will last as long as you like. When you and your crew are thoroughly familiar with every phase of her operation, bring the engineers back here to Base and go out on patrol.

"Somewhere in the galaxy you will find a pirate vessel of the new type. You lock to him, as I said before. You attach the Q-gun well forward, being sure that the point of attachment is far enough away from the power-rooms so that the essential mechanisms will not be destroyed. You board and storm—another revival of the technique of older times. Specialists in your crew, who will have done nothing much up to that time, will then find out what our scientists want to know. If at all possible they will send it in instantly via tight-beam communicator. If for any reason it should be impossible for them to communicate, the whole thing is again up to you."

The Port Admiral paused, his eyes boring into those of the younger man, then went on impressively:

"That information MUST get back to Base. If it does not, the *Brittania* is a failure; we will be back right where we started from; the slaughter of our men and the destruction of our ships will continue unchecked. As to how you are to do it we cannot give even general instructions. All I can say is that you have the most important assignment in the Universe today, and repeat—*that information* MUST GET BACK TO BASE. Now come aboard and meet your crew and the engineers."

Under the expert tutelage of the designers and builders of the *Brittania* Lieutenant Kinnison drove her hither and thither through the trackless wastes of the galaxy.* Inert and free, under every possible degree of power he maneuvered her; attacking imaginary foes and actual meteorites with equal zeal. Maneuvered and attacked until he and

---

* Navigation. Each ship has as reference sphere a galactic-inductor compass. This instrument, swinging freely in an almost frictionless mount, is held in one position relative to the galaxy as a whole by galactic lines of force, analogous to the Terrestrial lines of magnetic force which affect Terrestrial compasses. Its equator is always parallel to the galactic equator; its line of zeroes is always parallel to the line joining Centralia, the central solar system of the First Galaxy, with the system of Vandemar, which is on its very rim.

The position of the ship in the galaxy is known at all times by that of a moving dot in the tank. This dot is shifted automatically by calculating machines coupled inductively to the leads of the drives. When the ship is inert this device is inoperative, as any distance traversed in inert flight is entirely negligible in galactic computations. Due to various perturbations and other slight errors, cumulative discrepancies occur, for which the pilot must from time to time correct manually the position of the dot in the tank representing his ship.   E.E.S.

his ship were one; until he reacted automatically to her slightest demand; until he and every man of his eager and highly trained crew knew to the final volt and to the ultimate ampere her gargantuan capacity both to give it and to take it.

Then and only then did he return to Base, unload the engineers, and set out upon the quest. Trail after trail he followed, but all were cold. Alarm after alarm he answered, but always he arrived too late: arrived to find gutted merchantman and riddled Patrol vessel, with no life in either and with nothing to indicate in which direction the marauders might have gone.

Finally, however:

"QBT! Calling QBT!" The *Britannia's* code call blared from the sealed-band speaker, and a string of numbers followed—the spatial coordinates of the luckless vessel's position.

Chief Pilot Henry Henderson punched the figures upon his locator, and in the "tank"—the enormous, minutely cubed model of the galaxy—there appeared a redly brilliant point of light. Kinnison rocketed out of his narrow bunk, digging sleep out of his eyes, and shot himself into place beside the pilot.

"Right in our laps!" he exulted. "Scarcely ten light-years away! Start scrambling the ether!" and as the vengeful cruiser darted toward the scene of depredation all space became filled with blast after blast of static interference through which, it was hoped, the pirate could not summon the help he was so soon to need.

But that howling static gave the pirate commander pause. Surely this was something new? Before him lay a richly-laden freighter, its two convoying ships already practically out of action. A few more minutes and the prize would be his. Nevertheless he darted away, swept the ether with his detectors, saw the *Britannia*, and turned in headlong flight. For if this streamlined fighter was sufficiently convinced of its prowess to try to blanket the ether against *him*, that information was something that Boskone would value far above one shipload of material wealth.

But the pirate craft was now upon the visiplates of the *Britannia*, and, entirely ignoring the crippled space-ships, Henderson flung his vessel after the other. Manipulating his incredibly complex controls purely by touch, the while staring into his plate not only with his eyes, but with every fiber of his being as well, he hurled his huge mount hither and thither in frantic leaps. After what seemed an age he snapped down a toggle switch and relaxed long enough to grin at Kinnison.

"Holding 'em?" the young commander demanded.

"Got 'em, Skipper," the pilot replied, positively. "It was touch and go for ninety seconds, but I've got a CRX tracer on him now at full pull. He can't put out enough jets to get away from *that*—I can hold him forever!"

"Fine work, Hen!" Kinnison strapped himself into his seat and donned his headset. "General call! Attention! Battle stations! By stations, report!"

"Station One, tractor beams—hot!"

"Station Two, repellors—hot!"

"Station Three, projector One—hot!"

Thus station after station of the warship of the void reported, until:

"Station Fifty-Eight, the Q-gun—hot!" Kinnison himself reported; then gave to the pilot the words which throughout the spaceways of the galaxy had come to mean complete readiness to face any emergency.

"Hot and tight, Hen—let's take 'em!"

The pilot shoved his blast-lever, already almost at maximum, clear out against its stop and hunched himself even more intently over his instruments, varying by infinitesimals the direction of the thrust that was driving the *Britannia* toward the enemy at the unimaginable velocity of ninety parsecs an hour[*]—a velocity possible only to inertialess matter being urged through an almost perfect vacuum by a driving blast capable of lifting the stupendous normal tonnage of the immense sky-rover against a gravity ten times that of her native Earth.

Unimaginable? Completely so—the ship of the Galactic Patrol was hurling herself through space at a pace in comparison with which any speed that the mind can grasp would be the merest crawl: a pace to make light itself seem stationary.

Ordinary vision would have been useless, but the observers of that day used no antiquated optical systems. Their detector beams, converted into light only at their plates, were heterodyned upon and were carried by subetheral ultra-waves; vibrations residing far below the level

[*] With the neutralization of inertia it was discovered that there is no limit whatever to the velocity of inertialess matter. A free ship takes on instantaneously the velocity at which the force of her drive is exactly equalled by the friction of the medium.   E.E.S.

of the ether and thus possessing a velocity and a range infinitely greater than those of any possible ether-borne wave.

Although stars moved across the visiplates in flaming, zig-zag lines of light as pursued and pursuer passed solar system after solar system in fantastic, light-years-long hops, yet Henderson kept his cruiser upon the pirate's tail and steadily cut down the distance between them. Soon a tractor beam licked out from the Patrol ship, touched the fleeing marauder lightly, and the two space-ships flashed toward each other.

Nor was the enemy unprepared for combat. One of the crack raiders of Boskone, master pirate of the known Universe, she had never before found difficulty in conquering any vessel fleet enough to catch her. Therefore, her commander made no attempt to cut the beam. Or rather, since the two inertialess vessels flashed together to repellor-zone contact in such a minute fraction of a second that any human action within that time was impossible, it would be more correct to say that the pirate captain changed his tactics instantly from those of flight to those of combat.

He thrust out tractor beams of his own, and from the already white-hot refractory throats of his projectors there raved out horribly potent beams of annihilation; beams of dreadful power which tore madly at the straining defensive screens of the Patrol ship. Screens flared vividly, radiating all the colors of the spectrum. Space itself seemed a rainbow gone mad, for there were being exerted there forces of a magnitude to stagger the imagination; forces to be yielded only by the atomic might from which they sprang; forces whose neutralization set up visible strains in the very fabric of the ether itself.

The young commander clenched his fists and swore a startled deep-space oath as red lights flashed and alarm-bells clanged. His screens were leaking like sieves—practically down—needle after needle of force incredible stabbing at and through his wall-shield—four stations gone already and more going!

"Scrap the plan!" he yelled into his microphone. "Open everything to absolute top—short out all resistors—give 'em everything you can put through the bare bus-bars. Dalhousie, cut all your repellors; bring us right up to their zone. All you beamers, concentrate on Area Five. *Break down those screens!*" Kinnison was hunched rigidly over his panel, his voice came grittily through locked teeth. *"Get through to that wall-shield so I can use this Q-gun!"*

Under the redoubled force of the *Britannia's* attack the defenses of the enemy began to fail. Kinnison's hands flew over his controls. A port opened in the Patrol-ship's armored side and an ugly snout protruded—the projector-ringed muzzle of a squat and monstrous cannon. From its projector bands there leaped out with the velocity of light a tube of quasi-solid force which was in effect a continuation of the gun's grim barrel; a tube which crashed through the weakened third screen of the enemy with a space-wracking shock and struck savagely, with writhing, twisting thrusts, at the second. Aided by the massed concentration of the *Britannia's* every battery of short-range beams, it went through. And through the first. Now it struck the very-wall-shield of the outlaw—that impregnable screen which, designed to bear the brunt of any possible inert collision, had never been pierced or ruptured by any material substance, however applied.

To this inner defense the immaterial gun-barrel clung. Simultaneously the tractor beams, hitherto exerting only a few dynes of force, stiffened into unbreakable, inflexible rods of energy, binding the two ships of space into one rigid system; each, relative to the other, immovable.

Then Kinnison's flying finger tip touched a button and the Q-gun spoke. From its sullen throat there erupted a huge torpedo. Slowly the giant projectile crept along, watched in awe and amazement by the officers of both vessels. For to those space-hardened veterans the velocity of light was a veritable crawl; and here was a thing that would require four or five whole seconds to cover a mere ten kilometers of distance!

But, although slow, this bomb *might* prove dangerous, therefore the pirate commander threw his every resource into attempts to cut the tube of force, to blast away from the tractor beams, to explode the sluggish missile before it could reach his wall-shield. In vain; for the *Britannia's* every beam was set to protect the torpedo and the mighty rods of energy without whose grip the inertialess mass of the enemy vessel would offer no resistance whatever to the force of the proposed explosion.

Slowly, *so* slowly, as the age-long seconds crawled into eternity, there extended from Patrol ship almost to pirate wall a raging, white-hot pillar—the gases of combustion of the propellant heptadetonite—ahead of which there rushed the Q-gun's tremendous shell with its horridly destructive freight. What would happen? Could even the almost immeasurable force of that frightful charge of atomic explosive break down a wall-shield designed to withstand the cosmic assaults of meteoric missiles? And what would happen if that wall-screen held?

In spite of himself Kinnison's mind insisted upon painting the ghastly picture: the awful explosion; the pirate's screen still intact; the forward-rushing gases driven backward along the tube of force. The bare metal of the Q-gun's breech, he knew, was not and could not be reenforced by the infinitely stronger, although immaterial shields of pure energy which protected the hull; and no conceivable substance, however resistant, could impede save momentarily the unimaginable forces about to be unleashed.

Nor would there be time to release the Q-tube after the explosion but before the *Brittania's* own destruction; for if the enemy's shield stayed up for even a fraction of a second the unthinkable pressure of the blast would propagate backward through the already densely compressed gases in the tube, would sweep away as though it were nothing the immensely thick metallic barrier of the gun-breech, and would wreak within the bowels of the Patrol vessel a destruction even more complete than that intended for the foe.

Nor were his men in better case. ─ach knew that this was the climactic instant of his existence; that life itself hung poised upon the issue of the next split second. Hurry it up! Snap into it! Will that crawling, creeping thing *never* strike?

Some prayed briefly, some swore bitterly; but prayers and curses were alike unconscious and had precisely the same meaning—each man, white of face and grim of jaw, clenched his hands and waited, tense and straining, for the impact.

CHAPTER 3   *In the Lifeboats*

THE MISSILE STRUCK, AND IN THE INSTANT OF ITS STRIKING the coldly brilliant stars were blotted from sight in a vast globe of intolerable flame. The pirate's shield had failed, and under the cataclysmic force of that horrific detonation the entire nose-section of the enemy vessel had flashed into incandescent vapor and had added itself to the rapidly expanding cloud of fire. As it expanded the cloud cooled. Its fierce glare subsided to a rosy glow, through which the stars again began to shine. It faded, cooled, darkened—revealing the crippled hulk of the pirate ship. She was still fighting; but ineffectually, now that all her heavy forward batteries were gone.

"Needlers, fire at will!" barked Kinnison, and even that feeble resistance was ended. Keen-eyed needle-ray men, working at spy-ray visiplates, bored hole after hole into the captive, seeking out and destroying the control-panels of the remaining beams and screens.

"Pull 'er up!" came the next order. The two ships of space flashed together, the yawning, blasted-open fore-end of the raider solidly against the *Brittania's* armored side. A great port opened.

"Now, Bus, it's all yours. Classification to six places, straight A's—they're human or approximately so. Board and storm!"

Back of that port there had been massed a hundred fighting men; dressed in full panoply of space armor, armed with the deadliest weapons known to the science of the age, and powered by the gigantic accumulators of their ship. At their head was Sergeant vanBuskirk, six and a half feet of Dutch Valerian dynamite, who had fallen out of Valeria's Cadet Corps only because of an innate inability to master the intricacies of higher mathematics. Now the attackers swept forward in a black-and-silver wave.

Four squatly massive semi-portable projectors crashed down upon their magnetic clamps and in the fierce ardor of their beams the thick bulkhead before them ran the gamut of the spectrum and puffed outward. Some score of defenders were revealed, likewise clad in armor, and battle again was joined. Explosive and solid bullets detonated against and ricocheted from that highly efficient armor, the beams of De-Lameter hand-projectors splashed in torrents of man-made lightning off its protective fields of force. But that skirmish was soon over. The semi-portables, whose vast energies no ordinary personal armor could withstand, were brought up and clamped down; and in their holocaust of vibratory destruction all life vanished from the pirates' compartment.

"One more bulkhead and we're in their control room!" vanBuskirk cried. "Beam it down!"

But when the beamers pressed their switches nothing happened. The pirates had managed to jury-rig a screen generator, and with it had cut the power-beams behind the invading forces. Also they had cut loop-holes in the bulkhead, through which in frantic haste they were trying to bring heavy projectors of their own into alignment.

"Bring up the ferral paste," the sergeant commanded. "Get up as close to that wall as you can, so they can't blast us!"

The paste—successor to thermite—was brought up and the giant Dutchman troweled it on in furious swings, from floor up and around in a huge arc and back down to floor. He fired it, and simultaneously some of the enemy gunners managed to angle a projector sharply enough to reach the further ranks of the Patrolmen. Then mingled the flashing, scintillating, gassy glare of the thermite and the raving energy of the pirates' beam to make of that confined space a veritable inferno.

But the paste had done its work, and as the semi-circle of wall fell out the soldiers of the Lens leaped through the hole in the still-glowing wall to struggle hand-to-hand against the pirates, now making a desperate last stand. The semi-portables and other heavy ordnance powered from the *Brittania* were of course useless. Pistols were ineffective against the pirates' armor of hard alloy; hand-rays were equally impotent against its defensive shields. Now heavy hand-grenades began to rain down among the combatants, blowing Patrolmen and pirates alike to bits—for the outlaw chiefs cared nothing that they killed many of their own men if in so doing they could take toll of the Law. And worse, a crew of gunners was swiveling a mighty projector around upon its hastily-improvised mount to cover that sector of the compartment in which the policemen were most densely massed.

But the minions of the Law had one remaining weapon, carried expressly for this eventuality. The space-axe—a combination and sublimation of battle-axe, mace, bludgeon, and lumberman's picaroon, a massively needle-pointed implement of potentialities limited only by the physical strength and bodily agility of its wielder.

Now all the men of the *Britannia's* storming party were Valerians, and therefore were big, hard, fast, and agile; and of them all their sergeant leader was the biggest, hardest, fastest, and most agile. When the space-tempered apex of that thirty-pound monstrosity, driven by the four-hundred-odd pounds of rawhide and whalebone that was his body, struck pirate armor that armor gave way. Nor did it matter whether or not that hellish beak of steel struck a vital part after crashing through the armor. Head or body, leg or arm, the net result was the same; a man does not fight effectively when he is breathing space in lieu of atmosphere.

VanBuskirk perceived the danger to his men in the slowly turning projector and for the first time called his chief.

"Kim," he spoke in level tones into his microphone. "Blast that delta-ray, will you? . . . . . Or have they cut this beam, so you can't hear me? . . . . . Guess they have."

"They've cut our communication," he informed his troopers then. "Keep them off me as much as you can and I'll attend to that delta-ray outfit myself."

Aided by the massed interference of his men he plunged toward the threatening mechanism, hewing to right and to left as he strode. Beside the temporary projector-mount at last, he aimed a tremendous blow at the man at the delta-ray controls; only to feel the axe flash instantaneously to its mark and strike it with a gentle push, and to see his intended victim float effortless away from the blow. The pirate commander had played his last card: vanBuskirk floundered, not only weightless, but inertialess as well!

But the huge Dutchman's mind, while not mathematical, was even faster than his muscles, and not for nothing had he spent arduous weeks in inertialess tests of strength and skill. Hooking feet and legs around a convenient wheel he seized the enemy operator and jammed his helmeted head down between the base of the mount and the long, heavy steel lever by means of which it was turned. Then, throwing every ounce of his wonderful body into the effort, he braced both feet against the projector's grim barrel and heaved. The helmet flew apart like an eggshell, blood and brains gushed out in nauseous blobs: but the delta-ray projector was so jammed that it would not soon again become a threat.

Then vanBuskirk drew himself across the room toward the main control panel of the warship. Officer after officer he pushed aside, then reversed two double-throw switches, restoring gravity and inertia to the riddled cruiser.

In the meantime the tide of battle had continued in favor of the Patrol. Few survivors though there were of the black-and-silver force, of the pirates there were still fewer; fighting now a desperate and hopeless defensive. But in this combat quarter was not, *could* not be thought of, and Sergeant vanBuskirk again waded into the fray. Four times more his horribly effective hybrid weapon descended like the hammer of Thor, cleaving and crushing its way through steel and flesh' and bone. Then, striding to the control board, he manipulated switches and dials, then again spoke evenly to Kinnison.

"You can hear me now, can't you? . . . . . All mopped up—come and get the dope!"

The specialists, headed by Master Technician LaVerne Thorndyke, had been waiting strainingly for that word for minutes. Now they literally flew at their tasks; in furious haste, but following rigidly and in perfect coordination a prearranged schedule. Every control and lead, every bus-bar and immaterial beam of force was traced and checked. Instruments and machines were dismantled, sealed mechanisms were ruthlessly torn apart by jacks or sliced open with cutting beams. And everywhere, every thing and every movement was being photographed, charted, and diagrammed.

"Getting the idea now, Kim," Thorndyke said finally, during a brief lull in his work. "A sweet system . . . . ."

"Look at this!" a mechanic interrupted. "Here's a machine that's all shot to hell!"

The shielding cover had been torn from a monstrous fabrication of metal, apparently a motor or generator of an exceedingly complex type. The insulation of its coils and windings had fallen away in charred fragments, its copper had melted down in sluggish, viscous streams.

"That's what we're looking for!" Thorndyke shouted. "Check those leads! Alpha!"

"Seven-three-nine-four!" and the minutely careful study went on until:

"That's enough; we've got everything we need now. Have you draftsmen and photographers got everything down solid?"

"On the boards!" and "In the cans!" rapped out the two reports as one.

"Then let's go!"

"And go *fast!*" Kinnison ordered, briskly. "I'm afraid we're going to run out of time as it is!"

All hands hurried back into the *Brittania*, paying no attention to the bodies littering the decks. So desperate was the emergency, each man knew, that nothing could be done about the dead, whether friend or foe. Every resource of mechanism, of brain and of brawn, must needs be strained to the utmost if they themselves were not soon to be in similar case.

"Can you talk, Nels?" demanded Kinnison of his Communications Officer, even before the air-lock had closed.

"No, sir, they're blanketing us solid," that worthy replied instantly. "Space's so full of static you couldn't drive a power-beam through it, let alone a communicator. Couldn't talk direct, anyway—look where we are," and he pointed out in the tank their present location.

"Hm . . . m . . . m. Couldn't have got much farther away without jumping the galaxy entirely. Boskone got a warning, either from that ship back there or from the disturbance. They're undoubtedly concentrating on us now . . . . . One of them will spear us with a tractor, just as sure as hell's a man-trap . . . . ."

The fledgling commander rammed both hands into his pockets and thought in black intensity. He *must* get this data back to Base—but how? HOW? Henderson was already driving the vessel back toward Sol with every iota of her inconceivable top speed, but it was out of the question even to hope that she would ever get there. The life of the *Brittania* was now, he was coldly certain, to be measured in hours— and all too scant measure, even of them. For there must be hundreds of pirate vessels even now tearing through the void, forming a gigantic net to cut off her return to Base. Fast though she was, one of that barricading horde would certainly manage to clamp on a tractor—and when that happened her flight was done.

Nor could she fight. She had conquered one first-class war-vessel of the public enemy, it was true; but at what awful cost! One fresh vessel could blast his crippled mount out of space; nor would there be only one. Within a space of minutes after the attachment of a tracer the *Brittania* would be surrounded by the cream of Boskone's fighters. There was only one chance; and slowly, thoughtfully, and finally grimly, young Lieutenant Kinnison—now and briefly Captain Kinnison—decided to take it.

"Listen, everybody!" he ordered. "We *must* get this information back to Base, and we can't do it in the *Brittannia*. The pirates are bound to catch us, and our chance in another fight is exactly zero. We'll have to abandon ship and take to the lifeboats, in the hope that at least one will be able to get through.

"The technicians and specialists will take all the data they got—information, descriptions, diagrams, pictures, everything—boil it down, and put it on a spool of tape. They will make about a hundred copies of it. The crew and the Valerian privates will man boats starting with Number Twenty One and blast off as soon as you can get your tapes. Once away, use very little detectable power, or better yet no power at all, until you're sure the pirates have chased the *Brittania* a good many parsecs away from where you are.

"The rest of us—specialists and the Valerian non-coms —will go last. Twenty boats, two men to a boat, and each man will have a spool. We'll start launching when we're as far as it's safe to go. Each boat will be strictly on its own. Do it any way you can; but some way, *any* way, get your spool back to Base. There's no use in me trying to impress you with the importance of this stuff; you know what it means as well as I do.

"Boatmates will be drawn by lot. The quartermaster will write all our names—and his own, to make it forty even— on slips of paper and draw them out of a helmet two at a time. If two navigators, such as Henderson and I, are drawn together, both names go back into the pot. Get to work!"

Twice the name of "Kinnison" came out together with that of another skilled in astronautics and was replaced. The third time, however, it came out paired with "van-Buskirk," to the manifest joy of the giant Valerian and to the approval of the crowd as well.

"That was a break for me, Kim!" the sergeant called,

over the cheers of his fellows. "I'm *sure* of getting back now!"

"That's throwing the oil, big fellow—but I don't know of anybody I'd rather have at my back than you," Kinnison replied, with a boyish grin.

The pairings were made; DeLameters, spare batteries, and other equipment were checked and tested; the spools of tape were sealed in their corrosion-proof containers and distributed; and Kinnison sat talking with the Master Technician.

"So they've solved the problem· of the really efficient reception and conversion of cosmic radiation!" Kinnison whistled softly through his teeth. "And a sun—even a small one—radiates the energy given off by the annihilation of one-to-several million tons of matter per second! SOME power!"

"That's the story, Skipper, and it explains completely why their ships have been so much superior to ours. They could have installed faster drives even than the *Brittania's* —they probably will, now that it has become necessary. Also, if the bus-bars in that receptor-convertor had been a few square centimeters larger in cross-section, they could have held their wall-shield, even against our duodec bomb. Then what? . . . . . They had plenty of intake, but not quite enough distribution."

"They have atomic motors, the same as ours; just as big and just as efficient," Kinnison coagitated. "But those motors are all we *have* got, while they use them, and at full power, too, simply as first- stage exciters for the cosmic-energy screens. Blinding blue blazes, what power! Some of us have *got* to get back, Verne. If we don't, Boskone's got the whole galaxy by the tail, and civilization is sunk without a trace."

"I'll say so; but also I'll say this for those of us who don't get back—it won't be for lack of trying. Well, better I go check my boat. If I don't see you again, Kim old man, clear ether!"

They shook hands briefly and Thorndyke strode away. Enroute, however, he paused beside the quartermaster and signalled to him to disconnect his communicator.

"Clever lad, Allerdyce!" Thorndyke whispered, with a grin. "Kinda loaded the dice a trifle once or twice, didn't you? I don't think anybody but me smelled a rat, though. Certainly neither the skipper nor Henderson did, or you'd've had it to do over again."

"At least one team has got to get through," Allerdyce replied, quietly and obliquely, "and the strongest teams we can muster will find the going none too easy. Any team made up of strength and weakness is a weak team. Kinnison, our only Lensman, is of course the best man aboard this buzz-buggy. Who would you pick for number two?"

"VanBuskirk, of course, the same as you did. I wasn't criticising you, man, I was complimenting you, and thanking you, in a roundabout way, for giving me Henderson. He's got plenty of what it takes, too."

"It wasn't 'vanBuskirk, of course,' by any means," the quartermaster rejoined. "It's mighty hard to figure either you or Henderson third, to say nothing of fourth, in any kind of company, however fast—mentally and physically. However, it seemed to me that you fitted in better with the pilot. I could hand-pick only two teams without getting caught at it—you spotted me as it was—but I think I picked the two strongest teams possible. One of you will get through—if none of you four can make it, nobody could."

"Well, here's hoping, anyway. Thanks again. See you again some time, maybe—clear ether!"

Chief Pilot Henderson had, a few minutes since, changed the course of the cruiser from right-line flight to fantastic, zig-zag leaps through space, and now he turned frowningly to Kinnison.

"We'd better begin dumping them out pretty soon now, I think," he suggested. "We haven't detected anything yet, but according to the figures it won't be long now; and after they get their traps set we'll run out of time mighty quick."

"Right," and one after another, but even so several light-years apart in space, eighteen of the small boats were launched into the void. In the control room there were left only Henderson and Thorndyke with vanBuskirk and Kinnison, who were of course to be the last to leave the vessel.

"All right, Hen, now we'll try out your roulette-wheel director-by-chance," Kinnison said, then went on, in answer to Thorndyke's questioning glance: "A bouncing ball on an oscillating table. Every time the ball carroms off a pin it shifts the course through a fairly large, but unpredictable angle. Pure chance—we thought it might cross them up a little."

Hairline beams were connected from panels to pins, and soon four interested spectators looked on while, with no human guidance, the *Brittania* lurched and leaped even more erratically than she had done under Henderson's direction. Now, however, the ever-changing vectors of her course were as unexpected and surprising to her passengers as to any possible external observer.

One more lifeboat left the vessel, and only the Lensman and his giant aide remained. While they were waiting the required few minutes before their own departure, Kinnison spoke.

"Bus, there's one more thing we ought to do, and I've just figured out how to do it. We don't want this ship to fall into the pirates' hands intact, as there's a lot of stuff in her that would probably be as new to them as it was to us. They know we got the best of that ship of theirs, but they don't know what we did or how. On the other hand, we want her to drive on as long as possible after we leave her—the farther away from us she gets, the better our chance of getting away. We should have something to touch off those duodec torpedoes we have left—all seven at once—at the first touch of a spy beam; both to keep them from studying her and to do a little damage if possible—they'll go inert and pull her up close as soon as they get a tracer on her. Of course we can't do it by stopping the spy-ray altogether, with a spy-screen, but I think I can establish an R7TX7M field outside our regular screens that will interfere with a TX7 just enough—say one-tenth of one percent—to actuate a relay in the field-supporting beam."

"One-tenth of one percent of one milliwatt is one microwatt, isn't it? Not much power, I'd say, but that's a little out of my line. Go ahead—I'll observe while you're busy."

Thus it came about that, a few minutes later, the immense sky-rover of the Galactic Patrol darted along entirely untenanted. And it was her non-human helmsman, operating solely by chance, that prolonged the chase far more than even the most optimistic member of her crew could have hoped. For the pilots of the pirate pursuers were intelligent, and assumed that their quarry also was directed by intelligence. Therefore they aimed their vessels for points toward which the *Brittania* should logically go; only and maddeningly to watch her go somewhere else. Senselessly she hurled herself directly toward enormous suns, once grazing one so nearly that the harrying pirates gasped at the foolhardiness of such exposure to lethal radiation. For no reason at all she shot straight backward, almost into a cluster of pirate craft, only to dash off on another unexpected tangent before the startled outlaws could lay a beam against her.

But finally she did it once too often. Flying between two vessels, she held her line the merest fraction of a second too long. Two tractors lashed out and the three vessels flashed together, zone to zone to zone. Then, instantly, the two pirate ships became inert, to anchor in space their wildly fleeing prey. Then spy-beams licked out, to explore the *Brittania's* interior.

At the touch of those beams, light and delicate as they were, the relay clicked and the torpedoes let go. Those frightful shells were so designed and so charged that one of them could demolish any inert structure known to man: what of seven? There was an explosion to stagger the imagination and which must be left to the imagination, since no words in any language of the galaxy can describe it adequately.

The *Brittania*, literally blown to bits, more-than-half fused and partially volatilized by the inconceivable fury of the outburst, was hurled in all directions in streamers, droplets, chunks, and masses; each component part urged away from the center of pressure by the ragingly compressed gases of detonation. Furthermore, each component was now of course inert and therefore capable of giving up its full measure of kinetic energy to any inert object with which it should come in contact.

One mass of wreckage, so fiercely sped that its victim had time neither to dodge nor become inertialess, crashed full against the side of the nearer attacker. Meteorite screens flared brilliantly violet and went down. The full-driven wall-shield held; but so terrific was the concussion that what few of the crew were not killed outright would take no interest in current events for many hours to come.

The other, slightly more distant attacker was more fortunate. Her commander had had time to render her inertialess, and as she rode lightly away, ahead of the outermost, most tenuous fringe of vapor, he reported succinctly to his headquarters all that had transpired. There was a brief interlude of silence, then a speaker gave tongue.

"Helmuth, speaking for Boskone," snapped from it. "Your report is neither complete nor conclusive. Find, study, photograph, and bring in to headquarters every fragment and particle pertaining to the wreckage, paying particular attention to all bodies or portions thereof."

"Helmuth, speaking for Boskone!" roared from the general-wave unscrambler. "Commanders of all vessels, of every class and tonnage, upon whatever mission bound, attention! The vessel referred to in our previous message has been destroyed, but it is feared that some or all of her personnel were allowed to escape. Every unit of that personnel must be killed before he has opportunity to communicate with any Patrol base. Therefore cancel your present orders, whatever they may be, and proceed at maximum blast to the region previously designated. Scour that entire volume of space. Beam out of existence every vessel whose papers do not account unquestionably for every intelligent being aboard. Investigate every possible avenue of escape. More detailed orders will be given each of you upon your nearer approach to the neighborhood under search."

CHAPTER 4 *Escape*

SPACE-SUITED COMPLETE EXCEPT FOR HELMETS, AND WITH those ready to hand, Kinnison and vanBuskirk sat in the tiny control room of their lifeboat as it drifted inert through inter-stellar space. Kinnison was poring over charts taken from the *Brittania's* pilot room; the sergeant was gazing idly into a detector plate.

"No clear ether yet, I don't suppose," the captain remarked, as he rolled up a chart and tossed it aside.

"No let-up for a second; they're not taking any chances at all. Found out where we are? Alsakan ought to be hereabouts somewhere, hadn't it?"

"Yeah. Not close, though, even for a ship—out of the question for us. Nothing much inhabited around here, either, to say nothing of being civilized. Scarcely one to the block. Don't think I've ever been out here before; have you?"

"Off my beat entirely. How long do you figure it'll be before it's safe for us to blast off?"

"Can't start blasting until your plates are clear. Anything we can detect can detect us as soon as we start putting out power."

"We may be in for a spell of waiting, then . . . . . " Van-Buskirk broke off suddenly and his tone changed to one of tense excitement. "Help, Noshabkeming, help! Look at that!"

"Blinding blue blazes!" Kinnison exclaimed, staring into the plate. "With all macro-universal space and all eternity to play around in, why in all space's hells did she have to come back here and now?"

For there, right in their laps, not a hundred miles away, lay the *Brittania* and her two pirate captors!

"Better go free, hadn't we?" whispered vanBuskirk.

"Daren't!" Kinnison grunted. "At this range they'd spot us in a split second. Acting like a hunk of loose metal's our only chance. We'll be able to dodge any flying chunks, I think . . . . . there she goes!"

From their coign of vantage the two Patrolmen saw their gallant ship's terrific end; saw the one pirate vessel suffer collision with the flying fragment; saw the other escape inertialess; saw her disappear.

The inert pirate vessel had now almost exactly the same velocity as the lifeboat, both in speed and in direction; only very slowly were the large craft and the small approaching each other. Kinnison stood rigid, staring into his plate, his nervous hands grasping the switches whose closing, at the first sign of detection, would render them inertialess and would pour full blast into their driving projectors. But minute after minute passed and nothing happened.

"Why don't they *do* something?" he burst out, finally. "They know we're here—there isn't a detector made that could be badly enough out of order to miss us at this distance. Why, they can *see* us from there, with no detectors at all!"

"Asleep, unconscious, or dead," vanBuskirk diagnosed, "and they're not asleep. Believe me, Kim, that ship was nudged. She must've been hit hard enough to lay her whole crew out cold . . . . . and say, she's got a standard emergency inlet port—how about it, huh?"

Kinnison's mind leaped eagerly at the daring suggestion of his subordinate, but he did not reply at once: Their first, their *only* duty, concerned the safety of two spools of tape. But if the lifeboat lay there inert until the pirates regained control of their craft, detection and capture were certain.

The same fate was as certain should they attempt flight with all nearby space so full of enemy fliers. Therefore, hare-brained though it appeared at first glance, vanBuskirk's wild idea was actually the safest course!

"All right, Bus, we'll try it. We'll take a chance on going free and using a tenth of a dyne of drive for a hundredth of a second. Get into the lock with your magnets."

The lifeboat flashed against the pirate's armored side and the sergeant, by deftly manipulating his two small hand-magnets, worked it rapidly along the steel plating, toward the driving jets. There, in the conventional location just forward of the main driving projectors, was indeed the emergency inlet port, with its Galactic Standard controls.

In a few minutes the two warriors were inside, dashing toward the control room. There Kinnison glanced at the board and heaved a sigh of relief.

"Fine! Same type as the one we studied. Same race, too," he went on, eyeing the motionless forms scattered about the floor. Seizing one of the bodies, he propped it against a panel thus obscuring a multiple lens.

"That's the eye overlooking the control room," he explained unnecessarily. "We can't cut their headquarters visi-beams without creating suspicion, but we don't want them looking around in here until after we've done a little stage-setting."

"But they'll get suspicious anyway when we go free," vanBuskirk protested.

"Sure, but we'll arrange for that later. First thing we've got to do is to make sure that all the crew except possibly one or two in here, are really dead. Don't beam unless you have to; we want to make it look as though everybody got killed or fatally injured in the crash."

A complete tour of the vessel, with a grim and distasteful accompaniment, was made. Not all of the pirates were dead, or even disabled; but, unarmored as they were and taken completely by surprise, the survivors could offer but little resistance. A cargo port was opened and the *Brittania's* lifeboat was drawn inside. Then back to the control room, where Kinnison picked up another body and strode to the main panels.

"This fellow," he announced, "was hurt badly, but managed to get to the board. He threw in the free switch, like this, and then full-blast drive, so. Then he pulled himself over to the steering globe and tried to lay course back to-

ward headquarters, but couldn't quite make it. He died with
the course set right there. Not exactly toward Sol, you notice—that would be too much of a coincidence—but close
enough to help a lot. His bracelet got caught in the guard,
like this. There is clear evidence as to exactly what happened. Now we'll get out of range of that eye, and let the
body that's covering it float away naturally."

"Now what?" asked vanBuskirk, after the two had hidden
themselves.

"Nothing whatever until we have to," was the reply.
"Wish we could go on like this for a couple of weeks, but
no chance. Headquarters will get curious pretty quick as to
why we're shoving off."

Even as he spoke a furious burst of noise erupted from
the communicator; a noise which meant:

"Vessel F47U596! Where are you going, and why? Report!"

At that brusk command one of the still forms struggled
weakly to its knees and tried to frame words, but fell back
dead.

"Perfect!" Kinnison breathed into vanBuskirk's ear.
"Couldn't have been better. Now they'll probably take their
time about rounding us up . . . . . maybe we can get back
to somewhere near Tellus, after all . . . . . Listen, here
comes some more." The communicator was again sending.
"See if you can get a line on their transmitter."

"If there are any survivors able to report, do so at once!"
Kinnison understood the dynamic cone to say. Then, the
voice moderating as though the speaker had turned from
his microphone to someone nearby, it went on, "No one
answers, sir. This, you know, is the ship that was lying
closest to the new Patrol ship when she exploded; so close
that her navigator did not have time to go free before collision with the debris. The crew were apparently all killed
or incapacitated by the shock."

"If any of the officers survive have them brought in for
trial," a more distant voice commanded. savagely. "Boskone
has no use for bunglers except to serve as examples. Have
the ship seized and returned here as soon as possible."

"Could you trace it, Bus?" Kinnison demanded. "Even
one line on their headquarters would be mighty useful."

"No, it came in scrambled—couldn't separate it from the
rest of the static out there. Now what?"

"Now we eat and sleep. Particularly and most emphati-
cally, we sleep."

"Watches?"

"No need; I'll be awakened in plenty of time if anything happens. My Lens, you know."

They ate ravenously and slept prodigiously; then ate and slept again. Rested and refreshed, they studied charts, but vanBuskirk's mind was very evidently not upon the maps before them.

"You understand that jargon, and it doesn't even sound like a language to me," he pondered. "It's the Lens, of course. Maybe it's something that shouldn't be talked about?"

"No secret—not among us, at least," Kinnison assured him. "The Lens receives as pure thought any pattern of force which represents, or is in any way connected with, thought. My brain receives this thought in English, since that is my native language. At the same time my ears are practically out of circuit, so that I actually hear the English language instead of whatever noise is being made. I do not hear the foreign sounds at all. Therefore I haven't the slightest idea what the pirates' language sounds like, since I have never heard any of it.

"Conversely, when I want to talk to someone who doesn't know any language I do, I simply think into the Lens and direct its force at him, and he thinks I am talking to him in his own mother tongue. Thus, you are hearing me now in perfect Valerian Dutch, even though you know that I can speak only a dozen or so words of it, and those with a vile American accent. Also, you are hearing it in my voice, even though you know I am actually not saying a word, since you can see that my mouth is wide open and that neither my lips, tongue, nor vocal cords are moving. If you were a Frenchman you would be hearing this in French; or, if you were a Manarkan and couldn't talk at all, you would be getting it as regular Manarkan telepathy."

"Oh . . . . I see . . . . I think," the astounded Dutchman gulped. "Then why couldn't you talk back to them through their phones?"

"Because the Lens, although a mighty fine and versatile thing, is not omnipotent," Kinnison replied, dryly. "It sends out only thought; and thought-waves, lying below the level of the ether, cannot affect a microphone. The microphone, not being itself intelligent, cannot receive thought. Of course I can broadcast a thought—everybody does, more or less—but without a Lens at the other end

I can't reach very far. Power, they tell me, comes with practice—I'm not so good at it yet."

"You can receive a thought . . . . . everybody broadcasts . . . . . Then you can read minds?" vanBuskirk stated, rather than asked.

"When I want to, yes. That was what I was doing while we were mopping up. I demanded the location of their base from every one of them alive, but none of them knew it. I got a lot of pictures and descriptions of the buildings, layout, arrangements and personnel of the base, but not a hint as to where it is in space. The navigators were all dead, and not even the Arisians understand death. But that's getting pretty deep into philosophy and it's time to eat again. Let's go!"

Days passed uneventfully, but finally the communicator again began to talk. Two pirate ships were closing in upon the supposedly derelict vessel; discussing with each other the exact point of convergence of the three courses.

"I was hoping we'd be able to communicate with Prime Base before they caught up with us," Kinnison remarked. "But I guess it's no dice—I can't get anybody on my Lens and the ether's as full of interference as ever. They're a suspicious bunch, and they aren't going to let us get away with a single thing if they can help it. You've got that duplicate of their communications unscrambler built?"

"Yes—that was it you just listened to. I built it out of our own stuff, and I've gone over the whole ship with a cleaner. There isn't a trace, not even a finger-print, to show that anybody except her own crew has ever been aboard."

"Good work! This course takes us right through a planetary system in a few minutes and we'll have to unload there. Let's see . . . . . this chart marks planets two and three as inhabited, but with a red reference number, eleven twenty-seven. Um . . . m . . . that means practically unexplored and unknown. No landing ever made . . . no patrol representation or connection . . . . no commerce . . . . . state of civilization unknown . . . . scanned only once, in the Third Galactic Survey, and that was a hell of a long time ago. Not so good, apparently—but maybe all the better for us, at that. Anyway, it's a forced landing, so get ready to shove off."

They boarded their lifeboat, placed it in the cargo-lock, opened the outer port upon its automatic block, and waited. At their awful galactic speed the diameter of a solar system would be traversed in such a small fraction of a second that observation would be impossible, to say nothing of computation. They would have to act first and compute later.

They flashed into the strange system. A planet loomed terrifyingly close; at their frightful velocity almost invisible even upon their ultra-vision plates. The lifeboat shot out, becoming inert as it passed the screen. The cargo-port swung shut. Luck had been with them; the planet was scarcely a million miles away. While vanBuskirk drove toward it, Kinnison made hasty observations.

"Could have been better—but could have been a lot worse," he reported. "This is planet four. Uninhabited, which is very good. Three, though, is clear over across the sun, and Two isn't any too close for a space-suit flight—better than eighty million miles. Easy enough as far as distance goes—we've all made longer hops in our suits—but we'll be open to detection for about fifteen minutes. Can't be helped, though . . . . here we are!"

"Going to land her free, huh?" vanBuskirk whistled. "What a chance!"

"It'd be a bigger one to take the time to land her inert. Her power will hold—I hope. We'll inert her and match intrinsics with her when we come back—we'll have more time then."

The lifeboat stopped instantaneously, in a free landing, upon the uninhabited, desolate, rocky soil of the strange world. Without a word the two men leaped out, carrying fully packed knapsacks. A portable projector was then dragged out and its fierce beam directed into the base of the hill beside which they had come to earth. A cavern was quickly made, and while its glassy walls were still smoking hot the lifeboat was driven within it. With their DeLameters the two wayfarers then undercut the hill, so that a great slide of soil and rock obliterated every sign of the visit. Kinnison and vanBuskirk could find their vessel again, from their accurately-taken bearings; but, they hoped, no one else could.

Then, still without a word, the two adventurers flashed upward. The atmosphere of the planet, tenuous and cold though it was, nevertheless so sorely impeded their progress that minutes of precious time were required for the driving projectors of their suits to force them through its thin layer. Eventually, however, they were in interplanetary space and were flying at quadruple the speed of light. Then vanBuskirk spoke.

"Landing the boat, hiding it, and this trip are the danger spots. Heard anything yet?"

"No, and I don't believe we will. I think probably we've lost them completely. Won't know definitely, though, until after they catch the ship, and that won't be for ten minutes yet. We'll be landed by then."

A world now loomed beneath them; a pleasant, Earthly-appearing world of scattered clouds, green forests, rolling plains, wooded and snow-capped mountain-ranges, and rolling oceans. Here and there were to be seen what looked like cities, but Kinnison gave them a wide berth; electing to land upon an open meadow in the shelter of a black and glassy cliff.

"Ah, just in time: they're beginning to talk," Kinnison announced. "Unimportant stuff yet, opening the ship and so on. I'll relay the talk as nearly verbatim as possible when it gets interesting." He fell silent, then went on in a sing-song tone, as though he were reciting from memory, which in effect he was:

" 'Captains of ships P4J263 and EQ69B47 calling Helmuth! We have stopped and have boarded the F47U596. Everything is in order and as deduced and reported by your observers. Everyone aboard is dead. They did not all die at the same time, but they all died from the effects of the collision. There is no trace of outside interference and all the personnel are accounted for.'

" 'Helmuth, speaking for Boskone. Your report is inconclusive. Search the ship minutely for tracks, prints, scratches. Note any missing supplies or misplaced items of equipment. Study carefully all mechanisms, particularly converters and communicators, for signs of tampering or dismantling.'

"Whew!" whistled Kinnison. "They'll find where you took that communicator apart, Bus, just as sure as hell's a mantrap!"

"No, they won't," declared vanBuskirk as positively. "I did it with rubber-nosed pliers, and if I left a scratch or a scar or a print on it I'll eat it, tubes and all!"

A pause.

" 'We have studied everything most carefully, Oh Helmuth, and find no trace of tampering or visit.'

"Helmuth again: 'Your report is still inconclusive. Whoever did what has been done is probably a Lensman, and certainly has *brains*. Give me the present recorded serial

number of all port openings, and the exact number of
times you have opened each port.'

"Ouch!" groaned Kinnison. "If that means what I think
it does, all hell's out for noon. Did you see any numbering
recorders on those ports? I didn't—of course neither of us
thought of such a thing. Hold it—here comes some more
stuff.

" 'Port-opening recorder serial numbers are as follows'
. . . don't mean a thing to us . . . . . 'we have opened the
emergency inlet port once and the starboard main lock
twice. No other port at all.'

"And here's Helmuth again: 'Ah, as I thought. The
emergency port was opened once by outsiders, and the
starboard cargo port twice. The Lensman came aboard,
headed the ship toward Sol, took his lifeboat aboard, listened to us, and departed at his leisure. And this in the
very midst of our fleet, the entire personnel of which was
supposed to be looking for him! How supposedly intelligent
spacemen could be guilty of such utter and indefensible
stupidity . . . . ' He's tellin' 'em plenty, Bus, but there's no
use repeating it. The tone can't be reproduced, and it's
simply taking the hide right off their backs . . . . here's
some more . . . . . 'General broadcast! Ship F47U596 in its
supposedly derelict condition flew from the point of destruction of the Patrol ship, on course . . . . . ' No use quot-
ing, Bus, he's simply giving directions for scouring our
whole line of flight . . . . . Fading out—they're going on, or
back. This outfit, of course, is good for only the closest kind
of close-up work."

"And we're out of the frying pan into the fire, huh?"

"Oh, no; we're a lot better off than we were. We're on a
planet and not using any power they can trace. Also,
they've got to cover so much territory that they can't comb
it very fine, and that gives the rest of the fellows a break.
Furthermore . . . . . . "

A crushing weight descended upon his back, and the
Patrolmen found themselves fighting for their lives. From
the bare, supposedly evidently safe rack face of the cliff
there had emerged rope-tentacled monstrosities in a ravenously attacking swarm. In the savage blasts of DeLameters
hundreds of the gargoyle horde vanished in vivid flares of
radiance, but on they came; by thousands and, it seemed,
by millions. Eventually the batteries energizing the projectors became exhausted. Then flailing coil met shearing steel,
fierce-driven parrot beaks clanged against space-tempered

armor, bulbous heads pulped under hard-swung axes; but not for the fractional second necessary for inertialess flight could the two win clear. Then Kinnison sent out his SOS.

"A Lensman calling help! A Lensman calling help!" he broadcast with the full power of mind and Lens, and immediately a sharp, clear voice poured into his brain:

"Coming, wearer of the Lens! Coming at speed to the cliff of the Catlats. Hold until I come! I arrive in thirty . . . . ."

Thirty what? What possible intelligible relative measure of that unknown and unknowable concept, Time, can be conveyed by thought alone?

"Keep slugging, Bus!" Kinnison panted. "Help is on the way. A local cop—voice sounds like it could be a woman —will be here in thirty somethings. Don't know whether it's thirty minutes or thirty days; but we'll still be there."

"Maybe so and maybe not," grunted the Dutchman. "Something's coming besides help. Look up and see if you see what I think I do."

Kinnison did so. Through the air from the top of the cliff there was hurtling downward toward them a veritable dragon: a nightmare's horror of hideously reptilian head, of leathern wings, of viciously fanged jaws, of frightfully taloned feet, of multiple knotty arms, of long, sinuous, heavily-scaled serpent's body. In fleeting glimpses through the writhing tentacles of his opponents Kinnison perceived little by little the full picture of that unbelievable monstrosity: and, accustomed as he was to the outlandish denizens of worlds scarcely known to man, his very senses reeled.

CHAPTER 5   *Worsel to the Rescue*

As THE QUASI-REPTILIAN ORGANISM DESCENDED THE CLIFF-dwellers went mad. Their attack upon the two Patrolmen, already vicious, became insanely frantic. Abandoning the gigantic Dutchman entirely, every Catlat within reach threw himself upon Kinnison and so enwrapped the Lensman's head, arms, and torso that he could scarcely move a muscle. Then entwining captors and helpless man moved slowly toward the largest of the openings in the cliff's obsidian face.

Upon that slowly moving mass vanBuskirk hurled himself, deadly space-axe swinging. But, hew and smite as he would, he could neither free his chief from the grisly horde enveloping him nor impede measurably that horde's progress toward its goal. However, he could and did cut away the comparatively few cables confining Kinnison's legs.

"Clamp a leg-lock around my waist, Kim," he directed, the flashing thought in no whit interfering with his prodigious axe-play, "and as soon as I get a chance, before the real tussle comes, I'll couple us together with all the belt-snaps I can reach—wherever we're going we're going together! Wonder why they haven't ganged up on me, too, and what that lizard is doing? Been too busy to look, but thought he'd've been on my back before this."

"He won't be on your back. That's Worsel, the lad who answered my call. I told you his voice was funny? They can't talk or hear—use telepathy, like the Manarkans. He's cleaning them out in great shape. If you can hold me for three minutes he'll have the lot of them whipped."

"I can hold you for three minutes against all the vermin between here and Andromeda," vanBuskirk declared. "There, I've got four snaps on you."

"Not too tight, Bus," Kinnison cautioned. "Leave enough slack so you can cut me loose if you have to. Remember

49

that the spools are more important than any one of us. Once inside that cliff we'll be all washed up—even Worsel can't help us there—so drop me rather than go in yourself."

"Um," grunted the Dutchman, non-committally. "There, I've tossed my spool out onto the ground. Tell Worsel that if they get us he's to pick it up and carry on. We'll go ahead with yours, inside the cliff if necessary."

"I said cut me loose if you can't hold me!" Kinnison snapped, and I meant it. That's an official order. Remember it!"

"Official order be damned!" snorted vanBuskirk, still plying his ponderous mace. "They won't get you into that hole without breaking me in two, and that will be a job of breaking in anybody's language. Now shut your pan," he concluded grimly. "We're here, and I'm going to be too busy, even to think, very shortly."

He spoke truly. He had already selected his point of resistance, and as he reached it he thrust the head of his mace into the crack behind the open trap-door, jammed its shaft into the shoulder-socket of his armor, set blocky legs and Herculean arms against the cliffside, arched his mighty back, and held. And the surprised Catlats, now inside the gloomy fastness of their tunnel, thrust anchoring tentacles into crevices in the wall and pulled; harder, ever harder.

Under the terrific stress Kinnison's heavy armor creaked as its air-tight joints accommodated themselves to their new and unusual positions. That armor, or space-tempered alloy, of course would not give way—but what of its anchor?

Well it was for Kimball Kinnison that day, and well for our present civilization, that the *Brittania's* quartermaster had selected Peter vanBuskirk for the Lensman's mate; for death, inevitable and horrible, resided within that cliff, and no human frame of Earthly growth, however armored, could have borne for even a fraction of a second the violence of the Catlats' pull.

But Peter vanBuskirk, although of Earthly-Dutch ancestry, had been born and reared upon the planet Valeria, and that massive planet's gravity—over two and one half times Earth's—had given him a physique and a strength almost inconceivable to us life-long dwellers upon small, green Terra. His head, as has been said, towered seventy-eight inches above the ground; but at that he appeared squatty because of his enormous spread of shoulder and his startling girth. His bones were elephantine—they had to be, to furnish adequate support and leverage for the incredible masses of muscle overlaying and surrounding them. But even vanBuskirk's Valerian strength was now being taxed to the uttermost.

The anchoring chains hummed and snarled as the clamps bit into the rings. Muscles writhed and knotted, tendons stretched and threatened to snap; sweat rolled down his mighty back. His jaws locked in agony and his eyes started from their sockets with the effort; but still vanBuskirk held.

"Cut me loose!" commanded Kinnison at last. "Even you can't take much more of that. No use letting them break your back . . . . . *Cut*, I tell you . . . . . I said *CUT*, you big, dumb, Valerian ape!"

But if vanBuskirk heard or felt the savagely-voiced commands of his chief he gave no heed. Straining to the very ultimate fiber of his being, exerting every iota of loyal mind and every atom of Brobdingnagian frame: grimly, tenaciously, stubbornly the gigantic Dutchman held.

Held while Worsel of Velantia, that grotesquely hideous, that fantastically reptilian ally, plowed toward the two Patrolmen through the horde of Catlats; a veritable tornado of rending fang and shearing talon, of beating wing and crushing snout, of mailed hand and trenchant tail:

Held while that demon incarnate drove closer and closer, hurling entire Catlats and numberless dismembered fragments of Catlats to the four winds as he came:

Held until Worsel's snake-like body, a supple and sentient cable of living steel, tipped with its double-edged, razor-keen, scimitar-like sting, slipped into the tunnel beside Kinnison and wrought grisly havoc among the Catlats close-packed there!

As the terrific tension upon him was suddenly released vanBuskirk's own efforts hurled him away from the cliff. He fell to the ground, his overstrained muscles twitching uncontrollably, and on top of him fell the fettered Lensman. Kinnison, his hands now free, unfastened the clamps linking his armor to that of vanBuskirk and whirled to confront the foe—but the fighting was over. The Catlats had had enough of Worsel of Velantia; and, screaming and shrieking in baffled rage, the last of them were disappearing into their caves.

VanBuskirk got shakily to his feet. "Thanks for the help, Worsel, we were just about to run out of time . . . . ." he began, only to be silenced by an insistent thought from the grotesquely monstrous stranger.

"Stop that radiating! Do not think at all if you cannot screen your minds!" came urgent mental commands. "These Catlats are a very minor pest of this planet Delgon. There are others worse by far. Fortunately, your thoughts are upon a frequency never used here—if I had not been so very close to you I would not have heard you at all—but should the Overlords have a listener upon that band your unshielded thinking may already have done irreparable harm. Follow me. I will slow my speed to yours, but hurry all possible!"

"You tell 'im, Chief," vanBuskirk said, and fell silent; his mind as nearly a perfect blank as his iron will could make it.

"This is a screened thought, through my Lens," Kinnison took up the conversation. "You don't need to slow down on our account—we can develop any speed you wish. Lead on!"

The Velantian leaped into the air and flashed away in headlong flight. Much to his surprise the two human beings kept up with him effortlessly upon their inertialess drives, and after a moment Kinnison directed another thought.

"If time is an object, Worsel, know that my companion and I can carry you anywhere you wish to go at a speed hundreds of times greater than this that we are using," he vouchsafed.

It developed that time was of the utmost possible importance and the three closed in. Mighty wings folded back, hands and talons gripped armor chains, and the group, inertialess all, shot away at a pace that Worsel of Velantia had never imagined even in his wildest dreams of speed. Their goal, a small, featureless tent of thin sheet metal, occupying a barren spot in a writhing, crawling expanse of lushly green jungle, was reached in a space of minutes. Once inside, Worsel sealed the opening and turned to his armored guests.

"We can now think freely in open converse. This wall is the carrier of a screen through which no thought can make its way."

"This world you call by a name I have interpreted as Delgon," Kinnison began, slowly. "You are a native of Velantia, a planet now beyond the sun. Therefore I assumed that you were taking us to your space-ship. Where is that ship?"

"I have no ship," the Velantian replied, composedly,

"nor have I need of one. For the remainder of my life—which is now to be measured in a few of your hours—this tent is my only . . ."

"No ship!" vanBuskirk broke in. "I hope we won't have to stay on this Noshabkeming-forgotten planet forever—and I'm not very keen on going much further in that lifeboat, either."

"We may not have to do either of those things," Kinnison reassured his sergeant. "Worsel comes of a long-lived tribe, and the fact that he thinks his enemies are going to get him in a few hours doesn't make it true, by any means—there are three of us to reckon with now. Also, when we need a space-ship we'll get one, if we have to build it. Now, let's find out what this is all about. Worsel, start at the beginning and don't skip a thing. Between us we can surely find a way out, for all of us."

Then the Velantian told his story. There was much repetition, much roundabout thinking, as some of the concepts were so bizarre as to defy transmission, but finally the Patrolmen had a fairly complete picture of the situation then obtaining within that strange solar system.

The inhabitants of Delgon were bad, being characterized by a type and a depth of depravity impossible for a human mind to visualize. Not only were the Delgonians enemies of the Velantians in the ordinary sense of the word; not only were they pirates and robbers; not only were they their masters, taking them both as slaves and as food-cattle; but there was something more, something deeper and worse, something only partially transmissible from mind to mind—a horribly and repulsively Saturnalian type of mental and intellectual, as well as biological, parasitism. This relationship had gone on for ages, and during those ages rebellion was impossible, as any Velantian capable of leading such a movement disappeared before he could make any headway at all.

Finally, however, a thought screen had been devised, behind which Velantia developed a high science of her own. The students of this science lived with but one purpose in life, to free Velantia from the tyranny of the Overlords of Delgon. Each student, as he reached the zenith of his mental power, went to Delgon, to study and if possible to destroy the tyrants. And after disembarking upon the soil of that dread planet no Velantian, whether student or scientist or private adventurer, had ever returned to Velantia.

"But why don't you lay a complaint against them before

the Council?" demanded vanBuskirk. "They'd straighten things out in a hurry."

"We have not heretofore known, save by the most unreliable and roundabout reports, that such an organization as your Galactic Patrol really exists," the Velantian replied, obliquely. "Nevertheless, many years since, we launched a space-ship toward its nearest reputed base. However, since that trip requires three normal lifetimes, with deadly peril in every moment, it will be a miracle if the ship ever completes it. Furthermore, even if the ship should reach its destination, our complaint will probably not even be considered because we have not a single shred of real evidence with which to support it. No living Velantian has even seen a Delgonian, nor can anyone testify to the truth of anything I have told you. While we believe that that is the true condition of affairs, our belief is based, not upon evidence admissible in a court of law, but upon deductions from occasional thoughts radiated from this planet. Nor were these thoughts alike in tenor . . . . ."

"Skip that for a minute—we'll take the picture as correct," Kinnison broke in. "Nothing you have said so far shows any necessity for you to die in the next few hours."

"The only object in life for a trained Velantian is to liberate his planet from the horrors of subjection to Delgon. Many such have come here, but not one has found a workable idea; not one has either returned to or even communicated with Velantia after starting work here. I am a Velantian. I am here. Soon I shall open that door and get in touch with the enemy. Since better men than I am have failed, I do not expect to succeed. Nor shall I return to my native planet. As soon as I start to work the Delgonians will command me to come to them. In spite of myself I will obey that command, and very shortly thereafter I shall die, in what fashion I do not know."

"Snap out of it, Worsel!" Kinnison ordered, bruskly. "That's the rankest kind of defeatism, and you know it. Nobody ever got to the first check-station on that kind of fuel."

"You are talking about something now about which you know nothing whatever." For the first time Worsel's thoughts showed passion. "Your thoughts are idle—ignorant—vain. You know nothing whatever of the mental power of the Delgonians."

"Maybe not—I make no claim to being a mental giant —but I do know that mental power alone cannot overcome a definitely and positively opposed *will*. An Arisian could probably break my will, but I'll stake my life that no other mentality in the known Universe can do it!"

"You think so, Earthling?" and a seething sphere of mental force encompassed the Tellurian's brain. Kinnison's senses reeled at the terrific impact, but he shook off the attack and smiled.

"Come again. Worsel. That one jarred me to the heels, but it didn't quite ring the bell."

"You flatter me," the Velantian declared in surprise. "I could scarcely touch your mind—could not penetrate even its outermost defenses, and I exerted all my force. But that fact gives me hope. My mind is of course inferior to theirs, but since I could not influence you at all, even in direct contact and at full power, you may be able to resist the minds of the Delgonians. Are you willing to hazard the stake you mentioned a moment ago? Or rather, I ask you, by the Lens you wear, so to hazard it—with the liberty of an entire people dependent upon the outcome?"

"Why not? The spools come first, of course—but without you our spools would both be buried now inside the cliff of the Catlats. Fix it so your people will find these spools and carry on with them in case we fail, and I'm your man. There—now tell me what we're apt to be up against, and then let loose your dogs."

"That I cannot do. I know only that they will direct against us mental forces such as you have never even imagined—I cannot forewarn you in any respect whatever as to what forms those forces may appear to assume. I know, however, that I shall succumb to the first bolt of force. Therefore bind me with these chains before I open the shield. Physically I am extremely strong, as you know; therefore be sure to put on enough chains so that I cannot possibly break free, for if I can break away I shall undoubtedly kill both of you."

"How come all these things here, ready to hand?" asked vanBuskirk, as the two Patrolmen so loaded the passive Velantian with chains, manacles, hand-cuffs, leg-irons and straps that he could not move even his tail.

"It has been tried before, many times," Worsel replied bleakly, "but the rescuers, being Velantians, also succumbed to the force and took off the irons. Now I caution you, with all the power of my mind—no matter what you see, no matter what I may command you or beg of you, no matter how urgently you yourself may wish to do so—DO NOT LIB-

ERATE ME UNDER ANY CIRCUMSTANCES unless and until things appear exactly as they do now and that door is shut. Know fully and ponder well the fact that if you release me while that door is open it will be because you have yielded to Delgonian force; and that not only will all three of us die, lingeringly and horribly; but also and worse, that our deaths will not have been of any benefit to civilization. Do you understand? Are you ready?"

"I understand—I am ready," thought Kinnison and van-Buskirk as one.

"Open that door."

Kinnison did so. For a few minutes nothing happened. Then three-dimensional pictures began to form before their eyes—pictures which they knew existed only in their own minds, yet which were composed of such solid substance that they obscured from vision everything else in the material world. At first hazy and indistinct, the scene—for it was in no sense now a picture—became clear and sharp. And, piling horror upon horror, sound was added to sight. And directly before their eyes, blotting out completely even the solid metal of the wall only a few feet distant from them, the two outlanders saw and heard something which can be represented only vaguely by imagining Dante's Inferno an actuality and raised to the Nth power!

In a dull and gloomy cavern there lay, sat, and stood hordes of *things*. These beings—the "nobility" of Delgon—had reptilian bodies, somewhat similar to Worsel's, but they had no wings and their heads were distinctly apish rather than crocodilian. Every greedy eye in the vast throng was fixed upon an enormous screen which, like that in a motion-picture theater, walled off one end of the stupendous cavern.

Slowly, shudderingly, Kinnison's mind began to take in what was happening upon that screen. And it was really happening, Kinnison was sure of that—this was not a picture any more than this whole scene was an illusion. It was all an actuality—somewhere.

Upon that screen there were stretched out victims. Hundreds of these were Velantians, more hundreds were winged Delgonians, and scores were creatures whose like Kinnison had never seen. And all these were being tortured: tortured to death both in fashions known to the Inquisitors of old and in ways of which even those experts had never an inkling. Some were being twisted outrageously in three-dimensional frames. Others were being stretched upon racks.

Many were being pulled horribly apart, chains intermittently but relentlessly extending each helpless member. Still others were being lowered into pits of constantly increasing temperature or were being attacked by gradually increasing concentrations of some foully corrosive vapor which ate away their tissues, little by little. And, apparently the pièce de résistance of the hellish exhibition, one luckless Velantian, in a spot of hard, cold light, was being pressed out flat against the screen, as an insect might be pressed between two panes of glass. Thinner and thinner he became under the influence of some awful, invisible force; in spite of every exertion of inhumanly powerful muscles driving body, tail, wings, arms, legs, and head in every frantic maneuver which grim and imminent death could call forth.

Physically nauseated, brain-sick at the atrocious visions blasting his mind and at the screaming of the damned assailing his ears, Kinnison strove to wrench his mind away, but was curbed savagely by Worsel.

"You *must* stay! You *must* pay attention!" commanded the Velantian. "This is the first time any living being has seen so much—you *must* help me now! They have been attacking me from the first; but, braced by the powerful negatives in your mind, I have been able to resist and have transmitted a truthful picture so far. But they are surprised at my resistance and are concentrating more force . . . . . I am slipping fast . . . . . you *must* brace my mind! And when the picture changes—as change it must, and soon—do not believe it. Hold fast, brothers of the Lens, for your own lives and for the people of Velantia. There is more—and worse!"

Kinnison stayed. So did vanBuskirk, fighting with all his stubborn Dutch mind. Revolted, outraged, nauseated as they were at the sights and sounds, they stayed. Flinching with the victims as they were fed into the hoppers of slowly turning mills; wincing at the unbelievable acts of the boilers, the beaters, the scourgers, the flayers; suffering themselves every possible and many apparently impossible nightmares of slow and hideous torture—with clenched fists and locked teeth, with sweating foreheads over white and straining faces, Kinnison and vanBuskirk stayed.

The light in the cavern now changed to a strong, greenish-yellow glare; and in that hard illumination it was to be seen that each dying being was surrounded by a palely glowing aura. And now, crowning horror of that unutterably horrible orgy of Sadism resublimed, from the eyes of each one of the monstrous audience there leaped out visible beams of force. These beams touched the auras of the dying prisoners; touched and clung. And as they clung, the auras shrank and disappeared.

The Overlords of Delgon were actually FEEDING upon the ebbing life-forces of their tortured, dying victims!

CHAPTER 6 *Delgonian Hypnotism*

GRADUALLY AND SO INSIDIOUSLY THAT THE VELANTIAN'S DIRE warnings might as well never have been uttered, the scene changed. Or rather, the scene itself did not change, but the observers' perception of it slowly underwent such a radical transformation that it was in no sense the same scene it had been a few minutes before; and they felt almost abjectly apologetic as they realized how unjust their previous ideas had been.

For the cavern was not a torture-chamber, as they had supposed. It was in reality a hospital, and the beings they had thought victims of brutalities unspeakable were in reality patients undergoing treatments and operations for various ills. In proof whereof the patients—who should have been dead by this time were the early ideas well-founded—were now being released from the screen-like operating theater. And not only was each one completely whole and sound in body, but he was also possessed of a mental clarity, power, and grasp undreamed-of before his hospitalization and treatment by Delgon's super-surgeons!

Also the intruders had misunderstood completely the audience and its behavior. They were really medical students, and the beams which had seemed to be devouring rays were simply visibeams, by means of which each student could follow, in close-up detail, each step of the operation in which he was most interested. The patients themselves were living, vocal witnesses of the visitors' mistakenness, for each, as he made his way through the assemblage

of students, was voicing his thanks for the marvelous results
of his particular treatment or operation.

Kinnison now became acutely aware that he himself was
in need of immediate surgical attention. His body, which he
had always regarded so highly, he now perceived to be sadly
inefficient; his mind was in even worse shape than his physique; and both body and mind would be improved immeas-
urably if he could get to the Delgonian hospital before the
surgeons departed. In fact, he felt an almost irresistible
urge to rush away toward that hospital; instantly, without
the loss of a single precious second. And, since he had had
no reason to doubt the evidence of his own senses, his
conscious mind was not aroused to active opposition. However, in his—in his subconscious, or his essence, or whatever you choose to call that ultimate something of his that
made him a Lensman—a "dead slow bell" began to sound.

"Release me and we'll all go, before the surgeons leave
the hospital," came an insistent thought from Worsel. "But
hurry—we haven't much time!"

VanBuskirk, completely under the influence of the frantic compulsion, leaped toward the Velantian, only to be
checked bodily by Kinnison, who was foggily trying to iso-
late and identify one thing about the situation that did not
ring quite true.

"Just a minute, Bus—shut that door first!" he commanded.

"Never mind the door!" Worsel's thought came in a
roaring crescendo. "Release me instantly! Hurry! Hurry, or
it will be too late, for all of us!"

"All this terrific rush doesn't make any kind of sense at
all," Kinnison declared, closing his mind resolutely to the
clamor of the Velantian's thoughts. "I want to go just as
badly as you do, Bus, or maybe more so—but I can't help
feeling that there's something screwy somewhere. Anyway,
remember the last thing Worsel said, and let's shut the door
before we unsnap a single chain."

Then something clicked in the Lensman's mind.

"Hypnotism, through Worsel!" he barked, opposition now
aflame. "So gradual that it never occurred to me to build
up a resistance. Holy Klono, what a fool I've been! Fight
'em, Bus—*fight 'em!* Don't let 'em kid you any more, and
pay no attention to anything Worsel sends at you!" Whirling
around, he leaped toward the open door of the tent.

But as he leaped his brain was invaded by such a concentration of force that he fell flat upon the floor, physical-

ly out of control. He must *not* shut the door. He *must* release the Velantian. They *must* go to the Delgonian cavern. Fully aware now, however, of the source of the waves of compulsion, he threw the sum total of his mental power into an intense negation and struggled, inch-wise, toward the opening.

Upon him now, in addition to the Delgonians' compulsion, beat at point-blank range the full power of Worsel's mighty mind, demanding release and compliance. Also, and worse, he perceived that some powerful mentality was being exerted to make vanBuskirk kill him. One blow of the Valerian's ponderous mace would shatter helmet and skull, and all would be over—once more the Delgonians would have triumphed. But the stubborn Dutchman, although at the very verge of surrender, was still fighting. One step forward he would take, bludgeon poised aloft, only to throw it convulsively backward. Then in spite of himself, he would go over and pick it up, again to step toward his crawling chief.

Again and again vanBuskirk repeated his futile performance while the Lensman struggled nearer and nearer the door. Finally he reached it and kicked it shut. Instantly the mental turmoil ceased and the two white and shaking Patrolmen released the limp, unconscious Velantian from his bonds.

"Wonder what we can do to help him revive?" gasped Kinnison, but his solicitude was unnecessary—the Velantian recovered consciousness as he spoke.

"Thanks to your wonderful power of resistance, I am alive, unharmed, and know more of our foes and their methods than any other of my race has ever learned," Worsel thought, feelingly. "But it is of no value whatever unless I can send it back to Velantia. The thought-screen is carried only by the metal of these walls; and if I make an opening in the wall to think through, however small, it will now mean death. Of course the science of your Patrol has not perfected an apparatus to drive thought through such a screen?"

"No. Anyway, it seems to me that we'd better be worrying about something besides thought-screens," Kinnison suggested. "Surely, now that they know where we are, they'll be coming out here after us, and we haven't got much of any defense."

"They don't know where we are, or care . . . . ." began the Velantian.

"Why not?" broke in vanBuskirk. "Any spy-ray capable of such scanning as you showed us—I never saw anything like it before—would certainly be as easy to trace as an out-and-out atomic blast!"

"I sent out no spy-ray or anything of the kind," Worsel thought, carefully. "Since our science is so foreign to yours, I am not sure that I can explain satisfactorily, but I shall try to do so. First, as to what you saw. When that door is cpen, no barrier to thought exists. I merely broadcast a thought, placing myself en rapport with the Delgonian Overlords in their retreat. This condition established, of course I heard and saw exactly what they heard and saw—and so, equally of course, did you, since you were also en rapport with me. That is all."

"That's *all!*" echoed vanBuskirk. "What a system! You can do a thing like that, without apparatus of any kind, and yet say 'that's all'!"

"It is results that count," Worsel reminded him gently. "While it is true that we have done much—this is the first time in history that any Velantian has encountered the mind of a Delgonian Overlord and lived—it is equally true that it was the will-power of you Patrolmen that made it possible; not my mentality. Also, it remains true that we cannot leave this room and live."

"Why won't we need weapons?" asked Kinnison, returning to his previous line of thought.

"Thought-screens are the only defense we will require," Worsel stated positively, "for they use no weapons except their minds. By mental power alone they make us come to them; and, once there, their slaves do the rest. Of course, if my race is ever to rid the planet of them, we must employ offensive weapons of power. We have such, but we have never been able to use them. For, in order to locate the enemy, either by telepathy or by spy-ray, we must open our metallic shields—and the instant we release those screens we are lost. From those conditions there is no escape," Worsel concluded, hopelessly.

"Don't be such a pessimist," Kinnison commanded. "There's a lot of things not tried yet. For instance, from what I have seen of your generator equipment and the pattern of that screen, you don't need a metallic conductor any more than a snake needs hips. Maybe I'm wrong, but I think we're a bit ahead of you there. If a deVilbiss projector can handle that screen—and I think it can, with special tuning—vanBuskirk and I can fix things in an hour so that all three of us can walk out of here in perfect safety—from mental interference, at least. While we're trying it out, tell us all the new stuff you got on them just now, and anything else that by any possibility may prove useful. And remember you said this is the first time any of you had been able to cut them off. That fact ought to make them sit up and take notice—probably they'll stir around more than they ever did before. Come on, Bus—let's tear into it!"

The deVilbiss projectors were rigged and tuned. Kinnison had been right—they worked. Then plan after plan was made, only to be discarded as its weaknesses were pointed out.

"Whichever way we look there are too many 'ifs' and 'buts' to suit me," Kinnison summed up the situation finally. "*If* we can find them, and *if* we can get up close to them without losing our minds to them, we could clean them out *if* we had some power in our accumulators. So I'd say the first thing for us to do is to get our batteries charged. We saw some cities from the air, and cities always have power. Lead us to power, Worsel—almost *any* kind of power—and we'll soon have it in our guns."

"There are cities, yes," Worsel was not at all enthusiastic, "dwelling-places of the ordinary Delgonians; the people you saw being eaten in the cavern of the Overlords. As you saw, they resemble us Velantians to a certain extent. Since they are of a lower culture and are much weaker in life force than we are, however, the Overlords prefer us to their own slave races.

"To visit any city of Delgon is out of the question. Every inhabitant of every city is an abject slave and his brain is an open book. Whatever he sees, whatever he thinks, is communicated instantly to his master. And I now perceive that I may have misinformed you as to the Overlords' ability to use weapons. While the situation has never arisen, it is only logical to suppose that as soon as we are seen by any Delgonian the controllers will order all the inhabitants of the city to capture us and bring us to them."

"What a guy!" interjected vanBuskirk. "Did you ever see his top for looking at the bright side of life?"

"Only in conversation," the Lensman replied. "When the ether gets crowded, you notice, he's right in there, blasting away and not saying a word. But to get back to the question of power. I've got only a few minutes of free flight left in my battery; and with your mass, you must be just about out. Come to think of it, didn't you land a trifle hard when we sat down here?"

"Fairly—I went into the ground up to my knees."

"I thought so. We've *got* to get some power, and the nearest city—out of the question or not—is the best place to get it. Luckily, it isn't far."

VanBuskirk grunted. "As far as I'm concerned it might as well be on Mars, considering what's between here and there. You can take my batteries and I'll wait here."

"On your emergency food, water, and air? That's out!"

"What else, then?"

"I can spread my field to cover all three of us," proposed Kinnison. "That will give us at least one minute of free flight—almost, if not quite, enough to clear the jungle. They have night here; and, like us, the Delgonians are night-sleepers. We start at dusk, and tonight we recharge our batteries."

The following hour, during which the huge, hot sun dropped to the horizon, was spent in intense discussion, but no significant improvement upon the Lensman's plan could be devised.

"It is time to go," Worsel announced, curling out one extensile eye toward the vanishing orb. "I have recorded all my findings. Already I have lived longer and, through you, have accomplished more, than anyone has ever believed possible. I am ready to die—I should have been dead long since."

"Living on borrowed time's a lot better than not living at all," Kinnison replied, with a grin. "Link up . . . . Ready? . . . . Go!"

He snapped his switches and the close-linked group of three shot into the air and away. As far as the eye could reach in any direction extended the sentient, ravenous growth of the jungle; but Kinnison's eyes were not upon that fantastically inimical green carpet. His whole attention was occupied by two all-important meters and by the task of so directing their flight as to gain the greatest possible horizontal distance with the power at his command.

Fifty seconds of flashing flight, then:

"All right, Worsel, get out in front and get ready to pull!" Kinnison snapped. "Ten seconds of drive left, but I can hold us free for five seconds after my driver quits. Pull!"

Kinnison's driver expired, its small accumulator completely exhausted; and Worsel, with his mighty wings, took up the task of propulsion. Inertialess still, with Kinnison and vanBuskirk grasping his tail, each beat a mile-long leap, he struggled on. But all too soon the battery powering the neutralizers also went dead and the three began to plummet downward at a sharper and sharper angle, in spite of the Velantian's Herculean efforts to keep them aloft.

Some distance ahead of them the green of the jungle ended in a sharply cut line, beyond which there was a heavy growth of fairly open forest. A couple of miles of this and there was the city, their objective—so near and yet so far!

"We'll either just make the timber or we just won't," Kinnison, mentally plotting the course, announced dispassionately. "Just as well if we land in the jungle, I think. It'll break our fall, anyway—hitting solid ground inert at this speed would be bad."

"If we land in the jungle we will never leave it," Worsel's thought did not slow the incredible tempo of his prodigious pinions, "but it makes little difference whether I die now or later."

"It does to us, you pessimistic croaker!" flared Kinnison. "Forget that dying complex of yours for a minute! Remember the plan, and follow it! We're going to strike the jungle, about ninety or a hundred meters in. If you come in with us you die at once, and the rest of our scheme is all shot to hell. So when we let go, you go ahead and land in the woods. We'll join you there, never fear: our armor will hold long enough for us to cut our way through a hundred meters of any jungle that ever grew—even this one . . . . Get ready, Bus . . . . . Leggo!"

They dropped. Through the lush succulence of close-packed upper leaves and tentacles they crashed; through the heavier, woodier main branches below; through to the ground. And there they fought for their lives; for those voracious plants nourished themselves not only upon the soil in which their roots were imbedded, but also upon anything organic unlucky enough to come within their reach. Flabby but tough tentacles encircled them; ghastly sucking disks, exuding a potent corrosive, slobbered wetly at their armor; knobbed and spiky bludgeons whanged against tempered steel as the monstrous organisms began dimly to realize that these particular tid-bits were encased in something far more resistant than skin, scales, or bark.

But the Lensman and his giant companion were not

quiescent. They came down oriented and fighting. VanBuskirk, in the van, swung his frightful space-axe as a reaper swings his scythe—one solid, short step forward with each swing. And close behind the Valerian strode Kinnison, his own flying axe guarding the giant's head and back. Forward they pressed, and forward—not the strongest, toughest stems of that monstrous weed could stay vanBuskirk's Herculean strength; not the most agile of the striking tendrils and curling tentacles could gain a manacling hold in the face of Kinnison's flashing speed in cut, thrust, and slash.

Masses of the obscene vegetation crashed down upon their heads from above, revoltingly cupped orifices sucking and smacking; and they were showered continually with floods of the opaque, corrosive sap, to the action of which even their armor was not entirely immune. But, hampered as they were and almost blinded, they struggled on; while behind them an ever-lengthening corridor of demolition marked their progress.

"Ain't we got fun?" grunted the Dutchman, in time with his swing. "But we're quite a team at that, chief—brains and brawn, huh?"

"Uh uh," dissented Kinnison, his weapon flying. "Grace and poise; or, if you want to be really romantic, ham and eggs."

"Rack and ruin will be more like it if we don't break out before this confounded goo eats through our armor. But we're making it—the stuff's thinning out and I think I can see trees up ahead."

"It is well if you can," came a cold, clear thought from Worsel, "for I am sorely beset. Hasten or I perish!"

At that thought the two Patrolmen forged ahead in a burst of even more furious activity. Crashing through the thinning barriers of the jungle's edge, they wiped their lenses partially clear, glanced quickly about, and saw the Velantian. That worthy was "sorely beset" indeed. Six animals—huge, reptilian, but lithe and active—had him down. So helplessly immobile was Worsel that he could scarcely move his tail, and the monsters were already beginning to gnaw at his scaly, armored hide.

"I'll put a stop to that, Worsel!" called Kinnison; referring to the fact, well known to all us moderns, that any real animal, no matter how savage, can be controlled by any wearer of the Lens. For, no matter how low in the scale of intelligence the animal is, the Lensman can get in touch with whatever mind the creature has, and reason with it.

But these monstrosities, as Kinnison learned immediately, were not really animals. Even though of animal form and mobility, they were purely vegetable in motivation and behavior, reacting only to the stimuli of food and of reproduction. Weirdly and completely inimical to all other forms of created life, they were so utterly noisome, so completely alien that the full power of mind and Lens failed entirely to gain rapport.

Upon that confusedly writhing heap the Patrolmen flung themselves, terrible axes destructively a-swing. In turn they were attacked viciously, but this battle was not long to endure. VanBuskirk's first terrific blow knocked one adversary away, almost spinning end over end. Kinnison took out one, the Dutchman another, and the remaining three were no match at all for the humiliated and furiously raging Velantian. But it was not until the monstrosities had been gruesomely carved and torn apart, literally to bits, that they ceased their insensately voracious attacks.

"They took me by surprise," explained Worsel, unnecessarily, as the three made their way through the night toward their goal, "and six of them at once were too much for me. I tried to hold their minds, but apparently they have none."

"How about the Overlords?" asked Kinnison. "Suppose they have received any of our thoughts? Bus and I may have done some unguarded radiating."

"No," Worsel made positive reply. "The thought-screen batteries, while small and of very little actual power, have a very long service life. Now let us go over again the next steps of our plan of action."

Since no more untoward events marred their progress toward the Delgonian city, they soon reached it. It was for the most part dark and quiet, its somber buildings merely blacker blobs against a background of black. Here and there, however, were to be seen automotive vehicles moving about, and the three invaders crouched against a convenient wall, waiting for one to come along the "street" in which they were. Eventually one did.

As it passed them Worsel sprang into headlong, gliding flight, Kinnison's heavy knife in one gnarled fist. And as he sailed he struck—lethally. Before that luckless Delgonian's brain could radiate a single thought it was in no condition to function at all; for the head containing it was bouncing in the gutter. Worsel backed the peculiar conveyance along the curb and his two companions leaped into it, lying flat upon its floor and covering themselves from sight as best they could.

Worsel, familiar with things Delgonian and looking enough like a native of the planet to pass a casual inspection in the dark, drove the car. Streets and thoroughfares he traversed at reckless speed, finally drawing up before a long, low building; entirely dark. He scanned his surrounding with care, in every direction. Not a creature was in sight.

"All is clear, friends," he thought, and the three adventurers sprang to the building's entrance. The door—it had a door, of sorts—was locked, but vanBuskirk's axe made short work of that difficulty. Inside, they braced the wrecked door against intrusion, then Worsel led the way into the unlighted interior. Soon he flashed his lamp about him and stepped upon a black, peculiarly-marked tile set into the floor, whereupon a harsh, white light illuminated the room.

"Cut it, before somebody takes alarm!" snapped Kinnison.

"No danger of that," replied the Velantian. "There are no windows in any of these rooms; no light can be seen from outside. This is the control room of the city's power plant. If you can convert any of this power to your uses, help yourselves to it. In this building is also a Delgonian arsenal. Whether or not anything in it can be of service to you is of course for you to say. I am now at your disposal."

Kinnison had been studying the panels and instruments. Now he and vanBuskirk tore open their armor—they had already learned that the atmosphere of Delgon, while not as wholesome for them as that in their suits, would for a time at least support human life—and wrought diligently with pliers, screw-drivers, and other tools of the electrician. Soon their exhausted batteries were upon the floor beneath the instrument panel, absorbing greedily the electrical fluid from the bus-bars of the Delgonians.

"Now, while they're getting filled up, let's see what these people use for guns. Lead on, Worsel!"

WITH WORSEL IN THE LEAD, THE THREE INTERLOPERS hastened along a corridor, past branching and intersecting hallways, to a distant wing of the structure. There, it was evident, manufacturing of weapons was carried on; but a quick study of the queer-looking devices and mechanisms upon the benches and inside the storage racks lining the walls convinced Kinnison that the room could yield them nothing of permanent benefit. There were high-powered beam-projectors, it was true; but they were so heavy that they were not even semi-portable. There were also hand-weapons of various peculiar patterns, but without exception they were ridiculously inferior to the DeLameters of the Patrol in every respect of power, range, controllability, and storage capacity. Nevertheless, after testing them out sufficiently to make certain of the above findings, he selected an armful of the most powerful models and turned to his companions.

"Let's go back to the power room," he urged. "I'm nervous as a cat. I feel stark naked without my batteries; and if anyone should happen to drop in there and do away with them, we'd be sunk without a trace."

Loaded down with Delgonian weapons they hurried back the way they had come. Much to Kinnison's relief he found that his forebodings had been groundless; the batteries were still there, still absorbing myriawatt-hour after myriawatt-hour from the Delgonian generators. Staring fixedly at the innocuous-looking containers, he frowned in thought.

"Better we insulate those leads a little heavier and put the cans back in our armor," he suggested finally. "They'll charge just as well in place, and it doesn't stand to reason that this drain of power can go on for the rest of the night without *somebody* noticing it. And when that happens those

Overlords are bound to take plenty of steps—none of which we have any idea what are going to be."

"You must have power enough now so that we can all fly away from any possible trouble," Worsel suggested.

"But that's just exactly what we're *not* going to do!" Kinnison declared, with finality. "Now that we've found a good charger, we aren't going to leave it until our accumulators are chock-a-block. It's coming in faster than full draft will take it out, and we're going to get a full charge if we have to stand off all the vermin of Delgon to do it."

Far longer than Kinnison had thought possible they were unmolested, but finally a couple of Delgonian engineers came to investigate the unprecedented shortage in the output of their completely automatic generators. At the entrance they were stopped, for no ordinary tools could force the barricade vanBuskirk had erected behind that portal. With leveled weapons the Patrolmen stood, awaiting the expected attack, but none developed. Hour by hour the long night wore away, uneventfully. At daybreak, however, a storming party appeared and massive battering rams were brought into play.

As the dull, heavy concussions reverberated throughout the building the Patrolmen—each picked up two of the weapons piled before them and Kinnison addressed the Velantian.

"Drag a couple of those metal benches across that corner and coil up behind them," he directed. "They'll be enough to ground any stray charges—if they can't see you they won't know you're here, so probably nothing much will come your way direct."

The Velantian demurred, declaring that he would not hide while his two companions were fighting his battle, but Kinnison silenced him fiercely.

"Don't be a fool!" the Lensman snapped. "One of these beams would fry you to a crisp in ten seconds, but the defensive fields of our armor could neutralize a thousand of them, from now on. Do as I say, and do it quick, or I'll shock you unconscious and toss you in there myself!"

Realizing that Kinnison meant exactly what he said, and knowing that, unarmored as he was, he was utterly unable to resist either the Tellurian or their common foe, Worsel unwillingly erected his metallic barrier and coiled his sinuous length behind it. He hid himself just in time.

The outer barricade had fallen, and now a wave of reptilian forms flooded into the control room. Nor was this any ordinary investigation. The Overlords had studied the situation from afar, and this wave was one of heavily-armed—for Delgon—soldiery. On they came, projectors fiercely aflame; confident in their belief that nothing could stand before their blasts. But how wrong they were! The two repulsively erect bipeds before them neither burned nor fell. Beams, no matter how powerful, did not reach them at all, but spent themselves in crackingly incandescent fury, inches from their marks. Nor were these outlandish beings inoffensive. Utterly careless of the service-life of the pitifully weak Delgonian projectors, they were using them at maximum drain and at extreme aperture—and in the resultant beams the Delgonian soldier-slaves fell in scorched and smoking heaps. On came reserves, platoon after platoon, only and continuously to meet the same fate; for as soon as one projector weakened the invincibly armored man would toss it aside and pick up another. But finally the last commandeered weapon was exhausted and the beleaguered pair brought their own DeLameters—the most powerful portable weapons known to the military scientists of the Galactic Patrol—into play.

And what a difference! In *those* beams the attacking reptiles did not smoke or burn. They simply vanished in a blaze of flaming light, as did also the nearby walls and a good share of the building beyond! The Delgonian hordes having disappeared, vanBuskirk shut off his projector. Kinnison, however, left his on, angling its beam sharply upward; blasting into fiery vapor the ceiling and roof over their heads; remarking:

"While we're at it we might as well fix things so that we can make a quick get-away if we want to."

Then they waited. Waited, watching the needles of their meters creep ever closer to the "full-charge" marks; waited while, as they suspected, the distant, cowardly-hiding Overlords planned some other, more promising line of physical attack.

Nor was it long in developing. Another small army appeared, armored this time; or, more accurately, advancing behind metallic shields. Knowing what to expect, Kinnison was not surprised when the beam of his DeLameter not only failed to pierce one of those shields, but did not in any way impede the progress of the Delgonian column.

"Well, we're all done here, anyway, as far as I'm concerned," Kinnison grinned at the Dutchman as he spoke.

"My cans've been showing full back pressure for the last two minutes. How about yours?"

"Same here," vanBuskirk reported, and the two leaped lightly into the Velantian's refuge. Then, inertialess all, the three shot into the air at such a pace that to the slow senses of the Delgonian slaves they simply disappeared. Indeed, it was not until the barrier had been blasted away and every room, nook, and cranny of the immense structure had been literally and minutely combed that the Delgonians—and through their enslaved minds the Overlords—became convinced that their prey had in some uncanny and unknown fashion eluded them.

Now high in air, the three allies traversed in a matter of minutes the same distance that had cost them so much time and strife the day before. Over the monster-infested forest they sped, over the deceptively peaceful green lushness of the jungle, to slant down toward Worsel's thought-proof tent. Inside that refuge they snapped off their thought screens and Kinnison yawned prodigiously.

"Working days and nights both is all right for a while, but it gets monotonous in time. Since this seems to be the only really safe spot on the planet, I suggest that we take a day or so off and catch up on our eats and sleeps."

They slept and ate; slept and ate again.

"The next thing on the program," Kinnison announced then, "is to clean out that den of Overlords. Then Worsel will be free to help us get going about our own business."

"You speak lightly indeed of the impossible," Worsel, all glum despondency, reproved him. "I have already explained why the task is, and must remain, beyond our power."

"Yes, but you don't quite grasp the possibilities of the stuff we've got now to work with," the Tellurian replied. "Listen: you could never do anything because you couldn't see through or work through your thought screens. Neither we nor you could, even now, enslave a Delgonian and make him lead us to the cavern, because the Overlords would know all about it 'way ahead of time and the slave would lead us anywhere else except to the cavern. However, one of us can cut his screen and surrender; possibly keeping just enough screen up to keep the enemy from possessing his mind fully enough to learn that the other two are coming along. The big question is—which of us is to surrender?"

"That is already decided," Worsel made instant reply.

"I am the logical—in fact, the *only* one—to do it. Not only would they think it perfectly natural that they should overpower me, but also I am the only one of us three sufficiently able to control his thoughts as to keep from them the knowledge that I am being accompanied. Furthermore, you both know that it would not be good for your minds, unaccustomed as they are to the practice, to surrender their control voluntarily to an enemy."

"I'll say it wouldn't!" Kinnison agreed, feelingly. "I might do it if I had to, but I wouldn't like it and I don't think I'd ever quite get over it. I hate to put such a horrible job off onto you, Worsel, but you're undoubtedly the best equipped to handle it—and even you may have your hands full."

"Yes . . . . ." the Velantian said, thoughtfully. "While the undertaking is no longer an absolute impossibility, it is difficult . . . very. In any event you will probably have to beam me yourselves if we succeed in reaching the cavern . . . . The Overlords will see to that. If so, do it without regret—know that I expect it and am well content to die in that fashion. Any one of my fellows would be only too glad to be in my place; meaning what it does to all Velantia. Know also that I have already reported what is to occur, and that your welcome to Velantia is assured, whether or not I accompany you there."

"I don't think I'll have to kill you, Worsel," Kinnison replied, slowly, picturing in detail exactly what that steel-hard reptilian body would be capable of doing when, unshackled, its directing mind was completely taken over by an utterly soulless and conscienceless Overlord. "If you can't keep from going off the deep end, of course you'll get tough and I know you're mighty hard to handle. However, as I told you back there, I think I can beam you unconscious without killing you. I may have to burn off a few scales, but I'll try not to do any damage that can't be repaired."

"If you can so stop me it will be wonderful indeed. Are we ready?"

They were ready. Worsel opened the door and in a moment was hurtling through the air, his giant wings arrowing him along at a pace no winged creature of Earth could even approach. And, following him easily at a little distance, floated the two Patrolmen upon their inertialess drives.

During that long flight scarcely a thought was exchanged, even between Kinnison and vanBuskirk. To direct a thought at the Velantian was of course out of the question. All lines of communication with him had been cut; and furthermore his mind, able as it was, was being taxed to the ultimate cell in doing what he had set out to do. And the two Patrolmen were reluctant to converse with each other, even upon their tight-beams, radios, or sounders, for fear that some slight leakage of thought-energy might reveal their presence to the everwatchful Overlords. If this opportunity were lost, they knew, another chance to wipe out that hellish horde might never present itself.

Land was traversed, and sea; but finally a stupendous range of mountains reared before them and Worsel, folding back his tireless wings, shot downward in a screaming, full-weight dive. In his line of flight Kinnison saw the mouth of a cave, a darker spot of blackness in the black rock of the mountain's side. Upon the ledged approach there lay a Delgonian—a guard or lookout, of course.

The Lensman's DeLameter was already in his hand, and at sight of the guardian reptile he sighted and fired in one fast motion. But, rapid as it was, it was still too slow—the Overlords had seen that the Velantian had companions of whom he had been able to keep them in ignorance theretofore.

Instantly Worsel's wings again began to beat, bearing him off at a wide angle; and, although the Patrolmen were insulated against his thought, the meaning of his antics was very plain. He was telling them in every possible way that the hole below was *not* the cavern of the Overlords; that it was over this way; that they were to keep on following him to it. Then, as they refused to follow him, he rushed upon Kinnison in mad attack.

"Beam him down, Kim!" vanBuskirk yelled. "Don't take any chances with that bird!" and leveled his own DeLameter.

"Lay off, Bus!" the Lensman snapped. "I can handle him—a lot easier out here than on the ground."

And so it proved. Inertialess as he was, the buffetings of the Velantian affected him not at all; and when Worsel coiled his supple body around him and began to apply pressure, Kinnison simply expanded his thought screen to cover them both, thus releasing the mind of his temporarily inimical friend from the Overlord's grip. Instantly the Velantian became himself, snapped on his own shield, and the three continued as one their interrupted downward course.

Worsel came to a halt upon the ledge, beside the practically incinerated corpse of the lookout; knowing, unarmored as he was, that to go further meant sudden death. The armored pair, however, shot on into the gloomy passage. At first they were offered no opposition—the Overlords had had no time to muster an adequate defense. Scattering handfuls of slaves rushed them, only to be blasted out of existence as their hand weapons proved useless against the armor of the Galactic Patrol. Defenders became more numerous as the cavern itself was approached, but neither were they allowed to stay the Patrolman's progress. Finally a palely shimmering barrier of metal appeared to bar their way. Its fields of force neutralized or absorbed the blasts of the DeLameters, but its material substance offered but little resistance to a thirty-pound sledge, swung by one of the strongest men ever produced by any planet colonized by the humanity of Earth.

Now they were in the cavern itself—the sanctum sanctorum of the Overlords of Delgon. There was the hellish torture screen; now licked clean of life. There was the audience which had been so avid, now milling about in a mob frenzy of panic. There, upon a raised balcony, were the "big shots" of this nauseous clan; now doing their utmost to marshal some force able to cope effectively with this unheard-of violation of their ages-old immunity.

A last wave of Delgonian slaves hurled themselves forward, futile projectors furiously aflame, only to disappear in the DeLameters' fans of force. The Patrolmen hated to kill those mindless slaves, but it was a nasty job that had to be done. The slaves out of the way, those ravening beams bored on into the massed Overlords.

And now Kinnison and vanBuskirk killed, if not joyously, at least relentlessly, mercilessly, and with neither sign nor sensation of compunction. For this unbelievably monstrous tribe needed killing, root and branch—not a scion or shoot of it should be allowed to survive, to continue to contaminate the civilization of the galaxy. Back and forth, to and fro, up and down swept the raging beams; playing on until in all the vast volume of that gruesome chamber nothing lived save the two grim figures in its portal.

Assured of this fact, but with DeLameters still in hand, the two destroyers retraced their way to the tunnel's mouth, where Worsel anxiously awaited them. Lines of communication again established, Kinnison informed the Velantian of all that had taken place and the latter gradually cut down the power of his thought-screen. Soon it was at zero strength and he reported jubilantly that for the first time in untold ages, the Overlords of Delgon were off the air!

"But surely the danger isn't over yet!" protested Kinnison. "We couldn't have got them all in this one raid. Some of them must have escaped, and there must be other dens of them on this planet somewhere?"

"Possibly, possibly;" the Velantian waved his tail airily —the first sign of joyousness he had shown. "But their power is broken, definitely and forever. With these new screens, and with the arms and armament which, thanks to you, we can now fabricate, the task of wiping them out completely will be comparatively simple. Now you will accompany me to Velantia; where, I assure you, the resources of the planet will be put solidly behind you in your own endeavors. I have already summoned a space-ship—in less than twelve days we will be back in Velantia and at work upon your projects. In the meantime . . . . ."

"Twelve *days!* Noshabkeming the Radiant!" vanBuskirk exploded, and Kinnison put in:

"Sure—you forget they haven't got free drive. We'd better hop over and get our lifeboat, I think. It's not so good, either way, but in our own boat we'll be open to detection less than an hour, as against twelve days in the Velantians'. And the pirates may be here any minute. It's as good as certain that their ship will be stopped and searched long before it gets back to Velantia, and if we were aboard it'd be just too bad."

"And, since the crew knows about us, the pirates soon will, and it'll be just too bad, anyway," vanBuskirk reasoned.

"Not at all," interposed Worsel. "The few of my people who know of you have been instructed to seal that knowledge. I must admit, however, that I am greatly disturbed by your conceptions of these pirates of space. You see, until I met you I knew nothing more of the pirates than I did of your Patrol."

"What a world!" vanBuskirk exclaimed. "No Patrol and no pirates! But at that, life might be simpler without both of them and without the free space-drive—more like it used to be in the good old airplane days that the novelists rave about."

"Of course I could not judge as to that." The Velantian was very serious. "This in which we live seems to be an out-of-the-way section of the galaxy; or it may be that we have nothing the pirates want."

"More likely it's simply that, like the Patrol, they haven't got organized into this district yet," suggested Kinnison. "There are so many thousands of millions of solar systems in the galaxy that it will probably be thousands of years yet before the Patrol gets into them all."

"But about these pirates," Worsel went back to his point. "If they have such minds as those of the Overlords, they will be able to break the seals of our minds. However, I gather from your thoughts that their minds are not of that strength?"

"Not so far as I know," Kinnison replied. "You folks have the most powerful brains I ever heard of, short of the Arisians. And speaking of mental power, you can hear thoughts a lot farther than I can, even with my Lens or with this pirate receiver I've got. See if you can find out whether there are any pirates in space around here, will you?"

While the Velantian was concentrating, vanBuskirk asked:

"Why, if his mind is so strong, could the Overlords put him under so much easier than they could us 'weak-minded' human beings?"

"You are confusing 'mind' with 'will,' I think. Ages of submission to the Overlords made the Velantians' will-power zero, as far as the bosses were concerned. On the other hand, you and I could raise stubbornness to sell to most people. In fact, if the Overlords had succeeded in really breaking us down, back there, the chances are we'd have gone insane."

"Probably you're right—we break, but don't bend, huh?" and the Velantian was ready to report.

"I have scanned space to the nearer stars—some eleven of your light-years—and have encountered no intruding entities," he announced.

"Eleven light-years—what a range!" Kinnison exclaimed. "However, that's only a shade over two minutes for a pirate ship at full blast. But we've got to take a chance sometime, and the quicker we get started the sooner we'll get back. We'll pick you up here, Worsel. No use in you going back to your tent—we'll be back here long before you could reach it. You'll be safe enough, I think, especially with our spare DeLameters. Let's get going, Bus!"

Again they shot into the air, again they traversed the

airless depths of interplanetary space. To locate the temporary tomb of their lifeboat required only a few minutes, to disinter her only a few more. Then again they braved detection in the void; Kinnison tense at his controls, vanBuskirk in strained attention listening to and staring at his unscramblers and detectors. But the ether was still blank as the lifeboat struck Delgon's atmosphere; it remained blank while the lifeboat, inert, blasted frantically to match Worsel's intrinsic velocity.

"All right, Worsel, snap it up!" Kinnison called, and went on to vanBuskirk, "Now, you big, flat-footed Valerian spacehound, I hope that spaceman's god of yours will see to it our luck holds good for just fourteen minutes more. We've had more luck already than we had any right to expect, but we can put a little more to most God-awful good use!"

"Noshabkeming *does* bring spacemen luck," insisted the giant, grimacing a peculiar salute toward a small, golden image set inside his helmet, "and the fact that you warty, runty, atheistic little space-fleas of Tellus haven't got sense enough to know it—not even enough sense to really believe in your own gods, even Klono—doesn't change matters at all."

"That's tellin' 'em, Bus!" Kinnison applauded. "But if it helps charge your batteries, go to it . . . . . Ready to blast! Lift!"

The Velantian had come aboard, the tiny airlock was again tight, and the little vessel shot away from Delgon toward far Velantia. And still the ether remained empty as far as the detectors could reach. Nor was this fact surprising, in spite of the Lensman's fears to the contrary; for the Patrolmen had given the pirates such an extremely long line to cover that many days must yet elapse before the minions of Boskone would get around to visit that unimportant, unexplored, and almost unknown solar system. En route to his home planet Worsel got in touch with the crew of the Velantian vessel already in space, ordering them to return to port post-haste and instructing them in detail what to think and how to act should they be stopped and searched by one of Boskone's raiders. By the time these instructions had been given, Velantia loomed large beneath the flying midget. Then, with Worsel as guide, Kinnison drove over a mighty ocean upon whose opposite shore lay the great city in which Worsel lived.

"But I would like to have them welcome you as befits what you have done, and have you go to the Dome!"

mourned the Velantian. "Think of it! You have done a thing which for ages the massed power of the planet has been trying vainly to accomplish, and yet you insist that I alone take credit for it!"

"I don't insist on any such thing," argued Kinnison, "even though it's practically all yours, anyway. I insist only on your keeping us and the Patrol out of it, and you know as well as I do why you've got to do that. Tell them anything else you want to. Say that a couple of pink-haired Chickladorians helped you and then beat it back home. *That* planet's far enough away so that if the pirates chase them they'll get a real run for their money. After this blows over you can tell the truth—but *not until then*.

"And as for us going to the Dome for a grand hocus-pocus, that is completely and definitely OUT. We're not going anywhere except to the biggest airport you've got. You're not going to give us anything except a lot of material and a lot of highly-trained help that can keep their thoughts sealed.

"We've got to build a lot of heavy stuff fast; and we've got to get started on it just as quick as Klono and Noshabkeming will let us!"

CHAPTER 8   *The Quarry Strikes Back*

WORSEL KNEW HIS COUNCIL OF SCIENTISTS, AS WELL HE might; since it developed that he himself ranked high in that select circle. True to his promise, the largest airport of the planet was immediately emptied of its customary personnel, which was replaced the following morning by an entirely new group of workmen.

Nor were these replacements ordinarily laborers. They were young, keen, and highly trained; taken to a man from behind the thought-screens of the Scientists. It is true that they had no inkling of what they were to do, since none of them had ever dreamed of the possibility of such engines as they were to be called upon to construct.

But, on the other hand, they were well versed in the fundamental theories and operations of mathematics, and from pure mathematics to applied mechanics is but a step. Furthermore, they had *brains;* knew how to think logically, coherently, and effectively; and needed neither driving nor supervision—only instruction. And best of all, practically every one of the required mechanisms already existed, in miniature, within the *Brittania's* lifeboat; ready at hand for their dissection, analysis, and enlargement. It was not lack of understanding which was to slow up the work; it was simply that the planet did not boast machine tools and equipment large enough or strong enough to handle the necessarily huge and heavy parts and members required.

While the construction of this heavy machinery was being rushed through, Kinnison and vanBuskirk devoted their efforts to the fabrication of an ultra-sensitive receiver, tunable to the pirates' scrambled wave-bands. With their exactly detailed knowledge, and with the cleverest technicians and the choicest equipment of Velantia at their disposal, the set was soon completed.

Kinnison was giving its exceedingly delicate coils their final alignment when Worsel wriggled blithely into the radio laboratory.

"Hi, Kimball Kinnison of the Lens!" he called gaily. Throwing a few yards of his serpent's body in lightning loops about a convenient pillar, he made a horizontal bar of the rest of himself and dropped one wing-tip to the floor. Then, nonchalantly upside down, he thrust out three or four eyes and curled their stalks over the Lensman's shoulder, the better to inspect the results of the mechanics' efforts. Gone was the morose, pessimistic, death-haunted Worsel entirely; gay, happy, carefree, and actually frolicsome—if you can imagine a thirty-foot-long, crocodile-headed, leather-winged python as being frolicsome!

"Hi, your royal snakeship!" Kinnison retorted in kind. "Still here, huh? Thought you'd be back on Delgon by this time, cleaning up the rest of that mess."

"The equipment is not ready, but there's no hurry about that," the playful reptile unwrapped ten or twelve feet of tail from the pillar and waved it airily about. "Their power is broken, their race is done. You are about to try out the new receiver?"

"Yes—going out after them right now," and Kinnison

began deftly to manipulate the micrometric verniers of his dials.

Eyes fixed upon meters and gauges, he listened . . . . . listened. Increased his power and listened again. More and more power he applied to his apparatus, listening continually. Suddenly he stiffened, his hands becoming rock-still. He listened, if possible even more intently than before; and as he listened his face grew grim and granite-hard. Then the micrometers began again crawlingly to move, as though he were tracing a beam.

"Bus! Hook on the focusing beam-antenna!" he snapped. "It's going to take every milliwatt of power we've got in this hookup to tap his beam, but I think I've got Helmuth direct instead of through a pirate-ship relay!"

Again and again he checked the readings of his dials and of the directors of his antenna; each time noting the exact time of the Velantian day.

"There! As soon as we get some time, Worsel, I'd like to work out these figures with some of your astronomers. They'll give me a right line through Helmuth's headquarters —I hope. Some day, if I'm spared, I'll get another!"

"What kind of news did you get, chief?" asked vanBuskirk.

"Good and bad both," replied the Lensman. "Good in that Helmuth doesn't believe that we stayed with his ship as long as we did. He's a suspicious devil, you know, and is pretty well convinced that we tried to run the same kind of a blazer on him that we did the other time. Since he hasn't got enough ships on the job to work the whole line, he's concentrating on the other end. That means that we've got plenty of days left yet. The bad part of it is that they've got four of our boats already and are bound to get more. Lord, how I wish I could call the rest of them! Some of them could certainly make it here before they got caught."

"Might I then offer a suggestion?" asked Worsel, of a sudden diffident.

"Surely!" the Lensman replied in surprise. "Your ideas have never been any kind of poppycock. Why so bashful all at once?"

"Because this one is so . . . . ah . . . . so peculiarly personal, since you men regard so highly the privacy of your minds. Our two sciences, as you have already observed, are vastly different. You are far beyond us in mechanics, physics, chemistry, and the other applied sciences. We, on the other hand, have delved much deeper than you have into psychology and the other introspective studies. For that reason I know positively that the Lens you wear is capable of enormously greater things than you are at present able to make it perform. Of course I cannot use your Lens directly, since it is attuned to your own ego. However, if the idea appeals to you, I could, with your consent, occupy your mind and use your Lens to put you en rapport with your fellows. I have not volunteered the suggestion before because I know how averse your mind is to any foreign control."

"Not necessarily to foreign control," Kinnison corrected him. "Only to *enemy* control. The idea of friendly control never even occurred to me. That would be an entirely different breed of cats. Go to it!"

Kinnison relaxed his mind completely, and that of the Velantian came welling in; wave upon friendly, surging wave of benevolent power. And not only—or not precisely—power. It was more than power; it was a dynamic poignancy, a vibrant penetrance, a depth and clarity of perception that Kinnison in his most cogent moments had never dreamed a possibility. The possessor of that mind knew things, cameo-clear in microscopic detail, which the keenest minds of Earth could perceive only as chaotically indistinct masses of mental light and shade, of no recognizable pattern whatever!

"Give me the thought-pattern of him with whom you wish first to converse," came Worsel's thought, this time from deep within the Lensman's own brain.

Kinnison felt a subtle thrill of uneasiness at that new and ultra-strange dual personality, but thought back steadily: "Sorry—I can't."

"Excuse me, I should have known that you cannot think in our patterns. Think, then, of him as a person—as an individual. That will give me, I believe, sufficient data."

Into the Earthman's mind there leaped a picture of Henderson, sharp and clear. He felt his Lens actually tingle and throb as a concentration of vital force such as he had never known poured through his whole being and into that almost-living creation of the Arisians; and immediately thereafter he was in full mental communication with the Master Pilot! And there, seated across the tiny mess-table of their lifeboat, was LaVerne Thorndyke, the Master Technician.

Henderson came to his feet with a yell as the telepathic message bombshelled into his brain, and it required several seconds to convince him that he was not the victim of space-insanity or suffering from any other form of hallucination. Once convinced, however, he acted—his lifeboat shot toward far Velantia at maximum blast.

Then: "Nelson! Allerdyce! Thompson! Jenkins! Uhlenhuth! Smith! Chatway! . . . . . ." Kinnison called the roll.

Nelson, the specialist in communications, answered his captain's call. So did Allerdyce, the juggling quartermaster. So did Uhlenhuth, a technician. So did those in three other boats. Two of these three were apparently well within the danger zone and might get nipped in their dash, but their crews elected without hesitation to take the chance. Four boats, it was already known, had been captured by the pirates. The others . . . . .

"Only eight boats," Kinnison mused. "Not so good—but it could have been a lot worse—they might have got us all by this time—and maybe some of them are just out of our reach." Then, turning to the Velantian, who had withdrawn his mind as soon as the job was done:

"Thanks, Worsel," he said simply. "Some of those lads coming in have got plenty of just what it takes, and *how* we can use them!"

One by one the lifeboats made port, where their crews were welcomed briefly but feelingly before they were put to work. Nelson, one of the last pair to arrive, was particularly welcome.

"Nels, we need you badly," Kinnison informed him as soon as greetings had been exchanged. "The pirates have a beam, carrying a peculiarly scrambled signal, that they can receive and decode through any ordinary kind of blanketing interference, and you're the best man we've got to study their system. Some of these Velantian scientists can probably help you a lot on that—any race that can develop a screen against thought figures ought to know more than somewhat about vibration in general. We've got working models of the pirates' instruments, so you can figure out their patterns and formulas. When you've done that, I want you and your Velantians to design something that will scramble all the pirates' communicator beams in space, as far as you can reach. If you can fix things so they can't talk, any more than we can, it'll help a lot, believe me!"

"QX, Chief, we'll give it the works," and the radio man called for tools, apparatus, and electricians.

Then throughout the great airport the many Velantians and the handful of Patrolmen labored mightily, side by side, and to very good effect indeed. Slowly the port became ringed about by, and studded everywhere with, monstrous mechanisms. Everywhere there were projectors: refractory-throated demons ready to vomit forth every force known to the expert technicians of the Patrol. There were absorbers, too, backed by their bleeder resistors, air-gaps, ground-rods, and racks for discharged accumulators. There, too, were receptors and converters for the cosmic energy which was to empower many of the devices. There were, of course, atomic motor-generators by the score, and battery upon battery of gigantic accumulators. And Nelson's high-powered scrambler was ready to go to work.

These machines appeared crude, rough, unfinished; for neither time nor labor had been wasted upon non-essentials. But inside each one the moving parts fitted with micrometric accuracy and with hair-spring balance. All, without exception, functioned perfectly.

At Worsel's call, Kinnison climbed up out of a great beam-proof pit, the top of whose wall was practically composed of tractor-beam projectors. Pausing only to make sure that a sticking switch on one of the screen-dome generators had been replaced, he hurried to the heavily armored control room, where his little force of fellow Patrolmen awaited him.

"They're coming, boys," he announced. "You all know what to do. There are a lot more things we could have done if we'd had more time, but as it is we'll just go to work on them with what we've got," and Kinnison, again all brisk Captain, bent over his instruments.

In the ordinary course of events the pirate would have flashed up to the planet with spy-rays out and issuing a preemptory demand for the planet to show a clean bill of health or to surrender instantly such fugitives as might lately have landed upon it. But Kinnison did not—could not—wait for that. The spy-rays, he knew, would reveal the presence of his armament; and such armament most certainly did not belong to this planet. Therefore he acted first, and everything happened practically at once.

A tracer lashed out, the pilot-ray of the rim-battery of extraordinarily powerful tractors. Under their terrific pull the inertialess ship flashed toward their center of action. At the same moment there burst into activity Nelson's scrambler, a dome-screen against cosmic-energy intake, and a full circle of super-powered projectors.

All these things occurred in the twinkling of an eye, and

the vessel was being slowed down by the atmosphere of Velantia before her startled commander could even realize that he was being attacked. Only the automatically-reacting defensive screens saved that ship from instant destruction; but they did so save it and in seconds the pirates' every weapon was furiously ablaze.

In vain. The defenses of that pit could take it. They were driven by mechanisms easily able to absorb the output of any equipment mountable upon a mobile base, and to his consternation the pirate found that his cosmic-energy intake was at, and remained at, zero. He sent out call after call for help, but could not make contact with any other pirate station—ether and sub-ether alike were closed to him, his signals were blanketed completely. Nor could his drivers, even though operating at ruinous overload, move him from the geometrical center of that incandescently flaming pit, so inconceivably rigid were the tractors' clamps upon him.

And soon his power began to fail. His vessel, designed to operate upon cosmic-energy intake, carried only enough accumulators for stablization of power-flow, an amount ridiculously inadequate for a combat as profligate of energy as this. But strangely enough, as his defenses weakened, so lessened the power of the attack. It was no part of the Lensman's plan to destroy this superdreadnaught of the void.

"That was one good thing about the old *Brittania*," he gritted, as he cut down step by step the power of his beams, "what power she had, nobody could block her off from!"

Soon the stored-up energy of the battleship was exhausted and she lay there, quiescent. Then giant pressors went into action and she was lifted over the wall of the pit, to settle down in an open space beside it—open, but still under the domes of force.

Kinnison had no needle-rays as yet, the time at his disposal having been sufficient only for the construction of the absolutely essential items of equipment. Now, while he debated with his fellows as to what part of the vessel to destroy in order to wipe out its crew, the pirates themselves ended the debate. Ports yawned in the vessel's side and they came out fighting.

For they were not a breed to die like rats in a trap, and they knew that to remain inside their vessel was to die whenever and however their captors willed. They knew also that die they must if they could not conquer. Their surrender, even if it should be accepted, would mean only a somewhat later death in the lethal chambers of the Law. In the open, they could at least take some of their foes with them.

Furthermore, not being men as we know men, they had nothing in common with either human beings or Velantians. Both to them were vermin, as they themselves were to the beings manning this surprisingly impregnable fortress here in this waste corner of the galaxy. Therefore, space-hardened veterans all, they fought, with the insane ferocity and desperation of the ultimately last stand; but they did not conquer. Instead, and to the last man, they died.

As soon as the battle was over, before the interference blanketing the pirates' communicators was cut off, Kinnison went through the captured vessel, destroying the headquarters visiplates and every automatic sender which could transmit any kind of a message to any pirate base. Then the interference was stopped, the domes were released, and the ship was removed from the field of operations. Then, while Thorndyke and his reptilian aides—themselves now radio experts of no mean attainments—busied themselves at installing a high-powered scrambler aboard her, Kinnison and Worsel scanned space in search of more prey. Soon they found it, more distant than the first one had been— two solar systems away—and in an entirely different direction. Tracers and tractors and interference and domes of force again became the order of the day. Projectors again raved out in their incandescent might, and soon another immense cruiser of the void lay beside her sister ship. Another, and another; then for a long time space was blank.

The Lensman then energized his ultra-receiver, pointing his antenna carefully into the galatic line to Helmuth's base, as laid down for him by the Velantian astronomers. Again, so tight and hard was Helmuth's beam, he had to drive his apparatus so unmercilly that the tube-noise almost drowned out the signals, but again he was rewarded by hearing faintly the voice of the pirate Director of Operations:

" . . . . . four vessels, all within or near one of those five solar systems, have ceased communicating; each cessation being accompanied by a period of blanketing interference of a pattern never before registered. You two vessels who are receiving these orders are instructed to investigate that region with the utmost care. Go with screens out and everything on the trips, and with automatic recorders set on me here. It is not believed that the Patrol has anything to do with this, as ability has been shown transcending anything it has been known to possess. As a working hypothesis it is assumed that one of the solar systems, hitherto practically unexplored and unknown, is in reality the seat of a highly advanced race, which perhaps has taken offense at the attitude or conduct of our first ship to visit them. Therefore proceed with extreme caution, with a thorough spy-ray search at extreme range before approaching at all. If you land, use tact and diplomacy instead of the customary tactics. Find out whether our ships and crews have been destroyed, or are only being held: and remember, automatic reporters on me at all times. Helmuth speaking for Boskone—off!"

For minutes Kinnison manipulated his controls in vain —he could not get another sound.

"What are you trying to get, Kim?" asked Thorndyke. "Wasn't that enough?"

"No, that's only half of it," Kinnison returned. "Helmuth's nobody's fool. He's certainly trying to plot the boundaries of our interference, and I want to see how he's coming out with it. But no dice. He's so far away and his beam's so hard I can't work him unless he happens to be talking almost directly toward us. Well, it won't be long now until we'll give him some real interference to plot. Now let's see what we can do about those two other ships that are heading this way."

Carefully as those two ships investigated, and sedulously as they sought to obey Helmuth's instructions, all their precautions amounted to exactly nothing. As ordered, they began to spy-ray survey at extreme range; but even at that range Kinnison's tracers were effective and those pirates also ceased communicating in a blaze of interference. Then recent history repeated itself. The details were changed somewhat, since there were two vessels instead of one; but the pit was of ample size to accommodate two ships, and the tractors could hold two as well and as rigidly as one. The conflict was a little longer, the beaming a little hotter and more coruscant, but the ending was the same. Scramblers and other special appartus were installed and Kinnison called his men together.

"We're about ready to shove off again. Running away has worked twice so far and should work once more, if we can ring in enough variations on the theme to keep Helmuth guessing a while longer. Maybe, if the supply of pirate ships holds up, we can make Helmuth furnish us transportation clear back to Prime Base!

"Here's the idea. We've got six ships, and enough Velantians have volunteered to man them—in spite of the fact that they probably won't get back. Six ships, of course, isn't enough of a task force to fight its way through Helmuth's fleets; so we'll spread out, covering plenty of parsecs and broadcasting every watt of interference we can put out, in as many different shapes and sizes as our generators can figure. We won't be able to talk to each other, but nobody else can talk, either, anywhere near us, and that ought to give us a chance. Each ship will be on its own, like we were before, in the boats; the big difference being that we'll be in superdreadnaughts.

"Question—should we split up again or stick together? We'd better all go in one ship, I think—with spools aboard the others, of course. What do you think?"

They agreed with him to a man and he directed a thought at the Velantian.

"Now, Worsel, about you fellows here—you probably won't have it so easy, either. Sooner or later—and sooner would be my guess—Helmuth's boys will be coming to see you. In force and cocked and primed and with blood in their eyes. It'll be a battle, not a slaughter."

"Let them come, in whatever force they care to bring. The more who attack here, the less there will be to halt your progress. This armament represents the best of that possessed by both your Patrol and the pirates, with improvements developed by your scientists and ours in full cooperation. We understand thoroughly its construction, operation, and maintenance. You may rest assured that the pirates will never levy tribute upon us, and that any pirate visiting this system will remain in it—permanently!"

"At-a-snake, Worsel—long may you wiggle!" Kinnison exclaimed. Then, more seriously, "Maybe, after this is all over, I'll see you again sometime. If not, goodbye. Goodbye, all Velantia. All set, everybody? Clear ether—blast off!"

Six ships, one pirate craft, now vessels of the Galactic Patrol, hurled themselves into and through Velantian air; into and through interplanetary space; out into the larger, wider, opener emptiness of the interstellar void. Six ships, each broadcasting with prodigious power and volume an all-inclusive interference through which not even a CRX tracer could be driven.

CHAPTER 9   *Breakdown*

KIMBALL KINNISON SAT AT THE CONTROLS, SMOKING A RARE festive cigarette and smiling; at peace with the entire universe. For this new picture was in every element a different one from the old. Instead of being in a pitifully weak and defenseless lifeboat, skulking and hiding, he was in one of the most powerful battleships afloat, driving boldly at full blast almost directly toward home. While the Patrolmen were so terribly few in number that most of them had to work double shifts—Kinnison and Henderson had to do all the piloting and navigating—they had under them a full crew of alert and highly-trained Velantians. And the enemy, instead of being a close-knit group, keeping Helmuth informed moment by moment of the situation and instantly responsive to his orders, were now entirely out of communication with each other and with their headquarters; groping helplessly. Literally as well as figuratively the pirates were in the dark; the absolute blackness of interstellar space.

Thorndyke entered the room, frowning slightly. "You look like the fabled Cheshire cat, Kim. I hate to spoil such perfect bliss, but I'm here to tell you that we ain't out of the woods yet, by seven thousand rows of big, green, peppermint trees."

"Maybe not," the Lensman returned blithely, "but compared to the jam we were in a little while back we're not only sitting on top of the world; we're perched right on the exact apex of the universe. They can't send or receive reports or orders, and they can't communicate. Even their detectors are mighty lame—you know how far they can get on electromagnetics and visual apparatus. Furthermore, there isn't an identification number, symbol, or name on the outside of this buzz-buggy. If it ever had one the friction and attrition have worn it off, clear down to the armor. What can happen that we can't cope with?"

88

"These engines can happen," the technician responded, bluntly. "The Bergenholm is developing a meter-jump that I don't like a little bit."

"Does she knock? Or even tick?" demanded Kinnison.

"Not yet," Thorndyke confessed, reluctantly.

"How big a jump?"

"Pretty near two thousandths maximum. Average a thousandth and a half."

"That's hardly a wiggle on the recorder line. Drivers run for months with bigger jumps than that."

"Yeah—drivers. But of all the troubles anybody ever had with Bergenholms, a meter-kick was never one of them, and that's what's got me guessing as to the whichness of the why. I'm not trying to scare you—yet. I'm just telling you."

The machine referred to was the neutralizer of inertia, the sine qua non of interstellar speed, and it was not to be wondered at that the slightest irregularity in its performance was to the technician a matter of grave concern. Day after day passed, however, and the huge converter continued to function; taking in and sending out its wonted torrents of power. It developed not even a tick, and the meter-jump did not grow worse. And during those days they put an inconceivable distance behind them.

During all this time their visual instruments remained blank; to all optical apparatus space was empty save for the normal tenancy of celestial bodies. From time to time something invisible or beyond the range of vision registered upon one of the electromagnet detectors, but so slow were these instruments that nothing came of their signals. In fact, by the time the warnings were recorded, the objects causing the disturbance were probably far astern.

One day, however, the Bergenholm quit—cold. There was no laboring, no knocking, no heating up, no warning at all. One instant the ship was speeding along in free flight, the next she was lying inert in space. Practically motionless, for any possible velocity built up by inert acceleration is scarcely a crawl, as free space-speeds go.

Then the whole crew labored like mad. As soon as they had the massive covers off, Thorndyke scanned the interior of the machine and turned to Kinnison.

"I think we can patch her up, but it'll take quite a while. Maybe you'd be of more use in the control room—this ain't quite as safe as church, is it, lying here inert?"

"Most of the stuff is on automatic trip, but maybe I'd

better keep an eye on things, at that. Let me know occasionally how you're getting along," and the Lensman went back to his controls—none too soon.

For one pirate ship was already beaming him viciously. Only the fact that his defensive armament was upon its automatic trips had saved the stolen battleship from practically instantaneous destruction. And as the surprised Lensman began to check his other instruments another spaceship flashed into being upon his other side and also went to work.

As Kinnison had already remarked more than once, Helmuth was far from being a fool, and that new and amazingly effective blanketing of his every means of communication was a problem whose solution was of paramount importance. Almost every available ship had been for days upon the fringe of that interference; observing and reporting continuously. So rapidly was it moving, however, so peculiar was its apparent shape, and so contradictory were the directional readings obtained, that Helmuth's computers had been baffled.

Then Kinnison's Bergenholm failed and his ship went inert. In a space of minutes the location of one center of interference was known. Its coordinates were determined and half a dozen warships were ordered to rush that spot. The raider first to arrive had signalled, visually and audibly; then, obtaining no response, had anchored with a tractor and had loosed his bolts. Nor would the result have been different had everyone aboard, instead of no one, been in the control room at the time of the signalling. Kinnison could have read the messages, but neither he nor anyone else then aboard the erstwhile pirate craft could have answered them in kind.

The two space-ships attacking the turncoat became three, and still the Lensman sat unworried at his board. His meters showed no dangerous overload; his noble craft was taking everything her sister-ships could send.

Then Thorndyke stepped into the room, no longer a natty officer of space. Instead, he was stripped to sweat-soaked undershirt and overalls, he was covered with grease and grime, and what of his thickly smeared face was visible was almost haggard with fatigue. He opened his mouth to say something, then snapped it shut as his eye was caught by a flaring visiplate.

"Holy Klono's claws!" he exclaimed, "At us already? Why didn't you yell?"

"How much good would that have done?" Kinnison wanted to know. "Of course, if I had known that you were loafing on the job and could have snapped it up a little, I would have. But there's no particular hurry about this. It'll take at least four of them to break us down, and I was hoping you'd have us travelling before they overload us. What was on your mind?"

"I came up here—One, to tell you that we're ready to blast; Two, to suggest that you hit her easy at first; and Three, to ask if you know where there's any grease-soap. But you can cancel Two and Three. We don't want to play around with these boys much longer—they play too rough—and I ain't going to wash up until I see whether she holds together or not. Blast away—and won't those guys be surprised!"

"I'll say so—some of this stuff is NEW!"

The Lensman twirled a couple of knobs, then punched down hard upon three buttons. As he did so the flaring plates became dark; they were again alone in space. To the dumbfounded pirates it was as though their prey had slipped off into the fourth dimension. Their tractors gripped nothing whatever; their ravening beams bored unimpeded through the space occupied an instant before by resisting screens; tracers were useless. They did not know what had happened, or how, and they could neither report to nor be guided by the master mind of Boskone.

For minutes Thorndyke, vanBuskirk, and Kinnison waited tensely for they knew not what to happen; but nothing happened and then the tension gradually relaxed.

"What was the matter with it?" Kinnison asked, finally.

"Overloaded," was Thorndyke's terse reply.

"Overloaded—hooey!" snapped the Lensman. "How *could* they overload a Bergenholm? And, even if they could, why in all the nine hells of Valeria would they want to?"

"They *could* do it easily enough, in just the way they *did* do it; by banking accumulators onto it in series-parallel. As to why, I'll let you do the guessing. With no load on the Bergenholm you've got full inertia, with full load you've got zero inertia—you can't go any further. It looks just plain dumb to me. But then, I think all pirates are short a few jets somewhere—if they weren't they wouldn't be pirates."

"I don't know whether you're right or not. Hope so, but afraid not. Personally, I don't believe these folks are pirates at all, in the ordinary sense of the word."

"Huh? What are they, then?"

"Piracy implies similarity of culture, I would think," the Lensman said, thoughtfully. "Ordinary pirates are usually renegades, deficient somehow, as you suggested; rebelling against a constituted authority which they themselves have at one time acknowledged and of which they are still afraid. That pattern doesn't fit into this matrix at all, anywhere."

"So what? Now I say 'hooey' right back at you. Anyway, why worry about it?"

"Not worrying about it exactly, but somebody has got to do something about it, or else . . . . . ."

"I don't like to think; it makes my head ache," interrupted vanBuskirk. "Besides, we're getting away from the Bergenholm."

"You'll get a real headache there," laughed Kinnison, "because I'll bet a good Tellurian beefsteak that the pirates were trying to set up a negative inertia when they overloaded the Bergenholm; and thinking about that state of matter is enough to make *anybody's* head ache!"

"I knew that some of the dippier Ph.D.'s in higher mechanics have been speculating about it," Thorndyke offered, "but it can't be done that way, can it?"

"Nor any other way that anybody has tried yet, and if such a thing is possible the results may prove really startling. But you two had better shove off, you're dead from the neck up. The Berg's spinning like a top—as smooth as that much green velvet. You'll find a can of soap in my locker, I think."

"Maybe she'll hold together long enough for us to get some sleep." The technician eyed a meter dubiously, although its needle was not wavering a hair's breadth from the green line. "But I'll tell the cockeyed Universe that we gave her a jury rigging if there ever was one. You can't depend on it for an hour until after it's been pulled and gone over; and that, you know as well as I do, takes a real shop, with plenty of equipment: If you take my advice you'll sit down somewhere while you can and as soon as you can. That Bergenholm is in bad shape, believe me. We can hold her together for a while by main strength and awkwardness, but before very long she's going out for keeps—and when she does you don't want to find yourself fifty years from a machine shop instead of fifty minutes."

"I'll say not," the Lensman agreed. "But on the other hand, we don't want those birds jumping us the minute we land, either. Let's see, where are we? And where are the bases? Um . . . um . . . Sector bases are white rings, you know, sub-sector bases red stars . . . . . " Three heads bent over charts.

"The nearest red-star marker seems to be in System 240-16-37," Kinnison finally announced. "Don't know the name of the planet—never been there . . . . . "

"Too far," interrupted Thorndyke. "We'll never make it— might as well try direct for Prime Base on Tellus. If you can't find a red closer than that, look for an orange or a yellow."

"Bases of any kind seem to be scarce around here," the Lensman commented. "You'd think they'd be thicker. Here's a violet triangle, but that wouldn't help us—just an outpost. . . . . . How about this blue square? It's just about on our line to Tellus, and I can't see anything any better that we can possibly reach."

"That looks like our best bet," Thorndyke concurred, after a few minutes of study. "It's probably several break-downs away, but maybe we can make it—sometime. Blues are pretty low-grade space-ports, but they've got tools, any-way. What's the name of it, Kim—or is it only a number?"

"It's that very famous planet, Trenco," the Lensman an-nounced, after looking up the reference numbers in the atlas.

"*Trenco!*" exclaimed Thorndyke in diguest. "The nuttiest dopiest, wooziest planet in the galaxy—we *would* draw something like that to sit down on for repairs, wouldn't we? Well, I'm on plus time for sleep. Call me if we go inert before I wake up, will you?"

"I sure will; and I'll try to figure out a way of getting down to ground without bringing all the pirates in space along with us."

Then Henderson came in to stand his watch, Kinnison slept, and the mighty Bergenholm continued to hold the vessel inertialess. In fact, all the men were thoroughly rested and refreshed before the expected breakdown came. And when it did come they were more or less prepared for it. The delay was not sufficiently long to enable the pirates to find them again; but from that point in space to the ill-famed planet which was their destination, progress was one long series of hops.

The sweating, grunting, swearing engineers made one seemingly impossible repair after another, by dint of what dodge, improvisation, and makeshift only the fertile brain of LaVerne Thorndyke ever did know. The Master Techni-cian, one of the keenest and most highly trained engineers of the whole Solarian System, was not used to working with his hands. Although young in years, he was wont to use only his head, in directing the labors and the energies of others.

Nevertheless, he was now working like a stevedore. He was permanently grimy and greasy—their one can of mechanics' soap had been used up long since—his finger-nails were black and broken, his hands and face were burned, blistered, and cracked. His muscles ached and shrieked at the unaccustomed effort, until now they were on the build. But through it all he had stuck uncomplainingly, even buoyantly, to his task. One day, during an interlude of free flight, he strode into the control-room and glanced at the course-plotting goniometer, then started into the "tank."

"Still on the original course, I see. Have you got anything doped out yet?"

"Nothing very good, that's why I'm staying on this course until we reach the point closest to Trenco. I've figured until my alleged brain backfired on me, and here's all I can get:

"I've been shrinking and expanding our interference zone, changing its shape as much as I could, and cutting it off entirely now and then; to cross up their surveyors as much as I could. When we come to the jumping-off place we'll simply cut off everything that is sending out traceable vibrations. The Berg will have to run, of course, but it doesn't radiate much and we can ground out practically all of that. The drive is the bad feature—it looks as though we'll have to cut down to where we can ground out the radiation."

"How about the flare?" Thorndyke took the inevitable slide-rule from a pocket of his overalls.

"I've already had the Velantians build us some baffles—we've got lots of spare tantalum, tungsten, carballoy, and refractory, you know—just in case we should want to use them."

"Radiation . . . . detection . . . . decrement . . . . cosine squared theta . . . um . . . call it point zero zero three eight," the engineer mumbled, squinting at his "slip-stick." "Times half a million . . . . . . about nineteen hundred lights will have to be tops. Mighty slow, but we would get there sometime—maybe. Now about the baffles," and he went into another bout of computation during which could be distinguished a few such words as "temperature . . . inert corpuscles . . . velocity . . . fusion-point . . . Weinberger's Constant . . . . " Then:

"It figures that at about eighteen hundred lights your

baffles go out," he announced. "Pretty close check with the radiation limit. QX, I guess—but I shudder to think of what we may have to do to that Bergenholm to hold it together that long."

"It's not so hot. I don't think much of the scheme myself," admitted Kinnison frankly. "Probably you can think up something better before . . . ."

"Who, me? What with?" Thorndyke interrupted, with a laugh. "Looks to me like our best bet—anyway, ain't you the master mind of this outfit? Blast off!"

Thus it came about that, long later, the Lensman cut off his interference, cut off his driving power, cut off every mechanism whose operation generated vibrations which would reveal to enemy detectors the location of his cruiser. Space-suited mechanics emerged from the stern lock and fitted over the still white-hot vents of the driving projectors the baffles they had previously built.

It is of course well known that all ships of space are propelled by the inert projection, by means of high-potential static fields, of nascent fourth-order particles or "corpuscles," which are formed, inert, inside the inertialess projector, by the conversion of some form of energy into matter. This conversion liberates some heat, and a vast amount of light. This light, or "flare," shining as it does directly upon and through the highly tenuous gas formed by the projected corpuscles, makes of a speeding space-ship one of the most gorgeous spectacles known to man; and it was this very spectacular effect that Kinnison and his crew must do away with if their bold scheme were to have any chance at all of success.

The baffles were in place. Now, instead of shooting out in tell-tale luminescence, the light was shut in—but so, alas, was approximately three percent of the heat. And the generation of heat *must* be cut down to a point at which the radiation-equilibrium temperature of the baffles would be below the point of fusion of the refractories of which they were composed. This would cut down their speed tremendously; but on the other hand, they were practically safe from detection and would reach Trenco eventually—if the Bergenholm held out.

Of course there was still the chance of visual or electromagnetic detection, but that chance was vanishingly small. The proverbial task of finding a needle in a haystack would be an easy one indeed, compared to that of seeing in a telescope or upon visiplate or magneplate a dead-black, lightless ship in the infinity of space. No, the Bergenholm was their great, their only concern; and the engineers lavished upon that monstrous fabrication of metal a devotion to which could be likened only that of a corps of nurses attending the ailing baby of a multi-millionaire.

This concentration of attention did get results. The engineers still found it necessary to sweat and to grunt and to swear, but they did somehow keep the thing running— most of the time. Nor were they detected—then.

For the attention of the pirate high command was very much taken up with that fast-moving, that ever-expanding, that peculiarly-fluctuating volume of interference; utterly enigmatic as it was and impenetrable to their every instrument of communcation. In that system was the Prime Base of the Galactic Patrol. Therefore it *was* the Lensman's work —undoubtedly the same Lensman who had conquered one of their super-ships and, after having learned its every secret, had escaped in a lifeboat through the fine-meshed net set to catch him! And, piling Ossa upon Pelion, this same Lensman had—*must* have—captured ship after unconquerable ship of their best and was even now sailing calmly home with them! It was intolerable, unbearable, an insult that could not and would not be borne.

Therefore, using as tools every pirate ship in that sector of space, Helmuth and his computers and navigators were slowly but grimly solving the equations of motion of that volume of interference. Smaller and smaller became the uncertainties. Then ship after ship bored into the subethereal murk, to match course and velocity with, and ultimately to come to grips with, each focus of disturbance as it was determined.

Thus in a sense and although Kinnison and his friends did not then know it, it was only the failure of the Bergenholm that was to save their lives, and with those lives our present Civilization.

Slowly, hatingly, and, for reasons already given, undetected, Kinnison made pitiful progress toward Trenco; cursing impatiently and impartially his ship, the crippled generator, its designer and its previous operators as he went. But at long last Trenco loomed large beneath them and the Lensman used his Lens.

"Lensman of Trenco space-port, or any other Lensman within call!" he sent out clearly. "Kinnison of Tellus—Sol III—calling. My Bergenholm is almost out and I must sit down at Trenco space-port for repairs. I have avoided the pirates so far, but they may be either behind me or ahead of me, or both. What is the situation there?"

"I fear that I can be of no help," came back a weak thought, without the customary identification. "I am out of control. However, Tregonsee is in the . . . . . ."

Kinnison felt a poignant, unbearably agonizing mental impact that jarred him to the very core: a shock that, while of sledge-hammer force, was still of such a keenly penetrant timbre that it almost exploded every cell of his brain. It seemed as though some mighty fist, armed with yard-long needles, had slugged an actual blow into the most vitally sensitive nerve-centers of his being.

Communication ceased, and the Lensman knew, with a sick, shuddering certainty, that while in the very act of talking to him a Lensman had died.

CHAPTER 10 *Trenco*

JUDGED BY ANY EARTHLY STANDARDS THE PLANET TRENCO was—and is—a peculiar one indeed. Its atmosphere, which is not air, and its liquid, which is not water, are its two outstanding peculiarities and the sources of most of its others. Almost half of that atmosphere and by far the greater part of the liquid phase of the planet is a substance of extremely low latent heat of vaporization, with a boiling-point such that during the daytime it is a vapor and at night a liquid. To make matters worse, the other constituents of Trenco's gaseous envelope are of very feeble blanketing power, low specific heat, and of high permeability, so that its days are intensely hot and its nights are bitterly cold.

At night, therefore, it rains. Words are entirely inadequate to describe to anyone who has never been there just how it does rain during Trenco's nights. Upon Earth one inch of rainfall in an hour is a terrific downpour. Upon Trenco that amount of precipitation would scarcely be considered a mist; for along the equatorial belt, in less than thirteen Tellurian hours, it rains exactly forty-seven feet and five inches every night—no more no less, each and every night of every year.

Also there is lightning. Not in Terra's occasional flashes, but in one continuous, blinding glare which makes night as we know it unknown there; in nerve-wracking, battering, sense-destroying discharges which make ether and sub-ether alike impenetrable to any ray or signal short of a full-driven power beam. The days are practically as bad. The lightning is not violent then, but the bombardment of Trenco's monstrous sun, through that outlandishly peculiar atmosphere, produces almost the same effect.

Because of the difference in pressure set up by the enormous precipitation, always and everywhere upon Trenco there is wind—and what a wind! Except at the very poles, where it is too cold for even Trenconian life to exist, there is hardly a spot in which or a time at which an Earthly gale would not be considered a dead calm; and along the equator, at every sunrise and at every sunset, the wind blows from the day side to the night side at the rate of well over eight hundred miles an hour!

Through countless thousands of years wind and wave have planed and scoured the planet Trenco to a geometrically perfect oblate spheroid. It has no elevations and no depressions. Nothing fixed in an Earthly sense grows or exists upon its surface; no structure has ever been built there able to stay in one place through one whole day of the cataclysmic meteorological phenomena which constitute the natural Trenconian environment.

There live upon Trenco two types of vegetation, each type having innumerable sub-divisions. One type sprouts in the mud of morning; flourishes flatly, by dint of deeply sent and powerful roots, during the wind and the heat of the day; comes to full fruit in later afternoon; and at sunset dies and is swept away by the flood. The other type is free-floating. Some of its genera are remotely like footballs, others resemble tumbleweeds, still others thistledowns, hundreds of others have not their remotest counterparts upon Earth. Essentially, however, they are alike in habits of life. They can sink in the "water" of Trenco; then can burrow in its mud, from which they derive part of their sustenance; they can emerge therefrom into the sunlight; they can, undamaged float in or roll along before the ever-present Trenconian wind; and they can enwrap, entangle, or otherwise seize and hold anything with which they come in contact which by any chance may prove edible.

Animal life, too, while abundant and diverse, is characterized by three qualities. From lowest to very highest it is amphibious, it is streamlined, and it is omnivorous. Life upon Trenco is hard, and any form of life to evolve there must of stern necessity be willing, yes, even anxious, to eat literally *anything* available. And for that reason all surviving forms of life, vegetable and animal, have a voracity and a fecundity almost unknown anywhere else in the galaxy.

Thionite, the noxious drug referred to earlier in this narrative, is the sole reason for Trenco's galactic importance. As chlorophyll is to Earthly vegetation, so is thionite to that of Trenco. Trenco is the only planet thus far known upon which this substance occurs, nor have our scientists even yet been able either to analyze or to synthesize it. Thionite is capable of affecting only those races who breathe oxygen and possess warm blood, red with hæmoglobin. However, the planets peopled by such races are legion, and very shortly after the drug's discovery hordes of addicts, smugglers, peddlers, and out-and-out pirates were rushing toward the new Bonanza. Thousands of these adventurers died, either from each other's ray-guns or under an avalanche of hungry Trenconian life; but, thionite being what it is, thousands more kept coming. Also came the Patrol, to curb the evil traffic at its source by beaming down ruthlessly any being attempting to gather any Trenconian vegetation.

Thus between the Patrol and the drug syndicate there rages a bitterly continuous battle to the death. Arrayed against both factions is the massed life of the noisome planet, omnivorous as it is, eternally ravenous, and of an individual power and ferocity and a collective aggregate of numbers by no means to be despised. And eternally raging against all these contending parties are the wind, the lightning, the rain, the flood, and the hellish vibratory output of Trenco's enormous, malignant, blue-white sun.

This, then, was the planet upon which Kinnison had to land in order to repair his crippled Bergenholm—and in the end how well it was to be that such was the case!

"Kinnison of Tellus, greetings. Tregonsee of Rigel IV calling from Trenco space-port. Have you ever landed on this planet before?"

"No, but what . . . . ."

"Skip that for a time; it is most important that you

land here quickly and safely. Where are you in relation to this planet?"

"Your apparent diameter is a shade under six degrees. We are near the plane of your ecliptic and almost in the plane of your terminator, on the morning side."

"That is well, you have ample time. Place your ship between Trenco and the sun. Enter the atmosphere exactly fifteen G-P minutes from the present moment, at twenty degrees after meridian, as nearly as possible on the ecliptic, which is also our equator. Go inert as you enter atmosphere, for a free landing upon this planet is impossible. Synchronize with our rotation, which is twenty six point two G-P hours. Descend vertically until the atmospheric pressure is seven hundred millimeters of mercury, which will be at an altitude of approximately one thousand meters. Since you rely largely upon that sense called sight, allow me to caution you now not to trust it. When your external pressure is seven hundred millimeters of mercury your altitude will be one thousand meters, whether you believe it or not. Stop at that pressure and inform me of the fact, meanwhile holding yourself as nearly stationary as you can. Check so far?"

"QX—but do you mean to tell me that we can't locate each other at a *thousand meters?*" Kinnison's amazed thought escaped him. "What kind of . . . . ."

"I can locate you, but you cannot locate me," came the dry reply. "Everyone knows that Trenco is peculiar, but no one who has never been here can realize even dimly how peculiar it really is. Detectors and spy-rays are useless, electro-magnetics are practically paralyzed, and optical apparatus is distinctly unreliable. You cannot trust your vision here—do not believe anything you see. It used to require days to land a ship at this port, but with our Lenses and my 'sense of perception,' as you call it, it will be a matter of minutes."

Kinnison flashed his ship to the designated position.

"Cut the Berg, Thorndyke, we're all done with it. We've got to build up an inert velocity to match the rotation, and land inert."

"Thanks be to all the gods of space for that." The engineer heaved a sigh of relief. "I've been expecting it to blow its top for the last hour, and I don't know whether we'd ever have got it meshed in again or not."

"QX on location and orbit," Kinnison reported to the

as yet invisible space-port a few minutes later. "Now, what about that Lensman? What happened?"

"The usual thing," came the emotionless response. "It happens to altogether too many Lensmen who can see, in spite of everything we can tell them He insisted upon going out after his zwilniks in a ground car, and of course we had to let him go. He became confused, lost control, let something—possibly a zwilnik's bomb—get under his leading edge, and the wind and the trencos did the rest. He was Lageston of Mercator V—a good man, too. What is your pressure now?"

"Five hundred millimeters."

"Slow down. Now, if you cannot conquer the tendency to believe your eyes, you had better shut off your visiplates and watch only the pressure gauge."

"Being warned, I can disbelieve my eyes, I think," and for a minute or so communication ceased.

At a startled oath from vanBuskirk, Kinnison glanced into the plate and it needed all his nerve to keep from wrenching savagely at the controls. For the whole planet was tipping, lurching, spinning; gyrating madly in a frenzy of impossible motions; and even as the Patrolmen stared a huge mass of something shot directly toward the ship!

"Sheer off, Kim!" yelled the Valerian.

"Hold it, Bus," cautioned the Lensman. "That's what we've got to expect, you know—I passed all the stuff along as I got it. Everything, that is, except that a 'zwilnik' is anything or anybody that comes after thionite, and that a 'trenco' is anything, animal or vegetable, that lives on the planet. QX, Tregonsee—seven hundred, and I'm holding steady—I hope!"

"Steady enough, but you are too far away for our landing beam to grasp you. Apply a little drive . . . . . Shift course to your left and down . . . . . more left . . . . . up a trifle . . . that's it . . . . . slow down . . . . . QX."

There was a gentle, snubbing shock, and Kinnison again translated to his companions the stranger's thoughts:

"We have you. Cut off all power and lock all controls in neutral. Do nothing more until I instruct you to come out."

Kinnison obeyed; and, released from all duty, the visitors stared in fascinated incredulity into the visiplate. For that at which they stared was and must forever remain impossible of duplication upon Earth, and only in imagination can it be even faintly pictured. Imagine all the fantastic and monstrous creatures of a delirium-tremens vision incarnate and actual. Imagine them being hurled through the air, borne by a dust-laden gale more severe than any the great American dust-bowl or Africa's Sahara Desert ever endured. Imagine this scene as being viewed, not in an ordinary, solid distorting mirror, but in one whose falsely reflecting contours were changing constantly, with no logical or intelligible rhythm, into new and ever more grotesque warps. If imagination has been equal to the task, the resultant is what the visitors tried to see.

At first they could make nothing whatever of it. Upon nearer approach, however, the ghastly distortion grew less and the flatly level expanse took on a semblance of rigidity. Directly beneath them they made out something that looked like an immense, flat blister upon the otherwise featureless terrain. Toward this blister their ship was drawn.

A port opened, dwarfed in apparent size to a mere window by the immensity of the structure one of whose entrances it was. Through this port the vast bulk of the spaceship was wafted upon the landing-bars, and behind it the mighty bronze-and-steel gates clanged shut. The lock was pumped to a vacuum, there was a hiss of entering air, a spray of vaporous liquid bathed every inch of the vessel's surface, and Kinnison felt again the calm thought of Tregonsee, the Rigellian Lensman:

"You may now open your air-lock and emerge. If I have read aright our atmosphere is sufficiently like your own in oxygen content so that you will suffer no ill effects from it. It may be well, however, to wear your armor until you have become accustomed to its considerably greater density."

"That'll be a relief!" growled vanBuskirk's deep bass, when his chief had transmitted the thought. "I've been breathing this thin stuff so long I'm getting light-headed."

"That's gratitude!" Thorndyke retorted. "We've been running our air so heavy that all the rest of us are thick-headed now. If the air in this space-port is any heavier than what we've been having, I'm going to wear armor as long as we stay here!"

Kinnison opened the air-lock, found the atmosphere of the space-port satisfactory, and stepped out; to be greeted cordially by Tregonsee the Lensman.

This—this apparition was at least erect, which was something. His body was the size and shape of an oil-drum. Beneath this massive cylinder of a body were four short, blocky legs upon which he waddled about with surprising speed. Midway up the body, above each leg, there sprouted out a ten-foot-long, writhing, boneless, tentacular arm, which toward the extremity branched out into dozens of lesser tentacles, ranging in size from hair-like tendrils up to mighty fingers two inches or more in diameter. Tregonsee's head was merely a neckless, immobile, bulging dome in the center of the flat upper surface of his body—a dome bearing neither eyes nor ears, but only four equally-spaced toothless mouths and four single, flaring nostrils.

But Kinnison felt no qualm of repugnance at Tregonsee's monstrous appearance, for embedded in the leathery flesh of one arm was the Lens. Here, the Lensman knew, was in every essential a MAN—and probably a super-man.

"Welcome to Trenco, Kinnison of Tellus," Tregonsee was saying. "While we are near neighbors in space, I have never happened to visit your planet. I have encountered Tellurians here, of course, but they were not of a type to be received as guests."

"No, a zwilnik is not a high type of Tellurian," Kinnison agreed. "I have often wished that I could have your sense of perception, if only for a day. It must be wonderful indeed to be able to perceive a thing as a whole, inside and out, instead of having vision stopped at its surface, as is ours. And to be independent of light or darkness, never to be lost or in need of instruments; to know definitely where you are in relation to every other object or thing around you—that, I think, is the most marvelous sense in the Universe."

"Just as I have wished for sight and hearing, those two remarkable and to us entirely unexplainable senses. I have dreamed, I have studied volumes, on color and sound. Color in art and in nature; sound in music and in the voices of loved ones; but they remain meaningless symbols upon a printed page. However, such thoughts are vain. In all probability neither of us would enjoy the other's equipment if he had it, and this interchange is of no material assistance to you."

In flashing thoughts Kinnison then communicated to the other Lensman everything that had transpired since he left Prime Base.

"I perceive that your Bergenholm is of standard fourteen rating," Tregonsee said, as the Tellurian finished his story. "We have several spares here; and, while they all have regulation Patrol mountings, it would take much less time to change mounts than to overhaul your machine."

"That's so, too—I never thought of the possibility of your having spares on hand—and we've lost a lot of time already. How long will it take?"

"One shift of labor to change mounts; at least eight to rebuild yours enough to be sure that it will get you home."

"We'll change mounts, then, by all means. I'll call the boys . . . . ."

"There is no need of that. We are amply equipped, and neither you humans nor the Velantians could handle our tools." Tregonsee made no visible motion nor could Kinnison perceive a break in his thought, but while he was conversing with the Tellurian half a dozen of his blocky Rigellians had dropped whatever they had been doing and were scuttling toward the visiting ship. "Now I must leave you for a time, as I have one more trip to make this afternoon."

"Is there anything I can do to help you?" asked Kinnison.

"No," came the definite negative. "I will return in three hours, as well before sunset the wind makes it impossible to get even a ground-car into the port. I will then show you why you can be of little assistance to us."

Kinnison spent those three hours watching the Rigellians work upon the Bergenholm; there was no need for direction or advice. They knew what to do and they did it. Those tiny, hairlike fingers, literally hundreds of them at once, performed delicate tasks with surpassing nicety and dispatch; when it came to heavy tasks the larger digits or even whole arms wrapped themselves around the work and, with the solid bracing of the four block-like legs, exerted forces that even vanBuskirk's giant frame could not have approached.

As the end of the third hour neared, Kinnison watched with a spy-ray—there were no windows in Trenco spaceport—the leeward groundway of the structure. In spite of the weird antics of Trenco's sun—gyrating, jumping, appearing and disappearing—he knew that it was going down. Soon he saw the ground-car coming in, scuttling crabwise, nose into the wind but actually moving backward and sidewise. Although the "seeing" was very poor, at this close range the distortion was minimized and he could see that, like its parent craft, the ground-car was a blister. Its edges actually touched the ground all around, sloping upward and over the top in such a smooth reverse curve that the harder the wind blew the more firmly was the vehicle pressed downward.

The ground-flap came up just enough to clear the car's

top and the tiny craft crept up. But before the landing bars could seize her the ground-car struck an eddy from the flap—an eddy in a medium which, although gaseous, was at that velocity practically solid. Earth blasted away in torrents from the leading edge, the car leaped bodily into the air and was flung away, end over end. But Tregonsee, with consummate craftsmanship, forced her flat again, and again she crawled up toward the flap. This time the landing-bars took hold and, although the little vessel fluttered like a leaf in a gale, she was drawn inside the port and the flap went down behind her. She was then sprayed, and Tregonsee came out.

"Why the spray?" thought Kinnison, as the Rigellian entered his control-room.

"Trencos. Much of the life of this planet starts from almost imperceptible spores. It develops rapidly, attains considerable size, and consumes anything organic it touches. This port was depopulated time after time before the lethal spray was developed. Now turn your spy-ray again to the lee of the port."

During the few minutes that had elapsed the wind had increased in fury to such an extent that the very ground was boiling away from the trailing edge in the tumultuous eddy formed there, ultra-streamlined though the space-port was. And that eddy, far surpassing in violence any storm known to Earth, was to the denizens of Trenco a miraculously appearing quiet spot in which they could stop and rest, eat and be eaten.

A globular monstrosity had thrust pseudopodia deep into the boiling dirt. Other limbs now shot out, grasping a tumbleweedlike growth. The latter fought back viciously, but could make no impression upon the rubbery integument of the former. Then a smaller creature, slipping down the polished curve of the shield, was enmeshed by the tumbleweed. There ensued the amazing spectacle of one-half of the tumbleweed devouring the newcomer, even while its other half was being devoured by the globe!

"Now look out farther . . . . . still farther," directed Tregonsee.

"I can't. Things take on impossible motions and become so distorted as to be unrecognizable."

"Exactly. If you saw a zwilnik out there, where would you shoot?"

"At him, I suppose—why?"

"Because if you shot at where you think you see him.

not only would you miss him, but the beam might very well swing around and enter your own back. Many men have been killed by their own weapons in precisely that fashion. Since we know, not only what the object is, but exactly where it is, we can correct our lines of aim for the then existing values of distortion. This is of course the reason why we Rigellians and other races possessing the sense of perception are the only ones who can efficiently police this planet."

"Reason enough, I'd say, from what I've seen," and silence fell.

For minutes the two Lensmen watched, while creatures of a hundred kinds streamed into the lee of the space-port and killed and ate each other. Finally something came crawling up wind, against that unimaginable gale; a flatly streamlined creature resembling somewhat a turtle, but shaped as was the ground-car. Thrusting down long, hooked flippers into the dirt it inched along, paying no attention to the scores of lesser creatures who hurled themselves upon its armored back, until it was close beside the largest football-shaped creature in the eddy. Then, lightning-like, it drove a needle-sharp organ at least eight inches into the leathery mass of its victim. Struggling convulsively, the stricken thing lifted the turtle a fraction of an inch—and both were hurled instantly out of sight; the living ball still eating a luscious bit of prey despite the fact that it was impaled upon the poniard of the turtle and was certainly doomed.

"Good Lord, what was that?" exclaimed Kinnison.

"The flat? That was a representative of Trenco's highest life-form. It may develop a civilization in time—it is quite intelligent now."

"But the difficulties!" protested the Tellurian. "Building cities, even homes . . . . ."

"Neither cities nor homes are necessary here, nor even desirable. Why build? Nothing is or can be fixed on this planet, and since one place is exactly like every other place, why wish to remain in any one particular spot? They do very well, in their own mobile way. Here, you will notice, comes the rain."

The rain came—forty-four inches per hour of rain—and the incessant lightning. The dirt became first mud, then muddy water being driven in fiercely flying gouts and masses. Now, in the lee of the space-port, the outlandish denizens of Trenco were burrowing down into the mud—

still eating each other and anything else that came within reach.

The water grew deeper and deeper, its upper surface now whipped into frantic sheets of spray. The structure was now afloat, and Kinnison saw with astonishment that, small as was the exposed surface and flatly curved, yet it was pulling through the water at frightful speed the wide-spreading steel sea-anchors which were holding its head to the gale.

"With no reference points how do you know where you're going?" he demanded.

"We neither know nor care," responded Tregonsee, with a mental shrug. "We are like the natives in that. Since one spot is like every other spot, why choose between them?"

"What a world—*what* a world! However, I am beginning to understand why thionite is so expensive," and, overwhelmed by the ever-increasing fury raging outside, Kinnison sought his bunk.

Morning came, a reversal of the previous evening. The liquid evaporated, the mud dried, the flat-growing vegetation sprang up with shocking speed, the animals emerged and again ate and were eaten.

And eventually came Tregonsee's announcement that it was almost noon, and that now, for half an hour or so, it would be calm enough for the space-ship to leave the port.

"You are sure that I would be of no help to you?" asked the Rigellian, half-pleadingly.

"Sorry, Tregonsee, but I'm afraid you wouldn't fit into my matrix any better than I would into yours. But here's the spool I told you about. If you will take it to your base on your next relief you will do civilization and the Patrol more good than you could by coming with us. Thanks for the Bergenholm, which is covered by credits, and thanks a lot for your help and courtesy, which can't be covered. Goodbye," and the now entirely space-worthy craft shot out through the port, through Trenco's noxiously peculiar atmosphere, and into the vacuum of space.

CHAPTER 11   *Grand Base*

AT SOME LITTLE DISTANCE FROM THE GALAXY, YET SHACKLED to it by the flexible yet powerful bonds of gravitation, the small but comfortable planet upon which was Helmuth's base circled about its parent sun. This planet had been chosen with the utmost care, and its location was a secret guarded jealously indeed. Scarcely one in a million of Boskone's teeming myriads knew even that such a planet existed; and of the chosen few who had ever been asked to visit it, fewer still by far had been allowed to leave it.

Grand Base covered hundreds of square miles of that planet's surface. It was equipped with all the arms and armament known to the military genius of the age; and in the exact center of that immense citadel there arose a glittering metallic dome.

The inside surface of that dome was lined with visiplates and communicators, hundreds of thousands of them. Miles of catwalks clung precariously to the inward-curving wall. Control panels and instrument boards covered the floor in banks and tiers, with only narrow runways between them. And what a personnel! There were Solarians, Crevenians, Sirians. There were Antareans, Vandemarians, Arcturians. There were representatives of scores, yes, hundreds of other solar systems of the galaxy.

But whatever their external form they were all breathers of oxygen and they were all nourished by warm, red blood. Also, they were all alike mentally. Each had won his present high place by trampling down those beneath him and by pulling down those above him in the branch to which he had first belonged of the "pirate" organization. Each was characterized by a total lack of scruple; by a coldly ruthless passion for power and place.

Kinnison had been eminently correct in his belief that Boskone's was not a "pirate outfit" in any ordinary sense of the word, but even his ideas of its true nature fell far short indeed of the truth. It was a culture already inter-galactic in scope, but one built upon ideals diametrically opposed to those of the civilization represented by the Galactic Patrol.

It was a tyranny, an absolute monarchy, a despotism not even remotely approximated by the dictatorships of earlier ages. It had only one creed—"The end justifies the means." Anything—literally *anything at all*—that produced the desired result was commendable; to fail was the only crime. The successful named their own rewards; those who failed were disciplined with an impersonal, rigid severity exactly proportional to the magnitude of their failures.

Therefore no weaklings dwelt within that fortress; and of all its cold, hard, ruthless crew far and away the coldest, hardest, and most ruthless was Helmuth, the "speaker for Boskone," who sat at the great desk in the dome's geometrical center. This individual was almost human in form and build, springing as he did from a planet closely approximating Earth in mass, atmosphere, and climate. Indeed, only his general, all-pervasive aura of blueness bore witness to the fact that he was not a native of Tellus.

His eyes were blue, his hair was blue, and even his skin was faintly blue beneath its coat of ultra-violet tan. His intensely dynamic personality fairly radiated blueness—not the gentle blue of an Earthly sky, not the sweetly innocuous blue of an Earthly flower; but the keenly merciless blue of a delta-ray, the cold and bitter blue of a Polar iceberg, the unyielding, inflexible blue of quenched and drawn tungsten-chromium steel.

Now a frown sat heavily upon his arrogantly patrician face as his eyes bored into the plate before him, from the base of which were issuing the words being spoken by the assistant pictured in its deep surface:

". . . . . the fifth dove into the deepest ocean of Corvina II, in the depths of which all rays are useless. The ships which followed have not as yet reported, but they will do so as soon as they have completed their mission. No trace of the sixth has been found, and it is therefore assumed that it was destroyed . . . ."

"Who assumes so?" demanded Helmuth, coldly. "There is no justification whatever for such an assumption. Go on!"

"The Lensman, if there is one and if he is alive, must therefore be in the fifth ship, which is about to be taken."

"Your report is neither complete nor conclusive, and I

do not at all approve of your intimation that the Lensman is simply a figment of my imagination. That it was a Lensman is the only possible logical conclusion—none other of the Patrol forces could have done what has been done. Postulating his reality, it seems to me that instead of being a bare possibility, it is highly probable that he has again escaped us, and again in one of our own vessels—this time in the one you have so conveniently assumed to have been destroyed. Have you searched the line of flight?"

"Yes, sir. Everything in space and every planet within reach of that line has been examined with care; except, of course, Velantia and Trenco."

"Velantia is, for the time being, unimportant. The sixth ship left Velantia and did not go back there. Why Trenco?" and Helmuth pressed a series of buttons. "Ah, I see . . . . To recapitulate, one ship, the one which in all probability is now carrying the Lensman, is still unaccounted for. Where is it? We know that it has not landed upon or near any Solarian planet, and measures are being taken to see to it that it does not land upon or near any planet of 'Civilization.' Now, I think, it has become necessary to comb that planet Trenco, inch by inch."

"But sir, how . . . . ." began the anxious-eyed underling.

"When did it become necessary to draw diagrams and make blue-prints for you?" demanded Helmuth, harshly. "We have ships manned by Ordoviks and other races having the sense of perception. Find out where they are and get them there at full blast!" and he punched a button, to replace the image upon his plate by another.

"It has now become of paramount importance that we complete our knowledge of the Lens of the Patrol," he began, without salutation or preamble. "Have you traced its origin yet?"

"I believe so, but I do not certainly know. It has proved to be a task of such difficulty . . . . ."

"If it had been an easy one I would not have made a special assignment of it to you. Go on!"

"Everything seems to point to the planet Arisia, of which I can learn nothing definite whatever except . . . . ."

"Just a moment!" Helmuth punched more buttons and listened. "Unexplored . . . . unknown . . . . shunned by all spacemen . . . . .

"Superstition, eh?" he snapped. "Another of those haunted planets?"

"Something more than ordinary spacemen's superstition, sir, but just what I have not been able to discover. By combing my department I managed to make up a crew of those who either were not afraid of it or had never heard of it. That crew is now en route there."

"Whom have we in that sector of space? I find it desirable to check your findings."

The department head reeled off a list of names and numbers, which Helmuth considered at length.

"Gildersleeve, the Valerian," he decided. "He is a good man, coming along fast. Aside from a firm belief in his own peculiar gods, he has shown no signs of weakness. You considered him?"

"Certainly." The henchman, as cold as his icy chief, knew that explanations would not satisfy Helmuth, therefore he offered none. "He is raiding at the moment, but I will put you on him if you like."

"Do so," and upon Helmuth's plate there appeared a deep-space scene of rapine and pillage.

The convoying Patrol cruiser had already been blasted out of existence; only a few idly drifting masses of debris remained to show that it had ever been. Needle-beams were at work, and soon the merchantman hung inert and helpless. The pirates, scorning to use the emergency inlet port, simply blasted away the entire entrance panel. Then they boarded, an armored swarm; flaming DeLameters spreading death and destruction before them.

The sailors, outnumbered as they were and over-armed, fought heroically—but uselessly. In groups and singly they fell; those who were not already dead being callously tossed out into space in slitted space-suits and with smashed drivers. Only the younger women—the stewardesses, the nurses, the one or two such among the few passengers— were taken as booty; all others shared the fate of the crew.

Then, the ship plundered from nose to after-jets and every article or thing of value trans-shipped, the raider drew off, bathed in the blue-white glare of the bombs that were destroying every trace of the merchant-ship's existence. Then and only then did Helmuth reveal himself to Gildersleeve.

"A good, clean job of work, Captain," he commended. "Now, how would you like to visit Arisia for me—for *me*, direct?"

A pallor overspread the normally ruddy face of the Va-

lerian and an uncontrollable tremor shook his giant frame.
But as he considered the implications resident in Helmuth's
concluding phrase he licked his lips and spoke.

"I hate to say no, sir, if you order me to and if there
was any way of making my crew do it. But we were near
there once, sir, and we . . . . I . . . . they . . . . it
well, sir, I *saw* things, sir, and I was . . . . was *warned*,
sir!"

"Saw what? And was warned of what?"

"I can't describe what I saw, sir. I can't even think of
it in thoughts that mean anything. As for the warning,
though, it was very definite, sir. I was told very plainly that
if I ever go near that planet again I will die a worse death
than any I have dealt out to any other living being."

"But you will go there again?"

"I tell you, sir, that the crew will not do it," Gildersleeve replied, doggedly. "Even if I were anxious to go,
every man aboard will mutiny if I try it."

"Call them in right now and tell them that you have
been ordered to Arisia."

The captain did so, but he had scarcely started to talk
when he was stopped in no uncertain fashion by his first officer—also of course a Valerian—who pulled his DeLameter
and spoke savagely:

"Cut it, Gil! We are not going to Arisia. I was with
you before, you know. Set course within five points of that
accursed planet and I blast you where you sit!"

"Helmuth, speaking for Boskone!" ripped from the headquarters speaker. "This is rankest mutiny. You know the
penalty, do you not?"

"Certainly I do—what of it?" The first officer snapped
back.

"Suppose that I *tell* you to go to Arisia?" Helmuth's
voice was now soft and silky, but instinct with deadly
menace.

"In that case *I* tell *you* to go to the ninth hell—or to
Arisia, a million times worse!"

"What? You dare speak thus to *me*?" demanded the
arch-pirate, sheer amazement at the fellow's audacity blanketing his rising anger.

"I so dare," declared the rebel, brazen defiance and un-
alterable resolve in every line of his hard body and in every
lineament of his hard face. "All you can do is kill us. You
can order out enough ships to blast us out of the ether, but
that's all you *can* do. That would be only death and we'd

have the fun of taking a lot of the boys along with us. If
we go to Arisia, though, it would be different—very, *very*
different. No, Helmuth, and I throw this in your teeth: if
I ever go near Arisia again it will be in a ship in which you,
Helmuth, in person, are sitting at the controls. If you think
this is an empty dare and don't like it, don't take it. Send
on your dogs!"

"That will do! Report yourselves to Base D under . . . ."
Then Helmuth's flare of anger passed and his cold reason
took charge. Here was something utterly unprecedented;
an entire crew of the hardest-bitten marauders in space
offering open and barefaced mutiny—no, not mutiny, but
actual rebellion—to him, Helmuth, in his very person.
And not a typical, skulking, carefully planned uprising, but
the immovably brazen desperation of men making an ultimately last-ditch stand. Truly, it must be a powerful superstition indeed, to make that crew of hard-boiled hellions
choose certain death rather than face again the imaginary
—they *must* be imaginary—perils of a planet unknown to
and unexplored by Boskone's planetographers. But they
were, after all, ordinary space-men, of little mental force
and of small real ability. Even so, it was clearly indicated
that in this case precipitate action was to be avoided. Therefore he went on calmly and almost without a break. "Cancel all this that has been spoken and that has taken place.
Continue with your original orders pending further investigation," and switched his plate back to the department
head.

"I have checked your conclusions and have found them
correct," he announced, as though nothing at all out of the
way had transpired. "You did well in sending a ship to
investigate. No matter where I am or what I am doing,
notify me instantly at the first sign of irregularity in the
behavior of any member of that ship's personnel."

Nor was that call long in coming. The carefully-selected
crew—selected for complete lack of knowledge of the dread
planet which was their objective—sailed along in blissful
ignorance, both of the real meaning of their mission and of
what was to be its ghastly end. Soon after Helmuth's unsatisfactory interview with Gildersleeve and his mate, the luckless exploring vessel reached the barrier which the Arisians
had set around their system and through which no uninvited stranger was allowed to pass.

The free-flying ship struck that frail barrier and stopped.
In the instant of contact a wave of mental force flooded

the mind of the captain, who, gibbering with sheer, stark, panic terror, flashed his vessel away from that horror-impregnated wall and hurled call after frantic call along his beam, back to headquarters. His first call, in the instant of reception, was relayed to Helmuth at his central desk.

"Steady, man; report intelligently!" that worthy snapped, and his eyes, large now upon the cowering captain's plate, bored steadily, hypnotically into those of the expedition's leader. "Pull yourself together and tell me exactly what happened. Everything!"

"Well, sir, when we struck something—a screen of some sort—and stopped, something came aboard. It was . . . oh . . . ay-ay-e-e!" his voice rose to a shriek, but under Helmuth's dominating glare he subsided quickly and went on. "A monster, sir, if there ever was one. A fire-breathing demon, sir, with teeth and claws and cruelly barbed tail. He spoke to me in my own Crevenian language. He said . . . . ."

"Never mind what he said. I did not hear it, but I can guess what it was. He threatened you with death in some horrible fashion, did he not?" and the coldly ironical tones did more to restore the shaking man's equilibrium than reams of remonstrance could have done.

"Well, yes, that was about the size of it, sir," he admitted.

"And does that sound reasonable to you, the commander of a first class battleship of Boskone's Fleet?" sneered Helmuth.

"Well, sir, put on that way, it does seem a bit far-fetched," the captain replied, sheepishly.

"It *is* far-fetched." The director, in the safety of his dome, could afford to be positive. "We do not know exactly what caused that hallucination, apparition, or whatever it was—you were the only one who could see it, apparently; it certainly was not visible on our master-plates. It was probably some form of suggestion or hypnotism; and you know as well as we do that any suggestion can be thrown off by a definitely opposed will. But you did not oppose it, did you?"

"No, sir, I didn't have time."

"Nor did you have your screens out, nor automatic recorders on the trip. Not much of anything, in fact . . . . I think that you had better report back here, at full blast."

"Oh, no, sir—please!" He knew what rewards were granted to failures, and Helmuth's carefully chosen words had already produced the effect desired by their speaker. "They took me by surprise then, but I'll go through this next time."

"Very well, I will give you one more chance. When you get close to the barrier, or whatever it is, go inert and put out all your screens. Man your plates and weapons, for whatever can hypnotize can be killed. Go ahead at full blast, with all the acceleration you can get. Crash through anything that opposes you, and beam anything that you can detect or see. Can you think of anything else?"

"That should be sufficient, sir." The captain's equanimity was completely restored, now that the warlike preparations were making more and more nebulous the sudden, but single, thought wave of the Arisian.

"Proceed!"

The plan was carried out to the letter. This time the pirate craft struck the frail barrier inert, and its slight force offered no tangible bar to the prodigious mass of metal. But this time, since the barrier was actually passed, there was no mental warning and no possibility of retreat.

Many men have skeletons in their closets. Many have phobias, things of which they are consciously afraid. Many others have them, not consciously, but buried deep in the subconscious; specters which seldom or never rise above the threshold of perception. Every sentient being has, if not such specters as these, at least a few active or latent dislikes, dreads, or outright fears. This is true, no matter how quiet and peaceful a life the being has led.

These pirates, however, were the scum of space. They were beings of hard and criminal lives and of violent and lawless passions. Their hates and conscience-searing deeds had been legion, their count of crimes long, black, and hideous. Therefore, slight indeed was the effort required to locate in their conscious minds—to say nothing of the noxious depths of their subconscious ones—visions of horror fit to blast stronger intellects than theirs. And that is exactly what the Arisian Watchman did. From each pirate's total mind, a veritable charnel pit, he extracted the foulest, most unspeakable dregs, the deeply hidden things of which the subject was in the greatest fear. Of these things he formed a whole of horror incomprehensible and incredible, and this ghastly whole he made incarnate and visible to the pirate who was its unwilling parent; as visible as though it were composed of flesh and blood, of copper and steel. Is it any wonder that each member of that outlaw crew, seeing such an abhorrent materialization, went instantly mad?

It is of no use to go into the horribly monstrous shapes of the things, even were it possible; for each of them was visible to only one man, and none of them was visible to those who looked on from the safety of the distant base. To them the entire crew simply abandoned their posts and attacked each other, senselessly and in insane frenzy, with whatever weapons came first to hand. Indeed, many of them fought bare-handed, weapons hanging unused in their belts, gouging, beating, clawing, biting until life had been rived horribly away. In other parts of the ship DeLameters flamed briefly, bars crashed crunchingly, knives and axes sheared and trenchantly bit. And soon it was over—almost. The pilot was still alive, unmoving and rigid at his controls.

Then he, too, moved; rapidly and purposefully. He cut in the Bergenholm, spun the ship around, shoved her drivers up to maximum blast, and steadied her into an exact course —and when Helmuth read that course even his iron nerves failed him momentarily. For the ship was flying, not for its own home port, but directly toward Grand Base, the jealously secret planet whose spatial coordinates neither that pilot nor any other creature of the pirates' rank and file had ever known!

Helmuth snapped out orders, to which the pilot gave no heed. His voice—for the first time in his career—rose to a howl, but the pilot still paid no attention. Instead, eyes bulging with horror and fingers curved tensely into veritable talons, he reared upright upon his bench and leaped as though to clutch and to rend some unutterably appalling foe. He leaped over his board into thin and empty air. He came down a-sprawl in a maze of naked, high-potential bus-bars. His body vanished in a flash of searing flame and a cloud of thick and greasy smoke.

The bus-bars cleared themselves of their gruesome "short" and the great ship, manned now entirely by corpses, bored on.

". . . . . stinking klebots, the lily-livered cowards!" the department head, who had also been yelling orders, was still pounding his desk and yelling. "If they're *that* afraid—go crazy and kill each other without being touched—I'll have to go myself . . . ."

"No, Sansteed," Helmuth interrupted curtly. "You will not have to go. There is, after all, I think, something there —something that you may not be able to handle. You see, you missed the one essential key fact." He referred to the course, the setting of which had shaken him to the very core.

"Let be," he silenced the other's flood of question and protest. "It would serve no purpose to detail it to you now. Have the ship taken back to port."

Helmuth knew now that it was not superstition that made spacemen shun Arisia. He knew that, from his standpoint at least, there was something very seriously amiss. But he had not the faintest conception of the real situation, nor of the real and terrible power which the Arisians could, and upon occasion would, wield.

CHAPTER **12**   Kinnison Brings Home the Bacon

HELMUTH SAT AT HIS DESK, THINKING; THINKING WITH ALL the coldly analytical precision of which he was capable.

This Lensman was both powerful and tremendously resourceful. The cosmic-energy drive, developed by the science of a world about which the Patrol knew nothing, was Boskone's one great item of superiority. If the Patrol could be kept in ignorance of that drive the struggle would be over in a year; the culture of the iron hand would be unchallenged throughout the galaxy. If, however, the Patrol should succeed in learning Boskone's top secret, the war between the two cultures might well be prolonged indefinitely. This Lensman knew that secret and was still at large, of that he was all too certain. Therefore the Lensman must be destroyed. And that brought up the Lens.

What was it? A peculiar bauble indeed; impossible of duplication because of some subtlety of intra-atomic arrangement, and possessing peculiar and dire potentialities. The old belief that no one except a Lensman could wear a Lens was true—he had proved it. The Lens must account in some way for the outstanding ability of the Lensman, and it must tie in, somehow, with both Arisia and the

thought-screens. The Lens was the one thing possessed by
the Patrol which his own forces did not have. He must and
would have it, for it was undoubtedly a powerful arm. Not
to be compared, of course, with their own monopoly of
cosmic energy—but that monopoly was now threatened,
and seriously. That Lensman *must be destroyed*.

But how? It was easy to say "Comb Trenco, inch by
inch," but doing it would prove a Herculean task. Suppose
that the Lensman should again escape, in that volume of
so fantastically distorted media? He had already escaped
twice, in much clearer ether than Trenco's. However, if his
information should never get back to Prime Base little
harm would be done, and ships had been thrown around
every solar system the Lensman could reach. Not even a
grain-of-dust meteorite could pass those screens without
detection. So much for the Lensman. Now about getting the
secret of the Lens.

Again, how? There was *something* upon Arisia; something connected in some way with the Lens and with
thought—possibly also with those thought-screens . . . . .

His mind flashed back over the unorthodox manner of
his acquirement of those devices—unorthodox in that he had
neither stolen them nor murdered their inventor. A person
had come to him with pass-words and credentials which
could not be ignored; had handed him a heavily-sealed container, which, he said, had come from a planet named
Ploor; had remarked casually "Thought-screen data—you'll
know when you need 'em"; and had gone.

Whatever the Arisian was, it had mental power; of that
fact there could be no doubt. Out of the full sphere of
space, what was the mathematical probability that the pilot
of that deathship would have set by accident his course so
exactly upon Grand Base? Vanishingly small. Treachery
would not explain the facts—not only had the pilot been
completely insane when he laid the course, but also *he did
not know where Grand Base was*.

As an explanation mental force alone seemed fantastic,
but no other as yet presented itself as a possibility. Also, it
was supported by the unbelievable, the absolutely definite
refusal of Gildersleeve's normally fearless crew even to approach the planet. It would take an unheard-of mental
force so to affect such crime-hardened veterans.

Helmuth was not one to underestimate an enemy. Was
there a man beneath that dome, save himself, of sufficient
mental caliber to undertake the now necessary mission to

Arisia? There was not. He himself had the finest mind on
the planet; else that other had deposed him long since and
had sat at the control desk himself. He was sublimely confident that no outside thought could break down *his* definitely opposed will—and besides, there were the thought-
screens, the secret of which he had not as yet shared with
anyone. The time had come to use those screens.

It has already been made clear that Helmuth was not a
fool. No more was he a coward. If he himself could best of
all his force do a thing, that thing he did; with the coldly
ruthless efficiency that marked alike his every action and
his every thought.

How should he go? Should he accept that challenge,
and take Gildersleeve's rebellious crew of cutthroats to
Arisia? No. In the event of an outcome short of complete
success, it would not do to lose face before that band of
ruffians. Moreover, the idea of such a crew going insane behind him was not one to be relished. He would go alone.

"Wolmark, come to the center," he ordered. When that
worthy appeared he went on: "Be seated, as this is to be a
serious conference. I have watched with admiration and ap-
preciation, as well as some mild amusement, the development of your lines of information; especially those concerning affairs which are most distinctly not in your department. They are, however, efficient—you already know
exactly what has happened." A statement this, in no wise
a question.

"Yes, sir," quietly. Wolmark was somewhat taken aback,
but not at all abashed.

"That is the reason you are here now. I thoroughly approve of you. I am leaving the planet for a few days, and
you are the best man in the organization to take charge in
my absence."

"I suspected that you would be leaving, sir."

"I know you did: but I am now informing you, merely
to make sure that you develop no peculiar ideas in my absence, that there are at least a few things which you do not
suspect at all. That safe, for instance," nodding toward a
peculiarly shimmering globe of force anchoring itself in
air. "Even your highly efficient spy system has not been
able to learn a thing about that."

"No, sir, we have not—yet," he could not forbear adding.

"Nor will you, with any skill or force known to man.
But keep on trying, it amuses me. I know, you see, of all

your attempts. But to get on. I now say, and for your own good I advise you to believe, that failure upon my part to return to this desk will prove highly unfortunate for you."

"I believe that, sir. Any man of intelligence would make such arrangement, if he could. But sir, suppose that the Arisians . . . . ."

"If your 'if he could' implies a doubt, act upon it and learn wisdom," Helmuth advised him coldly. "You should know by this time that I neither gamble nor bluff. I have made arrangements to protect myself, both from enemies, such as the Arisians and the Patrol, and from friends, such as ambitious youngsters who are trying to supplant me. If I were not entirely confident of getting back here safely, my dear Wolmark, I would not go."

"You misunderstand me, sir. Really, I have no idea of supplanting you."

"Not until you get a good opportunity, you mean—I understand you thoroughly; and, as I have said before, I approve of you. Go ahead with all your plans. I have kept at least one lap ahead of you so far, and if the time should ever come when I can no longer do so, I shall no longer be fit to speak for Boskone. You understand, of course, that the most important matter now in work is the search for the Lensman, of which the combing of Trenco and the screening of the Patrol's systems are only two phases?"

"Yes, sir."

"Very well. I can, I think, leave matters in your hands. If anything really serious comes up, such as a development in the Lensman case, let me know at once. Otherwise do not call me. Take the desk," and Helmuth strode away.

He was whisked to the space-port, where there awaited him his special speedster, equipped long since with divers and sundry items of equipment whose functions were known only to himself.

For him the trip to Arisia was neither long nor tedious. The little racer was fully automatic, and as it tore through space he worked as coolly and efficiently as he was wont to do at his desk. Indeed, more so, for here he could concentrate without interruption. Many were the matters he planned and the decisions he made, the while his portfolio of notes grew thicker and thicker.

As he neared his destination he put away his work, actuated his special mechanisms, and waited. When the speedster struck the barrier and stopped Helmuth wore a faint, hard smile; but that smile disappeared with a snap as a thought crashed into his supposedly shielded brain.

"You are surprised that your thought-screens are not effective?" The thought was coldly contemptuous. "I know in essence what the messenger from Ploor told you concerning them when he gave them to you; but he spoke in ignorance. We of Arisia know thought in a way that no member of his race is now or ever will be able to understand.

"Know, Helmuth, that we Arisians do not want and will not tolerate uninvited visitors. Your presence is particularly distasteful, representing as you do a despotic, degrading, and antisocial culture. Evil and good are of course purely relative, so it cannot be said in absolute terms that your culture is evil. It is, however, based upon greed, hatred, corruption, violence, and fear. Justice it does not recognize, nor mercy, nor truth except as a scientific utility. It is basically opposed to liberty. Now liberty—of person, of thought, of action—is the basic and the goal of the civilization to which you are opposed, and with which any really philosophical mind must find itself in accord.

"Inflated overweeningly by your warped and perverted ideas, by your momentary success in dominating your handful of minions, tied to you by bonds of greed, of passion, and of crime, you come here to wrest from us the secret of the Lens; from us, a race as much abler than yours as we are older—a ratio of millions to one.

"You consider yourself cold, hard, ruthless. Compared to me, you are weak, soft, tender; as helpless as a newborn child. That you may learn and appreciate that fact is one reason why you are living at this present moment. Your lesson will now begin."

Then Helmuth, starkly rigid, unable to move a muscle, felt delicate probes enter his brain. One at a time they pierced his innermost being, each to a definitely selected center. It seemed that each thrust carried with it the ultimate measure of exquisitely poignant anguish possible of endurance, but each successive needle carried with it an even more keenly unbearable thrill of agony.

Helmuth was not now calm and cold. He could have screamed in wild abandon, but even that relief was denied him. He could not even scream; all he could do was sit there and suffer.

Then he began to see things. There, actually materializing in the empty air of the speedster, he saw in endless procession things he had done, either in person or by proxy, both during his ascent to his present high place in the pirates' organization and since the attainment of that place. Long was the list, and black. As it unfolded his torment grew more and ever more intense, until finally, after an interval that might have been a fraction of a second or might have been untold hours, he could stand no more. He fainted, sinking beyond the reach of pain into a sea of black unconsciousness.

He awakened white and shaking, wringing wet with perspiration and so weak that he could scarcely sit erect, but with a supremely blissful realization that, for the time being at least, his punishment was over.

"This, you will observe, has been a very mild treatment," the cold Arisian accents went on inside his brain. "Not only do you still live, you are even still sane. We now come to the second reason why you have not been destroyed. Your destruction by us would not be good for that struggling young civilization which you oppose.

"We have given that civilization an instrument by virtue of which it should become able to destroy you and everything for which you stand. If it cannot do so it is not yet ready to become a civilization and your obnoxious culture shall be allowed to conquer and to flourish for a time.

"Now go back to your dome. Do not return. I know that you will not have the temerity to do so in person. Do not attempt to do so by any form whatever of proxy."

There were no threats, no warnings, no mention of consequences; but the level and incisive tone of the Arisian put a fear into Helmuth's cold heart the like of which he had never before known.

He whirled his speedster about and hurled her at full blast toward his home planet. It was only after many hours that he was able to regain even a semblance of his customary poise, and days elapsed before he could think coherently enough to consider as a whole the shocking, the unbelievable thing that had happened to him.

He wanted to believe that the creature, whatever it was, had been bluffing—that it could not kill him, that it had done its worst. In similar case he would have killed without mercy, and that course seemed to him the only logical one to pursue. His cold reason, however, would not allow him to entertain that comforting belief. Deep down he *knew* that the Arisian could have killed him as easily as it had slain the lowest member of his band, and the thought chilled him to the marrow.

What could he do? What *could* he do? Endlessly, as the miles and light-years reeled off behind his hurtling racer, this question reiterated itself; and when his home planet loomed close it was still unanswered.

Since Wolmark believed implicitly his statement that it would be poor technique to oppose his return, the planet's screens went down at Helmuth's signal. His first act was to call all the department heads to the center, for an extremely important council of war. There he told them everything that had happened, calmly and concisely, concluding:

"They are aloof, disinterested, unpartisan to a degree I find it impossible to understand. They disapprove of us on purely philosophical grounds, but they will take no active part against us as long as we stay away from their solar system. Therefore we cannot obtain knowledge of the Lens by direct action, but there are other methods which shall be worked out in due course.

"The Arisians do approve of the Patrol, and have helped them to the extent of giving them the Lens. There, however, they stop. If the Lensmen do not know how to use their Lenses efficiently—and I gather that they do not—we 'shall be allowed to conquer and to flourish for a time.' We *will* conquer, and we will see to it that the time of our flourishing will be a long one indeed.

"The whole situation, then, boils down to this: our cosmic energy against the Lens of the Patrol. Ours is the much more powerful arm, but our only hope of immediate success lies in keeping the Patrol in ignorance of our cosmic-energy receptors and converters. One Lensman already has that knowledge. Therefore, gentlemen, it is very clear that the death of that Lensman has now become absolutely imperative. We *must* find him, if it means the abandonment of our every other enterprise throughout this galaxy. Give me a full report upon the screening of the planets upon which the Lensman may try to land."

"It is done, sir," came quick reply. "They are completely blockaded. Ships are spaced so closely that even the electromagnetic detectors have a five hundred percent overlap. Visual detectors have at least two hundred fifty percent overlap. Nothing as large as one millimeter in any dimension can get through without detection and observation."

"And how about the search of Trenco?"

"Results are still negative. One of our ships, with papers all in order, visited Trenco space-port openly. No one was there except the regular force of Rigellians. Our captain was in no position to be too inquisitive, but the missing ship was certainly not in the port and he gathered that he was the first visitor they had had in a month. We learned on Rigel IV that Tregonsee, the Lensman on duty on Trenco, has been there for a month and will not be relieved for another month. He was the only Lensman there. We are of course carrying on the search of the rest of the planet. About half the personnel of each vessel to land has been lost, but they started with double crews and replacements are being sent."

"The Lensman Tregonsee's story may or may not be true," Helmuth mused. "It makes little difference. It would be impossible to hide that ship in Trenco space-port from even a casual inspection, and if the ship is not there the Lensman is not. He may be in hiding elsewhere on the planet, but I doubt it. Continue to search nevertheless. There are many things he may have done . . . . I will have to consider them, one by one."

But Helmuth had very little time to consider what Kinnison might have done, for the Lensman had left Trenco long since. Because of the flare-baffles upon his driving projectors his pace was slow; but to compensate for this condition the distance to be covered was not too long. Therefore, even as Helmuth was cogitating upon what next to do, the Lensman and his crew were approaching the far-flung screen of Boskonian war-vessels investing the entire Solarian System.

To approach that screen undetected was a physical impossibility, and before Kinnison realized that he was in a danger zone six tractors had flicked out, had seized his ship, and had jerked it up to combat range. But the Lensman was ready for anything, and again everything happened at once.

Warnings screamed into the distant pirate base and Helmuth, tense at his desk, took personal charge of his mighty fleet. On the field of action Kinnison's screens flamed out in stubborn defense, tractors snapped under his slashing shears, the baffles disappeared in an incandescent flare as he shot maximum blast into his drive, and space again became suffused with the output of his now ultra-powered multiplex scramblers.

And through that murk the Lensman directed a thought, with the full power of mind and Lens.

"Port Admiral Haynes—Prime Base! Port Admiral Haynes—Prime Base! Urgent! Kinnison calling from the direction of Sirius—urgent!" he sent out the fiercely-driven message.

It so happened that at Prime Base it was deep night, and Port Admiral Haynes was sound asleep; but, trigger-nerved old space-cat that he was, he came instantly and fully awake. Scarcely had an eye flicked open than his answer had been hurled back:

"Haynes acknowledging—send it, Kinnison!"

"Coming in, in a pirate ship. All the pirates in space are on our necks, but we're coming in, in spite of hell and high water! Don't send up any ships to help us down—they could blast you out of space in a second, but they can't stop us. Get ready—it won't be long now!"

Then, after the Port Admiral had sounded the emergency alarm, Kinnison went on:

"Our ship carries no markings, but there's only one of us and you'll know which one it is—we'll be doing the dodging. They'd be crazy to follow us down into atmosphere, with all the stuff you've got, but they act crazy enough to do almost anything. If they do follow us down, get ready to give 'em hell—here we are!"

Pursued and pursuers had touched the outermost fringe of the stratosphere; and, slowed down to optical visibility by even that highly rarified atmosphere, the battle raged in incandescent splendor. One ship was spinning, twisting, looping, gyrating, jumping and darting hither and thither—performing every weird maneuver that the fertile and agile minds of the Patrolmen could improvise—to shake off the horde of attackers.

The pirates, on the other hand, were desperately determined that, whatever the cost, THE Lensman should not land. Tractors would not hold and the inertialess ship could not be rammed. Therefore their strategy was that which had worked so successfully four times before in similar case—to englobe the ship completely and thus beam her down. And while attempting this englobement they so massed their forces as to drive the Lensman's vessel as far as possible away from the grim and tremendously powerful fortifications of Prime Base, almost directly below them.

But the four ships which the pirates had recaptured had been manned by Velantians; whereas in this one Kinnison the Lensman and Henderson the Master Pilot were calling upon their every resource of instantaneous nervous reaction, of brilliant brain and of lightning hand to avoid that fatal trap. And avoid it they did, by series after series of fantastic maneuvers never set down in any manual of space combat.

Powerful as were the weapons of Prime Base, in that thick atmosphere their effective range was less than fifty miles. Therefore the gunners, idle at their controls, and the officers of the superdreadnaughts, chained by definite orders to the ground, fumed and swore as, powerless to help their battling fellows, they stood by and watched in their plates the furious engagement so high overhead.

But slowly, so slowly, Kinnison won his way downward, keeping as close over Base as he could without being englobed, and finally he managed to get within range of the gigantic projectors of the Patrol. Only the heaviest of the fixed-mount guns could reach that mad whirlpool of ships, but each one of them raved out against the same spot at precisely the same instant. In the inferno which that spot instantly became, not even a full-driven wall-shield could endure, and a vast hole yawned where pirate ships had been. The beams flicked off, and, timed by his Lens, Kinnison shot his ship through that hole before it could be closed and arrowed downward at maximum blast.

Ship after ship of the pirate horde followed him down in madly suicidal last attempts to blast him out of the ether; down toward the terrific armament of the base. Prime Base itself, the most dreaded, the most heavily armed, the most impregnable fortress of the Galactic Patrol! Nothing afloat could even threaten that citadel—the overbold attackers simply disappeared in brief flashes of coruscant vapor.

Kinnison, even before inerting his ship preparatory to landing, called his commander.

"Did any of the other boys beat us in, sir?" he asked.

"No, sir," came the curt response. Congratulations, felicitations, and celebration would come later; Haynes was now the Port Admiral receiving an official report.

"Then, sir, I have the honor to report that the expedition has succeeded," and he could not help adding informally, youthfully exultant at the success of his first real mission, "We've brought home the bacon!"

CHAPTER 13   *Maulers Afloat*

A POWERFUL FLEET HAD BEEN SENT TO RESCUE THOSE OF
the *Brittania's* crew who might have managed to stay out
of the clutches of the pirates. The wildly enthusiastic celebration inside Prime Base was over. Outside the force-walls
of the Reservation, however, it was just beginning. The
specialists and the Velantians were in the thick of it. No
one on Earth knew anything about Velantia, and those
highly intelligent reptilian beings knew just as little of
Tellus. Nevertheless, simply because they had aided the
Patrolmen, the visitors were practically given the keys to the
planet, and they were enjoying the experience tremendously.

"We want Kinnison—we want Kinnison!" the festive
crowd, led by Universal Telenews men, had been yelling;
and finally the Lensman came out. But after one pose before a lens and a few words into a microphone, he pleaded,
"There's my call, now—urgent!" and fled back inside Reservation. Then the milling tide of celebrants rolled back toward the city, taking with it every Patrolman who could
get leave.

Engineers and designers were swarming through and
over the pirate ship Kinnison had driven home, each armed
with a sheaf of blue-prints already prepared from the long-
cherished data-spool, each directing a corps of mechanics
in dismantling some mechanism of the great space-rover.
To this hive of bustling activity it was that Kinnison had
been called. He stood there, answering as best he could
the multitude of questions being fired at him from all sides,
until he was rescued by no less a personage than Port Admiral Haynes.

"You gentlemen can get your information from the data
sheets better than you can from Kinnison," he remarked

127

with a smile, "and I want to take his report without any more delay."

Hand under arm, the old Lensman led the young one away, but once inside his private office he summoned neither secretary nor recorder. Instead, he pushed the buttons which set up a complete-coverage shield and spoke.

"Now, son, open up. Out with it—everything that you have been holding back ever since you landed. I got your signal."

"Well, yes, I have been holding back," Kinnison admitted. "I haven't got enough jets to be sticking my neck out in fast company, even if it were something to be discussed in public, which it isn't. I'm glad you could give me this time so quick. I want to go over an idea with you, and with *no one else*. It may be as cockeyed as Trenco's ether— you're to be the sole judge of that—but you'll know I mean well, no matter how goofy it is."

"That certainly is not an overstatement," Haynes replied, dryly. "Go ahead."

"The great peculiarity of space combat is that we fly free, but fight inert," Kinnison began, apparently irrelevantly, but choosing his phraseology with care. "To force an engagement one ship locks to the other first with tracers, then with tractors, and goes inert. Thus, relative speed determines the ability to force or to avoid engagement; but it is relative power that determines the outcome. Heretofore the pirates—

"And by the way, we are belittling our opponents and building up a disastrous overconfidence in ourselves by calling them pirates. They are not—they can't be. Boskonia must be more than a race or a system—it is very probably a galaxy-wide culture. It is an absolute despotism, holding its authority by means of a rigid system of rewards and punishments. In our eyes it is fundamentally wrong, but it works—*how* it works! It is organized just as we are, and is apparently as strong in bases, vessels, and personnel.

"Boskonia has had the better of us, both in speed—except for the *Brittania's* momentary advantage—and in power. That advantage is now lost to them. We will have, then, two immense powers, each galactic in scope, each tremendously powerful in arms, equipment, and personnel; each having exactly the same weapons and defenses, and each determined to wipe out the other. A stalemate is inevitable; an absolute deadlock; a sheerly destructive war of attrition which will go on for centuries and which must end in the annihilation of both Boskonia and civilization."

"But our new projectors and screens!" protested the elder man. "They give us an overwhelming advantage. We can force or avoid engagement, as we please. You know the plan to crush them—you helped to develop it."

"Yes, I know the plan. I also know that we will not crush them. So do you. We both know that our advantage will be only temporary." The young Lensman, unimpressed, was in deadly earnest.

The Admiral did not reply for a time. Deep down, he himself had felt the doubt; but neither he nor any other of his school had ever mentioned the thing that Kinnison had now so baldly put into words. He knew that whatever one side had, of weapon or armor or equipment, would sooner or later become the property of the other; as was witnessed by the desperate venture which Kinnison himself had so recently and so successfully concluded. He knew that the devices installed in the vessels captured upon Velantia had been destroyed before falling into the hands of the enemy, but he also knew that with entire fleets so equipped the new arms could not be kept secret indefinitely. Therefore he finally replied:

"That may be true." He paused, then went on like the indomitable veteran that he was. "But we have the advantage now and we'll drive it while we've got it. After all, we *may* be able to hold it long enough."

"I've just thought of one more thing that would help—communication," Kinnison did not argue the previous point, but went ahead. "It seems to be impossible to drive any kind of a communicator beam through the double interference . . . . ."

"*Seems* to be!" barked Haynes. "It *is* impossible! Nothing but a thought . . . . ."

"That's it exactly—*thought!*" interrupted Kinnison in turn. "The Velantians can do things with a Lens that nobody would believe possible. Why not examine some of them for Lensmen? I'm sure that Worsel could pass, and probably many others. They can drive thoughts through anything except their own thought-screens—and what communicators they would make!"

"That idea has distinct possibilities and will be followed up. However, it is not what you wanted to discuss. Go ahead."

"QX." Kinnison went into Lens-to-Lens communication.

"I want some kind of a shield or screen that will neutralize or nullify a detector. I asked Hotchkiss, the communications expert, about it—under seal. He said it had never been investigated, even as an academic problem in research, but that it was theoretically possible."

"This room is shielded, you know." Haynes was surprised at the use of the Lenses. "Is it *that* important?"

"I don't know. As I said before, I may be cockeyed; but if my idea is any good at all that nullifier is the most important thing in the universe, and if word of it gets out it may be useless. You see, sir, over the long route, the only really permanent advantage that we have over Boskonia, the one thing they can't get, is the Lens. There must be some way to use it. If that nullifier is possible, and if we can keep it secret for a while, I believe I've found it. At least, I want to try something. It may not work—probably it won't, it's a mighty slim chance—but if it does, we may be able to wipe out Boskonia in a few months instead of carrying on forever a war of attrition. First, I want to go . . . . ."

"Hold on!" Haynes snapped. "I've been thinking, too. I can't see any possible relation between such a device and any real military weapon, or the Lens, either. If I can't, not many others can, and that's a point in your favor. If there's anything at all in your idea, it's too big to share with anyone, even me. Keep it to yourself."

"But it's a peculiar hook-up, and may not be any good at all." protested Kinnison. "You might want to cancel it."

"No danger of that," came the positive statement. "You know more about the pirates—pardon me, about Boskonia —than any other Patrolman. You believe that your idea has some slight chance of success. Very well—that fact is enough to put every resource of the Patrol back of you. Put your idea on a tape under Lensman's Seal, so that it will not be lost in case of your death. Then go ahead. If it is possible to develop that nullifier you shall have it. Hotchkiss will take charge of it, and have any other Lensmen he wants. No one except Lensmen will work on it or know anything about it. No records will be kept. It will not even exist until you yourself release it to us."

"Thanks, sir," and Kinnison left the room.

Then for weeks Prime Base was the scene of an activity furious indeed. New apparatus was designed and tested— new shears, new generators, new scramblers, and many other new things. Each item was designed and tested, redesigned and retested, until even the most skeptical of the Patrol's engineers could no longer find in it anything to criticize. Then throughout the galaxy the ships of the Patrol were recalled to their sector bases to be rebuilt.

There were to be two great classes of vessels. Those of the first—special scouting cruisers—were to have speed and defense—nothing else. They were to be the fastest things in space, and able to defend themselves against attack—that was all. Vessels of the second class had to be built from the keel upward, since nothing even remotely like them had theretofore been conceived. They were to be huge, ungainly, slow—simply storehouses of incomprehensibly vast powers of offense. They carried projectors of a size and power never before set upon movable foundations, nor were they dependent upon cosmic energy. They carried their own, in bank upon bank of stupendous accumulators. In fact, each of these monstrous floating fortresses was to be able to generate screens of such design and power that no vessel anywhere near them could receive cosmic energy!

This, then, was the bolt which civilization was preparing to hurl against Boskonia. In theory the thing was simplicity itself. The ultra-fast cruisers would catch the enemy, lock on with tractors so hard that they could not be sheared, and go inert, thus anchoring the enemy in space. Then, while absorbing and dissipating everything that the opposition could send, they would put out a peculiarly patterned interference, the center of which could easily be located. The mobile fortresses would then come up, cut off the Boskonians' power intake, and finish up the job.

Not soon was that bolt forged; but in time civilization was ready to launch its terrific and, it was generally hoped and believed, conclusive attack upon Boskonia. Every sector base and sub-base was ready; the zero hour had been set.

At Prime Base Kimball Kinnison, the youngest Tellurian ever to wear the four silver bars of captain, sat at the conning-plate of the heavy battle cruiser *Brittania,* so named at his own request. He thrilled inwardly as he thought of her speed. Such was her force of drive that, streamlined to the ultimate degree although she was, she had special wall-shields, and special dissipators to radiate into space the heat of friction of the medium through which she tore so madly. Otherwise she would have destroyed herself in an hour of full blast, even in the hard vacuum of interstellar space!

And in his office Port Admiral Haynes watched a chronometer. Minutes to go—then seconds.

"Clear ether!" His deep voice was gruff with unexpressed emotion. "Five seconds—four—three—two—one—Lift!" and the Fleet shot into the air.

The first objective of this Tellurian fleet was very close indeed to home, for the Boskonians had established a base upon Neptune's moon, right here in the Solarian System. So close to Prime Base that only intensive screening and constant vigilance had kept its spy-rays out; so powerful that the ordinary battleships of the Patrol had not been sent against it. Now it was to be reduced.

Short as was the time necessary to traverse any interplanetary distance, the Solarians were detected and were met in force by the ships of Boskone. But scarcely had battle been joined when the enemy began to realize that this was to be a battle the like of which they had never before seen; and when they began to understand it, it was too late. They could not run, and all space was so full of interference that they could not even report to Helmuth what was going on. These first, peculiarly tear-drop-shaped vessels of the Patrol did not fight at all. They simply held on like bull-dogs, taking without response everything that the white-hot projectors could throw at them. Their defensive screens radiated fiercely, high into the violet, under the appalling punishment being dealt out to them by the batteries of ship and shore, but they did not go down. Nor did the grip of a single tractor loosen from its anchorage. And in minutes the squat and monstrous maulers came up. Out went their cosmic-energy blocking screens, out shot their tractor beams, and out from the refractory throats of their stupendous projectors raved the most terrifically destructive forces ever generated by mobile machinery.

Boskonian outer screens scarcely even flickered as they went down before the immeasurable, the incredible violence of that thrust. The second course offered a briefly brilliant burst of violet radiance as it gave way. The inner screen resisted stubbornly as it ran the spectrum in a wildly coruscant display of pyrotechnic splendor; but it, too, went through the ultra-violet and into the black. Now the wall-shield itself—that inconceivably rigid fabrication of pure force which only the detonation of twenty metric tons of duodec had ever been known to rupture—was all that barred from the base metal of Boskonian walls the utterly indescribable fury of the maulers' beams. Now force was streaming from that shield in veritable torrents. So terrible were the conflicting energies there at grips that their neutralization was actually visible and tangible. In sheets and masses, in terrific, ether-wracking vortices, and in miles-long, pillaring streamers and flashes, those energies were being hurled away. Hurled to all the points of the sphere's full compass, filling and suffusing all nearby space.

The Boskonian commanders stared at their instruments, first in bewildered amazement and then in sheer, stark, unbelieving horror as their power-intake dropped to zero and their wall-shields began to fail—and still the attack continued in never-lessening power. Surely that beaming *must* slacken down soon—no conceivable mobile plant could throw such a load for long!

But those mobile plants could—and did. The attack kept up, at the terrifically high level upon which it had begun. No ordinary storage cells fed those mighty projectors; along no ordinary bus-bars were their Titanic amperages borne. Those maulers were designed to do just one thing—to *maul*—and that one thing they did well; relentlessly and thoroughly.

Higher and higher into the spectrum the defending wall-shields began to radiate. At the first blast they had leaped almost through the visible spectrum, in one unbearably fierce succession of red, orange, yellow, green, blue, and indigo; up to a sultry, coruscating, blindingly hard violet. Now the doomed shields began leaping erratically into the ultra-violet. To the eye they were already invisible; upon the recorders they were showing momentary flashes of black.

Soon they went down; and in the instant of each failure one vessel of Boskonia was no more. For, that last defense gone, nothing save unresisting metal was left to withstand the ardor of those ultra-powerful, ravening beams. As has already been said, no substance, however refractory or resistant or inert, can endure even momentarily in such a field of force. Therefore every atom, alike of vessel and of contents, went to make up the searing, seething burst of brilliant, incandescently luminous vapor which suffused all circumambient space.

Thus passed out of the Scheme of Things the vessels of the Solarian Detachment of Boskonia. Not a single vessel escaped; the cruisers saw to that. And then the attack thundered on to the base. Here the cruisers were useless; they merely formed an observant fringe, the while con-

tinuing to so blanket all channels of communication that
the doomed pirates could send out no word of what was
happening. The maulers moved up and grimly, doggedly,
methodically went to work.

Since a base is always much more powerfully armored
than is a battleship, the reduction of the fortresses took
longer than had the destruction of the fleet. But their receptors could no longer draw power from the sun or from
any other heavenly body, and their other sources of power
were comparatively weak. Therefore their defenses also
failed under that incessant assault. Course after course
their screens went down, and with the last ones went every
structure. The maulers' beams went through metal and
masonry as effortlessly as steel-jacketed bullets go through
butter, and bored on, deep into the planet's bed-rock, before
their frightful force was spent.

Then around and around they spiralled until nothing
whatever was left of the Boskonian works; until only a
seething, white-hot lake of molten lava in the midst of the
satellite's frigid waste was all that remained to show that
anything had ever been built there.

Surrender had not been thought of. Quarter or clemency
had not been asked or offered. Victory of itself was not
enough. This was, and of stern necessity had to be, a war
of utter, complete, and merciless extinction.

CHAPTER 14   *Unattached*

THE ENEMY STRONGHOLD SO INSULTINGLY CLOSE TO PRIME
Base having been obliterated, Regional Fleets, in loose for-
mations, began to scour the various Galactic Regions. For
a few weeks game was plentiful enough. Hundreds of raiding vessels were overtaken and held by the Patrol cruisers,
then blasted to vapor by the maulers.

Many Boskonian bases were also reduced. The locations
of most of these had long been known to the Intelligence

Service, others were detected or discovered by the fast-flying cruisers themselves. Marauding vessels revealed the sites of others by succeeding in reaching them before being overtaken by the cruisers. Others were found by the tracers and loops of the Signal Corps.

Very few of these bases were hidden or in any way difficult of access, and most of them fell before the blasts of a single mauler. But if one mauler was not enough, others were summoned until it did fall. One fortress, a hitherto unknown and surprisingly strong Secor Base, required the concentration of every mauler of Tellus, but they were brought up and the fortress fell. As had been said, this was a war of extinction and every pirate base that was found was wiped out.

But one day a cruiser found a base which had not even a spy-ray shield up, and a cursory inspection showed it to be completely empty. Machinery, equipment, stores, and personnel had all been evacuated. Suspicious, the Patrol vessels stood off and beamed it from afar, but there were no untoward occurrences. The structures simply slumped down into lava, and that was all.

Every base discovered thereafter was in the same condition, and at the same time the ships of Boskone, formerly so plentiful, disappeared utterly from space. Day after day the cruisers sped hither and thither throughout the vast reaches of the void, at the peak of their unimaginably high pace, without finding a trace of any Boskonian vessel. More remarkable still, and for the first time in years, the ether was absolutely free from Boskonian interference.

Following an impulse, Kinnison asked and received permission to take his ship on scouting duty. At maximum blast he drove toward the Velantian system, to the point at which he had picked up Helmuth's communication line. Along that line he drove for days, halting only when well outside the galaxy. Ahead of him there was nothing reachable except a few star-clusters. Behind him there extended the immensity of the galactic lens in all its splendor, but Captain Kinnison had no eye for astronomical beauty that day.

He held the *Brittania* there for an hour, while he mulled over in his mind what the apparent facts could mean. He knew that he had covered the line, from its point of determination out beyond the galaxy's edge. He knew that his detectors, operating as they had been in clear and undistorted ether, could not possibly have missed a thing as large as Helmuth's base must be, if it had been anywhere near that line; that their effective range was immensely greater than the largest possible error in the determination or the following of the line. There were, he concluded, four possible explanations, and only four.

First, Helmuth's base might also have been evacuated. This was unthinkable. From what he himself knew of Helmuth that base would be as nearly impregnable as anything could be made, and it was no more apt to be vacated than was Prime Base of the Patrol. Second, it might be subterranean; buried under enough metal-bearing rock to ground out all radiation. This possibility was just as unlikely as the first. Third, Helmuth might already have the device he himself wanted so badly, and upon which Hotchkiss and the other experts had been at work so long, a detector nullifier. This was possible, distinctly so. Possible enough, at least, to warrant filing the idea for future consideration. Fourth, that base might not be in the galaxy at all, but in that starcluster out there straight ahead of him, or possibly in one even farther away. That idea seemed the best of the four. It would necessitate ultra-powerful communicators, of course, but Helmuth could very well have them. It squared up in other ways—its pattern fitted into the matrix very nicely.

But if that base were out there . . . . . it could stay there—for a while . . . . . a battle cruiser just wasn't enough ship for that job. Too much opposition out there, and not—enough—ship . . . . Or too much ship? But he wasn't ready, yet, anyway. He needed, and would get, another line on Helmuth's base. Therefore, shrugging his shoulders, he whirled his vessel about and set out to rejoin the fleet.

While a full day short of junction, Kinnison was called to his plate, to see upon its lambent surface the visage of Port Admiral Haynes.

"Did you find out anything on your trip?" he asked.

"Nothing definite, sir. Just a couple of things to think about, is all. But I can say that I don't like this at all—I don't like anything about it or any part of it."

"No more do I," agreed the admiral. "It looks very much as though your forecast of a stalemate might be about to eventuate. Where are you headed for now?"

"Back to the Fleet."

"Don't do it. Stay on scouting duty for a while longer. And, unless something more interesting turns up, report back here to me—we have something that may interest you. The boys have been . . . . ."

The admiral's picture was broken up into flashes of blinding light and his words became a meaningless, jumbled roar of noise. A distress call had begun to come in, only to be blotted out by a flood of Boskonian static interference, of which the ether had for so long been clear. The young Lensman used his Lens.

"Excuse me, sir, while I see what this is all about?"

"Certainly, son."

"Got its center located?" Kinnison yelped at his communications officer. "They're close—right in our laps!"

"Yes, sir!" and the radio man snapped out numbers.

"Blast!" the captain commanded, unnecessarily; for the alert pilot had already set the course and was kicking in full-blast drive. "If that baby is what I think it is, all hell's out for noon."

Toward the center of disturbance the *Brittania* flashed, emitting now a scream of peculiarly patterned interference which was not only a scrambler of all un-Lensed communication throughout that whole part of the galaxy, but also an imperative call for any mauler within range. So close had the cruiser been to the scene of depredation that for her to reach it required only minutes.

There lay the merchantman and her Boskonian assailant. Emboldened by the cessation of piratical activities, some shipping concern had sent out a freighter, loaded probably with highly "urgent" cargo; and this was the result. The marauder, inert now, had gripped her with his tractors and was beaming her into submission. She was resisting, but feebly now; it was apparent that her screens were failing. Her crew must soon open ports in token of surrender or roast to a man; and they would probably prefer to roast.

Thus the situation obtaining in one instant. The next instant it was changed; the Boskonian discovering suddenly that his beams, instead of boring through the weak defenses of the freighter, were not even exciting to a glow the mighty protective envelopes of a battle-cruiser of the Patrol. He switched from the diffused heat-beam he had been using upon the merchantman to the hardest, hottest, most penetrating beam of annihilation he mounted—with but little more to show for it and with no better results. For the *Brittania's* screens had been designed to stand up almost indefinitely against the most potent beams of any ordinary war-ship, and they stood up.

Kinnison had tremendously powerful beams of his own, but he did not use them. It would take the super-powerful offense of a mauler to produce a definite answer to the question seething in his mind.

Increase power as the pirate would, to whatever ruinous overload, he could not break down Kinnison's screens; nor, dodge as he would, could he again get in position to attack his former prey. And eventually the mauler arrived; fortunately it, too, had been fairly close by. Out reached its mighty tractors. Out raved one of its tremendous beams, striking the Boskonian's defenses squarely amidships.

That beam struck and the pirate ship disappeared—but not in a hazily incandescent flare of volatilized metal. The raider disappeared bodily, and still all in one piece. He had put out super-shears of his own, snapping the mauler's supposedly unbreakable tractors like threads; and the velocity of his departure was due almost as much to the pressor effect of the Patrol beam as it was to the thrust of his own drivers.

It was the beginning of the stalemate Kinnison had foreseen.

"I was afraid of that," the young captain muttered; and, paying no attention whatever to the merchantman, he called the commander of the mauler. At this close range, of course, no ether scrambler could interfere with visual apparatus, and there on his plate he saw the face of Clifford Maitland, the man who had graduated number two in his own class.

"Hi, Kim, you old space-flea!" Maitland exclaimed in delight. "Oh, pardon me, sir," he went on in mock deference, with an exaggerated salute. "To a guy with four jets, I should say . . . ."

"Seal that, Cliff, or I'll climb up you like a squirrel, first chance I get!" Kinnison retorted. "So they've got you skippering an El Ponderoso, huh? Think of a mere infant like you being let play with so much high-power! What'll we do about this heap here?"

"Damfino. It isn't covered, so you'll have to tell me, Captain."

"Who'm I to be passing out orders? As you say, it isn't covered in the book—it's against G I regs for them to be cutting our tractors. But he's all yours, not mine—I've got to flit. You might find out what he's carrying, from where, to where, and why. Then, if you want to, you can escort him either back where he came from or on to where he's going; whichever you think best. If this interference doesn't let up, maybe you'd better Lens Prime Base for orders. Or use your own judgment, if any. Clear ether, Cliff, I've got to buzz along."

"Clear ether, spacehound!"

"Now, Hank," Kinnison turned to his pilot, "we've got urgent business at Prime Base—and when I say 'urgent' I don't mean perchance. Let's see you burn a hole in the ether."

The *Brittania* streaked Earthward, and scarcely had she touched ground when Kinnison was summoned to the office of the Port Admiral. As soon as he was announced, Haynes bruskly cleared his office and sealed it against any possible form of intrusion or eavesdropping. He had aged noticeably since these two had had that memorable conference in this same room. His face was lined and careworn, his eyes and his entire mien bore witness to days and nights of sleeplessly continuous work.

"You were right, Kinnison," he began, Lens to Lens. "A stalemate it is; a hopeless deadlock. I called you in to tell you that Hotchkiss has your nullifier done, and that it works perfectly against all long-range stuff. Against electromagnetics, however, it is not very effective. About all that can be done, it seems, is to shorten the range; and it doesn't interfere with vision at all."

"I can get by with that, I think—I will be out of electromagnetic range most of the time, and nobody watches their electos very close, anyway. Thanks a lot. It's ready to install?"

"Doesn't need installation. It's such a little thing you can put it in your pocket. It's self-contained and will work anywhere."

"Better and better. In that case I'll need two of them—and a ship. I would like to have one of those new automatic speedsters.* Lots of legs, cruising range, and screens. Only

---

* Unlike the larger war-vessels of the Patrol, speedsters are very narrow in proportion to their length, and in their design nothing is considered save speed and maneuverability. Very definitely they are not built for comfort. Thus, although their gravity plates are set for horizontal flight, they have braking jets, under jets, side jets, and top jets, as well as driving jets; so that in inert maneuvering any direction whatever may seem "down," and that direction may change with bewildering rapidity.

Nothing can be loose in a speedster—everything, even to food-

one beam, but I probably won't use even that one . . . . ."

"Going *alone*?" interrupted Haynes. "Better take your battle-cruiser, at least. I don't like the idea of you going into deep space alone."

"I don't particularly relish the prospect, either, but it's got to be that way. The whole fleet, maulers and all, isn't enough to do by force what's got to be done, and even two men is too many to do it in the only way it can be done. You see, sir . . . ."

"No explanations, please. It's on the spool, where we can get it if we need it. Are you informed as to the latest developments?"

"No, sir. I heard a little coming in, but not much."

"We are almost back where we were before you took off in the first *Brittania*. Commerce is almost at a standstill. All shipping firms are practically idle, but that is neither all of it nor the worst of it. You may not realize how important interstellar trade is; but as a result of its stoppage general business has slowed down tremendously. As is only to be expected, perhaps, complaints are coming in by the thousand because we have not already blasted the pirates out of space, and demands that we do so at once. They do not understand the true situation, nor realize that we are doing everything we can. We cannot send a mauler with every freighter and liner, and mauler-escorted vessels are the only ones to arrive at their destinations."

"But why? With tractor shears on all ships, how can they hold them?" asked Kinnison.

"Magnets!" snorted Haynes. "Plain, old-fashioned electromagnets. No pull to speak of, at a distance, of course, but with the raider running free they don't need much. Close up—lock on—board and storm—all done!"

"Hm . . m . . m. That changes things. I've got to find a pirate ship. I was planning on following a freighter or liner out toward Alsakan, but if there aren't any to follow . . . . I'll have to hunt around . . . . ."

---

supplies in the refrigerators, must be clamped into place. Sleeping is done in hammocks, not in beds. All seats and resting-places have heavy safety-straps, and there are no loose items of furniture or equipment anywhere on board.

Because they are designed for the utmost possible speed in the free condition, speedsters are extremely cranky and tricky in inert flight unless they are being handled upon their under jets, which are designed and placed specifically and only for inert flight.

Some of the ultra-fast vessels of the pirates, as will be brought out later, were also of this shape and design.   E.E.S.

"That is easily arranged. Lots of them want to go. We will let one go, with a mauler accompanying her, but well outside detector range."

"That covers everything, then, except the assignment. I can't very well ask for leave, but maybe I could be put on special assignment, reporting direct to you?"

"Something better than that," and Haynes smiled broadly, in genuine pleasure. "Everything is fixed. Your Release has been entered in the books. Your commission as captain has been cancelled, so leave your uniform in your former quarters. Here is your credit book and here is the rest of your kit. You are now an Unattached Lensman."

The Release! The goal toward which all Lensmen strive, but which so few attain! He was now a free agent, responsible to no one and to nothing save his own conscience. He was no longer of Earth, nor of the Solarian System, but of the galaxy as a whole. He was no longer a tiny cog in the immense machine of the Galactic Patrol; wherever he might go, throughout the immensity of the entire Island Universe, he *would be* the Galactic Patrol!

"Yes, it's real." The older man was enjoying the youngster's stupefaction at his Release, reminding him as it did of the time, long years before, when he had won his own. "You go anywhere you please and do anything you please, for as long as you please. You take anything you want, whenever you want it, with or without giving reasons—although you will usually give a thumb-printed credit slip in return. You report if, as, when, where, how, and to whom you please—or not, as you please. You don't even get a salary any more. You help yourself to that, too, wherever you may be; as much as you want, whenever you want it."

"But, sir . . . I . . . . you . . . I mean . . . . that is . . . . ." Kinnison gulped three times before he could speak coherently. "I'm not ready, sir. Why, I'm nothing but a kid—I haven't got enough jets to swing it. Just the bare thought of it scares me into hysterics!"

"It would—it always does." Haynes was very much in earnest now, but it was a glad, proud earnestness. "You are to be as nearly absolutely free an agent as it is possible for a living, flesh-and-blood creature to be. To the man on the street that would seem to spell a condition of perfect bliss. Only a Gray Lensman knows what a frightful load it really is; but it is a load that such a Lensman is glad and proud to carry."

"Yes, sir, he would be, of course, if he . . . . ."

"That thought will bother you for a time—if it did not, you would not be here—but don't worry about it any more than you can help. All I can say is that in the opinion of those who should know, not only have you proved yourself ready for Release, but also you have earned it."

"How do they figure that out?" Kinnison demanded, hotly. "All that saved my bacon on that trip was luck—a burned-out Bergenholm—and at the time I thought it was bad luck, at that. And vanBuskirk and Worsel and the other boys and the Lord knows who else pulled me out of jam after jam. I'd like awfully well to believe that I'm ready, sir, but I'm not. I can't take credit for pure dumb luck and for other men's abilities."

"Well, cooperation is to be expected, and we like to make Gray Lensmen out of the lucky ones." Haynes laughed deeply. "It may make you feel better, though, if I tell you two more things. First, that so far you have made the best showing of any man yet graduated from Wentworth Hall. Second, that we of the Court believe that you would have succeeded in that almost impossible mission without van-Buskirk, without Worsel, and without the lucky failure of the Bergenholm. In a different, and now of course unguessable fashion, but succeeded, nevertheless. Nor is this to be taken as in any sense a belittlement of the very real abilities of those others, nor a denial that luck, or chance, does exist. It is merely our recognition of the fact that you have what it takes to be an Unattached Lensman.

"Seal it now, and buzz off!" he commanded, as Kinnison tried to say something; and, clapping him on the shoulder, he turned him around and gave him a gentle shove toward the door. "Clear ether, lad!"

"Same to you, sir—all of it there is. I still think that you and all the rest of the Court are cockeyed; but I'll try not to let you down," and the newly unattached Lensman blundered out. He stumbled over the threshold, bumped against a stenographer who was hurrying along the corridor, and almost barged into the jamb of the entrance door instead of going through the opening. Outside he regained his physical poise and walked on air toward his quarters; but he never could remember afterward what he did or whom he met on that long, fast hike. Over and over the one thought pounded in his brain: unattached! *Unattached! ! UNATTACHED! ! !*

And behind him, in the Port Admiral's office, that high official sat and mused, smiling faintly with lips and eyes, staring unseeingly at the still open doorway through which Kinnison had staggered. The boy had measured up in every particular. He would be a good man. He would marry. He did not think so now, of course—in his own mind his life was consecrate—but he would. If necessary, the Patrol itself would see to it that he did. There were ways, and such stock was altogether too good not to be propagated. And, fifteen years from now—if he lived—when he was no longer fit for the grinding, grueling life to which he now looked forward so eagerly, he would select the Earth-bound job for which he was best fitted and would become a good executive. For such were the executives of the Patrol. But this day-dreaming was getting him nowhere, fast: he shook himself and plunged again into his work.

Kinnison reached his quarters at last, realizing with a thrill that they were no longer his. He now had no quarters, no residence, no address. Wherever he might be, throughout the whole of illimitable space, there was his home. But, instead of being dismayed by the thought of the life he faced, he was filled by a fierce eagerness to be actually living it.

There was a tap at his door and an orderly entered, carrying a bulky package.

"Your Grays, sir," he announced, with a crisp salute.

"Thanks." Kinnison returned the salute as smartly; and, almost before the door had closed, he was yanking off the space-black-and-silver-and-gold gorgeousness of the uniform he wore.

Stripped bare, he made the quick, meaningful gesture he had not really expected ever to be able to make. Gray Seal. No entity has ever donned or ever will don the Gray unmoved, nor without dedicating himself anew to that for which it stands.

The Gray—the unadorned, neutral-colored leather that was the proud garb of that branch of the Patrol to which he was thenceforth to belong. It had been tailored to his measurements, and he could not help studying with approval his reflection in the mirror. The round, almost visorless cap, heavily and softly quilted in protection against the helmet of his armor. The heavy goggles, opaque to all radiation harmful to the eyes. The short jacket, emphasizing broad shoulders and narrow waist. The trim breeches and high boots, encasing powerful, tapering legs.

"What an outfit—*what* an outfit!" he breathed. "And maybe I ain't such a bad-looking ape, at that, in these Grays!"

He did not then, and never did realize that he was wearing the plainest, drabbest, most strictly utilitarian uniform in existence; for to him, as to all others who knew it, the sheer, stark simplicity of the Unattached Lensman's plain gray leather transcended by far the gaudy trappings of the other branches of the Service. He had admired himself boyishly, as men do, feeling a trifle ashamed in so doing; but he did not then and never did appreciate what a striking figure of a man he really was as he strode out of Quarters and down the wide avenue toward the *Brittania's* dock.

He was glad indeed that there had been no ceremony or public show connected with this, his real and only important graduation. For as his fellows—not only his own crew, but also his friends from all over the Reservation—thronged about him, mauling and pummeling him in congratulation and acclaim, he knew that he couldn't stand much more. If there were to be much more of it, he discovered suddenly, he would either pass out cold or cry like a baby—he didn't quite know which.

That whole howling, chanting mob clustered about him; and, considering it an honor to carry the least of his personal belongings, formed a yelling, cap-tossing escort. Traffic meant nothing whatever to that pleasantly mad crew; nor, temporarily, did regulations. Let traffice detour—let pedestrians, no matter how august, cool their heels—let cars, trucks, yes, even trains, wait until they got past—let everything wait, or turn around and go back, or go some other way. Here comes Kinnison! Kimball Kinnison! Kimball Kinnison, Gray Lensman! Make way! And way was made; from the *Brittania's* dock clear across the base to the slip in which the Lensman's new speedster lay.

And what a ship this little speedster was! Trim, trig, streamlined to the ultimate she lay there; quiescent but surcharged with power. Almost sentient she was, this power-packed, ultraracy little fabrication of space-toughened alloy; instantly ready at his touch to liberate those tremendous energies which were to hurl him through the infinite reaches of the cosmic void.

None of the mob came aboard, of course. They backed off, still frantically waving and throwing whatever came closest to hand; and as Kinnison touched a button and shot into the air he swallowed several times in a vain attempt to dispose of an amazing lump which had somehow appeared in his throat.

CHAPTER 15 *The Decoy*

IT SO HAPPENED THAT FOR MANY LONG WEEKS THERE HAD been lying in New York Spaceport an urgent shipment for Alsakan, and that urgency was not merely a one-way affair. For, with the possible exception of a few packets whose owners had locked them in vaults and would not part with them at any price, there was not a single Alsakanite cigarette left on Earth!

Luxuries, then as now, soared feverishly in price with scarcity. Only the rich smoked Alsakanite cigarettes, and to those rich the price of anything they really wanted was a matter of almost complete indifference. And plenty of them wanted, and wanted badly, their Alsakanite cigarettes—there was no doubt of that. The current market report upon them was:

"Bid, one thousand credits per packet of ten. Offered, none at any price."

With that ever-climbing figure in mind, a merchant prince named Matthews had been trying to get an Alsakan-bound ship into the ether. He knew that one cargo of Alsakanite cigarettes safely landed in any Tellurian spaceport would yield more profit than could be made by his entire fleet in ten years of normal trading. Therefore he had for weeks been pulling every wire, and even every string, that he could reach; political, financial, even at times verging altogether too close for comfort upon the criminal —but without results.

For, even if he could find a crew willing to take the risk, to launch the ship without an escort would be out of the question. There would be no profit in a ship that did not return to Earth. The ship was his, to do with as he pleased, but the escorting maulers were assigned solely by the Galactic Patrol, and the Patrol would not give his ship an escort.

In answer to his first request, he had been informed that only cargoes classed as "necessary" were being escorted at all regularly; that "semi-necessary" loads were escorted occasionally, when of a particularly useful or desirable commodity and if opportunity offered; that "luxury" loads such as his were not being escorted at all; that he would be notified if, as, and when the *Prometheus* could be given escort. Then the merchant prince began his siege.

Politicians of high rank, local and national, sent in "requests" of varying degrees of diplomacy. Financiers first offered inducements, then threatened to "bear down," then put on all the various kinds of pressure known to their pressure-loving ilk. Pleas, demands, threats, and pressures were alike, however, futile. The Patrol could not be coaxed or bullied, cajoled, bribed, or cowed; and all further communications upon the subject, from whatever source originating were ignored.

Having exhausted his every resource of diplomacy, politics, guile, and finance, the merchant prince resigned himself to the inevitable and stopped trying to get his ship off the ground. Then New York Base received from Prime Base an open message, not even coded, which read:

"Authorize space-ship *Prometheus* to clear for Alsakan at will, escorted by Patrol ship B 42 TC 838, whose present orders are hereby cancelled. Signed, Haynes."

A demolition bomb dropped into that sub-base would not have caused greater excitement than did that message. No one could explain it—the base commander, the mauler's captain, the captain of the *Prometheus*, or the highly pleased but equally surprised Matthews—but all of them did whatever they could to expedite the departure of the freighter. She was, and had been for a long time, practically ready to sail.

As the base commander and Matthews sat in the office, shortly before the scheduled time of departure, Kinnison arrived—or, more correctly, let them know that he was there. He invited them both into the control-room of his speedster; and invitations from Gray Lensmen were accepted without question or demur.

"I suppose you are wondering what this is all about," he began. "I'll make it as short as I can. I asked you in here because this is the only convenient place in which I *know* that what we say will not be overheard. There are lots of spy-rays around here, whether you know it or not. The *Prometheus* is to be allowed to go to Alsakan, because that is where pirates seem to be most numerous, and we do not want to waste time hunting all over space to find one. Your vessel was selected, Mr. Matthews, for three reasons, and in spite of the attempts you have been making to obtain special privileges, not because of them. First, because there is no necessary or semi-necessary freight waiting for clearance into that region. Second, because we do not want your firm to fail. We do not know of any other large shipping line in such a shaky position as yours, nor of any firm anywhere to which one single cargo would make such an immense financial difference."

"You are certainly right there, Lensman!" Matthews agreed, whole-heartedly. "It means bankruptcy on the one hand and a fortune on the other."

"Here's what is to happen. The ship and the mauler blast off on schedule, fourteen minutes from now. They get about to Valeria, when they are both recalled—urgent orders for the mauler to go on rescue work. The mauler comes back, but your captain will, in all probability, keep on going, saying that he started out for Alsakan and that's where he's going . . . . ."

"But he wouldn't—he wouldn't *dare*!" gasped the shipowner.

"Sure he would," Kinnison insisted, cheerfully enough. "That is the third good reason your vessel is being allowed to set out, because it certainly will be attacked. You didn't know it until now, but your captain and over half of your crew are pirates themselves, and are going to . . . . ."

"What? Pirates!" Matthews bellowed. "I'll go down there and . . . . .".

"You'll do nothing whatever, Mr. Matthews, except watch things, and you will do that from here. The situation is under control."

"But my ship! My cargo!" the shipper wailed. "We'll be ruined if they . . . . ."

"Let me finish, please," the Lensman interrupted. "As soon as the mauler turns back it is practically certain that your captain will send out a message, letting the pirates know that he is easy prey. Within a minute after sending that message, he dies. So does every other pirate aboard. Your ship lands on Valeria and takes on a crew of space-fighting wildcats, headed by Peter vanBuskirk. Then it goes on toward Alsakan, and when the pirates board that ship, after its pre-arranged half-hearted resistance and easy surrender, they are going to think that all hell's out for noon. Especially since the mauler, back from her 'rescue work,' will be tagging along, not too far away."

"Then my ship will really go to Alsakan, and back, safely?" Matthews was almost dazed. Matters were entirely out of his hands, and things had moved so rapidly that he hardly knew what to think. "But if my own crews are pirates, some of them may . . . . . but I can of course get police protection if necessary."

"Unless something entirely unforeseen happens, the *Prometheus* will make the round trip in safety, cargoes and all—under mauler escort all the way. You will of course have to take the other matter up with your local police."

"When is the attack to take place, sir?" asked the base commander.

"That's what the mauler skipper wanted to know when I told him what was ahead of him," Kinnison grinned. "He wanted to sneak up a little closer about that time. I'd like to know, myself, but unfortunately that will have to be decided by the pirates after they get the signal. It will be on the way out, though, because the cargo she has aboard now is a lot more valuable to Boskone than a load of Alsakanite cigarettes would be."

"But do you think you can take the pirate ship that way?" asked the commander, dubiously.

"No, but we will cut down his personnel to such an extent that he will have to head back for his base."

"And that's what you want—the base. I see."

He did not see—quite—but the Lensman did not enlighten him further.

There was a brilliant double flare as freighter and mauler lifted into the air, and Kinnison showed the ship-owner out.

"Hadn't I better be going, too?" asked the commander. "Those orders, you know."

"A couple of minutes yet. I have another message for you—official. Matthews won't need a police escort long— if any. When that ship is attacked it is to be the signal for cleaning out every pirate in Greater New York—the worst pirate hot-bed on Tellus. Neither you nor your force will be in on it directly, but you might pass the word around, so that our own men will be informed ahead of the Telenews outfits."

"Good! That has needed doing for a long time."

"Yes, but you know it takes a long time to line up every man in such a big organization. They want to get them all, without getting any innocent bystanders."

"Who's doing it—Prime Base?"

"Yes. Enough men will be thrown in here to do the whole job in an hour."

"That *is* good news—clear ether, Lensman!" and the base commander went back to his post.

As the air-lock toggles rammed home, sealing the exit behind the departing visitor, Kinnison eased his speedster into the air and headed for Valeria. Since the two vessels ahead of him had left atmosphere inertialess, as would he, and since several hundred seconds had elapsed since their take-off, he was of course some ten thousand miles off their line as well as being uncounted millions of miles behind them. But the larger distance meant no more than the smaller, and neither of them meant anything at all to the Patrol's finest speedster. Kinnison, on easy touring blast, caught up with them in minutes. Closing up to less than one light-year, he slowed his pace to match theirs and held his distance.

Any ordinary ship would have been detected long since, but Kinnison rode no ordinary ship. His speedster was immune to all detection save electromagnetic or visual, and therefore, even at that close range—the travel of half a minute for even a slow space-ship in open space—he was safe. For electromagnetics are useless at that distance: and visual apparatus, even with subether converters, is reliable only up to a few mere thousands of miles, unless the observer knows exactly what to look for and where to look for it.

Kinnison, then, closed up and followed the *Prometheus* and her mauler escort; and as they approached the Valerian solar system the recall message came booming in. Also, as had been expected, the renegade captain of the freighter sent his defiant answer and his message to the pirate high command. The mauler turned back, the merchantman kept on. Suddenly, however, she stopped, inert, and from her ports were ejected discrete bits of matter—probably the bodies of the Boskonian members of her crew. Then the *Prometheus*, again inertialess, flashed directly toward the planet Valeria.

An inertialess landing is, of course, highly irregular, and is made only when the ship is to take off again immediately. It saves all the time ordinarily lost in spiraling and deceleration, and saves the computation of a landing orbit, which is no task for an amateur computer. It is, however, dangerous. It takes power, plenty of it, to maintain the force which neutralizes the inertia of mass, and if that force fails even for an instant while a ship is upon a planet's surface, the consequences are usually highly disastrous. For in the neutralization of inertia there is no magic, no getting of something for nothing, no violation of Nature's law of the conservation of matter and energy. The instant that force becomes inoperative the ship possesses exactly the same velocity, momentum, and inertia that it possessed at the instant the force took effect. Thus, if a space-ship takes off from Earth, with its orbital velocity of about eighteen and one-half miles per second relative to the sun, goes free, dashes to Mars, lands free, and then goes inert, its original velocity, both in speed and in direction, is instantly restored; with consequences better imagined than described. Such a velocity of course *might* take the ship harmlessly into the air; but it probably would not.

Inertialess vessels do not ordinarily load freight. They do, however, take on passengers, especially military personnel accustomed to open-space maneuvers in powered space-suits. Men and ship must go inert—separately, of course—immediately after leaving the planet, so that the men can match their intrinsic velocity to the ship's; but that takes only a very small fraction of the time required for an inert landing.

Hence the *Prometheus* landed free, and so did Kinnison. He stepped out, fully armored against Valeria's extremely heavy atmosphere, and laboring a trifle under its terrific gravitation, to be greeted cordially by *Lieutenant* vanBuskirk, whose fighting men were already streaming aboard the freighter.

"Hi, Kim!" the Dutchman called, gaily. "Everything went off like clockwork. Won't hold you up long—be blasting off in ten minutes."

"Ho, Lefty!" the Lensman acknowledged, as cordially, but saluting the newly commissioned officer with an exaggerated formality. "Say, Bus, I've been doing some thinking. Why wouldn't it be a good idea to . . . . ."

"Uh-uh, it would *not*," denied the fighter, positively. "I know what you're going to say—that you want in on this party—but don't say it."

"But I . . . . ." Kinnison began to argue.

"Nix," the Valerian declared flatly. "You've got to stay

with your speedster. No room for her inside; she's clear full of cargo and my men. You can't clamp on outside, because that would give the whole thing away. And besides, for the first and last time in my life I've got a chance to give a Gray Lensman orders. Those orders are to stay out of and away from this ship—and I'll see to it that you do, too, you little Tellurian shrimp! Boy, what a kick I get out of that!"

"You would, you big, dumb Valerian ape—you always were a small-souled type!" Kinnison retorted. "Piggy-piggy . . . . Haynes, huh?"

"Uh-huh." VanBuskirk nodded. "How else could I talk so rough to *you* and get away with it? However, don't feel too bad—you aren't missing a thing, really. It's in the cans already, and your fun is up ahead somewhere. And by the way, Kim, congratulations. You had it coming. We're all behind you, from here to the Magellanic Clouds and back."

"Thanks. The same to you, Bus, and many of 'em. Well, if you won't let me stow away, I'll tag along behind, I guess. Clear ether—or rather, I hope it's full of pirates by tomorrow morning. Won't be, though, probably; don't imagine they'll move until we're almost there."

And tag along Kinnison did, through thousands and thousands of parsecs of uneventful voyage.

Part of the time he spent in the speedster dashing hither and yon. Most of it, however, he spent in the vastly more comfortable mauler; to the armored side of which his tiny vessel clung with its magnetic clamps while he slept and ate, gossiped and read, exercised and played with the mauler's officers and crew, in deep-space comradery. It so happened, however, that when the long-awaited attack developed he was out in his speedster, and thus saw and heard everything from the beginning.

Space was filled with the old, familiar interference. The raider flashed up, locked on with magnets, and began to beam. Not heavily—scarcely enough to warm up the defensive screens—and Kinnison probed into the pirate with his spy-ray.

"Terrestrials—North Americans!" he exclaimed, half-aloud, startled for an instant. "But naturally they would be, since this is a put-up job and over half the crew were New York gangsters."

"The blighter's got his spy-ray screens up," the pilot was grumbling to his captain. The fact that he spoke in English was immaterial to the Lensman; he would have understood equally well any other possible form of communication or of thought exchange. "That wasn't part of the plan, was it?"

If Helmuth or one of the other able minds at Grand Base had been directing that attack it would have stopped right there. The pilot had shown a flash of feeling that, with a little encouragement, might have grown into a suspicion. But the captain was not an imaginative man. Therefore:

"Nothing was said about it, either way," he replied. "Probably the mate's on duty—he isn't one of us, you know. The captain will open up. If he doesn't do it pretty quick I'll open her up myself . . . . . there, the port's opening. Slide a little forward . . . hold it! Go get 'em, men!"

Men, hundreds of them, armed and armored, swarmed through the freighter's locks. But as the last man of the boarding party passed the portal something happened that was most decidedly not on the program. The outer port slammed shut and its toggles drove home!

"Blast those screens! Knock them down—get in there with a spray-ray!" barked the pirate captain. He was not one of those hardy and valiant souls who, like Gildersleeve, led in person the attacks of his cut-throats. He emulated instead the higher Boskonian officials and directed his raids from the safety of his control-room; but, as has been intimated, he was not exactly like those officials. It was only after it was too late that he became suspicious. "I wonder if somebody could have double-crossed us? . . . . . Highjackers?"

"We'll bally soon know," the pilot growled, and even as he spoke the spy-ray got through, revealing a very shambles.

For vanBuskirk and his Valerians had not been caught napping, nor were they a crew—unarmored, partially armed, and rendered even more impotent by internal mutiny, strife, and slaughter—such as the pirates had expected to find.

Instead, the boarders met a force that was overwhelmingly superior to their own. Not only in the strength and agility of its units, but also in that at least one semi-portable projector commanded every corridor of the freighter. In the blasts of those projectors most of the pirates died instantly, not knowing what struck them.

They were the fortunate ones. The others knew what was coming and saw it as it came, for the Valerians did not even draw their DeLameters. They knew that the pirates' armor could withstand for minutes any hand-weapon's beams, and they disdained to remount the heavy semi-portables. They came in with their space-axes, and at the sight the pirates broke and ran screaming in panic fear. But they could not escape. The toggles of the exit port were socketed and locked.

Therefore the storming party died to the last man; and, as vanBuskirk had foretold, it was scarcely even a struggle. For ordinary armor is so much tin-plate against a Valerian swinging a space-axe.

The spy-ray of the pirate captain got through just in time to see the ghastly finale of the massacre, and his face turned first purple, then white.

"The Patrol!" he gasped. "Valerians—a whole company of them! I'll say we've been double-crossed!"

"Righto—we've been jolly well had," the pilot agreed. "You don't know the half of it, either. Somebody's coming, and it isn't a boy scout. If a mauler should suck us in, we'd be very much a spent force, what?"

"Cut the gabble!" snapped the captain. "Is it a mauler, or not?"

"A bit too far away yet to say, but it probably is. They wouldn't have sent those jaspers out without cover, old bean—they know we can burn that freighter's screens down in an hour. Better get ready to run, what?"

The commander did so, wild thoughts racing through his mind. If a mauler got close enough to him to use magnets, he was done. His heaviest beams wouldn't even warm up a mauler's screens; his defenses wouldn't stand up for a second against a mauler's blasts . . . . , and he'd be ordered back to base . . . . .

"Tally ho, old fruit!" The pilot slammed on maximum blast. "It's a mauler and we've been bloody well jobbed. Back to base?"

"Yes," and the discomfited captain energized his communicator, to report to his immediate superior the humiliating outcome of the supposedly carefully-planned coup.

CHAPTER 16

*Kinnison Meets
the Wheelmen*

As THE PIRATE FLED INTO SPACE KINNISON FOLLOWED, matching his quarry in course and speed. He then cut in the automatic controller on his drive, the automatic recorder on his plate, and began to tune in his beam-tracer; only to be brought up short by the realization that the spy-ray's point would not stay in the pirate's control room without constant attention and manual adjustment. He had known that, too. Even the most precise of automatic controllers, driven by the most carefully stabilized electronic currents, are prone to slip a little at even such close range as ten million miles, especially in the bumpy ether near solar systems, and there was nothing to correct the slip. He had not thought of that before; the pilot always made those minor corrections as a matter of course.

But now he was torn between two desires. He wanted to listen to the conversation that would ensue as soon as the pirate captain got into communication with his superior officers; and, especially should Helmuth put in his beam, he very much wanted to trace it and thus secure another line on the headquarters he was so anxious to locate. He now feared that he could not do both—a fear that soon was to prove well grounded—and wished fervently that for a few minutes he could be two men. Or at least a Velantian; they had eyes and hands and separate brain-compartments enough so that they could do half-a-dozen things at once and do each one well. He could not; but he could try. Maybe he should have brought one of the boys along, at that. No, that would wreck everything, later on; he would have to do the best he could.

Communication was established and the pirate captain began to make his report; and by using one hand on the ray and the other on the tracer, he managed to get a partial line and to record scraps of the conversation. He missed, however, the essential part of the entire episode, that part in which the base commander turned the unsuccessful captain over to Helmuth himself. Therefore Kinnison was surprised indeed at the disappearance of the beam he was so laboriously trying to trace, and to hear Helmuth conclude his castigation of the unlucky captain with: .

". . . . . not entirely your fault, I will not punish you at all severely this time. Report to our base on Aldebaran I, turn your vessel over to commander there, and do anything he tells you to for thirty of the days of that planet."

Frantically Kinnison drew back his tracer and searched for Helmuth's beam; but before he could synchronize with it the message of the pirates' high chief was finished and his beam was gone. The Lensman sat back in thought.

Aldebaran! Practically next door to his own Solarian System, from which he had come so far. How had they possibly managed to keep concealed, or to re-establish, a base so close to Sol, through all the intensive searching that had been done? But they *had*—that was the important thing. Anyway, he knew where he was going, and that helped. One other thing he hadn't thought of, and one that might have spoiled everything, was the fact that he couldn't stay awake indefinitely to follow that ship! He had to sleep sometime, and while he was asleep his quarry was bound to escape. He of course had a CRX tracer, which would hold a ship without attention as long as it was anywhere within even extreme range; and it would have been a simple enough matter to have had a photo-cell relay put in between the plate of the CRX and the automatic controls of the spacer and driver—but he had not asked for it. Well, luckily, he now knew where he was going, and the trip to Aldebaran would be long enough for him to build a dozen such controls. He had all the necessary parts and plenty of tools.

Therefore, following the pirate ship easily as it tore through space, Kinnison built his automatic "chaser," as he called it. During each of the first four or five "nights" he lost the vessel he was pursuing, but found it without any great difficulty upon awakening. Thereafter he held it continuously; improving day by day the performance of his apparatus until it could do almost anything except talk. After that he devoted his time to an intensive study of the general problem before him. His results were highly unsatisfactory; for in order to solve any problem one must have enough data to set it up, either in actual equations or in logical sequences, and Kinnison did not have enough data.

He had altogether too many unknowns and not enough knowns.

The first specific problem was that of getting into the pirate base. Since the searchers of the Patrol had not found it, that base must be very well hidden indeed. And hiding anything as large as a base on Aldebaran I, as he remembered it, would be quite a feat in itself. He had been in that system only once, but . . . . .

Alone in his ship, and in deep space although he was, he blushed painfully as he remembered what had happened to him during that visit. He had chased a couple of dope runners to Aldebaran II, and there he had encountered the most vividly, the most flawlessly, the most remarkably and intriguingly beautiful girl he had ever seen. He had seen beautiful women, of course, before and in plenty. He had seen beauties amateur and professional; social butterflies, dancers, actresses, models, and posturers; both in the flesh and in Telenewscasts; but he had never supposed that such an utterly ravishing creature as she was could exist outside of a thionite dream. As a timidly innocent damsel in distress she had been perfect, and if she had held that pose a little longer Kinnison shuddered to think of what might have happened.

But, having known too many dope-runners and too few Patrolmen, she misjudged entirely, not only the cadet's sentiments, but also his reactions. For, even as she came amorously into his arms, he had known that there was something screwy. Women like that did not play that kind of game for nothing. She must be mixed up with the two he had been chasing. He got away from her, with only a couple of scratches, just in time to capture her confederates as they were making their escape—and he had been afraid of beautiful women ever since. He'd like to see that Aldebaranian hell-cat again—just once. He'd been just a kid then, but now . . . . .

But that line of thought was getting him nowhere, fast. It was Aldebaran I that he had better be thinking of. Barren, lifeless, desolate, airless, waterless. Bare as his hand, covered with extinct volcanoes, cratered, jagged, and torn. To hide a base on that planet would take plenty of doing, and, conversely, it would be correspondingly difficult to approach. If on the surface at all, which he doubted very strongly, it would be covered. In any event, all its approaches would be thoroughly screened and equipped with lookouts on the ultra-violet and on the infra-red, as well as on the visible. His detector nullifier wouldn't help him much there. Those screens and lookouts were bad—very, very bad. Question—could *anything* get into that base without setting off an alarm?

His speedster could not even get close, that was certain. Could he, alone? He would have to wear armor, of course, to hold his air, and it would radiate. Not necessarily—he could land out of range and walk, without power; but there were still the screens and the lookouts. If the pirates were on their toes it simply wasn't in the cards; and he had to assume that they would be alert.

What, then, could pass those barriers? Prolonged consideration of every fact of the situation gave definite answer and marked out clearly the course he must take. Something admitted by the pirates themselves was the only thing that could get in. The vessel ahead of his was going in. Therefore he must and would enter that base within the pirate vessel itself. With that point decided there remained only the working out of a method, which proved to be almost ridiculously simple.

Once inside the base, what should he—or rather, what *could* he—do? For days he made and discarded plans, but finally he tossed them all out of his mind. So much depended upon the location of the base, its personnel, its arrangement, and its routine, that he could develop not even the rough draft of a working plan. He knew what he wanted to do, but he had not even the remotest idea as to how he could go about doing it. Of the openings that appeared, he would have to choose the most feasible and fit his actions to whatever situation then and there obtained.

So deciding, he shot his spy-ray toward the planet and studied it with care. It was indeed as he had remembered it, or worse. Bleakly, hotly arid, it had no soil whatever, its entire surface being composed of igneous rock, lava, and pumice. Stupendous ranges of mountains criss-crossed and intersected each other at random, each range a succession of dead volcanic peaks and blown-off craters. Mountainside and rocky plain, crater-wall and valley floor, alike and innumerably were pockmarked with sub-craters and with immensely yawning shell-holes, as though the whole planet had been throughout geologic ages the target of an incessant cosmic bombardment.

Over its surface and through and through its volume he drove his spy-ray; finding nothing. He bored into its substance with his detectors and his tracers; with results com-

pletely negative. Of course, closer up, his electromagnetics
would report iron—plenty of it—but that information would
also be meaningless. Practically all planets had iron cores.
As far as his instruments could tell—and he had given
Aldebaran I a more thorough going-over by far than any
ordinary surveying ship would have given it—there was no
base of any kind upon or within the planet. Yet he *knew*
that a base was there. So what?—maybe—Helmuth's base
might be inside the galaxy after all, protected from detection in the same way; probably by solid miles of iron or
of iron ore. A second line upon that base had now become
imperative. But they were approaching the system fast; he
had better get ready.

He belted on his personal equipment, including a nullifier, then inspected his armor, checking its supplies and
apparatus carefully before he hooked it ready to his hand.
Glancing into the plate, he noted with approval that his
"chaser" was functioning perfectly. Pursued and pursuer
were now both well inside the solar system of Aldebaran;
and, as slowed the pirate so slowed the speedster. Finally
the leader went inert in preparation for his spiral, but Kinnison was no longer following. Before he went inert he
flashed down to within fifty thousand miles of the planet's
forbidding surface. He then cut his Bergenholm, threw the
speedster into an almost circular orbit, well away from the
landing orbit selected by the pirate, cut off all his power,
and drifted. He stayed in the speedster, observing and
computing, until he had so exactly defined its path that
he could find it unerringly at any future instant. Then he
went into the airlock, stepped out into space, and, waiting
only to be sure that the portal had snapped shut behind
him, set his course toward the pirate's spiral.

Inert now, his progress was so slow as to seem imperceptible, but he had plenty of time. And it was only relatively that his speed was low. He was actually hurtling
through space at the rate of well over two thousand miles
an hour, and his powerful little driver was increasing that
speed constantly by an acceleration of two Earth gravities.

Soon the vessel crept up, beneath him now, and Kinnison, increasing his drive to five gravities, shot toward it in
a long, slanting dive. This was the most ticklish minute of
the trip, but the Lensman had assumed correctly that the
ship's officers would be looking ahead of them and down,
not backward and up. They were, and he made his approach
unseen. The approach itself, the boarding of an inert space-

ship at its frightful landing-spiral velocity, was elementary to any competent space-man. There was not even a flare to bother him or to reveal him to sight, as the braking jets were now doing all the work. Matching course and velocity ever more closely, he crept up—flung his magnet—pulled up, hand over hand—opened the emergency inlet lock—and there he was.

Unconcernedly he made his way along the sternway and into the now deserted quarters of the fighters. There he lay down in a hammock, snapped the acceleration straps, and shot his spy-ray into the control room. And there, in the pirate captain's own visiplate, he observed the rugged and torn topography of the terrain below as the pilot fought his ship down, mile by mile. Tough going, this, Kinnison reflected, and the bird was doing a nice job, even if he was taking it the hard way, bringing her down straight on her nose instead of taking one more spiral around the planet and then sliding in on her under jets, which were designed and placed specifically for such work. But taking it the hard way he was, and his vessel was bucking, kicking, bouncing and spinning on the terrific blasts of her braking jets. Down she came, fast; and it was only after she was actually inside one of those stupendous craters, well below the level of its rim, that the pilot flattened her out and assumed normal landing position.

They were still going too fast, Kinnison thought, but the pirate pilot knew what he was doing. Five miles the vessel dropped, straight down that Titanic shaft, before the bottom was reached. The shaft's wall was studded with windows; in front of the craft loomed the outer gate of a gigantic airlock. It opened, the ship was trundled inside, landing-cradle and all, and the massive gate closed behind it. This was the pirates' base, and Kinnison was inside it!

"Men, attention!" The pirate commander snapped then. "The air is deadly poison, so put on your armor and be sure your tanks are full. They have rooms for us, having good air, but don't open your suits a crack until I tell you to. Assemble! All of you that are not here in this control room in five minutes will stay on board and take your own chances!"

Kinnison decided instantly to assemble with the crew. He could do nothing in the ship, and it would be inspected, of course. He had plenty of air, but space-armor all looked alike, and his Lens would warn him in time of any unfriendly or suspicious thought. He had better go. If they called a roll . . . . but he would cross that bridge when he came to it.

No roll was called; in fact, the captain paid no attention at all to his men. They would come along or not, just as they pleased. But since to stay in the ship meant death, every man was prompt. At the expiration of the five minutes the captain strode away, followed by the crowd. Through a doorway, left turn, and the captain was met by a creature whose shape Kinnison could not make out. A pause, a straggling forward, then a right turn.

Kinnison decided that he would not take that turn. He would stay here, close to the shaft, where he could blast his way out if necessary, until he had studied the whole base thoroughly enough to map out a plan of campaign. He soon found an empty and apparently unused room, and assured himself that through its heavy, crystal-clear window he could indeed look out into the vastly cylindrical emptiness of a volcanic shaft.

Then with his spy-ray he watched the pirates as they were escorted to the quarters prepared for them. Those might have been rooms of state, but it looked to Kinnison very much as though his former shipmates were being jailed ignominiously, and he was glad that he had taken leave of them. Shooting his ray here and there throughout the structure, he finally found what he was looking for; the communicator room. That room was fairly well lighted, and at what he saw there his jaw dropped in sheerest amazement.

He had expected to see men, since Aldebaran II, the only inhabited planet in the system, had been colonized from Tellus and its people were as truly human and Caucasian as those of Chicago or of Paris. But there . . . these *things* . . . . . he had been around quite a bit, but he had never seen nor heard of their like. They were wheels, really. When they went anywhere they rolled. Heads where hubs ought to be . . . . eyes . . . . arms, dozens of them, and very capable-looking hands . . . . .

"Vogenar!" a crisp thought flashed from one of the peculiar entities to another, impinging also upon Kinnison's Lens. "Someone—some outsider—is looking at me. Relieve me while I abate this intolerable nuisance."

"One of those creatures from Tellus? We will teach them very shortly that such intrusion is not to be borne."

"No, it is not one of them. The touch is similar, but the tone is entirely different. Nor could it be one of them, for not one of them is equipped with the instrument which is such a clumsy substitute for inherent power of mind. There, I will now . . . . "

Kinnison snapped on his thought-screen, but the damage had already been done. In the violated Communications Room the angry observer went on:

" . . . . attune myself and trace the origin of that prying look. It has disappeared now, but its sender cannot be distant, since our walls are shielded and screened . . . . Ah, there is a blank space, which I cannot penetrate, in the seventh room of the fourth corridor. In all probability it is one of our guests, hiding now behind a thought screen." Then his orders boomed out to a corps of guards. "Take him and put him with the others!"

Kinnison had not heard the order, but he was ready for anything, and those who came to take him found that it was much easier to issue such orders than to carry them out.

"Halt!" snapped the Lensman, his Lens carrying the crackling command deep into the Wheelmen's minds. "I do not wish to harm you, but come no closer!"

"You? Harm us?" came a cold, clear thought, and the creatures vanished. But not for long. They or others like them were back in moments, this time armed and armored for strife.

Again Kinnison found that DeLameters were useless. The armor of the foe mounted generators as capable as his own; and, although the air in the room soon became one intolerably glaring field of force, in which the very walls themselves began to crumble and to vaporize, neither he nor his attackers were harmed. Again, then, the Lensman had recourse to his mediæval weapon; sheathing his De-Lameter and wading in with his axe. Although not a vanBuskirk, he was, for an Earthman, of unusual strength, skill, and speed: and to those opposing him he was a very Hercules.

Therefore, as he struck and struck and struck again, the cell became a gorily reeking slaughter-pen, its every corner high-piled with the shattered corpses of the Wheelmen and its floor running with blood and slime. The last few of the attackers, unwilling to face longer that irresistible steel, wheeled away, and Kinnison thought flashingly of what he should do next.

This trip was a bust so far. He couldn't do himself a bit of good here now, and he'd better flit while he was still in one piece. How? The door? No. Couldn't make it—he'd run out of time quick that way. His screens would stop small-arms projectiles, but they knew that as well as he did. They'd use a young cannon—or, more probably, a semi-portable. Better take out the wall. That would give them something else to think about, too, while he was doing his flit.

Only a fraction of a second was taken up by these thoughts, then Kinnison was at the wall. He set his De-Lamater to minimum aperture and at maximum blast, to throw an irresistible cutting pencil. Through the wall that pencil pierced; up, over, and around.

But, fast as the Lensman had acted, he was still too late. There came trundling into the room behind him a low, four-wheeled truck, bearing a complex and monstrous mechanism. Kinnison whirled to face it. As he turned the section of the wall upon which he had been at work blew outward with a crash. The ensuing rush of escaping atmosphere swept the Lensman up and whisked him out through the opening and into the shaft. In the meantime the mechanism upon the truck had begun a staccato, grinding roar, and as it roared Kinnison felt slugs ripping through his armor and tearing through his flesh; each as crushing, crunching, paralyzing a blow as though it had been inflicted by vanBuskirk's space axe.

This was the first time Kinnison had ever been really badly wounded, and it made him sick. But. sick and numb, senses reeling at the shock of his slug-torn body, his right hand flashed to the external controller of his neutralizer. For he was falling inert. Only ten or fifteen meters to the bottom, as remembered it—he had mightly little time to waste if he were not to land inert. He snapped the controller. Nothing happened. Something had been shot away. His driver, too, was dead. Snapping the sleeve of his armor into its clamp he began to withdraw his arm in order to operate the internal controls, but he ran out of time. He crashed; on the top of a subsiding pile of masonry which had preceded him, but which had not yet attained a state of equilibrium; underneath a shower of similar material which rebounded from his armor in a boiler-shop clangor of noise.

Well it was that that heap of masonry had not yet had time to settle into form, for in some slight measure it acted as a cushion to break the Lensman's fall. But an inert fall of forty feet, even cushioned by sliding rocks, is in no sense a light one. Kinnison crashed. It seemed as though a thousand pile-drivers struck him at once. Surges of almost unbearable agony swept over him as bones snapped and bruised flesh gave way; and he knew dimly that a merciful tide of oblivion was reaching up to engulf his shrieking, suffering mind.

But, foggily at first in the stunned confusion of his entire being, something stirred; that unknown and unknowable something, that indefinable ultimate quality that had made him what he was. He lived, and while a Lensman lived he did not quit. To quit was to die then and there, since he was losing air fast. He had plastic in his kit, of course, and the holes were small. He *must* plug those leaks, and plug them quick. His left arm, he found, he could not move at all. It must be smashed pretty badly. Every shallow breath was a searing pain—that meant a rib or two gone out. Luckily, however, he was not breathing blood, therefore his lungs must still be intact. He could move his right arm, although it seemed like a lump of clay or a limb belonging to someone else. But, mustering all his power of will, he made it move. He dragged it out of the armor's clamped sleeve; and forced the leaden hand to slide through the welter of blood that seemed almost to fill the bulge of his armor. He found his kit-box, and, after an eternity of pain-wracked time, he compelled his sluggish hand to open it and to take out the plastic.

Then, in a continuously crescendo throbbing of agony, he forced his maimed, crushed, and broken body to writhe and to wriggle about, so that his one sound hand could find and stop the holes through which his precious air was whistling out and away. Find them he did, and quickly, and seal them tight; but when he had plugged the last one he slumped down, spent and exhausted. He did not hurt so much, now; his suffering had mounted to such terrific heights of intolerable keenness that the nerves themselves, in outraged protest at carrying such a load, had blocked it off.

There was much more to do, but he simply could not do it without a rest. Even his iron will could not drive his tortured muscles to any further effort until they had been allowed to recuperate a little from what they had gone through.

How much air did he have left, if any, he wondered: foggily and with an entirely detached and disinterested impersonality. Maybe his tanks were empty. Of course it couldn't have taken him so long to plug those leaks as it had seemed to, or he wouldn't have had any air left at all, in tanks or suit. He couldn't, however, have much left. He would look at his gauges and see.

But now he found that he could not move even his eyeballs, so deep was the coma that was enveloping him. Away off somewhere there was a billowy expanse of blackness, utterly heavenly in its deep, softly-cushioned comfort; and from that sea of peace and surcease there came reaching to embrace him huge, soft, tender arms. Why suffer, something crooned at him. It was *so* much easier to let go!

CHAPTER 17   *Nothing Serious at All*

KINNISON DID NOT LOSE CONSCIOUSNESS—QUITE. THERE was too much to do, too much that *had* to be done. He *had* to get out of here. He *had* to get back to his speedster. He *had*, by hook or by crook, to get back to Prime Base! Therefore, grimly, doggedly, teeth tight-locked in the enhancing agony of every movement, he drew again upon those hidden, those deeply buried resources which even he had no idea he possessed. His code was simple: the code of the Lens. While a Lensman lived he did not quit. Kinnison was a Lensman. Kinnison lived. Kinnison did not quit.

He fought back that engulfing tide of blackness, wave by wave as it came. He beat down by sheer force of will those tenderly beckoning, those sweetly seducing arms of oblivion. He forced the mass of protesting putty that was his body to do what *had* to be done. He thrust styptic gauze into the most copiously bleeding of his wounds. He was burned, too, he discovered then—they must have had a high-powered needle-beam on that truck, as well as the rifle—but he could do nothing about burns. There simply wasn't time.

He found the power lead that had been severed by a bullet. Stripping the insulation was an almost impossible job, but it was finally accomplished, after a fashion. Bridging the gap proved to be even a worse one. Since there was no slack, the ends could not be twisted together, but had to be joined by a short piece of spare wire, which in turn had to be stripped and then twisted with each end of the severed lead. That task, too, he finally finished; working purely by feel although he was, and half-conscious withal in a wracking haze of pain.

Soldering those joints was of course out of the question. He was afraid even to try to insulate them with tape, lest the loosely-twined strands should fall apart in the attempt. He did have some dry handkerchiefs, however, if he could reach them. He could, and did; and wrapped one carefully about the wires' bare joints. Then, apprehensively, he tried his neutralizer. Wonder of wonder, it worked! So did his driver!

In moments then he was rocketing up the shaft, and as he passed the opening out of which he had been blown he realized with amazement that what had seemed to him like hours must have been minutes only, and few even of them. For the frantic Wheelmen were just then lifting into place the temporary shield which was to stem the mighty outrush of their atmosphere. Wonderingly, Kinnison looked at his air-gauges. He had enough—if he hurried.

And hurry he did. He *could* hurry, since there was practically no atmosphere to impede his flight. Up the five-miles-deep shaft he shot and out into space. His chronometer, built to withstand even severer shocks than that of his fall, told him where his speedster was to be found, and in a matter of minutes he found her. He forced his rebellious right arm into the sleeve of his armor and fumbled at the lock. It yielded. The port swung open. He was inside his own ship again.

Again the encroaching universe of blackness threatened, but again he fought it off. He *could not* pass out—yet! Dragging himself to the board, he laid his course upon Sol, too distant by far to permit of the selection of such a tiny objective as its planet Earth. He connected the automatic controls.

He was weakening fast, and he knew it. But from somewhere and in some fashion he *must* get strength to do what *must* be done—and somehow he did it. He cut in the Berg, cut in maximum blast. Hang on, Kim! Hang on for just a second more! He disconnected the spacer. He killed the detector nullifiers. Then, with the utterly last remnant of his strength he thought into his Lens.

"Haynes." The thought went out blurred, distorted, weak. "Kinniston. I'm coming . . . . . com . . . . . "

He was done. Out, cold. Utterly spent. He had already done too much—far, far too much. He had driven that pitifully mangled body of his to its ultimately last possible . movement; his wracked and tortured mind to its ultimately last possible thought. The last iota of even his tremendous reserve of vitality was consumed and he plunged, parsecs deep, into the black depths of oblivion which had so long and so unsuccessfully been trying to engulf him. And on and on the speedster flashed at the very peak of her unimaginably high speed; carrying the insensible, the utterly spent, the sorely wounded, the abysmally unconscious Lensman toward his native Earth.

*   *   *   *   *

But Kimball Kinnison, Gray Lensman, had done everything that had *had* to be done before he blacked out. His final thought, feeble though it was, and incomplete, did its work.

Port Admiral Haynes was seated at his desk, discussing matters of import with an office-full of executives, when that thought arrived. Hardened old spacehound that he was, and survivor of many encounters and hospitalizations, he knew instantly what that thought connoted and from the depths of what dire need it had been sent.

Therefore, to the amazement of the officers in the room, he suddenly leaped to his feet, seized his microphone, and snapped out orders. Orders, and still more orders. Every vessel in seven sectors, of whatever class or tonnage, was to shove its detectors out to the limit. Kinnison's speedster is out there somewhere. Find her—get her—kill her drive and drag her in here, to number ten landing field. Get a pilot here, fast—no, two pilots, in armor. Get them off the top of the board, too—Henderson and Watson or Schermerhorn if they're anywhere within range. He then Lensed his lifelong friend Surgeon-Marshal Lacy, at Base Hospital.

"Sawbones, I've got a boy out that's badly hurt. He's coming in free—you know what that means. Send over a good doctor. And have you got a nurse who knows how to use a personal neutralizer and who isn't afraid to go into the net?"

"Coming myself. Yes." The doctor's thought was as crisp as the admiral's. "When do you want us?"

"As soon as they get their tractors on that speedster—you'll know when that happens."

Then, neglecting all other business, the Port Admiral directed in person the far-flung screen of ships searching for Kinnison's flying midget.

Eventually she was found; and Haynes, cutting off his plates, leaped to a closet, in which was hanging his own armor. Unused for years, nevertheless it was kept in readiness for instant service; and now, at long last, the old space-hound had a good excuse to use it again. He could have sent out one of the younger men, of course, but this was one job that he was going to do himself.

Armored, he strode out into the landing field across the paved way. There awaiting him were two armored figures, the two top-bracket pilots. There were the doctor and the nurse. He barely saw—or, rather, he saw without noticing —a saucy white cap atop a riot of red-bronze-auburn curls; a symmetrical young body in its spotless white. He did not notice the face at all. What he saw was that there was a neutralizer strapped snugly into the curve of her back, that it was fitted properly, and that it was not yet functioning.

For this that faced them was no ordinary job. The speedster would land free. Worse, the admiral feared—and rightly—that Kinnison would also be free, but independently; with an intrinsic velocity different from that of his ship. They must enter the speedster, take her out into space, and inert her. Kinnison must be taken out of the speedster, inerted, his velocity matched to that of the flier, and brought back aboard. Then and only then could doctor and nurse begin to work on him. Then they would have to land as fast as a landing could be made—the boy should have been in hospital long ago.

And during all these evolutions and until their return to ground the rescuers themselves would remain inertialess. Ordinarily such visitors left the ship, inerted themselves, and came back to it inert, under their own power. But now there was no time for that. They had to get Kinnison to the hospital; and besides, the doctor and the nurse—particularly the nurse—could not be expected to be space-suit navigators. They would all take it in the net, and that was another reason for haste. For while they were gone their intrinsic velocity would remain unchanged, while that of their present surroundings would be changing constantly. The longer they were gone the greater would become the discrepancy. Hence the net.

The net—a leather-and-canvas sack, lined with sponge-rubber-padded coiled steel, anchored to ceiling and to walls and to floor through every shock-absorbing artifice of beryllium-copper springs and of rubber and nylon cable that the mind of man had been able to devise. It takes something to absorb and to dissipate the kinetic energy which may reside within a human body when its intrinsic velocity does not match the intrinsic velocity of its surroundings—that is, if that body is not to be mashed to a pulp. It takes something, also, to enable any human being to face without flinching the prospect of going into that net, especially in ignorance of exactly how much kinetic energy will have to be dissipated. Haynes cogitated, studying the erect, supple young back, then spoke:

"Maybe we'd better cancel the nurse, Lacy, or get her a suit . . . . ."

"Time is too important," the girl herself put in, crisply. "Don't worry about me, Port Admiral; I've been in the net before."

She turned toward Haynes as she spoke, and for the first time he really saw her face. Why, she was a real beauty —a knockout—a seven-sector callout . . . . .

"Here she is!" In the grip of a tractor the speedster flashed to ground in front of the waiting five, and they hurried aboard.

They hurried, but there was no flurry, no confusion. Each knew exactly what to do, and each did it.

Out into space shot the little vessel, jerking savagely downward and sidewise as one of the pilots cut the Bergenholm. Out of the airlock flew the Port Admiral and the helpless, unconscious Kinnison, inertialess both and now chained together. Off they darted, in a new direction and with tremendous speed as Haynes cut Kinnison's neutralizer. There was a mighty double flare as the drivers of both space-suits went to work.

As soon as it was safe to do so, out darted an armored figure with a space-line, whose grappling end clinked into a socket of the old man's armor as the pilot rammed it home. Then, as an angler plays a fish, two husky pilots, feet wide-braced against the steel portal of the air-lock and bodies sweating with effort, heaving when they could and giving line only when they must helped the laboring drivers to overcome the difference in velocity.

Soon the Lensmen, young and old, were inside. Doctor and nurse went instantly to work, with the calmness and precision so characteristic of their highly-skilled crafts. In a trice they had him out of his armor, out of his leather, and into a hammock; perceiving at once that except for a few pads of gauze they could do nothing for their patient until they had him upon an operating table. Meanwhile the pilots, having swung the hammocks, had been observing, computing and conferring.

"She's got a lot of speed, Admiral—most of it straight down," Henderson reported. "On her landing jets it'll take close to two G's on a full revolution to bring her in. Either one of us can balance her down, but it'll have to be straight on her tail and it'll mean over five G's most of the way. Which do you want?"

"Which is more important, Lacy, time or pressure?" Haynes transferred decision to the surgeon.

"Time." Lacy decided instantly. "Fight her down!" His patient had been through so much already of force and pressure that a little more would not do additional hurt, and time was most decidedly of the essence. Doctor, nurse, and admiral leaped into hammocks; pilots at their controls tightened safety belts and acceleration straps—five gravities for over half an hour is no light matter—and the fight was on.

Starkly incandescent flares ripped and raved from driving jets and side jets. The speedster spun around viciously, only to be curbed, skilfully if savagely, at the precisely right instant. Without an orbit, without even a corkscrew or other spiral, she was going down—straight down. And not upon her under jets was this descent to be, nor upon her even more powerful braking jets. Master Pilot Henry Henderson, Prime Base's best, was going to kill the awful inertia of the speedster by "balancing her down on her tail." Or, to translate from the jargon of space, he was going to hold the tricky, cranky little vessel upright upon the terrific blasts of her main driving projectors, against the Earth's gravitation and against all other perturbing forces, while her driving force counteracted, overcame, and dissipated the full frightful measure of the kinetic energy of her mass and speed!

And balance her down he did. Haynes was afraid for a

minute that that intrepid wight was actually going to *land* the speedster on her tail. He didn't—quite—but he had only a scant hundred feet to spare when he nosed her over and eased her to ground on her under-jets.

The crash-wagon and its crew were waiting, and as Kinnison was rushed to the hospital the others hurried to the net room. Doctor Lacy first, of course, then the nurse; and, to Haynes' approving surprise, she took it like a veteran. Hardly had the surgeon let himself out of the "cocoon" than she was in it; and hardly had the terrific surges and recoils of her own not inconsiderable one hundred and forty-five pounds of mass abated than she herself was out and sprinting across the sward toward the hospital.

Haynes went back to his office and tried to work, but he could not concentrate, and made his way back to the hospital. There he waited, and as Lacy came out of the operating room he buttonholed him.

"How about it, Lacy, will he live?" he demanded.

"Live? Of course he'll live." the surgeon replied, gruffly. "Can't tell you details yet—we won't know, ourselves, for a couple of hours yet. Do a flit, Haynes. Come back at sixteen forty—not a second before—and I'll tell you all about it."

Since there was no help for it the Port Admiral did go away, but he was back promptly on the tick of the designated hour.

"How is he?" he demanded without preamble. "Will he really live, or were you just giving me a shot in the arm?"

"Better than that, much better," the surgeon assured him. "Definitely so; yes. He's in much better shape than we dared hope. Must have been a very light crash indeed—nothing seriously the matter with him at all. We won't even have to amputate, from what we can see now. He should make a one hundred percent recovery, not only without artificial members, but with scarcely a scar. He couldn't have been in a space crack-up at all, or he wouldn't have come out with so little injury."

"Fine, Doc—wonderful! Now the details."

"Here's the picture." The doctor unrolled a full-length X-ray print, showing every anatomical detail of the Lensman's interior structure. "First, just notice that skeleton. It is really remarkable. Slightly out of true here and there right now, of course, but I believe it's going to turn out to be the first absolutely perfect male skeleton I have ever seen. That young man will go far, Haynes."

"Sure he will. Why else do you suppose we put him in

Gray? But I didn't come over here to be told that—show me the damage."

"Look at the picture—see for yourself. Multiple and compound fractures, you notice, of legs and arm; and a few ribs. Scapula, of course—there. Oh, yes, there's a skull fracture, too, but it doesn't amount to much. That's all—the spine, you see, isn't injured at all."

"What d'you mean, 'that's all'? How about his wounds? I saw some of them myself, and they were *not* pin-pricks."

"Nothing of the least importance. A few punctured wounds and a couple of incised ones, but nothing even close to a vital part. He won't need even a transfusion, since he stopped the major hemorrhages himself, shortly after he was wounded. There are a few burns, of course, but they are mostly superficial—none that will not yield quite readily to treatment."

"Mighty glad of that. He'll be here six weeks, then?"

"Better call it twelve, I think—ten at least. You see, some of the fractures, especially those in the left leg, and a couple of burns, are rather severe, as such things go. Then, too, the length of time elapsing between injury and treatment didn't do anything a bit of good."

"In two weeks he'll be wanting to get up and go places and do things; and in six he'll be tearing down your hospital, stone by stone."

"Yes." The surgeon smiled. "He isn't the type to make an ideal patient; but, as I have told you before, I like to have patients that we do not like."

"And another thing. I want the files on his nurses, particularly the red-headed one."

"I suspected that you would, so I had them sent down. Here you are. Glad you noticed MacDougall—she's by way of being my favorite. Clarrissa MacDougall—Scotch, of course, with that name—twenty years old. Height, five feet six; weight, one forty-five and a half. Here are her pictures, conventional and X-ray. Man, look at that skeleton! Beautiful! The only really perfect skeleton I ever saw in a woman . . . . ."

"It isn't the skeleton I'm interested in," grunted Haynes. "It's what is outside the skeleton that my Lensman will be looking at."

"You needn't worry about MacDougall," declared the surgeon. "One good look at that picture will tell you that. She classifies—with that skeleton she *has* to. She couldn't leave the beam a millimeter, even if she wanted to. Good, bad, or indifferent; male or female; physical, mental, moral, and psychological; the skeleton tells the whole story."

"Maybe it does to you, but not to me," and Haynes took up the "conventional" photograph a stereoscope in full, true color; an almost living duplicate of the girl in question. Her thick, heavy hair was not red, but was a vividly intense and brilliant auburn; a coppery bronze, flashed with red and gold. Her eyes . . . . . bronze was all that he could think of, with flecks of topaz and of tawny gold. Her skin, too, was faintly bronze, glowing with even more than healthy youth's normal measure of sparkling vitality. Not only was she beautiful, the Port Admiral decided; in the words of the surgeon, she "classified."

"Hm . . . . m. Dimples, too," Haynes muttered. "Worse even than I thought—she's a menace to civilization," and he went on to read the documents. "Family . . . . . hm. History . . . . experiences . . . reactions and characteristics . . . . behavior patterns . . . . psychology . . . . mentality . . . . ."

"She'll do, Lacy," he advised the surgeon finally. "Keep her on with him . . . . ."

"Do!" Lacy snorted. "It isn't a question of whether *she* rates. Look at that hair—those eyes. Pure Samms. A man to match her would have to be one in a hundred thousand million. With that skeleton, though, he is."

"Of course he is. You don't seem to realize, you myopic old appendix-snatcher, that *he's* pure *Kinnison!*"

"Ah . . . so maybe we could . . . . but he won't be falling for anybody yet, since he's just been unattached. He'll be bullet-proof for quite a while. You ought to know that young Lensmen—especially young Gray Lensmen—can't see anything but their jobs; for a couple of years, anyway."

"His skeleton tells you that, too, huh?" Haynes grunted, skeptically. "Ordinarily, yes; but you never can tell, especially in hospitals . . . . ."

"More of your layman's misinformation!" Lacy snapped. "Contrary to popular belief, romance does not thrive in hospitals; except, of course, among the staff. Patients oftentimes think that they fall in love with nurses, but it takes two people to make one romance. Nurses do not fall in love with patients, because a man is never at his best under hospitalization. In fact, the better a man is, the poorer a showing he is apt to make."

"And, as I forget who said, a long time ago, 'no generalization is true, not even this one'," retorted the Port Admiral. "When it does hit him it will hit hard, and we'll take no chances. How about the black-haired one?"

"Well, I just told you that MacDougall has the only perfect skeleton I ever saw in a woman. Brownlee is very good, too, of course, but . . . ."

"But not good enough to rate Lensman's Mate, eh?" Haynes completed the thought. "Then take her out. Pick the best skeletons you've got for this job, and see that no others come anywhere near him. Transfer them to some other hospital—to some other floor of this one, at least. Any woman that he ever falls for will fall for him, in spite of your ideas as to the one-wayness of hospital romance; and I don't want him to have such a good chance of making a dive at something that doesn't rate up. Am I right or wrong, and for how much?"

"Well, I haven't had time yet to really study his skeleton, but . . . . ."

"Better take a week off and study it. I've studied a lot of people in the last sixty-five years, and I'll match my experience against your knowledge of bones, any time. Not saying that he *will* fall this trip, you understand—just playing safe."

CHAPTER 18   *Advanced Training*

KINNISON CAME TO—OR, RATHER, TO SAY THAT HE CAME half-to would be a more accurate statement—with a yell directed at the blurrily-seen figure in white which he knew must be a nurse.

"Nurse!" Then, as a searing stab of pain shot through him at the effort, he went on, thinking at the figure in white through his Lens:

"My speedster! I must have landed her free! Get the space-port . . . . ."

"There, there, Lensman," a low, rich voice crooned, and a red head bent over him. "The speedster has been taken care of. Everything is on the green; go to sleep and rest."

"Never mind your ship," the unctuous voice went on. "It was landed and put away . . . ."

"Listen, dumb-bell!" snapped the patient, speaking aloud now, in spite of the pain, the better to drive home his meaning. "Don't try to soothe me! What do you think I am, delirious? Get this and get it straight. I said I landed that speedster *free*. If you don't know what that means, tell somebody that does. Get the space-port—get Haynes—get . . . ."

"We got them, Lensman, long ago." Although her voice was still creamily, sweetly soft, an angry color burned into the nurse's face. "I said everything is on zero. Your speedster was inerted; how else could you be here, inert? I helped do it myself, so I *know* she's inert."

"QX." The patient relapsed instantly into unconsciousness and the nurse turned to an interne standing by—wherever *that* nurse was, at least one doctor could almost always be found.

"But my ship . . . ."

"Dumb-bell!" she flared. "What a sweet mess *he's* going to be to take care of! Not even conscious yet, and he's calling names and picking fights already!"

In a few days Kinnison was fully and alertly conscious. In a week most of the pain had left him, and he was beginning to chafe under restraint. In ten days he was "fit to be tied," and his acquaintance with his head nurse, so inauspiciously begun, developed even more inauspiciously as time went on. For, as Haynes and Lacy had each more than anticipated, the Lensman was by no means an ideal patient.

Nothing that could be done would satisfy him. All doctors were fat-heads, even Lacy, the man who had put him together. All nurses were dumb-bells, even—or especially?—"Mac," who with almost superhuman skill, tact, and patience had been holding him together. Why, even fat-heads and dumb-bells, even high-grade morons, ought to know that a man needed food!

Accustomed to eating everything he could reach, three or four or five times a day, he did not realize—nor did his stomach—that his now quiescent body could no longer use the five thousand or more calories that it had been wont to burn up, each twenty-four hours, in intense effort. He was always hungry, and he was forever demanding food.

And food, to him, did not mean orange juice or grape juice or tomato juice or milk. Nor did it mean weak tea and hard, dry toast and an occasional anemic soft-boiled egg. If he ate eggs at all he wanted them fried; three or four of them, accompanied by two or three thick slices of ham.

He wanted—and demanded in no uncertain terms, argumentatively and persistently—a big, thick, rare beefsteak. He wanted baked beans, with plenty of fat pork. He wanted bread in thick slices, piled high with butter, and not this quadruply-and-unmentionably-qualified toast. He wanted roast beef, rare, in big, thick slabs. He wanted potatoes and thick brown gravy. He wanted corned beef and cabbage. He wanted pie—any kind of pie—in large, thick quarters. He wanted peas and corn and asparagus and cucumbers, and also various other-worldly staples of diet which he often and insistently mentioned by name.

But above all he wanted beefsteak. He thought about it days and dreamed about it nights. One night in particular he dreamed about it—an especially luscious porterhouse, fried in butter and smothered in mushrooms—only to wake up, mouth watering, literally starved, to face again the weak tea, dry toast, and, horror of horrors, this time a flabby, pallid, flaccid *poached* egg! It was the last straw.

"Take it away," he said, weakly; then, when the nurse did not obey, he reached out and pushed the breakfast, tray and all, off the table. Then, as it crashed to the floor, he turned away, and, in spite of all his efforts, two hot tears forced themselves between his eyelids.

It was a particularly trying ordeal, and one requiring all of even Mac's skill, diplomacy, and forbearance, to make the recalcitrant patient eat the breakfast prescribed for him. She was finally successful, however, and as she stepped out into the corridor she met the ubiquitous interne.

"How's your Lensman?" he asked, in the privacy of the diet kitchen.

"Don't call him *my* Lensman!" she stormed. She was about to explode with the pent-up feelings which she of course could not vent upon such a pitiful, helpless thing as her star patient. "Beefsteak! I almost wish they *would* give him a beefsteak, and that he'd choke on it—which of course he would. He's worse than a baby. I never saw such a . . . . such a *brat* in my life. I'd like to spank him—he needs it. I'd like to know how *he* ever got to be a Lensman, the big cantankerous clunker! I'm *going* to spank him, too, one of these days, see if I don't!"

"Don't take it so hard, Mac," the interne urged. He was,

however, very much relieved that relations between the handsome young Lensman and the gorgeous red-head were not upon a more cordial basis. "He won't be here very long. But I never saw a patient clog *your* jets before."

"You probably never saw a patient like *him* before, either. I certainly hope he never gets cracked up again."

"Huh?"

"Do I have to draw you a chart?" she asked, sweetly. "Or, if he does get cracked up again, I hope they send him to some other hospital," and she flounced out.

Nurse MacDougall thought that when the Lensman could eat the meat he craved her troubles would be over; but she was mistaken. Kinnison was nervous, moody, brooding; by turns irritable, sullen, and pugnacious. Nor is it to be wondered at. He was chained to that bed, and in his mind was the gnawing consciousness that he had failed. And not only failed—he had made a complete fool of himself. He had underestimated an enemy, and as a result of his own stupidity the whole Patrol had taken a setback. He was anguished and tormented. Therefore:

"Listen, Mac," he pleaded one day. "Bring me some clothes and let me take a walk. I need exercise."

"Uh uh, Kim, not yet," she denied him gently, but with her entrancing smile in full evidence. "But pretty quick, when that leg looks a little less like a Chinese puzzle, you and nursie go bye-bye."

"Beautiful, but dumb!" the Lensman growled. "Can't you and those cockeyed croakers realize that I'll never get any strength back if you keep me in bed all the rest of my life? And don't talk baby-talk at me, either. I'm well enough at least so you can wipe that professional smile off your pan and cut that soothing bedside manner of yours."

"Very well—I think so, too!" she snapped, patience at long last gone. "Somebody should tell you the truth. I always supposed that Lensmen had to have *brains*, but you've been a perfect *brat* ever since you've been here. First you wanted to eat yourself sick, and now you want to get up, with bones half-knit and burns half-healed, and undo everything that has been done for you. Why don't you snap out of it and act your age for a change?"

"I never did think nurses had much sense, and now I know they haven't." Kinnison eyed her with intense disfavor, not at all convinced. "I'm not talking about going back to work. I mean a little gentle exercise, and I know what I need."

"You'd be surprised at what you don't know," and the nurse walked out, chin in air. In five minutes, however, she was back, her radiant smile again flashing.

"Sorry, Kim, I shouldn't have blasted off that way—I know that you're bound to back-fire and to have brainstorms. I would, too, if I were . . . . ."

"Cancel it, Mac," he began, awkwardly. "I don't know why I have to be crabbing at you all the time."

"QX, Lensman," she replied, entirely serene now. "I do. You're not the type to stay in bed without it griping you; but when a man has been ground up into such hamburger as you are, he has to stay in bed whether he likes it or not, and no matter how much he pops off about it. Roll over here, now, and I'll give you an alcohol rub. But it won't be long now, really—pretty soon we'll have you out in a wheel-chair . . . . ."

Thus it went for weeks. Kinnison knew his behavior was atrocious, abominable; but he simply could not help it. Every so often the accumulated pressure of his bitterness and anxiety *would* blow off; and, like a jungle tiger with a toothache, he would bite and claw anything or anybody within reach.

Finally, however, the last picture was studied, the last bandage removed, and he was discharged as fit. And he was not discharged, bitterly although he resented his "captivity," as he called it, until he really *was* fit. Haynes saw to that. And Haynes had allowed only the most sketchy interviews during that long convalescence. Discharged, however, Kinnison sought him out.

"Let me talk first," Haynes instructed him at sight. "No self-reproaches, no destructive criticism. Everything constructive. Now, Kimball, I'm mighty glad to hear that you made a perfect recovery. You were in bad shape. Go ahead."

"You have just about shut my mouth by your first order." Kinnison smiled sourly as he spoke. "Two words— flat failure. No, let me add two more—as yet."

"That's the spirit!" Haynes exclaimed. "Nor do we agree with you that it was a failure. It was merely not a success—so far—which is an altogether different thing. Also, I may add that we had very fine reports indeed on you from the hospital."

"Huh?" Kinnison was amazed to the point of being inarticulate.

"You just about tore it down, of course, but that was only to be expected."

"But, sir, I made such a . . . ."

"Exactly. As Lacy tells me quite frequently, he likes to have patients over there that they don't like. Mull that one over for a bit—you may understand it better as you get older. The thought, however, may take some of the load off your mind."

"Well, sir, I am feeling a trifle low, but if you and the rest of them still think . . . . ."

"We do so think. Cheer up and get on with the story."

"I've been doing a lot of thinking, and before I go around sticking out my neck again I'm going to . . . . ."

"You don't need to tell me, you know."

"No, sir, but I think I'd better. I'm going to Arisia to see if I can get me a few treatments for swell-head and lame-brain. I still think that I know how to use the Lens to good advantage, but I simply haven't got enough jets to do it. You see, I . . . . ." he stopped. He would not offer anything that might sound like an alibi: but his thoughts were plain as print to the old Lensman.

"Go ahead, son. We know you wouldn't."

"If I thought at all, I assumed that I was tackling men, since those on the ship were men, and men were the only known inhabitants of the Aldebaranian system. But when those wheelers took me so easily and so completely, it became very evident that I didn't have enough stuff. I ran like a scared pup, and I was lucky to get home at all. It wouldn't have happened if . . . . ." he paused.

"If what? Reason it out, son," Haynes advised, pointedly. "You are wrong, dead wrong. You made no mistake, either in judgment or in execution. You have been blaming yourself for assuming that they were men. Suppose you had assumed that they were the Arisians themselves. Then what? After close scrutiny, even in the light of after-knowledge, we do not see how you could have changed the outcome." It did not occur, even to the sagacious old admiral, that Kinnison need not have gone in. Lensmen always went in.

"Well, anyway, they licked me, and that hurts," Kinnison admitted, frankly. "So I'm going back to Arisia for more training, if they'll give it to me. I may be gone quite a while, as it may take even Mentor a long time to increase the permeability of my skull enough so that an idea can filter through it in something under a century."

"Didn't Mentor tell you never to go back there?"

"No, sir." Kinnison grinned boyishly. "He must've forgot it in my case—the only slip he ever made, I guess. That's what gives me an out."

"Um . . . m . . . m." Haynes pondered this startling bit of information. He knew, far better than young Kinnison could, the Arisian power of mind: he did not believe that Mentor of Arisia had ever forgotten anything, however tiny or unimportant. "It has never been done . . . . they are a peculiar race; incomprehensible . . . . but not vindictive. He may refuse you, but nothing worse—that is, if you do not cross the barrier without invitation. It's a splendid idea, I think; but be very careful to strike that barrier free and at almost zero power—or else don't strike it at all."

They shook hands, and in a space of minutes the speedster was again tearing through space. Kinnison now knew exactly what he wanted to get, and he utilized every waking hour of that long trip in physical and mental exercise to prepare himself to take it. Thus the time did not seem long. He crept up to the barrier at a snail's pace, stopping instantly as he touched it, and through that barrier he sent a thought.

"Kimball Kinnison of Sol Three calling Mentor of Arisia. Is it permitted that I approach your planet?" He was neither brazen nor obsequious, but was matter-of-factly asking a simple question and expecting a simple reply.

"It is permitted, Kimball Kinnison of Tellus," a slow, deep, measured voice resounded in his brain. "Neutralize your controls. You will be landed."

He did so, and the inert speedster shot forward, to come to ground in a perfect landing at a regulation space-port. He strode into the office, to confront the same grotesque entity who had measured him for his Lens not so long ago. Now, however, he stared straight into that entity's unblinking eyes, in silence.

"Ah, you have progressed. You realize now that vision is not always reliable. At our previous interview you took it for granted that what you saw must really exist, and did not wonder as to what our true shapes might be."

"I am wondering now, seriously," Kinnison replied, "and if it is permitted, I intend to stay here until I can see your true shapes."

"This?" and the figure changed instantly into that of an old, white-bearded, scholarly gentleman.

"No. There is a vast difference between seeing something myself and having you show it to me. I realize fully that you can make me see you as anything you choose. You could appear to me as a perfect copy of myself, or as any other thing, person or object conceivable to my mind." .

"Ah; your development has been eminently satisfactory. It is now permissible to tell you, youth, that your present quest, not for mere information, but for real knowledge, was expected."

"Huh? How could that be? I didn't decide definitely, myself, until only a couple of weeks ago."

"It was inevitable. When we fitted your Lens we knew that you would return if you lived. As we recently informed that one known as Helmuth . . . . ."

"*Helmuth!* You know, then, where . . . . ." Kinnison choked himself off. He would not ask for help in that—he would fight his own battles and bury his own dead. If they volunteered the information, well and good; but he would not ask it. Nor did the Arisian furnish it.

"You are right," the sage remarked, imperturbably. "For proper development it is essential that you secure that information for yourself." Then he continued his previous thought:

"As we told Helmuth recently, we have given your civ-ilization an instrumentality—the Lens—by virtue of which it should be able to make itself secure throughout the galaxy. Having given it, we could do nothing more of real or permanent benefit until you Lensmen yourselves began to understand the true relationship between mind and Lens. That understanding has been inevitable; for long we have known that in time a certain few of your minds would be-come strong enough to discover that theretofore unknown relationship. As soon as any mind made that discovery it would of course return to Arisia, the source of the Lens, for additional instruction; which, equally of course, that mind could not have borne previously.

"Decade by decade your minds have become stronger. Finally you came to be fitted with a Lens. Your mind, while pitifully undeveloped, had a latent capacity and a power that made your return here certain. There are several others who will return. Indeed, it has become a topic of discus-sion among us as to whether you or one other would be the first advanced student."

"Who is that other, if I may ask?"

"Your friend, Worsel the Velantian."

"He's got a real mind—'way, 'way ahead of mine," the Lensman stated, as a matter of self-evident fact.

"In some ways, yes. In other and highly important characteristics, no."

"Huh?" Kinnison exclaimed. "In what possible way have I got it over him?"

"I am not certain that I can explain it exactly in thoughts which you can understand. Broadly speaking, his mind is the better trained, the more fully developed. It is of more grasp and reach, and of vastly greater present power. It is more controllable, more responsive, more adaptable than is yours—now. But your mind, while undeveloped, is of considerable greater capacity than his, and of greater and more varied latent capabilities. Above all, you have a driving force, a will to do, an undefeatable mental urge that no one of his race will ever be able to develop. Since I predicted that you would be the first to return, I am naturally gratified that you have developed in accordance with that prediction."

"Well, I have been more or less under pressure, and I got quite a few lucky breaks. But at that, it seemed to me that I was progressing backward instead of forward."

"It is ever thus with the really competent. Prepare yourself!"

He launched a mental bolt, at the impact of which Kinnison's mind literally turned inside out in a wildly gyrating spiral vortex of dizzyingly confused images.

"Resist!" came the harsh command.

"Resist! How?" demanded the writhing, sweating Lensman. "You might as well tell a fly to resist an inert spaceship!"

"Use your will—your force—your adaptability. Shift your mind to meet mine at every point. Apart from these fundamentals neither I nor anyone else can tell you how; each mind must find its own medium and develop its own technique. But this is a very mild treatment indeed; one conditioned to your present strength. I will increase it gradually in severity, but rest assured that I will at no time raise it to the point of permanent damage. Constructive exercises will come later; the first step must be to build up your resistance. Therefore resist!"

The force, which had not slackened for an instant, waxed slowly to the very verge of intolerability; and grimly, doggedly, the Lensman fought it. Teeth locked, muscles straining, fingers digging savagely into the hard leather upholstery of his chair he fought it; mustering his every ultimate resource to the task . . . . .

Suddenly the torture ceased and the Lensman slumped down, a mental and physical wreck. He was white, trembling, sweating: shaken to the very core of his being. He was ashamed of his weakness. He was humiliated and bitterly disappointed at the showing he had made; but from the Arisian there came a calm, encouraging thought.

"You need not feel ashamed; you should instead feel proud, for you have made a start which is almost surprising, even to me, your sponsor. This may seem to you like needless punishment, but it is not. This is the only possible way in which that which you seek may be found."

"In that case, go to it," the Lensman declared. "I can take it."

The "advanced instruction" went on, with the pupil becoming ever stronger; until he was taking without damage thrusts that would at first have slain him instantly. The bouts became shorter and shorter, requiring as they did such terrific outpourings of mental force that no human mind could stand the awful strain for more than half an hour at a time.

And now these savage conflicts of wills and minds were interspersed with real instruction; with lessons neither painful nor unpleasant. In these the aged scientists probed gently into the youngster's mind, opening it out and exposing to its owner's gaze vast caverns whose very presence he had never even suspected. Some of these storehouses were already partially or completely filled; needing only arrangement and connection. Others were nearly empty. These were catalogued and made accessible. And in all, permeating everything, was the Lens.

"Just like clearing out a clogged-up water system; with the Lens the pump that couldn't work!" exclaimed Kinnison one day.

"More like that than you at present realize," assented the Arisian. "You have observed, of course, that I have not given you any detailed instructions nor pointed out any specific abilities of the Lens which you have not known how to use. You will have to operate the pump yourself; and you have many surprises awaiting you as to what your Lens will pump, and how. Our sole task is to prepare your mind to work with the Lens, and that task is not yet done. Let us on with it."

After what seemed to Kinnison like weeks the time came

when he could block out Mentor's suggestions completely; nor, now blocked out, should the Arisian be able to discern that fact. The Lensman gathered all his force together, concentrated it, and hurled it back at his teacher; and there ensued a struggle none the less Titanic because of its essential friendliness. The very ether seethed and boiled with the fury of the mental forces there at grips, but finally the Lensman beat down the other's screens. Then, boring deep into his eyes, he willed with all his force to see that Arisian as he really was. And instantly the scholarly old man subsided into a . . . . a BRAIN! There were a few appendages, of course, and appurtenances, and incidentalia to nourishment, locomotion, and the like, but to all intents and purposes the Arisian was simply and solely a brain.

Tension ended, conflict ceased, and Kinnison apologized.

"Think nothing of it," and the brain actually smiled into Kinnison's mind. "Any mind of power sufficient to neutralize the forces which I have employed is of course able to hurl no feeble bolts of its own. See to it, however, that you thrust no such force at any lesser mind, or it dies instantly."

Kinnison started to stammer a reply, but the Arisian went on:

"No, son, I knew and know that the warning is superfluous. If you were not worthy of this power and were you not able to control it properly you would not have it. You have obtained that which you sought. Go, then, with power."

"But this is only one phase, barely a beginning!" protested Kinnison.

"Ah, you realize even that? Truly, youth, you have come far, and fast. But you are not yet ready for more, and it is a truism that the reception of forces for which a mind is not prepared will destroy that mind. Thus, when you came to me you knew exactly what you wanted. Do you know with equal certainty what more you want from us?"

"No."

"Nor will you for years, if ever. Indeed, it may well be that only your descendants will be ready for that for which you now so dimly grope. Again I say, young man, go with power."

Kinnison went.

IT HAD TAKEN THE LENSMAN A LONG TIME TO WORK OUT IN his mind exactly what it was that he had wanted from the Arisians, and from no single source had the basic idea come. Part of it had come from his own knowledge of ordinary hypnosis; part from the ability of the Overlords of Delgon to control from a distance the minds of others; part from Worsel, who, working through Kinnison's own mind, had done such surprising things with a Lens; and a great part indeed from the Arisians themselves, who had the astounding ability literally and completely to super-impose their own mentalities upon those of others, wherever situate. Part by part and bit by bit the Tellurian Lensman had built up his plan, but he had not had the sheer power of intellect to make it work. Now he had that, and was ready to go.

Where? His first impulse was to return to Aldebaran I and to invade again the stronghold of the Wheelmen, who had routed him so ignominiously in his one encounter with them. Ordinary prudence, however, counseled against that course.

"You'd better lay off them a while, Kim, old boy," he told himself quite frankly. "They've got a lot of jets and you don't know how to use this new stuff of yours yet. Better pick out something easier to take!"

Ever since leaving Arisia he had been subconsciously aware of a difference in his eyesight. He was seeing things much more clearly than he had ever seen them before; more sharply and in greater detail. Now this awareness crept into his consciousness and he glanced toward his tube-lights. They were out—except for the tiny lamps and bulls-eyes of his instrument board the vessel must be in complete darkness. He remembered then with a shock that when he entered the speedster he had not turned on his lights—he could see, and had not thought of them at all!

This, then, was the first of the surprises the Arisian had promised him. He now had the sense of perception of the Rigellians. Or was it that of the Wheelmen? Or both? Or were they the same sense? Intently aware now, he focused his attention upon a meter before him. First upon its dial, noting that the needle was exactly upon the green hair-line of normal operation. Then deeper. Instantly the face of the instrument disappeared—moved behind his point of sight, or so it seemed—so that he could see its coils, pivots, and other interior parts. He could look into and study the grain and particle-size of the dense, hard condensite of the board itself. His vision was limited, apparently, only by his will to see!

"Well—ain't—that—something?" he demanded of the universe at large; then, as a thought struck him; "I wonder if they blinded me in the process?"

He switched on his lamps, discovering that his vision was unimpaired and normal in every respect; and a rigid investigation proved to him conclusively that in addition to ordinary vision he now had an extra sense—or perhaps two of them—and that he could change from one to the other, or use them simultaneously, at will! But the very fact of this discovery gave Kinnison pause.

He hadn't better go anywhere, or do anything, until he had found out something about his new equipment. The fact was that he didn't even know what he had, to say nothing of knowing how to use it. If he had the sense of a Zabriskan fontema he would go somewhere where he could do a little experimenting without getting his jets burned off in case something slipped at a critical moment. Where was the nearest Patrol base? A big one, fully defended . . . . . Let's see . . . . . . Radelix would be about the closest Sector Base, he guessed—he'd find out if he could raid that outfit without getting caught at it.

Off he shot, and in due course a fair, green, Earthlike planet lay beneath his vessel's keel. Since it was Earthlike in climate, age, atmosphere, and mass, its people were of course more or less similar to humanity in general characteristics, both of body and of mind. If anything, they were even more intelligent than Earthlings, and their Patrol base was a very strong one indeed. His spy-ray would be useless, since all Patrol bases were screened thoroughly and continuously—he would see what a sense of perception

would do. From Tregonsee's explanation, it ought to work
at this range.

It did. When Kinnison concentrated his attention upon
the base he saw it. He advanced toward it at the speed of
thought and entered it; passing through screens and metal
walls without hindrance and without giving alarm. He
saw men at their accustomed tasks and heard, or rather sensed,
their conversation: the everyday chat of their professions.
A thrill shot through him at a dazzling possibility thus revealed.

If he could make one of those fellows down there do
something without his knowing that he was doing it, the
problem was solved. That computer, say; make him un-
cover that calculator and set up a certain integral on it.
It would be easy enough to get into touch with him and
have him do it, but this was something altogether different.

Kinnison got into the computer's mind easily enough,
and willed intensely what he was to do; but the officer did
not do it. He got up; then, staring about him in bewilder-
ment, sat down again.

"What's the matter?" asked one of his fellows. "Forget
something?"

"Not exactly," the computer still stared. "I was going
to set up an integral. I didn't want it, either—I could swear
that somebody *told* me to set it up."

"Nobody did," grunted the other, "and you'd better start
staying home nights—then maybe you wouldn't get funny
ideas."

This wasn't so good, Kinnison reflected. The guy should
have done it, and shouldn't have remembered a thing about
it. Well, he hadn't really thought he could put it across at
that distance, anyway—he didn't have the brain of an
Arisian. He'd have to follow his original plan, of close-up
work.

Waiting until the base was well into the night side of
the planet and making sure that his flare-baffles were in
place, he allowed the speedster to drop downward, landing
at some little distance from the fortress. There he left the
ship and made his way toward his objective in a rapid series
of long, inertialess hops. Lower and shorter became the
hops. Then he cut off his power entirely and walked until
he saw before him, rising from the ground and stretching
interminably upward, an almost invisibly shimmering web
of force. This, the prowler knew, was the curtain which
marked the border of the Reservation; the trigger upon

which a touch, either of solid object or of beam, would initiate a succession of events which he was in no position to stop.

To the eye that base was not impressive, being merely a few square miles of level ground, outlined with low, broad pill-boxes and studded here and there with harmless-looking, bulging domes. There were a few clusters of buildings. That was all—to the eye—but Kinnison was not deceived. He knew that the base itself was a thousand feet underground; that the pill-boxes housed lookouts and detectors; and that those domes were simply weathershields which, rolled back, would expose projectors second in power not even to those of Prime Base itself.

Far to the right, between two tall pylons of metal, was a gate; the nearest opening in the web. Kinnison had avoided it purposely; it was no part of his plan to subject himself yet to the scrutiny of the all-inclusive photo-cells of that entrance. Instead, with his new sense of perception, he sought out the conduits leading to those cells and traced them down, through concrete and steel and masonry, to the control room far below. He then superimposed his mind upon that of the man at the board and flew boldly toward the entrance. He now actually had a dual personality; since one part of his mind was in his body, darting through the the air toward the portal, while the other part was deep in the base below, watching him come and acknowledging his signals!

A trap lifted, revealing a sloping, tunneled ramp, down which the Lensman shot. He soon found a convenient storeroom; and, slipping within it, he withdrew his control carefully from the mind of the observer, wiping out all traces of that control as he did so. He then watched apprehensively for a possible reaction. He was almost sure that he had performed the operation correctly, but he had to be absolutely certain; more than his life depended upon the outcome of this test. The observer, however, remained calm and placid at his post; and a close reading of his thoughts showed that he had not the faintest suspicion that anything out of the ordinary had occurred.

One more test and he was through. He must find out how many minds he could control simultaneously, but he'd better do that openly. No use making a man feel like a fool needlessly—he'd done that once already, and once was one time too many.

Therefore, reversing the procedure by which he had

come, he went back to his speedster, took her out into the ether, and slept. Then, when the light of morning flooded the base, he cut his detector nullifier and approached it boldly.

"Radelix base! Lensman Kinnison of Tellus, Unattached, asking permission to land. I wish to confer with your commanding officer, Lensman Gerrond."

A spy-ray swept through the speedster, the web disappeared, and Kinnison landed, to be greeted with a quiet and cordial respect. The base commander knew that his visitor was not there purely for pleasure—Gray Lensmen did not take pleasure jaunts. Therefore he led the way into his private office and shielded it.

"My announcement was not at all informative," Kinnison admitted then, "but my errand is nothing to be advertised. I've got to try out something, and I want to ask you and three of your best and—'stubbornest,' if I may use the term—officers to cooperate with me for a few minutes. QX?"

"Of course."

Three officers were called in and Kinnison explained. "I've been working for a long time on a mind-controller, and I want to see if it works. I'll put your books on this table, one in front of each of you. Now I would like to try to make two or three of you—all four of you if I can—each bend over, pick up his book, and hold it. Your part of the game will be for each of you to try not to pick it up, and to put it back as soon as you possibly can if I do make you obey. Will you?"

"Sure!" three of them chorused, and "There will be no mental damage, of course?" asked the commander.

"None whatever, and no after-effects. I've had it worked on myself, a lot."

"Do you want any apparatus?"

"No, I have everything necessary. Remember, I want top resistance."

"Let her come! You'll get plenty of resistance. If you can make any one of us pick up a book, after all this warning, I'll say you've got something."

Officer after officer, in spite of strainingly resisting mind and body, lifted his book from the table, only to drop it again as Kinnison's control relaxed for an instant. He could control two of them—*any* two of them—but he could not quite handle three. Satisfied, he ceased his efforts; and, as the base commander poured long, cold drinks for the sweating five, one of his fellows asked:

"What did you do, anyway, Kinnison—oh, pardon me, I shouldn't have asked."

"Sorry," the Tellurian replied uncomfortably, "but it isn't ready yet. You'll all know about it as soon as possible, but not just now."

"Sure," the Radeligian replied. "I knew I shouldn't have blasted off as soon as I spoke."

"Well, thanks a lot, fellows." Kinnison set his empty glass down with a click. "I can make a nice progress report on this do-jig now. And one more thing. I did a little long-range experimenting on one of your computers last night . . . . ."

"Desk Twelve? The one who thought he wanted to integrate something?"

"That's the one. Tell him I was using him for a mind-ray subject, will you, and give him this fifty-credit bill? Don't want the boys needling him *too* much."

"Yes, and thanks . . . . . and . . . . . I wonder . . . . ." the Radeligian Lensman had something on his mind. "Well . . . . can you make a man tell the truth with that? And if you can, will you?"

"I think so. Certainly I will, if I can. Why?" Kinnison knew that he could, but did not wish to seem cocksure.

"There's been a murder." The other three glanced at each other in understanding and sighed with profound relief. "A particularly fiendish murder of a woman—a girl, rather. Two men stand accused. Each has a perfect alibi, supported by honest witnesses; but you know how much an alibi means now. Both men tell perfectly straight stories, even under a lie-detector, but neither will let me—or any other Lensman so far—touch his mind." Gerrond paused.

"Uh-huh." Kinnison understood. "Lots of innocent people simply can't stand Lensing and have mighty strong blocks."

"Glad you've seen such. One of those men is lying with a polish I wouldn't have believed possible, or else both are innocent. And one of them *must* be guilty; they are the only suspects. If we try them now we make fools of ourselves, and we can't put the trial off very much longer without losing face. If you can help us out you'll be doing a lot for the Patrol, throughout this whole sector."

"I can help you," Kinnison declared. "For this, though,

better have some props. Make me a box—double Burbank controls, with five baby spots on it—orange, blue, green, purple, and red. The biggest set of headphones you've got, and a thick, black blindfold. How soon can you try 'em?"

"The sooner the better. It can be arranged for this afternoon."

The trial was announced, and long before the appointed hour the great court-room of that world's largest city was thronged. The hour struck. Quiet reigned. Kinnison, in his somber gray, strode to the judge's desk and sat down behind the peculiar box upon it. In dead silence two Patrol officers approached. The first invested him reverently with the headphones, the second so enwrapped his head in black cloth that it was apparent to all observers that his vision was completely obscured.

"Although from a world far distant in space, I have been asked to try two suspects for the crime of murder," Kinnison intoned. "I do not know the details of the crime nor the identity of the suspects. I do know that they and their witnesses are within these railings. I shall now select those who are about to be examined."

Piercing beams of intense, vari-colored light played over the two groups, and the deep, impressive voice went on:

"I know now who the suspects are. They are about to rise, to walk, and to seat themselves as I shall direct."

They did so; it being plainly evident to all observers that they were under some awful compulsion.

"The witnesses may be excused. Truth is the only thing of importance here; and witnesses, being human and therefore frail, obstruct truth more frequently than they further its progress. I shall now examine these two accused."

Again the vivid, weirdly distorting glares of light lashed out; bathing in intense monochrome and in various ghastly combinations first one prisoner, then the other; the while Kinnison drove his mind into theirs, plumbing their deepest depths. The silence, already profound, became the utter stillness of outer space as the throng, holding its very breath now, sat enthralled by that portentous examination.

"I have examined them fully. You are all aware that any Lensman of the Galactic Patrol may in case of need serve as judge, jury, and executioner. I am, however, none of these; nor is this proceeding to be a trial as you may have understood the term. I have said that witnesses are superfluous. I will now add that neither judge nor jury are necessary. All that is required is to discover the truth; since truth is all-powerful. For that same reason no executioner is needed here—the discovered truth will in and of itself serve us in that capacity.

"One of these men is guilty, the other is innocent. From the mind of the guilty one I am about to construct a composite, not of this one fiendish crime alone, but of all the crimes he has ever committed. I shall project that composite into the air before him. No innocent mind will be able to see any iota of it. The guilty man, however, will perceive its every revolting detail; and, so perceiving, he will forthwith cease to exist in this plane of life."

One of the men had nothing to fear—Kinnison had told him so, long since. The other had been trembling for minutes in uncontrollable paroxysms of terror. Now this one leaped from his seat, clawing savagely at his eyes and screaming in mad abandon.

"I did it! Help! Mercy! Take her away! Oh . . . h . . h! !" he shrieked, and died, horribly, even as he shrieked.

Nor was there noise in the court-room after the thing was over. The stunned spectators slunk away, scarcely daring even to breathe until they were safely outside.

Nor were the Radeligian officers in much better case. Not a word was said until the five were back in the base commander's office. Then Kinnison, still white of face and set of jaw, spoke. The others knew that he had found the guilty man, and that he had in some peculiarly terrible fashion executed him. He knew that they knew that the man was hideously guilty. Nevertheless:

"He was guilty," the Tellurian jerked out. "Guilty as all the devils in hell. I never had to do that before and it gripes me—but I couldn't shove the job off onto you fellows. I wouldn't want anybody to see that picture that didn't have to, and without it you could never begin to understand just how atrociously and damnably guilty that hell-hound really was."

"Thanks, Kinnison," Gerrond said, simply. "Kinnison. Kinnison of Tellus. I'll remember that name, in case we ever need you as badly again. But, after what you just did, it will be a long time—if ever. You didn't know, did you, that all the inhabitants of four planets were watching you?"

"Holy Klono, no! Were they?"

"They were; and if the way you scared *me* is any criterion, it will be a long, cold day before anything like that comes up again in this system. And thanks again, Gray

Lensman. You have done something for our whole Patrol this day."

"Be sure to dismantle that box so thoroughly that nobody will recognize any of its component parts," and Kinnison managed a rather feeble grin. "One more thing and I'll buzz along. Do you fellows happen to know where there's a good, strong pirate base around here anywhere? And, while I don't want to seem fussy, I would like it all the better if they were warm-blooded oxygen-breathers, so I won't have to wear armor all the time."

"What are you trying to do, give us the needle, or something?" This is not precisely what the Radeligian said, but it conveys the thought Kinnison received as the base commander stared at him in amazement.

"Don't tell me that there is such a base around here!" exclaimed the Tellurian in delight. "Is there, really?"

"There is. So strong that we haven't been able to touch it; manned and staffed by natives of your own planet, Tellus of Sol. We reported it to Prime Base some eighty-three days ago, just after we discovered it. You're direct from there . . . . ." He fell silent. This was no way to be talking to a Gray Lensman.

"I was in the hospital then, fighting with my nurse because she wouldn't give me anything to eat," Kinnison explained with a laugh. "When I left Tellus I didn't check up on the late data—didn't think I'd need it quite so soon. If you've got it, though . . . . ."

"Hospital! You?" queried one of the younger Radeligians.

"Yeah—bit off more than I could chew," and the Tellurian described briefly his misadventure with the Wheelmen of Aldebaran I. "This other thing has come up since then, though, and I won't be sticking my neck out that way again. If you've got such a made-to-order base as that in this region, it'll save me a long trip. Where is it?"

They gave him its coordinates and what little information they had been able to secure concerning it. They did not ask him why he wanted that data. They may have wondered at his temerity in daring to scout alone a fortress whose strength had kept at bay the massed Patrol forces of the sector: but if they did so they kept their thoughts well screened. For this was a Gray Lensman, and very evidently a super-powered individual, even of that select group whose weakest members were powerful indeed. If he felt like talking they would listen; but Kinnison did not talk. He listened; then, when he had learned everything they knew of the Boskonian base:

"Well, I'd better be flitting. Clear ether, fellows!" and he was gone.

CHAPTER 20 Mac Is a Bone of Contention

OUT FROM RADELIX AND INTO DEEP SPACE SHOT THE SPEED-ster, bearing the Gray Lensman toward Boyssia II, where the Boskonian base was situated. The Patrol forces had not been able to locate it definitely, therefore it must be clever-ly hidden indeed. Manned and staffed by Tellurians—and this was fairly close to the line first taken by the pilot of the pirate vessel whose crew had been so decimated by vanBuskirk and his Valerians. There couldn't be so many Boskonian bases with Tellurian personnel, Kinnison re-flected. It was well within the bounds of possibility, even of probability, that he might encounter here his former, but unsuspecting, shipmates again.

Since the Boyssian system was less than a hundred par-secs from Radelix, a couple of hours found the Lensman staring down upon another strange planet; and this one was a very Earthly world indeed. There were polar ice-caps, areas of intensely dazzling white. There was an atmosphere, deep and sweetly blue, filled for the most part with sun-light, but flecked here and there with clouds, some of which were slow-moving storms. There were continents, bearing mountains and plains, lakes and rivers. There were oceans, studded with islands great and small.

But Kinnison was no planetographer, nor had he been gone from Tellus sufficiently long so that the sight of this beautiful and home-like world aroused in him any qualm of nostalgia. He was looking for a pirate base; and, drop-ping his speedster as low into the night side as he dared, he began his search.

Of man or of the works of man he at first found little

enough trace. All human or near-human life was apparently still in a savage state of development; and, except for a few scattered races, or rather tribes, of burrowers and of cliff- or cave-dwellers, it was still nomadic, wandering here and there without permanent habitation or structure. Animals of scores of genera and species were there in myriads, but neither was Kinnison a biologist. He wanted pirates; and, it seemed, that was the one form of life which he was *not* going to find!

But finally, through sheer, grim, bull-dog pertinacity, he was successful. That base was there, somewhere. He would find it, no matter how long it took. He would find it, if he had to examine the entire crust of the planet, land and water alike, kilometer by plotted cubic kilometer! He set out to do just that; and it was thus that he found the Boskonian stronghold.

It had been built directly beneath a towering range of mountains, protected from detection by mile upon mile of native copper and of iron ore.

Its entrances, invisible before, were even now not readily perceptible, camouflaged as they were by outer layers of rock which matched exactly in form, color, and texture the rocks of the cliffs in which they were placed. Once those entrances were located, the rest was easy. Again he set his speedster into a carefully-observed orbit and came to ground in his armor. Again he crept forward, furtively and skulkingly, until he could perceive again a shimmering web of force.

With minor variations his method of entry into the Boskonian base was similar to that he had used in making his way into the Patrol base upon Radelix. He was, however, working now with a surety and a precision which had then been lacking. His practise with the Patrolmen had given him knowledge and technique. His sitting in judgment, during which he had touched almost every mind in the vast assemblage, had taught him much. And above all, the grisly finale of that sitting, horribly distasteful and soul-wracking as it had been, had given him training of inestimable value; necessitating as it had the infliction of the ultimate penalty.

He knew that he might have to stay inside that base for some time, therefore he selected his hiding-place with care. He could of course blank out the knowledge of his presence in the mind of anyone chancing to discover him; but since such an interruption might come at a critical instant, he preferred to take up his residence in a secluded place. There were, of course, many vacant suites in the officers' quarters—all bases must have accommodations for visitors—and the Lensman decided to occupy one of them. It was a simple matter to obtain a key, and, inside the bare but comfortable little room, he stripped off his armor with a sigh of relief.

Leaning back in a deeply upholstered leather arm-chair, he closed his eyes and let his sense of perception roam throughout the great establishment. With all his newly developed power he studied it, hour after hour and day after day. When he was hungry the pirate cooks fed him, not knowing that they did so—he had lived on iron rations long enough. When he was tired he slept, with his eternally vigilant Lens on guard.

Finally he knew everything there was to be known about that stronghold and was ready to act. He did not take over the mind of the base commander, but chose instead the chief communications officer as the one most likely and most intimately to have dealings with Helmuth. For Helmuth, he who spoke for Boskone, had for many months been the Lensman's definite objective.

But this game could not be hurried. Bases, no matter how important, did not call Grand Base except upon matters of the most dire urgency, and no such matter eventuated. Nor did Helmuth call that base, since nothing out of the ordinary was happening—to any pirates' knowledge, that is—and his attention was more necessary elsewhere.

One day, however, there came crackling in a triumphant report—a ship working out of that base had taken noble booty indeed; no less a prize than a fully-supplied hospital ship of the Patrol itself! As the report progressed Kinnison's heart went down into his boots and he swore bitterly to himself. How in all the nine hells of Valeria had they managed to take such a ship as that? Hadn't she been escorted?

Nevertheless, as chief communications officer he took the report and congratulated heartily, through the ship's radio man, its captain, its officers, and its crew.

"Mighty fine work; Helmuth himself shall hear of this," he concluded his words of praise. "How did you do it? With one of the new maulers?"

"Yes, sir," came the reply. "Our mauler, accompanying us just out of range, came up and engaged theirs. That left us free to take this ship. We locked on with magnets, cut our way in, and here we are."

There they were indeed. The hospital ship was red with blood; patients, doctors, internes, officers and operating crew alike had been butchered with the horribly ruthless savagery which was the customary technique of all the agencies of Boskone. Of all that ship's personnel only the nurses lived. They were not to be put to death—yet. In fact, and under certain conditions, they need not die at all.

They huddled together, a little knot of white-clad misery in that corpse-littered room, and even now one of them was being dragged away. She was fighting viciously, with fists and feet, with nails and teeth. No one pirate could handle her; it took two strong men to subdue that struggling fury. They hauled her upright and she threw back her head, in panting defiance. There was a cascade of red-bronze hair and Kinnison saw—Clarrissa MacDougall! And remembered that there *had* been some talk that they were going to put her back into space service! The Lensman decided instantly what to do.

"Stop, you swine!" he roared through his pirate mouthpiece. "Where do you think you're going with that nurse?"

"To the captain's cabin, sir." The huskies stopped short in amazement as that roar filled the room, but answered the question concisely.

"Let her go!" Then, as the girl fled back to the huddled group in the corner: "Tell the captain to come out here and assemble every officer and man of the crew. I want to talk to you all at once."

He had a minute or two in which to think, and he thought furiously, but accurately. He had to do something, but whatever he did must be done strictly according to the pirates' own standards of ethics; if he made one slip it might be Aldebaran I all over again. He knew how to keep from making that slip, he thought. But also, and this was the hard part, he must work in something that would let those nurses know that there was still hope; that there were more acts of this drama yet to come. Otherwise he knew with a stark, cold certainty what would happen. He knew of what stuff the space-nurses of the Patrol were made; knew that they could be driven just so far, and no farther—alive.

There was a way out of that, too. In the childishness of his hospitalization he had called Nurse MacDougall a dumb-bell. He had thought of her, and had spoken to her quite frankly, in uncomplimentary terms. But he knew that there was a real brain back of that beautiful face, that a quick and keen intelligence resided under that red-bronze thatch. Therefore when the assembly was complete he was ready, and in no uncertain or ambiguous language he opened up.

"Listen, you—all of you" he roared. "This is the first time in months that we have made such a haul as this, and you fellows have the brazen gall to start helping yourselves to the choicest stuff before anybody else gets a look at it. I tell you now to lay off, and that goes exactly as it lays. I, personally, will kill any man that touches one of those women before they arrive here at base. Now you, captain, are the first and worst offender of the lot," and he stared directly into the eyes of the officer whom he had last seen entering the dungeon of the Wheelmen.

"I admit that you're a good picker." Kinnison's voice was now venomously soft, his intonation distinct with thinly veiled sarcasm "Unfortunately, however, your taste agrees too well with mine. You see, captain, I'm going to need a nurse myself. I think I'm coming down with something. And, since I've got to have a nurse, I'll take that red-headed one. I had a nurse once with hair just that color, who insisted on feeding me tea and toast and a soft-boiled egg when I wanted beefsteak; and I'm going to take my grudge out on this one here for all the red-headed nurses that ever lived. I trust that you will pardon the length of this speech, but I want to give you my reasons in full for cautioning you that that particular nurse is my own particular personal property. Mark her for me, and see to it that she gets here—exactly as she is now."

The captain had been afraid to interrupt his superior, but now he erupted.

"But see here, Blakeslee!" he stormed. "She's mine, by every right. I captured her, I saw her first, I've got her here . . . ."

"Enough of that back-talk, captain!" Kinnison sneered elaborately. "You know, of course, that you are violating every rule by taking booty for yourself before division at base, and that you can get shot for doing it."

"But everybody does it!" protested the captain.

"Except when a superior officer catches him at it. Superiors get first pick, you know," the Lensman reminded him suavely.

"But I protest, sir! I'll take it up with . . . . ."

"Shut up!" Kinnison snarled, with cold finality. "Take

it up with whom you please, but remember this, my last warning. Bring her in to me as she is and you live. Touch her and you die! Now, you nurses, come over here to the board!"

Nurse MacDougall had been whispering furtively to the others and now she led the way, head high and eyes blazing defiance. She was an actress, as well as a nurse.

"Take a good, long look at this button, right here, marked 'Relay 46,'" came curt instructions. "If anybody aboard this ship touches any one of you, or even looks at you as though he wants to, press this button and I'll do the rest. Now, you big, red-headed dumb-bell, look at me. Don't start begging—yet. I just want to be sure you'll know me when you see me."

"I'll know you, never fear, you . . . . . you *brat!*" she flared, thus informing the Lensman that she had received his message. "I'll not only know you—I'll scratch your eyes out on sight!"

"That'll be a good trick if you can do it," Kinnison sneered, and cut off.

"What's it all about, Mac? What has got into you?" demanded one of the nurses, as soon as the women were alone.

"I don't know," she whispered. "Watch out, they may have spy-rays on us. I don't know anything, really, and the whole thing is too wildly impossible, too utterly fantastic to make sense. But pass the word along to all the girls to ride this out, because my Gray Lensman is in on it, somewhere and somehow. I don't see how he can be, possibly, but I just know he is."

For, at the first mention of tea and toast, before she perceived even an inkling of the true situation, her mind had flashed back instantly to Kinnison, the most stubborn and rebellious patient she had ever had. More, the only man she had ever known who had treated her precisely as though she were a part of the hospital's very furniture. As is the way of women—particularly of beautiful women—she had orated of women's rights and of women's status in the scheme of things. She had decried all special privileges, and had stated, often and with heat, that she asked no odds of any man living or yet to be born. Nevertheless, and also beautiful-womanlike, the thought had bitten deep that here was a man who had never even realized that she *was* a woman, to say nothing of realizing that she was an ex-

traordinarily beautiful one! And deep within her and stern-
ly suppressed the thought had still rankled.

At the mention of beefsteak she had all but screamed,
gripping her knees with frantic hands to keep her emotion
down. For she had had no real hope; she was simply fighting with everything she had until the hopeless end, which
she had known could not long be delayed. Now she gathered
herself together and began to act.

When the word "dumb-bell" boomed from the speaker
she knew, beyond doubt or peradventure, that it was Kinnison, the Gray Lensman, who was really doing that talking.
It was crazy—it didn't make any kind of sense at all—but
it was, it must be, true. And, again womanlike, she knew
with a calm certainty that as long as that Gray Lensman
were alive and conscious, he would be completely the master of any situation in which he might find himself. Therefore she passed along her illogical but cheering thought,
and the nurses, being also women, accepted it without
question as the actual and accomplished fact.

They carried on, and when the captured hospital ship
had docked at base, Kinnison was completely ready to
force matters to a conclusion. In addition to the chief
communications officer, he now had under his control a
highly capable observer. To handle two such minds was
child's play to the intellect which had directed, against
their full fighting wills, the minds of two and three quarters alert, powerful, and fully warned officers of the Galactic Patrol!

"Good girl, Mac" he put his mind en rapport with
hers and sent his message. "Glad you got the idea. You did
a good job of acting, and if you can do some more as good
we'll be all set. Can do?"

"I'll say I can!" she assented fervently. "I don't know
what you are doing, how you can possibly do it, or where
you are, but that can wait. Tell me what to do and I'll
do it!"

"Make passes at the base commander," he instructed
her. "Hate me—the ape I'm working through, you know;
Blakeslee, his name is—like poison. Go into it big—all jets
wide open. You maybe could love him, but if I get you
you'll blow out your brains—if any. You know the line—
play up to him with everything you can bring to bear, and
hate me to hell and back. Help all you can to start a fight
between us. If he falls for you hard enough the blow-off
comes then and there. If not, he'll be able to do us all

plenty of dirt. I can kill a lot of them, but not enough of them quick enough."

"He'll fall," she promised him gleefully, "like ten thousand bricks falling down a well. Just watch my jets!"

And fall he did. He had not even seen a woman for months, and he expected nothing except bitter-end resistance and suicide from any of these women of the Patrol. Therefore he was rocked to the heels—set back upon his very haunches—when the most beautiful woman he had ever seen came of her own volition into his arms, seeking in them sanctuary from his own chief communications officer.

"I hate him!" she sobbed, nestling against the huge bulk of the commander's body and turning upon him the full blast of the high powered projectors which were her eyes. "*You* wouldn't be so mean to me, I just know you wouldn't!" and her subtly perfumed head sank upon his shoulder. The outlaw was just so much soft wax.

"I'll say I wouldn't be mean to you" his voice dropped to a gentle bellow. "Why, you little sweetheart, I'll *marry* you. I will so, by all the gods of space!"

It thus came about that nurse and base commander entered the control room together, arms about each other.

"There he is!" she shrieked, pointing at the chief communications officer. "He's the one! Now let's see you start something, you rat-faced clunker! There's one real man around here, and he won't let you touch me—ya-a-a!" She gave him a resounding Bronx cheer, and her escort swelled visibly.

"Is—that—so?" Kinnison sneered. "Get this, glamor-puss, and get it straight. I marked you for mine as soon as I saw you, and mine you're going to be, whether you like it or not and no matter what anybody says or does about it. As for you, captain, you're too late—I saw her first. And now, you red-headed tomato, come over here where you belong."

She snuggled closer into the commander's embrace and the big man turned purple.

"What d'you mean, too late!" he roared. "You took her away from the ship's captain, didn't you? You said that superior officers get first choice, didn't you? I'm the boss here and I'm taking her away from you, get me? You'll stand for it, too, Blakeslee, and like it. One word out of you and I'll have you spread-eagled across the mouth of number six projector!"

"Superior officers don't *always* get first choice," Kinnison replied; with bitter, cold ferocity, but choosing his words with care. "It depends entirely on who the two men are."

Now was the time to strike. Kinnison knew that if the commander kept his head, the lives of those valiant women were forfeit, and his own whole plan seriously endangered. He himself could get away, of course—but he could not see himself doing it under these conditions. No, he must goad the commander to a frenzy. And without swearing would be better—the ape was used to invectives that would raise blisters on armor plate. Mac would help. In fact, and without his suggestion, she was even then hard at work fomenting trouble between the two men.

"You don't have to take that kind of stuff off of anybody, big boy," she was whispering, urgently. "Don't call in a crew to spread-eagle him, either; beam him out yourself. You're a better man than he is, any time. Blast him down—that'll show him who's who around here!"

"When the inferior is such a man as I am, and the superior such a louse as you are;" the biting, contemptuously sneering voice went on without a break, "Such a bloated swine; such a mangy, low-down cur; such a pussy-gutted tub of lard; such a brainless, filthy spawn of the lowest dregs of the rottenest scum of space; such an utterly incompetent, self-opinionated, misbegotten abortion as you are . . . . ."

The outraged pirate, bellowing profanity in wildly mounting rage, tried to break in; but Kinnison-Blakeslee's voice, if no louder than his, was far more penetrant.

". . . . then, in that case, the inferior keeps the red-headed wench himself. Put that on a tape, you white-livered coward, and eat it!"

Still bellowing, the fat man had turned and was leaping toward the arms cabinet.

"Blast him! Blast him down!" the nurse had been shrieking; and, as the raging commander neared the cabinet, no one noticed that her latest and loudest scream was "Kim! Blast him down! Don't wait any longer—beam him before he gets a gun!"

But the Lensman did not act—yet. Although almost every man of the pirate crew stared spell-bound, Kinnison's enslaved observer had for many seconds been jamming the sub-ether with Helmuth's personal and urgent call. It was

of almost vital importance to his plan that Helmuth himself
should see the climax of this scene. Therefore Blakeslee
stood immobile while his profanely raving superior reached
the cabinet and tore it open.

CHAPTER 21   *The Second Line*

BLAKESLEE WAS ALREADY ARMED—KINNISON HAD SEEN TO
that—and as the base commander wrenched open the arms
cabinet Helmuth's private look-out set began to draw current. Helmuth himself was now looking on and the enslaved observer had already begun to trace his beam.
Therefore as the furious pirate whirled around with raised
DeLameter he faced one already ablaze; and in a matter of
seconds there was only a charred and smoking heap where
he had stood.

Kinnison wondered that Helmuth's cold voice was not
already snapping from the speaker, but he was soon to discover the reason for that silence. Unobserved by the Lensman, one of the observers had recovered sufficiently from
his shocked amazement to turn in a riot alarm to the
guard-room. Five armed men answered that call on the
double, stopped and glanced around.

"Guards! Blast Blakeslee down!" Helmuth's unmistak-
able voice blared from his speaker.

Obediently and manfully enough the five guards tried;
and, had it actually been Blakeslee confronting them so de-
fiantly, they probably would have succeeded. It was the
body of the communications officer, it is true. The mind
operating the muscles of that body, however, was the mind
of Kimball Kinnison, Gray Lensman, the fastest man with
a hand-gun old Tellus had ever produced; keyed up, expecting the move, and with two DeLameters out and poised
at hip! *This* was the being whom Helmuth was so nonchalantly ordering his minions to slay! Faster than any
watching eye could follow, five bolts of lightning flicked

from Blakeslee's DeLameters. The last guard went down, his head a shrivelled cinder, before a single pirate bolt could be loosed. Then:

"You see, Helmuth," Kinnison spoke conversationally to the board, his voice dripping vitriol, "Playing it safe from a distance, and making other men pull your chestnuts out of the fire, is a very fine trick as long as it works. But when it fails to work, as now, it puts you exactly where I want you. I, for one, have been for a long time completely fed up with taking orders from a mere voice; especially from the voice of one whose entire method of operation proves him to be the prize coward of the galaxy."

"Observer! You other at the board!" snarled Helmuth, paying no attention to Kinnison's barbed shafts. "Sound the assembly—armed!"

"No use, Helmuth, he's stone deaf," Kinnison explained, voice smoothly venomous. "I'm the only man in this base you can talk to, and you won't be able to do even that very much longer."

"And you really think that you can get away with this mutiny—this barefaced insubordination—this defiance of *my authority?*"

"Sure I can—that's what I've been telling you. If you were here in person, or ever had been; if any of the boys had ever seen you, or had ever known you as anything except a disembodied voice; maybe I couldn't. But, since nobody has ever seen even your face, that gives me a chance . . . . . ."

In his distant base Helmuth's mind had flashed over every aspect of this unheard-of situation. He decided to play for time; therefore, even as his hands darted to buttons here and there, he spoke:

"Do *you* want to see my face?" he demanded. "If you do see it, no power in the galaxy . . . . ."

"Skip it, Chief," sneered Kinnison. "Don't try to kid me into believing you wouldn't kill me now, under any conditions, if you possibly could. As for your face, it makes no difference to me whether I ever see your ugly pan or not."

"Well, you shall!" and Helmuth's visage appeared; concentrating upon the rebellious officer a glare of such fury and such power that any ordinary man must have quailed. But not Blakeslee-Kinnison!

"Well! Not so bad, at that—the guy looks almost human!" Kinnison exclaimed, in the tone most carefully designed to drive even more frantic the helpless and inwardly raging pirate leader. "But I've got things to do. You can guess at what goes on around here from now on," and in the blaze of a DeLameter Helmuth's plate, set, and "eye" disappeared. Kinnison had also been playing for time, and his observer had checked and rechecked this second and highly important line to Helmuth's ultra-secret base.

Then, throughout the fortress, there blared out the urgent assembly call, to which the Lensman added, verbally:

"This is a one hundred percent callout, including crews of ships in dock, regular base personnel, and all prisoners. Come as you are and come fast—the doors of the auditorium will be locked in five minutes and any man outside those doors will be given ample reason to wish that he had been inside."

The auditorium was immediately off the control room, and was so arranged that when a partition was rolled back the control room became its stage. All Boskonian bases were arranged thus, in order that the supervising officers at Grand Base could oversee through their instruments upon the main panel just such assemblies as this one was supposed to be. Every man hearing that call assumed that it came from Grand Base, and every man hurried to obey it.

Kinnison rolled back the partition between the two rooms and watched for weapons as the men came streaming into the auditorium. Ordinarily only the guards went armed, but possibly a few of the ships' officers would be wearing their DeLameters . . . . . four—five—six. The captain and the pilot of the battleship that had taken the hospital ship, Vice-Commander Krimsky of the base, and three guards. Knives, billies, and such did not count.

"Time's up. Lock the doors. Bring the keys and the nurses up here," he ordered the six armed men, calling each by name. "You women take these chairs over here, you men sit there."

Then, when all were seated, Kinnison touched a button and the steel partition slid smoothly into place.

"What's coming off here?" demanded one of the officers. "Where's the commander? How about Grand Base? Look at that board!"

"Sit tight." Kinnison directed. "Hands on knees—I'll burn any or all of you that make a move. I have already burned the old man and five guards, and have put Grand Base out of the picture. Now I want to find out just how us seven stand." The Lensman already knew, but he was not tipping his hand.

"Why us seven?"

"Because we are the only ones who happened to be wearing side-arms. Everyone else of the entire personnel is unarmed and is now locked in the auditorium. You know how apt they are to get out until one of us lets them out."

"But Helmuth—he'll have you blasted for this!"

"Hardly—my plans were not made yesterday. How many of you fellows are with me?"

"What's your scheme?"

"To take these nurses to some Patrol base and surrender. I'm sick of this whole game; and, since none of them have been hurt, I figure they're good for a pardon and a fresh start—a light sentence at least."

"Oh, so *that's* the reason . . . . ." growled the captain.

"Exactly—but I don't want anyone with me whose only thought would be to burn me down at the first opportunity."

"Count me in," declared the pilot. "I've got a strong stomach, but enough of these jobbies is altogether too much. If you wangle anything short of a life sentence for me I'll go along, but I bloody well won't help you against . . . . ."

"Sure not. Not until after we're out in space. I don't need any help here."

"Do you want my DeLameter?"

"No, keep it. You won't use it on me. Anybody else?"

One guard joined the pilot, standing aside; the other four wavered.

"Time's up!" Kinnison snapped. "Now, you four fellows, either go for your DeLameters or turn your backs, and do it right now!"

They elected to turn their backs and Kinnison collected their weapons, one by one. Having disarmed them, he again rolled back the partition and ordered them to join the wondering throng in the auditorium. He then addressed the assemblage, telling them what he had done and what he had it in mind to do.

"A good many of you must be fed up on this lawless game of piracy and anxious to resume association with decent men, if you can do so without incurring too great a punishment," he concluded. "I feel quite certain that those of us who man the hospital ship in order to return these nurses to the Patrol will get light sentences, at most. Miss MacDougall is a head nurse—a commissioned officer of the Patrol. We will ask her what she thinks."

"I can say more than that," she replied clearly. "I am

not 'quite certain,' either—I am absolutely sure that whatever men Mr. Blakeslee selects for his crew will not be given any sentences at all. They will be pardoned, and will be given whatever jobs they can do best."

"How do you know, Miss?" asked one. "We're a black lot."

"I know you are." The head nurse's voice was serenely positive. "I won't say *how* I know, but you can take my word for it that I *do* know."

"Those of you who want to take a chance with us line up over here," Kinnison directed, and walked rapidly down the line, reading the mind of each man in turn. Many of them he waved back into the main group, as he found thoughts of treachery or signs of inherent criminality. Those he selected were those who were really sincere in their desire to quit forever the ranks of Boskone, those who were in those ranks because of some press of circumstance rather than because of a mental taint. As each man passed inspection he armed himself from the cabinet and stood at ease before the group of women.

Having selected his crew, the Lensman operated the controls that opened the exit nearest the hospital ship, blasted away the panel, so that that exit could not be closed, unlocked a door, and turned to the pirates.

"Vice-Commander Krimsky, as senior officer, you are now in command of this base," he remarked. "While I am in no sense giving you orders, there are a few matters about which you should be informed. First, I set no definite time as to when you may leave this room—I merely state that you will find it decidedly unhealthy to follow us at all closely as we go from here to the hospital ship. Second, you haven't a ship fit to take the ether; your main injector toggles have all been broken off at the pivots. If your mechanics work at top speed, new ones can be put on in exactly two hours. Third, there is going to be a severe earthquake in precisely two hours and thirty minutes, one which should make this base merely a memory."

"An earthquake! Don't bluff, Blakeslee—you couldn't do *that!*"

Well, perhaps not a regular earthquake, but something that will do just as well. If you think I'm bluffing, wait and find out. But common sense should give you the answer to that—I know exactly what Helmuth is doing now, whether you do or not. At first I intended to wipe you all out without warning, but I changed my mind. I decided to leave you alive, so that you could report to Helmuth exactly what happened. I wish I could be watching him when he finds out how easily one man took him, and how far from fool-proof his system is—but we can't have everything. Let's go!"

As the group hurried away, Mac loitered until she was near Blakeslee, who was bringing up the rear.

"Where are you, Kim?" she whispered urgently.

"I'll join up at the next corridor. Keep farther ahead, and get ready to run when we do!"

As they passed that corridor a figure in gray leather, carrying an extremely heavy object, stepped out of it. Kinnison himself set his burden down, yanked a lever, and ran —and as he ran fountains of intolerable heat erupted and cascaded from the mechanism he had left upon the floor. Just ahead of him, but at some distance behind the others, ran Blakeslee and the girl.

"Gosh, I'm glad to see you, Kim!" she panted as the Lensman caught up with them and all three slowed down. "What is that thing back there?"

"Nothing much—just a KJ4Z hot-shot. Won't do any real damage—just melt this tunnel down so they can't interfere with our get-away."

"Then you *were* bluffing about the earthquake?" she asked, a shade of disappointment in her tone.

"Hardly," he reproved her. "That isn't due for two hours and a half yet, but it'll happen on scheduled time."

"How?"

"You remember about the curious cat, don't you? However, no particular secret about it, I guess—three lithium-hydride bombs placed where they'll do the most good and timed for exactly simultaneous detonation. Here we are—don't tell anybody I'm here."

Aboard the vessel, Kinnison disappeared into a state-room while Blakeslee continued in charge. Men were divided into watches, duties were assigned, inspections were made, and the ship shot into the air. There was a brief halt to pick up Kinnison's speedster; then, again on the way, Blakeslee turned the board over to Crandall, the pilot, and went into Kinnison's room.

There the Lensman withdrew his control, leaving intact the memory of everything that had happened. For minutes Blakeslee was almost in a daze, but struggled through it and held out his hand.

"Mighty glad to meet you, Lensman. Thanks. All I can say is that after I got sucked in I couldn't . . . . ."

"Sure, I know all about it—that was one of the reasons I picked you out. Your subconscious didn't fight back a bit, at any time. You're to be in charge, from here to Tellus. Please go and chase everybody out of the control room except Crandall."

"Say, I just thought of something!" exclaimed Blakeslee when Kinnison joined the two officers at the board. "You must be that particular Lensman who has been getting in Helmuth's hair so much lately!"

"Probably—that's my chief aim in life."

"I'd like to see Helmuth's face when he gets the report of this. I've said that before, haven't I? But I mean it now, even more than I did before."

"I'm thinking of Helmuth, too, but not that way." The pilot had been scowling at his plate, and now turned to Blakeslee and the Lensman, glancing curiously from one to the other. "Oh I say . . . . . A Lensman, what? A bit of good old light begins to dawn; but that can wait. Helmuth is after us, foot, horse, and marines. Look at that plate!"

"Four of 'em already!" exclaimed Blakeslee. "And there's another! And we haven't got a beam hot enough to light a cigarette, nor a screen strong enough to stop a firecracker. We've got legs, but not as many as they've got. You knew all about that, though, before we started; and from what you've pulled off so far you've got something left on the hooks. What is it? What's the answer?"

"For some reason or other they can't detect us. All you have to do is to stay out of range of their electros and drill for Tellus."

"Some reason or other, eh? Nine ships on the plate now —all Boskonians and all looking for us—and not seeing us—some reason! But I'm not asking questions . . . . ."

"Just as well not to. I'd rather you'd answer one. Who or what is Boskone?"

"Nobody knows. Helmuth speaks for Boskone, and nobody else ever does, not even Boskone himself—if there is such a person. Nobody can prove it, but everybody knows that Helmuth and Boskone are simply two names for the same man. Helmuth, you know, is only a voice—nobody ever saw his face until today."

"I'm beginning to think so, myself," and Kinnison strode away, to call at the office of Head Nurse MacDougall.

"Mac, here's a small, but highly important box," he told her, taking the neutralizer from his pocket and handing it to her. "Put it in your locker until you get to Tellus. Then take it, yourself, in person, and give it to Haynes, himself, in person, and to nobody else. Just tell him I sent it—he knows all about it."

"But why not keep it and give it to him yourself? You're coming with us, aren't you?"

"Probably not all the way. I imagine I'll have to do a flit before long."

"But I want to talk to you!" she exclaimed. "Why, I've got a million questions to ask you!"

"That would take a long time," he grinned at her, "and time is just what we ain't got right now, neither of us," and he strode back to the board.

There he labored for hours at a calculating machine and in the tank; finally to squat down upon his heels, staring at two needle-like rays of light in the tank and whistling softly between his teeth. For those two lines, while exactly in the same plane, did not intersect in the tank at all! Estimating as carefully as he could the point of intersection of the lines, he punched the "cancel" key to wipe out all traces of his work and went to the chart-room. Chart after chart he hauled down, and for many minutes he worked with calipers, compass, goniometer, and a carefully-set adjustable triangle. Finally he marked a point—exactly upon a numbered dot already upon the chart—and again whistled. Then:

"Huh!" he grunted. He rechecked all his figures and retraversed the chart, only to have his needle pierce again the same tiny hole. He stared at it for a full minute, studying the map all around his marker.

"Star cluster AC 257-4736," he ruminated. "The smallest most insignificant, least-known star-cluster he could find, and my largest possible error can't put it anywhere else . . . . kind of thought it might be in a cluster, but I never would have looked *there*. No wonder it took a lot of stuff to trace his beam—it would have to be four numbers Brinnell harder than a diamond drill to work from there."

Again whistling tunelessly to himself he rolled up the chart upon which he had been at work, stuck it under his arm, replaced the others in their compartments, and went back to the control room.

"How's tricks, fellows?" he asked.

"QX," replied Blakeslee. "We're through them and into

clear ether. Not a ship on the plate, and nobody gave us even a tumble."

"Fine! You won't have any trouble, then, from here in to Prime Base. Glad of it, too—I've got to flit. That'll mean long watches for you two, but it can't very well be helped."

"But I say, old bird, I don't mind the watches, but....."

"Don't worry about that, either. This crew can be trusted, to a man. Not one of you joined the pirates of your own free will, and not one of you has ever taken active part....."

"What are you, a mind-reader or something?" Crandall burst out.

"Something like that," Kinnison assented with a grin, and Blakeslee put in:

"More than that, you mean. Something like hypnosis, only more so. You think I had something to do with this, but I didn't—the Lensman did it all himself."

"Um.....m." Crandall stared at Kinnison, new respect in his eyes. "I knew that Unattached Lensmen were good, but I had no idea they were *that* good. No wonder Helmuth has been getting his wind up about you. I'll string along with any one who can take a whole base, single-handed, and make such a bally ass to boot out of such a keen old bird as Helmuth is. But I'm in a bit of a dither, not so say a funk, about what's going to happen when we pop into Prime Base without you. Every man jack of us, you know, is slated for the lethal chamber without trial. Miss Mac-Dougall will do her bit, of course, but what I mean is has she enough jets to swing it, what?"

"She has, but to avoid all argument I've fixed that up, too. Here's a tape, telling all about what happened. It ends up with my recommendation for a full pardon for each of you, and for a job at whatever he is found best fitted for. Signed with my thumb-print. Give it or send it to Port Admiral Haynes as soon as you land. I've got enough jets, I think, so that it will go as it lays."

"Jets? You? Right-o! You've got jets enough to lift fourteen freighters off the North Pole of Valeria. What next?"

"Stores and supplies for my speedster. I'm doing a long flit and this ship has supplies to burn, so load me up, Plimsoll down."

The speedster was stocked forthwith. Then, with nothing more than a casually waved salute in the way of farewell, Kinnison boarded his tiny space-ship and shot away toward his distant goal. Crandall, the pilot, sought his bunk; while Blakeslee started his long trick at the board. In an hour or so the head nurse strolled in.

"Kim?" she queried, doubtfully.

"No, Miss MacDougall—Blakeslee. Sorry . . . . ."

"Oh, I'm glad of that—that means that everything's settled. Where's the Lensman—in bed?"

"He has gone, Miss."

"Gone! Without a word? Where?"

"He didn't say."

"He wouldn't, of course." The nurse turned away, exclaiming inaudibly; "Gone! I'd like to cuff him for that, the lug! GONE! Why, the great, big, lobsterly clunker!"

CHAPTER 22   *Preparing for the Test*

BUT KINNISON WAS NOT HEADING FOR HELMUTH'S BASE— yet. He was splitting the ether toward Aldebaran instead, as fast as his speedster could go; and she was one of the fastest things in the galaxy. He had two good reasons for going there before tackling Boskone's Grand Base. First, to try out his skill upon non-human intellects. If he could handle the Wheelmen he was ready to take the far greater hazard. Second, he owed those wheelers something, and he did not like to call in the whole Patrol to help him pay his debts. He could, he thought, handle that base himself.

Knowing exactly where it was, he had no difficulty in finding the volcanic shaft which was its entrance. Down that shaft his sense of perception sped. He found the lookout plates and followed their power leads. Gently, carefully, he insinuated his mind into that of the Wheelman at the board; discovering, to his great relief, that that monstrosity was no more difficult to handle than had been the Radeligian observer. Mind or intellect, he found, were not affected at all by the shape of the brains concerned; quality, reach, and power were the essential factors. Therefore he let himself in and took position in the same room from which he had been driven so violently. Kinnison examined with interest the wall through which he had been blown, noting that it had been repaired so perfectly that he could scarcely find the joints which had been made.

These wheelers, the Lensman knew, had explosives; since the bullets which had torn their way through his armor and through his flesh had been propelled by that agency. Therefore, to the mind within his grasp he suggested "the place where explosives are kept?" and the thought of that mind flashed to the store-room in question. Similarly, the thought of the one who had access to that room pointed out to the Lensman the particular Wheelman he wanted. It was as easy as that, and since he took care not to look at any of the weird beings, he gave no alarm.

Kinnison withdrew his mind delicately, leaving no trace of its occupancy, and went to investigate the arsenal. There he found a few cases of machine-rifle cartridges, and that was all. Then into the mind of the munitions officer, where he discovered that the heavy bombs were kept in a distant crater, so that no damage would be done by any possible explosion.

"Not quite as simple as I thought," Kinnison ruminated, "but there's a way out of that, too."

There was. It took an hour or so of time; and he had to control two Wheelmen instead of one, but he found that he could do that. When the munitions master took out a bomb-scow after a load of H.E., the crew had no idea that it was anything except a routine job. The only Wheelman who would have known differently, the one at the lookout board, was the other whom Kinnison had to keep under control. The scow went out, got its load, and came back. Then, while the Lensman was flying out into space, the scow dropped down the shaft. So quietly was the whole thing done that not a creature in that whole establishment knew that anything was wrong until it was too late to act—and then none of them knew anything at all. Not even the crew of the scow realized that they were dropping too fast.

Kinnison did not know what would happen if a mind—to say nothing of two of them—died while in his mental grasp, and he did not care to find out. Therefore, a fraction of a second before the crash, he jerked free and watched.

The explosion and its consequences did not look at all impressive from the Lensman's coign of vantage. The mountain trembled a little, then subsided noticeably. From its summit there erupted an unimportant little flare of flame, some smoke, and an insignificant shower of rock and debris.

However, when the scene had cleared there was no longer any shaft leading downward from that crater; a floor of solid rock began almost at its lip. Nevertheless the Lensman explored thoroughly all the region where the stronghold had been, making sure that the clean-up had been one hundred percent effective.

Then, and only then, did he point the speedster's streamlined nose toward star cluster AC 257-4736.

* * * * *

In his hidden retreat so far from the galaxy's crowded suns and worlds, Helmuth was in no enviable or easy frame of mind. Four times he had declared that that accursed Lensman, whoever he might be, must be destroyed; and had mustered his every available force to that end; only to have his intended prey slip from his grasp as effortlessly as a droplet of mercury eludes the clutching fingers of a child.

That Lensman, with nothing except a speedster and a bomb, had taken and had studied one of Boskone's new battleships, thus obtaining for his Patrol the secret of cosmic energy. Abandoning his own vessel, then crippled and doomed to capture or destruction, he had stolen one of the ships searching for him and in it he had calmly sailed to Velantia right through Helmuth's screen of blockading vessels. He had in some way so fortified Velantia as to capture six Boskonian battleships. In one of those ships he had won his way back to Prime Base, with information of such immense importance that it had robbed the Boskonian organization of its then overwhelming superiority. More, he had found or had developed new items of equipment which, save for Helmuth's own success in obtaining them, would have given the Patrol a definite and decisive superiority over Boskonia. Now both sides were equal, except for that Lensman and . . . . the Lens.

Helmuth still quailed inwardly whenever he thought of

what he had undergone at the Arisian barrier, and he had given up all thought of securing the secret of the Lens by force or from Arisia. But there must be other ways of getting it . . . . .

And just then there came in the urgent call from Boyssia II, followed by the stunningly successful revolt of the hitherto innocuous Blakeslee, culminating as it did in the destruction of Helmuth's every Boyssian device of vision or of communication. Blue-white with fury, the Boskonian flung his net abroad to take the renegade; but as he settled back to await results a thought struck him like a blow from a fist. Blakeslee *was* innocuous. He never had had, did not now have and never would have, the cold nerve and the sheer, dominating power he had just shown. Toward what conclusion did that fact point?

The furious anger disappeared from Helmuth's face as though it had been wiped therefrom with a sponge, and he became again the cold calculating mechanism of flesh and blood that he ordinarily was. This conception changed matters entirely. This was not an ordinary revolt of an ordinary subordinate. The man had done something which he could not possibly do. So what? The Lens again . . . . . again that accursed Lensman, the one who had somehow learned really to *use* his Lens!

"Wolmark, call every vessel at Boyssia base," he directed crisply. "Keep on calling them until someone answers. Get whoever is in charge there now and put him on me here."

A few minutes of silence followed, then Vice-Commander Krimsky reported in full everything that had happened and told of the threatened destruction of the base.

"You have an automatic speedster there, have you not?"

"Yes, sir."

"Turn over command to the next in line, with orders to move to the nearest base, taking with him as much equipment as is possible. Caution him to leave on time, however, for I very strongly suspect that it is now too late to do anything to prevent the destruction of the base. You, alone, take the speedster and bring away the personal files of the men who went with Blakeslee. A speedster will meet you at a point to be designated later and relieve you of the records."

An hour passed. Two, then three.

"Wolmark! Blakeslee and the hospital ship have vanished, I presume?"

"They have." The underling, expecting a verbal flaying, was greatly surprised at the mildness of his chief's tone and at the studious serenity of his face.

"Come to the center." Then, when the lieutenant was seated, "I do not suppose that you as yet realize what—or rather, who—it is that is doing this?"

"Why, Blakeslee is doing it, of course."

"I thought so, too, at first. That was what the one who really did it wanted us to think."

"It must have been Blakeslee. We saw him do it, sir—how could it have been anyone else?"

"I do not know. I do know, however, and so should you, that he could not have done it. Blakeslee, of himself, is of no importance whatever."

"We'll catch him, sir, and make him talk. He can't get away."

"You will find that you will not catch him and that he can get away. Blakeslee alone, of course, could not do so, any more than he could have done the things he apparently did do. No. Wolmark, we are not dealing with Blakeslee."

"Who then, sir?"

"Haven't you deduced that yet? The Lensman, fool—the same Lensman who has been thumbing his nose at us ever since he took one of our first-class battleships with a speed-boat and a firecracker."

"But—how *could* he?"

"Again I admit that I do not know—yet. The connection, however, is quite evident. Thought. Blakeslee was thinking thoughts utterly beyond him. The Lens comes from Arisia. The Arisians are masters of thought—of mental forces and processes incomprehensible to any of us. These are the elements which, when fitted together, will give us the complete picture."

"I don't see how they fit."

"Neither do I—yet. However, surely he can't trace . . . . ."

"Just a moment! The time has come when it is no longer safe to say what that Lensman can or cannot do. Our communicator beams are hard and tight, yes. But any beam can be tapped if enough power be applied to it, and any beam that can be tapped can be traced. I expect him to visit us here, and we shall be prepared for his visit. That is the reason for this conference with you. Here is a device which generates a field through which no thought can penetrate. I have had this device for some time, but for obvious reasons have not released it. Here are the diagrams and complete constructional data. Have a few hundred of them made with all possible speed, and see to it that every being upon this planet wears one continuously. Impress upon everyone, and I will also, that it is of the utmost importance that absolutely continuous protection be maintained, even while changing batteries.

"Experts have been working for some time upon the problem of protecting the entire planet with a screen, and there is some little hope of success in the near future; but individual protection will still be of the utmost importance. We cannot impress it too forcibly upon everyone that every man's life is dependent upon each one maintaining his thought-screen in full operation at all times. That is all."

When the messenger brought in the personal files of Blakeslee and the other deserters, Helmuth and his psychologists went over them with minutely painstaking care. The more they studied them the clearer it became that the chief's conclusion was the correct one. THE Lensman could read minds.

Reason and logic told Helmuth that the Lensman's only purpose in attacking the Boyssian base was to get a line on Grand Base; that Blakeslee's flight and the destruction of the base were merely diversions to obscure the real purpose of the visit; that the Lensman had staged that theatrical performance especially to hold him, Helmuth, while his beam was being traced, and that that was the only reason why the visiset was not sooner put out of action; and finally, that the Lensman had scored another clean hit.

He, Helmuth himself, had been caught flat-footed; and his face hardened and his jaw set at the thought. But he had not been taken in. He was forewarned and he would be ready, for he was coldly certain that Grand Base and he himself were the real objectives of the Lensman. That Lensman knew full well that any number of ordinary bases, ships, and men could be destroyed without damaging materially the Boskonian cause.

Steps must be taken to make Grand Base as impregnable to mental forces as it already was to physical ones. Otherwise, it might well be that even Helmuth's own life would presently be at stake—a thing precious indeed. Therefore council after council was held, every contingency that could be thought of was brought up and discussed, every possible precaution was taken. In short, every resource of Grand

Base was devoted to the warding off of any possible mental threat which might be forthcoming.

* * * * *

Kinnison approached that star cluster with care. Small though it was, as cosmic groups go, it yet was composed of some hundreds of stars and an unknown number of planets. Any one of those planets might be the one he sought, and to approach it unknowingly might prove disastrous. Therefore he slowed down to a crawl and crept up, light-year by light-year, with his ultra-powered detectors fanning out before him to the limit of their unimaginable reach.

He had more than half expected that he would have to search that cluster, world by world; but in that, at least, he was pleasantly disappointed. One corner of one of his plates began to show a dim glow of detection. A bell tinkled and Kinnison directed his most powerful master plate into the region indicated. This plate, while of very narrow field, had tremendous resolving power and magnification; and in it he saw that there were eighteen small centers of radiation surrounding one vastly larger one.

There was no doubt then as to the location of Helmuth's base, but there arose the question of approach. The Lensman had not considered the possibility of a screen of lookout ships—if they were close enough together so that the electromagnetics had even a fifty percent overlap, he might as well go back home. What were those outposts, and exactly how closely were they spaced? He observed, advanced, and observed again; computing finally that, whatever they were, they were so far apart that there could be no possibility of any electro overlap at all. He could get between them easily enough—he wouldn't even have to baffle his flares. They could not be guards at all, Kinnison concluded, but must be simply outposts, set far outside the solar system of the planet they guarded; not to ward off one-man speedsters, but to warn Helmuth of the possible approach of a force large enough to threaten Grand Base.

Closer and closer Kinnison flashed; discovering that the central object was indeed a base, startling in its immensity and completely and intensively fortified; and that the outposts were huge, floating fortresses, practically stationary in space relative to the sun of the solar system they surrounded. The Lensman aimed at the center of the imaginary square formed by four of the outposts and drove in as close to the planet as he dared. Then, going inert, he set his speedster into an orbit—he did not care particularly about its shape, provided that it was not too narrow an ellipse—and cut off all his power. He was now safe from detection. Leaning back in his seat and closing his eyes, he hurled his sense of perception into and through the massed fortifications of Grand Base.

For a long time he did not find a single living creature. Hundreds of miles he traversed, perceiving only automatic machinery, bank after towering, miles-square bank of accumulators, and remote-controlled projectors and other weapons and apparatus. Finally, however, he came to Helmuth's dome; and in that dome he received another severe shock. The personnel in that dome were to be numbered by the hundreds, but he could not make mental contact with any one of them. He could not touch their minds at all; he was stopped cold. Every member of Helmuth's band was protected by a thought-screen as effective as the Lensman's own!

Around and around the planet the speedster circled, while Kinnison struggled with this new and entirely unexpected setback. This looked as though Helmuth knew what was coming. Helmuth was nobody's fool, Kinnison knew; but how could he possibly have suspected that a mental attack was in the book? Perhaps he was just playing safe. If so, the Lensman's chance would come. Men would be careless; batteries weakened and would have to be changed.

But this hope was also vain, as continued watching revealed that each battery was listed, checked, and timed. Nor was any screen released, even for an instant, when its battery was changed; the fresh power source being slipped into service before the weakening one was disconnected.

"Well, that tears it—Helmuth *knows*," Kinnison cogitated, after watching vainly several such changes. "He's a wise old bird. The guy really has jets—I still don't see what I did that could have put him wise to what was going on."

Day after day the Lensman studied every detail of construction, operation, and routine of that base, and finally an idea began to dawn. He shot his attention toward a barracks he had inspected frequently of late, but stopped, irresolute.

"Uh uh, Kim, maybe better not," he advised himself.

"Helmuth's mighty quick on the trigger, to figure out that Boyssian thing so fast . . . . ."

His projected thought was sheared off without warning, thus settling the question definitely. Helmuth's big apparatus was at work, the whole planet was screened against thought.

"Oh well, probably better, at that," Kinnison went on arguing with himself. "If I'd tried it out maybe he'd've got onto it and laid me a stymie next time, when I really need it."

He went free and hurled his speedster toward Earth, now distant indeed. Several times during that long trip he was sorely tempted to call Haynes through his Lens and get things started; but he always thought better of it. This was altogether too important a thing to be sent through so much sub-ether, or even to be thought about except inside an absolutely thought-tight room. And besides, every waking hour of even that long trip could be spent very profitably in digesting and correlating the information he had obtained and in mapping out the salient features of the campaign that was to come. Therefore, before time began to drag, Kinnison landed at Prime Base and was taken directly to Port Admiral Haynes.

"Mighty glad to see you, son," Haynes greeted the young Lensman cordially as he sealed the room thought-tight. "Since you came in under your own power, I assume that you are here to make a constructive report?"

"Better than that, sir—I'm here to start something in a big way. I know at last where their Grand Base is, and have detailed plans of it. I think I know who and where Boskone is. I know where Helmuth is, and I have worked out a plan whereby, if it works, we can wipe out that base. Boskone, Helmuth, and all the lesser master minds, at one wipe."

"Mentor *did* come through, huh?" For the first time since Kinnison had known him the old man lost his poise. He leaped to his feet and seized Kinnison by the arm. "I knew you were good, but not *that* good! He gave you what you wanted?"

"He sure did," and the younger man reported as briefly as possible everything that had happened.

"I'm just as sure that Helmuth is Boskone as I can be of anything that can't be proved," Kinnison continued, unrolling a sheaf of drawings. "Helmuth speaks for Boskone, and nobody else ever does, not even Boskone himself. None of the other big shots know anything about Boskone or ever heard him speak; but they all jump through their hoops when Helmuth, 'speaking for Boskone,' cracks the whip. And I couldn't get a trace of Helmuth ever taking anything up with any higher-ups. Therefore I'm dead certain that when we get Helmuth we get Boskone.

"But that's going to be a job of work. I scouted his headquarters from stem to gudgeon, as I told you; and Grand Base is absolutely impregnable as it stands. I never imagined anything like it—it makes Prime Base here look like a deserted cross-roads after a hard winter. They've got screens, pits, projectors, accumulators, all on a gigantic scale. In fact, they've got everything—but you can get all that from the tape and these sketches. They simply can't be taken by any possible direct frontal attack. Even if we used every ship and mauler we've got they could stand us off. And they can match us, ship for ship—we'd never get near Grand Base at all if they knew we were coming . . . . '

"Well, if it's such an impossible job, what . . . . . "

"I'm coming to that. It's impossible as it stands; but there's a good chance that I'll be able to soften it up," and the young Lensman went on to outline the plan upon which he had been working so long. "You know, like a worm—bore from within. That's the only possible way to do it. You'll have to put detector nullifiers on every ship assigned to the job, but that'll be easy. We'll need everything we've got."

"The important thing, as I gather it, is timing."

"Absolutely. To the minute, since I won't be able to communicate, once I get inside their thought-screens. How long will it take to assemble our stuff and put it in that cluster?"

"Seven weeks—eight at the outside."

"Plus two for allowances. QX—at exactly hour 20, ten weeks from today, let every projector of every vessel you can possibly get there cut loose on that base with everything they can pour in. There's a detailed drawing in here somewhere . . . . . here—twenty-six main objectives, you see. Blast them all, simultaneously to the second. If they all go down, the rest will be possible—if not, it'll be just too bad. Then work along these lines here, straight from those twenty-six stations to the dome, blasting everything as you go. Make it last exactly fifteen minutes, not a minute more or less. If, by fifteen minutes after twenty, the main dome hasn't surrendered by cutting its screen, blast that, too, if you can—it'll take a lot of blasting, I'm afraid. From then on you and the five-star admirals will have to do whatever is appropriate to the occasion."

"Your plan doesn't cover that, apparently. Where will you be—how will *you* be fixed—if the main dome does not cut its screens?"

"I'll be dead, and you'll be just starting the damndest war that this galaxy ever saw."

CHAPTER 23   Tregonsee Turns Zwilnik

WHILE SERVICING AND CHECKING THE SPEEDSTER REQUIRED only a couple of hours, Kinnison did not leave Earth for almost two days. He had requisitioned much special equipment, the construction of one item of which—a suit of armor such as had never been seen before—caused almost all of the delay. When it was ready the greatly interested Port Admiral accompanied the young Lensman out to the steel-lined, sand-filled concrete dugout, in which the suit had already been mounted upon a remote-controlled dummy. Fifty feet from that dummy there was a heavy, water-cooled machine rifle, with its armored crew standing by. As the two approached the crew leaped to attention.

"As you were," Haynes instucted, and:

"You checked those cartridges against those I brought in from Aldebaran I?" asked Kinnison of the officer in charge, as, accompanied by the Port Admiral, he crouched down behind the shields of the control panel.

"Yes, sir. These are twenty-five percent over, as you specified."

"QX—commence firing!" Then, as the weapon clamored out its stuttering, barking roar, Kinnison made the dummy stoop, turn, bend, twist, and dodge, so as to bring its every plate, joint, and member into that hail of steel. The uproar stopped.

"One thousand rounds, sir," the officer reported.

"No holes—no dents—not a scratch or a scar," Kinnison reported, after a minute examination, and got into the thing. "Now give me two thousand rounds, unless I tell you to stop. Shoot!"

Again the machine rifle burst into its ear-shattering song of hate; and, strong as Kinnison was and powerfully braced by the blast of his drivers, he could not stand against the awful force of those bullets. Over he went, backward, and the firing ceased.

"Keep it up!" he snapped. "Think they're going to quit shooting at me because I fall down?"

"But you had had nineteen hundred!" protested the officer.

"Keep on pecking until you run out of ammunition or until I tell you to stop," ordered Kinnison. "I've got to learn how to handle this thing under fire," and the storm of metal again began to crash against the reverberating shell of steel.

It hurled the Lensman down, rolled him over and over, slammed him against the back-stop. Again and again he struggled upright, only to be hurled again to ground as the riflemen, really playing the game now, swung their leaden hail from part to part of the armor, and varied their attack from steady fire to short but savage bursts. But finally, in spite of everything the gun crew could do, Kinnison learned his controls.

Then, drivers flaring, he faced that howling, chattering muzzle and strode straight into the stream of smoke- and flame-enshrouded steel. Now the air was literally full of metal. Bullets and fragments of bullets whined and shrieked in mad abandon as they ricocheted in all directions off that armor. Sand and bits of concrete flew hither and yon, filling the atmosphere of the dugout. The rifle yammered at maximum, with its sweating crew laboring mightily to keep its voracious maw full-fed. But, in spite of everything, Kinnison held his line and advanced. He was barely six feet from that yelling, steel-vomiting muzzle when the firing again ceased.

"Twenty thousand, sir," the officer reported, crisply. "We'll have to change barrels before we can give you any more."

"That's enough!" snapped Haynes. "Come out of there!"

Out Kinnison came. He removed heavy ear-plugs, swallowed four times, blinked and grimaced. Finally he spoke.

"It works perfectly, sir, except for the noise. 'Sa good thing I've got a Lens—in spite of the plugs I won't be able to hear anything for three days!"

"How about the springs and shock-absorbers? Are you bruised anywhere? You took some real bumps."

"Perfect—not a bruise. Let's look her over."

Every inch of that armor's surface was now marked by blurs, where the metal of the bullets had rubbed itself off upon the shining alloy, but that surface was neither scratched, scored, nor dented.

"QX, boys—thanks," Kinnison dismissed the riflemen. They probably wondered how any man could see out through a helmet built up of inches-thick laminated alloys, with neither window nor port through which to look; but if so, they made no mention of their curiosity. They, too, were Patrolmen.

"Is that thing an armor or a personal tank?" asked Haynes. "I aged ten years while that was going on; but at that I'm glad you insisted on testing it. You can get away with anything now."

"It's much better technique to learn things among friends than enemies," Kinnison laughed. "It's heavy, of course—pretty close to a ton. I won't be walking around in it, though; I'll be flying it. Well, sir, since everything's all set, I think I'd better fly it over to the speedster and start flitting, don't you? I don't know exactly how much time I'm going to need on Trenco."

"Might as well," the Port Admiral agreed, as casually, and Kinnison was gone.

"What a man!" Haynes stared after the monstrous figure until it vanished in the distance, then strolled slowly toward his office, thinking as he went.

Nurse MacDougall had been highly irked and incensed at Kinnison's casual departure, without idle conversation or formal leave-takings. Not so Haynes. That seasoned campaigner knew that Gray Lensmen—especially young Gray Lensmen—were prone to get that way. He knew, as she would one day learn, that Kinnison was no longer of Earth.

He was now only of the galaxy, not of any one tiny dust-grain of it. He was of the Patrol. He *was* the Patrol, and he was taking his new responsibilities very seriously indeed. In his fierce zeal to drive his campaign through to a successful end he would use man or woman, singly or in groups; ships; even Prime Base itself; exactly as he had used them: as pawns, as mere tools, as means to an end. And, having used them, he would leave them as unconcernedly and as unceremoniously as he would drop pliers and spanner, and with no more realization that he had violated any of the nicer amenities of life as it is lived!

And as he strolled along and thought, the Port Admiral smiled quietly to himself. He knew, as Kinnison would learn in time, that the universe was vast, that time was long, and that the Scheme of Things, comprising the whole of eternity and the Cosmic All, was a something incomprehensibly immense indeed: with which cryptic thought the space-hardened veteran sat down at his desk and resumed his interrupted labors.

But Kinnison had not yet attained Haynes' philosophic viewpoint, any more than he had his age, and to him the trip to Trenco seemed positively interminable. Eager as he was to put his plan of campaign to the test, he found that mental urgings, or even audible invective, would not make the speedster go any faster than the already incomprehensible top speed of her drivers' maximum blast. Nor did pacing up and down the little control room help very much. Physical exercise he had to perform, but it did not satisfy him. Mental exercise was impossible; he could think of nothing except Helmuth's base.

Eventually, however, he approached Trenco and located without difficulty the Patrol's space-port. Fortunately, it was then at about eleven o'clock, so that he did not have to wait long to land. He drove downward inert, sending ahead of him a thought:

"Lensman of Trenco Space-port—Tregonsee or his relief? Lensman Kinnison of Sol III asking permission to land."

"It is Tregonsee," came back the thought. "Welcome, Kinnison. You are on the correct line. You have, then, perfected an apparatus to see truly in this distorting medium?"

"I didn't perfect it—it was given to me."

The landing bars lashed out, seized the speedster, and eased her down into the lock; and, as soon as she had been disinfected, Kinnison went into consultation with Tregonsee. The Rigellian was a highly important factor in the Tellurian's scheme; and, since he was also a Lensman, he was to be trusted implicitly. Therefore Kinnison told him briefly what occurred and what he had it in mind to do, concluding:

"So you see, I need about fifty kilograms of thionite. Not fifty milligrams, or even grams, but fifty *kilograms*; and, since there probably isn't that much of the stuff loose in the whole galaxy, I came over here to ask you to make it for me."

Just like that. Calmly asking a Lensman, whose duty it was to kill any being even attempting to gather a single Treconian plant, to make for him more of the prohibited drug than was ordinarily processed throughout the galaxy during a Solarian month! It would be just such an errand were one to walk into the Treasury Department at Washington and inform the Chief of the Narcotics Bureau, quite nonchalantly, that he had dropped in to pick up ten tons of heroin! But Tregonsee did not flinch or question—he was not even surprised. This was a Gray Lensman.

"That should not be too difficult," Tregonsee replied, after a moment's study. "We have several thionite processing units, confiscated from zwilnik outfits and not yet sent in; and all of us are of course familiar with the technique of extracting and purifying the drug."

He issued orders and shortly Trenco Space-port presented the astounding spectacle of a full crew of the Galactic Patrol devoting its every energy to the whole-hearted breaking of the one law it was supposed most rigidly, and without fear or favor, to enforce!

It was a little after noon, the calmest hour of Trenco's day. The wind had died to "nothing"; which, on the planet, meant that a strong man could stand against it; could even, if he were agile as well as strong, walk about in it. Therefore Kinnison donned his light armor and was soon busily harvesting broad-leaf, which, he had been informed, was the richest source of thionite.

He had been working for only a few minutes when a flat came crawling up to him; and, after ascertaining that his armor was not good to eat, drew off and observed him intently. Here was another opportunity for practice and in a flash the Lensman availed himself of it. Having practiced for hours upon the minds of various Earthly animals, he entered this mind easily enough, finding that the trenco was considerably more intelligent than a dog. So much so, in fact, that the race had already developed a fairly comprehensive language. Therefore it did not take long for the Lensman to learn to use his subject's peculiar limbs and other members, and soon the flat was working as though he were in the business for himself. And, since he was ideally adapted to his wildly raging Trenconian environment, he actually accomplished more than all the rest of the force combined.

"It's a dirty trick I'm playing on you, Spike," Kinnison told his helper after a while. "Come on into the receiving room and I'll see if I can square it with you."

Since food was the only logical tender, Kinnison brought out from his speedster a small can of salmon, a package of cheese, a bar of chocolate, a few lumps of sugar, and a potato, offering them to the Trenconian in order. The salmon and cheese were both highly acceptable fare. The morsel of chocolate was a delightfully surprising delicacy. The lump of sugar, however, was what really rang the bell —Kinnison's own mind felt the shock of pure ecstasy as that wonderful substance dissolved in the trenco's mouth. He also ate the potato, of course—any Trenconian animal will, at any time, eat practically anything—but it was merely food; nothing to rave about.

Knowing now what to do, Kinnison led his assistant out into the howling, shrieking gale and released him from control, throwing a lump of sugar up-wind as he did so. The trenco seized it in the air, ate it, and went into a very hysteria of joy.

"More! More!" he insisted, attempting to climb up the Lensman's armored leg.

"You must work for more of it, if you want it," Kinnison explained. "Break off broad-leaf plants and carry them over into that empty thing over there, and you get more."

This was an entirely new idea to the native, but after Kinnison had taken hold of his mind and had shown him how to do consciously that which he had been doing unconsciously for an hour, he worked willingly enough. In fact, before it started to rain, thereby putting an end to the labor of the day, there were a dozen of them toiling at the harvest and the crop was coming in as fast as the entire crew of Rigellians could process it. And even after the spaceport was sealed they crowded up, paying no attention to the rain, bringing in their small loads of leaves and plaintively asking admittance.

It took some little time for Kinnison to make them understand that the day's work was done, but that they were to come back tomorrow morning. Finally, however, he succeeded in getting the idea across; and the last disconsolate turtle-man swam reluctantly away. But sure enough, next morning, even before the mud had dried, the same twelve were back on the job; and the two Lensmen wondered simultaneously—how *could* those trencos have found the space-port? Or had they stayed near it through the storm and flood of the night.

"I don't know," Kinnison answered the unasked question, "but I can find out." Again and more carefully he examined the minds of two or three of them. "No, they didn't follow us," he reported then. "They're not as dumb as I thought they were. They have a sense of perception, Tregonsee, about the same thing, I judge, as yours—perhaps even more so. I wonder . . . . why couldn't they be trained into mighty efficient police assistants on this planet?"

"The way *you* handle them, yes. I can converse with them a little, of course, but they have never before shown any willingness to cooperate with us."

"You never fed them sugar," Kinnison laughed. "You have sugar, of course—or do you? I was forgetting that many races do not use it at all."

"We Rigellians are one of those races. Starch is so much tastier and so much better adapted to our body chemistry that sugar is used only as a chemical. We can, however, obtain it easily enough. But there is something else—you can tell these trencos what to do and make them really understand you. I can not."

"I can fix that up with a simple mental treatment that I can give you in five minutes. Also, I can let you have enough sugar to carry on with until you can get in a supply of your own."

In the few minutes during which the Lensman had been discussing their potential allies, the mud had dried and the amazing coverage of vegetation was springing visibly into being. So incredibly rapid was its growth that in less than an hour some species were large enough to be gathered. The leaves were lush and rank in color or a vivid crimsonish purple.

"These early morning plants are the richest of any in thionite—much richer than broad-leaf—but the zwilniks can never get more than a handful of them because of the wind," remarked the Rigellian. "Now, if you will give me that treatment, I will see what I can do with the flats."

Kinnison did so, and the trencos worked for Tregonsee as industriously as they had for Kinnison—and ate his sugar as rapturously.

"That's enough," decided the Rigellian presently. "This will finish your fifty kilograms and to spare."

He then paid off his now enthusiastic helpers, with instructions to return when the sun was directly overhead, for more work and more sugar. And this time they did not complain, nor did they loiter around or bring in unwanted vegetation. They were learning fast.

Well before noon the last kilogram of impalpable, purplish blue powder was put into its impermeable sack. The machinery was cleaned; and untouched leaves, the waste, and the contaminated air were blown out of the space-port; and the room and its occupants were sprayed with anti-thionite. Then and only then did the crew remove their masks and air-filters. Trenco Space-port was again a Patrol post, no longer a zwilnik's paradise.

"Thanks, Tregonsee and all you fellows . . . ." Kinnison paused, then went on, dubiously, "I don't suppose that you will . . . ."

"We will not," declared Tregonsee. "Our time is yours, as you know, without payment; and time is all that we gave you, really."

"Sure—that and a thousand million credits' worth of thionite."

"That, of course, does not count, as you also know. You have helped us, I think, even more than we have helped you."

"I hope I've done you some good, anyway. Well, I've got to flit. Thanks again—I'll see you again sometime, maybe," and again the Tellurian Lensman was on his way.

CHAPTER 24   *Kinnison Bores from Within*

KINNISON APPROACHED STAR CLUSTER AC 257-4736 WARILY, as before; and as before he insinuated his speedster through the loose outer cordon of guardian fortresses. This time, however, he did not steer even remotely near Helmuth's world. He would be there too long—there was altogether too much risk of electromagnetic detection to set his ship into any kind of an orbit around *that* planet. Instead, he had computed a long, narrow, elliptical orbit around its sun; well inside the zone guarded by the maulers. He could compute it only approximately, of course, since he did not know exactly either the masses involved or the perturbing forces; but he thought that he could find his ship again with an electro. If not, she would not be an irreplaceable loss. He set the speedster, then, into the outward leg of that orbit and took off in his new armor.

He knew that there was a thought-screen around Helmuth's planet, and suspected that there might be other screens as well. Therefore, shutting off every watt of power, he dropped straight down into the night side, almost half-way around the planet from Grand Base. His flares were of course heavily baffled, but even so he did not put on his brakes until it was absolutely necessary. He landed heavily, then sprang away in long, free hops, until he reached his previously-selected destination; a great cavern thickly shielded with iron ore and within working range of his objective. Deep within the cavern he hid himself, then searched intently for any sign that his approach had been observed. There was no such sign—so far, so good.

But during his search he had perceived with a slight shock that Helmuth had tightened his defenses even more. Not only was every man in the dome screened against thought, but also each was now wearing full armor. Had he protected the dogs, too? Or killed them? No real matter if he had—any kind of a pet animal would do; or, in a pinch, even a wild rock-lizard! Nevertheless he shot his perception into the particular barracks he had noted so long before, and found with some relief that the dogs were still there, and that they were still unprotected. It had not occurred, even to Helmuth's cautious mind, that a dog could be a source of mental danger.

With all due precaution against getting even a single grain of the stuff into his own system, Kinnison transferred his thionite into the special container in which it was to be used. Another day sufficed to observe and to memorize the personnel of the gateway observers, their positions, and the sequence in which they took the boards. Then the Lensman, still almost a week ahead of schedule, settled down to wait the time when he should make his next move. Nor was this waiting unduly irksome; now that everything was ready he could be as patient as a cat on duty at a mouse-hole.

The time came to act. Kinnison took over the mind of the dog, which at once moved over to the bunk in which one particular observer lay asleep. There would be no chance whatever of gaining control of any observer while he was actually on the board, but here in barracks it was almost ridiculously easy. The dog crept along on soundless paws—a long, slim nose reached out and up—sharp teeth closed delicately upon a battery lead—out came the plug. The thought-screen went down, and instantly Kinnison was in charge of the fellow's mind.

And when that observer went on duty his first act was to let Kimball Kinnison, Gray Lensman, into Boskone's Grand Base! Low and fast Kinnison flew, while the observer so placed his body as to shield from any chance passer-by the all too revealing surface of his visiplate. In a few minutes the Lensman reached a portal of the dome itself. That door also opened—and closed behind him. He released the mind of the observer and watched briefly. Nothing happened. All was still well!

Then, in every barracks save one, using whatever came to hand in the way of dog or other unshielded animal, Kinnison wrought briefly but effectively. He did not slay

by mental force—he did not have enough of that to spare
—but the mere turn of an inconspicuous valve would do
just as well. Some of those now idle men would probably
live to answer Helmuth's call to extra duty, but not too
many—nor would those who obeyed that summons live long
thereafter.

Down stairway after stairway he dove, down to the compartment in which was housed the great air-purifier. Now
let them come! Even if they had a spy-ray on him now it
would be too late to do them a bit of good. And now, by
Klono's golden gills, that fleet had better be out there,
getting ready to blast!

It was. From all over the galaxy Grand Fleet had come;
every Patrol base had been stripped of almost everything
mobile that could throw a beam. Every vessel carried either
a Lensman or some other highly trusted officer; and each
such officer had two detector nullifiers—one upon his person, the other in his locker—either of which would protect
his whole ship from detection.

In long lines, singly and at intervals, those untold thousands of ships had crept between the vessels . guarding
Grand Base. Nor were the outpost crews to blame. They
had been on duty for months, and not even an asteroid had
relieved the monotony. Nothing had happened or would.
They watched their plates steadily enough—and, if they
did nothing more, why should they have? And what could
they have done? How could they suspect that such a thing
as a detector nullifier had been invented?

The Patrol's Grand Fleet, then, was already massing
over its primary objectives, each vessel in a rigidly assigned
position. The pilots, captains, and navigators were chatting
among themselves; jerkily and in low tones, as though even
to raise their voices might reveal prematurely to the enemy
the concentration of the Patrol forces. The firing officers
were already at their boards, eyeing hungrily the small
switches which they could not throw for so many long
minutes yet.

And far below, beside the pirates' air-purifier, Kinnison
released the locking toggles of his armor and leaped out. To
burn a hole in the primary duct took only a second. To drop
into that duct his container of thionite; to drench that
container with the reagent which would in sixty seconds
dissolve completely the container's substance without affecting either its contents or the metal of the duct; to slap

a flexible adhesive patch over the hole in the duct; and to leap back into his armor: all these things required only a trifle over one minute. Eleven minutes to go—QX.

In the nearest barracks, even while the Lensman was arrowing up the stairways, a dog again deprived a sleeping man of his thought-screen. That man, however, instead of going to work, took up a pair of pliers and proceeded to cut the battery leads of every sleeper in the barracks; severing them so closely that no connection could be made without removing the armor.

As those leads were severed men woke up and dashed into the dome. Along catwalk after catwalk they raced, and apparently that was all they were doing. But each runner, as he passed a man on duty, flicked a battery plug out of its socket; and that observer, at Kinnison's command, opened the face-plate of his armor and breathed deeply of the now drug-laden atmosphere.

Thionite, as has been intimated, is perhaps the worst of all known habit-forming drugs. In almost infinitesimal doses it gives rise to a state in which the victim seems actually to experience the gratification of his every desire, whatever that desire may be. The larger the dose, the more intense the sensation, until—and very quickly—the dosage is reached at which he passes into an ecstasy so unbearable that death ensues forthwith.

Thus there was no alarm, no outcry, no warning. Each observer sat or stood entranced, holding exactly the pose he had been in at the instant of opening his face-plate. But now, instead of paying attention to his duty, he was plunging deeper and deeper into the paroxysmally ecstatic profundity of a thionite debauch from which there was to be no awakening. Therefore half of that mighty dome was unmanned before Helmuth even realized that anything out of order was going on.

As soon as he realized that something was amiss, however, he sounded the "all hands on duty" alarm and rapped out instructions to the officers in the barracks. But the cloud of death had arrived there first, and to his consternation not one-quarter of those officers responded. Quite a number of men did get into the dome, but every one of them collapsed before reaching the catwalks. And three-fourths of his working force died before he located Kinnison's speeding messengers.

"Blast them down!" Helmuth shrieked, pointing, gesticulating madly.

Blast whom down? The minions of the Lensmen were themselves blasting away now, right and left, shouting contradictory but supposedly authoritative orders.

"Blast those men not on duty!" Helmuth's raging voice now filled the dome. "You, at board 479! Blast that man on catwalk 28, at board 495!"

With such detailed instructions, Kinnison's agents one by one ceased to be. But as one was beamed down another took his place, and soon every one of the few remaining living pirates in the dome was blasting indiscriminately at every other one. And then, to cap the Saturnalian climax, came the zero second.

* * * * *

The Galactic Patrol's Grand Fleet had assembled. Every cruiser, every battleship, every mauler hung poised above its assigned target. Every vessel was stripped for action. Every accumulator cell was full to its ultimate watt, every generator and every arm was tuned and peaked to its highest attainable efficiency. Every firing officer upon every ship, sat tensely at his board; his hand hovering near, but not touching, his firing key; his eyes fixed glaringly upon the second-hand of his precisely synchronized timer; his ears scarcely hearing the droning, soothing voice of Port Admiral Haynes.

For the Old Man had insisted upon giving the firing order himself, and he now sat at the master timer, speaking into the master microphone. Beside him sat von Hohendorff, the grand old Commandant of Cadets. Both of these veterans had thought long since that they were done with space-war forever, but only an order of the full Galactic Council could have kept either of them at home. They were grimly determined that they were going to be in at the death, even though they were not at all certain whose death it was to be. If it should turn out that it was to be Helmuth's, well and good—everything would be on the green. If, on the other hand, young Kinnison had to go, they would in all probability have to go, too—and so be it.

"Now, remember, boys, keep your hands off of those keys until I give you the word," Haynes' soothing voice droned on, giving no hint of the terrific strain he himself was under. "I'll give you lots of warning . . . . . I am going to count the last five seconds for you. I know that you all want to shoot the first bolt, but remember that I personally will strangle any and every one of you who beats my signal by a thousandth of a second. It won't be long now, the second hand is starting around on its last lap . . . . . Keep your hands off of those keys . . . . keep away from them, I tell you, or I'll smack you down . . . . fifteen seconds yet . . . . stay away, boys, let 'em alone . . . . going to start counting now." His voice dropped lower and lower. "Five —four—three—two—one—FIRE!" he yelled.

Perhaps some of the boys did beat the gun a trifle; but not many, or much. To all intents and purposes it was one simultaneous blast of destruction that flashed down from a hundred thousand projectors, each delivering the maximum blast of which it was capable. There was no thought now of service life of equipment or of holding anything back for a later effort. They had to hold that blast for only fifteen minutes; and if the task ahead of them could not be done in those fifteen minutes it probably could not be done at all.

Therefore it is entirely useless even to attempt to de-scribe what happened then, or to portray the spectacle that ensued when beam met screen. Why try to describe pink to a man born blind? Suffice it to say that those Patrol beams bored down, and that Helmuth's automatic screens resisted to the limit of their ability. Nor was that resistance small.

Had Helmuth's customary staff of keen-eyed, quick-witted lieutenants been at their posts, to reenforce those primary screens with the practically unlimited power which could have been put behind them, his defense would not have failed under even the unimaginable force of that Titanic thrust; but those lieutenants were not at their posts. The screens of the twenty-six primary objectives failed, and the twenty-six stupendous flotillas moved slowly, grandly, voraciously, each along its designated line.

*   *   *   *   *

Every alarm in Helmuth's dome had burst into frantic warning as the massed might of the Galactic Patrol was hurled against the twenty-six vital points of Grand Base, but those alarms clamored in vain. No hands were raised to the switches whose closing would unleash the hellish energies of Boskone's irresistible projectors, no eyes were upon the sighting devices which would align them against the attacking ships of war. Only Helmuth, in his inner-shielded control compartment, was left; and Helmuth was the directing intelligence, the master mind, and not a mere operator. And, now that he had no operators to direct, he was utterly helpless. He could see the stupendous fleet of the Patrol, he could understand fully its dire menace; but he could neither stiffen his screens nor energize a single beam. He could only sit, grinding his teeth in helpless fury, and watch the destruction of the armament which, if it could only have been in operation, would have blasted those battleships and maulers from the skies as though they had been so many fluffy bits of thistledown.

Time after time he leaped to his feet, as if about to dash across to one of the control stations, but each time he sank back into his seat at the desk. One firing-station would be little, if any, better than none at all. Besides, that accursed Lensman was back of this. He was—must be—right here in the dome, somewhere. He *wanted* him to leave this desk—that was what he was waiting for! As long as he stayed at the desk he himself was safe. For that matter, this whole dome was safe. The projector had never been mounted that could break down *those* screens. No—no matter what happened, he would stay at the desk!

Kinnison, watching, marveled at his fortitude. He himself could not have stayed there, he knew; and he also knew now that Helmuth was going to stay. Time was flying; five of the fifteen minutes were gone. He had hoped that Helmuth would leave that well-protected inner sanctum, with its unknown potentialities; but if the pirate would not come out, the Lensman would go in. The storming of that inner stronghold was what his new armor was for.

In he went, but he did not catch Helmuth napping. Even before he crashed the screens his own defensive zones burst into furiously coruscant activity, and through that flame there came tearing the metallic slugs of a high-power machine rifle.

Ha! There *was* a rifle, even though he had not been able to find it! Clever guy, that Helmuth! And what a break that he had taken time to learn how to hold this suit up against the trickiest kind of machine-rifle fire!

Kinnison's screens were almost those of a battleship; his armor almost, relatively, as strong. And he could hold that armor upright. Therefore through the raging beam of the semi-portable projector he plowed and straight up that torrent of raging steel he drove his way. And now from his own mighty projector, against Helmuth's armor, there raved out a beam scarcely less potent than that of a semi-portable. The Lensman's armor did not mount a water-cooled machine rifle—there was a limit to what even that powerful structure could carry—but grimly, with every faculty of his newly enlarged mind concentrated upon that thought-screened, armored head behind the belching gun, Kinnison held his line and forged ahead.

Well it was that the Lensman *was* concentrating upon that screened head; for when the screen weakened slightly and a thought began to seep through it toward an enigmatically sparkling ball of force, Kinnison was ready. He blanketed the thought savagely, before it could take form, and attacked the screen so viciously that Helmuth had either to restore full coverage instantly or die then and there. For the Lensman had studied that ball long and earnestly. It was the one thing about the whole base that he could not understand; the one thing, therefore, of which he had been afraid.

But he was afraid of it no longer. It was operated, he now knew, by thought; and, no matter how terrific its potentialities might be, it now was and would remain perfectly harmless; for if the pirate chief softened his screen enough to emit a thought, he would never think again.

Therefore he rushed. At full blast he hurdled the rifle and crashed full against the armored figure behind it. Magnetic clamps locked and held; and, driving projectors furiously ablaze, he whirled around and forced the madly struggling Helmuth back, toward the line along which the bellowing rifle was still spewing forth a continuous storm of metal.

Helmuth's utmost efforts sufficed only to throw the Lensman out of balance, and both figures crashed to the floor. And now the madly fighting armored pair rolled over and over—straight into the line of fire.

First Kinnison; the bullets whining, shrieking off the armor of his personal battleship and crashing through or smashing ringingly against whatever happened to be in the ever-changing line or ricochet. Then Helmuth; and a fierce-driven metal slugs tore in their multitudes thre his armor and through and through his body, riddling every vital organ, that was   THE END

EXCITING SCIENCE FICTION BESTSELLERS!